Travesty of Justice
Preface

Ryan Thomas closed the book and put it down on his desk. He stood up and stretched his legs, slowly moving over to his office window. He looked down, noticing how busy the early morning streets of Chicago already were. It was nearly ten in the morning, and he was full of hope today. Not just for him, but for her too. He was excited to sign this deal and wrap things up.

He couldn't remember when a story had touched him so much. All he could think of now, was his pending meeting with the author of the book, he was about to get published. Nicole Butler was meeting with him later today, and he needed to get her to sign on with his company.

He and Nicole would be working together as co-writers; her book was being adapted into a movie script. His company had just negotiated a deal for the story rights, and they already told him that they wanted it to be a hit at the box office. He needed to get her to sign the contracts today at all cost.

It's all about the money he thought, especially for his company. But he knew it was about something much more than just money for her. When they'd spoken on the phone about their upcoming project earlier that week, he could hear the passion in her voice, and could tell just how important this story was to her, and how significant it was to tell the world this story.

He looked at his watch. In just a few minutes, he would meet the woman whose story had left him with such deep thoughts. He had written many movie scripts in his lifetime, yet this time it felt different to him – he had a very real sense of this woman's despair. The haunting realities of the book had left him with a nagging, sick feeling inside his gut. He guessed it was because he knew that the contents of this book were based on her life.

He ran his hands through his thick black hair and smoothed his black mustache, pondering about the woman who he would meet in just a few minutes. He looked handsome, as he gazed out the window in his navy blue sports jacket, white T-shirt, and faded blue jeans. He left his office, and as he walked down the long corridor to the

1

conference room, where he'd told Nicole he would meet her, he wondered what she would look like. Would she be fragile after such an experience, or would he see the strength she portrayed in her book?

Ryan quietly opened the conference room door, and saw a woman standing in the far corner of the room with her back to him, unaware of his presence. As she stood staring out the window, he quietly watched her for a few moments. She seemed to be a million miles away, deep in her own thoughts. She stood about five feet six inches tall, with silky golden-blonde hair that fell in waves around her shoulders. Nicole worn a finely-tailored light grey suit which stopped just above her knee, revealing her shapely legs.

Ryan cleared his throat, making his presence known, slightly embarrassed now because he had been staring at her for so long. Nicole spun around, suddenly realizing she was no longer alone. She looked somewhat startled to see him just standing there looking at her.

"I'm sorry. I didn't mean to scare you. I'm Ryan Thomas your agent and hopefully co-writer on the screenplay. We spoke on the phone."

For a moment Nicole stared at Ryan, as if she were sizing him up for new suit. Then just as if someone had turned on the lights, she flashed him a huge smile. "Hello. I'm Nicole, Mr. Thomas. I'm so sorry I didn't hear you come in. I'm so very pleased to meet you."

She walked over and offered Ryan a hand shake. He looked into Nicole's dark brown eyes as she came towards him. He noticed the grace of her movement; she looked younger then perhaps she was. She had a presence that did indeed command a gentle strength. He found it hard to take his eyes off of her. She had a hidden allure which seem to captivate him. He couldn't put his finger on it just yet, but he was anxious to speak with her further.

"I'm so happy to be working with you Mr. Thomas. I have dreamed of this day for the last year." Nicole spoke with a warmth and kindness.

Her smile was the kind that could easily melt one's heart he decided. He loved the sound of her voice, soft and gentle, yet steady as a rock – it made him want to listen to every word she said. "May I call you Nicole?" Ryan asked, eyeing her body language.

"Yes... you may, and thank you for seeing me today. I think before this project is over we will have spent a lot of time together, so I hope we can be comfortable with each other." She nodded, hoping that he would agree.

Ryan said yes with his eyes, and then motioned with his hand towards the conference table and chairs. "Shall we sit?"

Nicole walked over to the table but instead of sitting in front of him, she took a seat closer to the window. Ryan continued to look at her. He couldn't help but notice the lost look in her eyes, there was a sadness that was buried in them. It almost gave him an eerie feeling, like she could sense his thoughts, and was questioning his motives for being there. There was an unspoken question that he needed to answer.

"I just finished reading your book Nicole, and I'm honored to work with you and help you bring this story to life on the big screen. I just want you to know that you can trust me to follow your instructions, and to get this done the way you want it done." Somehow he knew the question in her eyes was about trust.

She looked at him. "Trust! Yes... I believe I can trust you Ryan.

Most of the time my gut instincts are right. I believe you do actually want to help, and I thank you so much for that. It's important for me to have the opportunity to produce something that will allow the world to see the many faces of injustice. I need to let the suffering stare straight at them. I want them to deal with it where they live, down deep inside themselves, in a place where most of us refuse to go – our conscience... our very souls."

"Nicole would you mind telling me this story in your own words? I've read your book, but I'd like to hear it from you personally."

Nicole agreed then turned her head away from him, and stared out the window into the vast empty space. Slowly she began to tell her true life travesty of justice to Ryan, allowing the empty space to become her vehicle to walk once again down memory lane.

Chapter One

The Zapata's Nightclub was the latest hotspot in Halifax Nova Scotia in 1999. The night in question was balmy and moonlit. It was a Saturday evening, and the club was jumping. All the university students were out and ready to play. A black soulful group out of Detroit, had the crowded dance floor jammed up with people, dancing and laughing like they had no troubles in the world.

Nicole sat facing the dance floor, watching her best friend Cathy dancing with a guy who looked like he'd had a few too many, and owned two left feet. Nicole loved to dance, and get all dressed up. Even at her young age of twenty, she had a certain class about her – she stood out in the crowd.

The band started to play a song with a slow and easy groove. She felt a hand on her shoulder, and a deep voice from behind her say, "May I have this dance please?"

She turned around and there stood a tall black man, clean-shaven and dressed in a dark green suit. He had a perfect muscle physique. He looked to be in his late Twenties. He stood looking at her, and then decided to ask again. "May I have a dance with you... please?"

She shakily got to her feet, and followed him out onto the dance floor. They danced in perfect rhythm for hours, just staring into each other's eyes, with no conversation, just a strange feeling of belonging, settling in between the two of them.

When the music stopped and the band decided to take a break, they wandered off the dance floor, and headed outside to catch a breath of fresh air. It was still warm, and comfortable enough to take a walk.

"Hi, I'm Samuel by the way. And what would your name be pretty lady?"

"Nicole."

"Well I think I'll just call you pretty lady. I had a great time dancing with you tonight, and you have very good rhythm by the way."

"Oh I see, you mean for a white girl," she said with a mocking little smile.

"Well... I guess that is kind of what I mean... yes. It's just that not a lot of white females can dance to funky music so easily and naturally as you do. Where did you

4

learn how?"

"Let just say I was born with it?" She laughed at herself then, realizing it was probably one line the poor guy had heard a lot in his lifetime, only about himself.

"Oh it's like that is it? I see you're a quick one."

"I'm sorry Samuel. Sometimes I can be a touch sarcastic. I think it runs in my family."

"Well in that case, I guess I cannot possibly hold it against you. We all have our burdens to bear when it comes to our heritage." He smiled. It was fun playing with her. "Will I see you again pretty lady?"

"How does tomorrow afternoon sound? Around two o'clock in the public gardens. We can meet near the bridge with the little creek running under it."

"I would love that." Samuel flashed his award-winning smile at Nicole.

Nicole looked at him with a mounting wonder in her eyes, then she became slightly embarrassed because she was just standing there staring at this handsome dark stranger, like she couldn't get enough of him.

"I'm sorry, I didn't mean to stare... it's just that I love your smile."

"If that's your reason, then you may look for as long as you like. There is no charge tonight," he said warmly.

She noticed that he spoke with an accent. He was possibly a foreigner studying here, she thought. "Ok then I guess I'll see you tomorrow. I should be getting home; I really must go back inside, and find my friend Cathy, and drag her home with me." Nicole decided that standing beside him just felt right.

"May I give you two a ride home?" he asked.

"Oh no thanks. It's such a nice night we can walk. I don't live far from here, just a few blocks away."

Nicole stood there and watched him drive off in an old red mustang. Just then she heard her name being called out. She looked up to see Cathy, her rather full-figured friend with curly blond hair, coming running toward her. She was not the most graceful girl, but sweet nonetheless.

"Just where have you been all night? I've been looking all over for you," Cathy said, trying to catch her breath.

"I'm so sorry Cathy. I thought you could see me on the dance floor. I just now stepped out for a little fresh air."

"Oh really! Well where did tall dark and handsome go then? That much I did see."

"He left for home just a few minutes ago. Come on sweetie; that's exactly where we should be heading for too. It's getting late." She put her arm inside her friend's arm as they walked along.

"Who was that good-looking man you were dancing with all night – who was he?" Cathy asked staring at Nicole with her curious big blue eyes.

"I really don't know. I guess he goes to one of the universities here. His name is Samuel."

"Yes I think you're most likely right. He looks like a foreigner. Are you going to see him again?" Cathy eyed her for an answer.

Nicole started walking faster, hoping to avoid the twenty questions routine with her. She knew just how persistent her friend could be when she wanted to know something.

"Okay, okay… yes I am going to see him tomorrow in the public gardens, but you have to promise me that you will not say a word to my mother about Samuel. She still thinks I am a child, even though I'm twenty years old. I'm sure my mother may very well have a slight nervous breakdown when she finds out that he is black, and a foreigner too."

Nicole laughed to herself with the image of her mother's reaction in her mind. Her mother was somewhat of a character. A most endearing woman, she had to admit, she could make almost anyone laugh by just being herself. She had a dry sense of humor, but she was always very fair to all her children, which Nicole hoped would continue in this case.

"But why keep it a secret Nicole? I don't get it!" Cathy asked.

"Well the reason is simple. I want a chance to at least see him in the daylight. You know how sometimes you meet someone at night, and you think they are great, but when you actually see them closer and in the daylight, you have to ask yourself, what was I thinking – because they are downright scary."

Cathy nodded. "Oh yes believe me I know exactly what you mean – just look what happened to me with Bill. I thought he looked good in the dark the night I met him, and I made another date. Then when he showed up the next day for lunch, his hair kind of stood up all on its own, and if that wasn't bad enough, he had on shabby orange plaid pants with a red shirt. He called it fashion-forward; I called it frightening. Yep... come to think of it, you had better see him again first, just to see if in the light of day, he turns out to be a monster. But somehow I don't think there will be any monster in sight. He looked pretty fine to me girl."

They laughed and held each other's arms. "A monster wow, I always wondered what happened to poor old Bill." They giggled softly as they crept up the staircase to Nicole's bedroom.

Early the next morning Nicole's family was up and off to church, her younger sister Marilyn complaining bitterly because she had to go to church, and Nicole got to sleep in. But Nicole's mother Sarah just smiled and said, "Never mind dear. We'll have a good time singing, and listening to the sermon."

Grandma Millie was already sitting in the car waiting for them. Sarah's oldest daughter had already moved out, and now lived in a different city. Her twin boys had been a big help to her around their old home over the years, fixing whatever had broken from too much ware. Sarah loved the fact that she had a large family; she'd taken great comfort in it ever since her husband had passed on. She devoted her whole life to raising her family the best she could, and was thankful that her husband's mother Millie had come to live with them, to help raise the children. They didn't always get along, but there was still a mad love between Millie and Sarah.

She left Nicole a note, letting her know it was her turn to make Sunday lunch for everyone, and off they went to church.

The sun was streaming through Nicole's window as her alarm went off. "OH! Kill that thing, Nick," Cathy moaned as she rolled over in bed.

"Hey sleepyhead get up. It's almost ten thirty, and you'll miss your eleven o'clock bus home. You know your mother will not be happy if that happens. You hit the shower, and I'll make us some coffee."

Nicole climbed out of her bed. She put on her white cotton robe, and ran downstairs to the kitchen.

7

A few minutes later, Cathy joined her fully clothed and ready to go. She took one long sip of coffee, and was ready to run and catch her bus. "Now remember to call me as soon as you come back from your date today. I want details." Cathy gave Nicole a quick hug, picked up her overnight bag, and ran to catch her bus.

"Get some rest and say hello to your mom for me," Nicole called out.

She headed upstairs to shower and change. She went into the bathroom. She turned on the water, and filled the bathtub with light floral-scented bath oil. Letting her robe fall to the ground, she climbed into the bath, allowing her whole body to sink into the hot water. A little while later, she stood in front of her closet wondering what to wear, finally she picked out a short sleeve cream linen shirt and shorts. She looked into the mirror and decided she looked okay. She ran downstairs to make lunch for her family.

She tossed a green salad and set it on the table, next to the plate of egg salad sandwiches she'd already prepared. She sliced up bananas, strawberries, and kiwi and mixed them all together to make colorful fruit salad. "There... that should hold them until dinner."

She ate a banana, and some berries as she was preparing lunch. Glancing at her watch, she saw that it was time to go. She picked up a pen and wrote on a piece of paper "Mommy I have gone to visit a friend. Be home for supper. Love Nicole."

Nicole walked along the tree-lined streets; it was a lovely summer's day. As she reached the park, she could smell the rich, abundant flowers. The park was full of Sunday walkers, enjoying their surroundings and eating ice cream. The bridge was straight ahead now.

"Oh my goodness... there he is," she said silently to herself. She was slightly nervous, and her heart began to beat faster as she walked closer to him.

"Hello there pretty lady," Samuel said with a smile from ear to ear, and then he kissed her on her cheek.

"Hi yourself... you have such a great smile." She let out a sigh of relief, thinking to herself, no monster in sight here. In fact he is a great big wow!

"Do you like ice cream?"

"Yes I love ice cream." She beamed up at him.

"How about we go and get some, and then find a cool spot to sit?"

"Sounds wonderful let's do that."

They walked along and found a shaded bench near the brook to sit on. They were surrounded by red roses, and there was a little rippling brook just at the back of the bench where they sat.

"So Samuel exactly where are you from?"

"Nigeria. Do you know where that is?"

"Not exactly, but I would guess somewhere... in Africa?" Nicole answered with hesitation in her voice, not sure if she was right.

"'*A dom wor'* means wonderful in my language, and a gold star goes to the pretty lady with the chocolate ice cream."

They both laughed, and Samuel gestured for them to take a seat on the bench.

"You know, there are many people here that don't even know where Africa is."

"Really? I guess its hard being so far away from home for you. Especially when there aren't a lot of people here that would understand your culture, or even know where your country is.' Nicole stared up at him with her big brown eyes, sensing that there was a lot that he wasn't telling her just yet.

"Yes it is my dear, it is harder than you could possibly imagine." Samuel's tone was somewhat serious and his eyes held a sadness, even those he was still smiling.

Nicole always noticed everyone's eyes. You just had to look close enough, and you could see the truth there behind them she believed.

He sensed her innocence, and he knew he shouldn't get her mixed up in something she would never understand, and she would be left to live with for the rest of her life. Although he loved what he was looking at, he didn't want to subject her to his world. He knew he has just met her, but in his heart, he felt if there was such a thing, as love at first sight then this must be it.

He cleared his throat and begin to explain.

"It just that the culture here in Nova Scotia is very difficult if you are dark-skinned, you know black." He smiled; Samuel was trying to sugarcoat reality for her.

"I guess I'm not really aware of these things Samuel, because basically I was bought up in a Christian home. You know following the golden rule and all."

"The golden rule?" he asked, pretending not to know what that was.

"Yes. Treat others the same way you want to be treated yourself silly." She laughed.

"OH... that golden rule!" He smiled trying to keep the mood light. "Well there are a lot of people here that have forgotten that rule my lady."

"Oh really! But I know there are a lot of people here that remember it too. There will always be good and bad everywhere you go. I believe that there are a lot of people that think black and white people shouldn't mix, but really the same red blood runs through all of our veins. So okay there is a difference in our skin tones, and yes different backgrounds, but that doesn't make one any better than the other. And the more we can learn about one another, the better we can come to understand each other, and learn to see that good in each other's differences. For heaven's sake, we only have one world. We need to take better care of it and each other. I think that's what he wants us to do."

"He?"

"You know... our higher power. I call him God. Many people call him by different names."

Samuel was quite taken with her. She was so intuitive and bright, in her own simple kind of way. The things she spoke of came from her heart. His world he knew would be very difficult for her. But the more he looked at her, the more his attraction for her grew, and it was getting the better of him. He knew he wanted her in his life.

Samuel stood up, "Should we stretch our legs, and take a walk around these lovely gardens? May I be your tour guide?" Samuel smiled and held out his arm for her to take.

Nicole nodded with a huge grin on her face as she followed by his side. When she slipped her arm into his, she felt how muscular his arm was, and noticed how good it felt wrapped around hers.

Samuel was keenly aware of the many disapproving eyes which glanced in their direction as they walked along. Nicole seemed to notice none of it; she was far too busy enjoying all the colorful flowers.

She loved the smell of his cologne. Everything about him just felt good to her. In less than a few short hours together, she had already decided in her heart, that he felt like home.

"So Samuel, are you going to university here?"

"Yes. I'm finishing my first degree in biochemistry and science. My life's goal is to become a medical doctor just like my father. Back in my village in Nigeria he took care of a lot of people, and I used to go to his office and watch him sometimes. I knew from a young age that I wanted to help people just like him."

"Really, oh how wonderful. I believe you will be a good doctor too."

"Why do you think so?"

"You have a way about you that makes people feel at ease when you're around them. They just want to trust you, and trust is so very important – don't you think so?" She looked up at him now with her innocent eyes.

He flinched a little at her words, and a wave of guilt washed over his face for a moment, but he quickly regained his composure. "I think I am going to nickname you Lady, because that is exactly what you are, and a very sweet one at that." Samuel reached out, and held her hand next to his heart, and looked her in the eye. "May I ask you a question?"

"I guess you are allowed one question," she smiled up at him.

He stopped and paused for just a moment, then looked at her again, this time with an overcast look on his face.

"What is it Samuel? You look so concerned."

"Well... I was just wondering... what your family would say if they knew you were in the company of a black man today."

"Oh that. Well to be perfectly honest, they would probably lock me away for the rest of my natural born days." She grinned in amusement at the look on his face at what she had just said.

She then laughed out loud, and kissed him on the cheek. "Don't mind me; I'm just joking with you. I really don't know how they would feel, but this much I know for sure about my family. My dad helped everyone. It didn't matter to him, he just gave help wherever it was needed – black, oriental, white, Indian. That's how he was, right up to the day he died.

"My mother is the same way; I think she would want me to have whoever makes me happy and treats me well. My Grandmother, well she's the best. She has a kind of sixth sense about a lot of things, like she just knows things sometimes before they even happen. It's some kind of very strong intuition. Most people that know me and her, say I am very much like her. Grand says we all have intuition. We call her Grand, because she really is, in every sense of the word Grand. But sometimes just Gran too. It's just that many of us don't know how to be still, and silent enough to listen to the universe when it talks to us. But my Gran does. The universe's energy speaks in many ways, but usually it's the little voice inside of us that guides us, and is life ward bound. I'm sorry. I know I'm going on about things you may not be interested in. But I hope I answered your question?"

Her intuition was telling her to tread carefully, that he was uneasy with this subject, and that he was hiding many fears – and maybe something else too she wasn't sure yet.

"I have an idea," Nicole declared in an almost childlike way.

"Oh really? What is your idea?"

"Well how about we start out just as friends nothing heavy." She had a little smile playing on her lips.

"A friend... you say." Samuel scratched his head, like he was toying with her idea. "Well as it turns out, I happen to have an opening in the friendship department, and I do believe you have the right qualifications." He smiled and relaxed a little.

"And just what are your requirements, may I ask?" she said wanting to laugh again.

"Well the person must be so lovely that they take my breath away, and they absolutely must make me smile on a regular basis." He held her hand and kissed it.

"Tell me is it proper for a friend to ask, when they might see each other again?" he asked.

"Oh yes it is absolutely proper. In fact it is almost mandatory in our case." She laughed in such a way that made him want to laugh along with her.

Her warm and caring nature left him with the feeling that all was well, when he was with her, and he just wanted to stay in her company.

Nicole looked at her watch and realized she was late for supper. She stood on her tiptoes, and kissed Samuel on the cheek. "Here's my phone number," she said as she jotted her number down on a piece of paper. "Call me any time. I have to run now because my family is expecting me for supper."

***

Nicole hurried quickly back home to her family, and their Sunday evening dinner. She walked in the door breathless.

"Hello dear. Where have you been all day?" Sarah asked, looking over the top of her eye glasses.

"Oh hi Mommy. I was in the public gardens this afternoon. It's so lovely there. The flowers were so colorful and beautiful, and it was such a sunny warm day. I loved it."

"You were there a long time dear, are you hungry?"

"Yes starving, what's for dinner?" Nicole looked around the kitchen to see what she was preparing. She realized she had hardly eaten all day.

"Roast chicken, mashed potatoes, and fresh green beans. And for dessert Grandma Millie made an apple pie." Sarah knew apple pie was the thing her daughter loved the best. In fact she would just eat the pie, and nothing else if Sarah let her.

"Yummy that sounds great. Where is Grand?"

"She's in the dining room setting the table dear, and your poor sister has been looking for you all day too."

Nicole made a beeline for the dining room. She ran over and kissed her grandmother on the cheek, picked up the glasses, and started setting the table with her.

"Hello child. I haven't seen you all day. What have you been up to?" She looked at her with wise old eyes.

Nicole looked at her grandmother knowing full well there was no use in telling her a lie; she would know the difference, because she always did. She could always get things past her Mother, but never her Grandmother; they were too much alike, no matter their age difference.

"What makes you think I'm up to something Gran?"

"My dear save it for your mother. Give me the truth – remember who you're talking to. Why didn't you get up and come to church with all of us? "

"Well if you must know, I met a new friend in the public gardens today, and I believed that the person needed a friend. So that's what I did, I was a friend to someone who needed one. And this morning Cathy was here, and she can never get up in time for church, so I couldn't just leave her alone now could I?" She smiled sweetly at her.

"Oh I see dear; it was Cathy who was too tired to get up and serve the Lord this morning, not you."

"Oh Grand he knows I love him anyway." Nicole hugged her, and went back out into the kitchen to help with supper.

Marilyn, Nicole's sister, came running in. "Hey where have you been Sis? I've been looking all over for you."

"Sorry kid, I was out. How are you doing? How was church? Did you sing a lot?"

"My day was boring, church was boring, and you should have taken me with you!"

"Next time I will okay?" She said this with her fingers crossed behind her back. She loved her little sister, but didn't want her along on her dates.

"Okay next time then Nick." Marilyn was easy to satisfy. She was all about family, and loved just being with them, doing different activities. But she always wanted Nicole to be there too; they were close in age, and that made them very close friends.

Nicole's twin brothers Randy and Ken came running in just in time to sit down to dinner.

"Hey girl, where have you been all day?" Ken asked.

"I was just out for a while."

They all sat down and began to eat their Sunday dinner, chatting about church that day and what was coming up in school next week. Sarah sat quietly, listening to her family chatting together. She smiled knowing she had loving children and that she was blessed.

"Mom... May I be excused? I promised Cathy I would call her tonight," Nicole said.

"What, no dessert dear? It's your favorite – apple pie with cheese and ice cream." Sarah eyed her daughter; she knew that she never passed up dessert.

"If it's okay I'll take it upstairs with me and eat it in my room."

"It's all right. But why are you in such a hurry to call Cathy tonight?'

"Oh I just wanted to let her know, that I didn't see any monster today in the garden." She ran upstairs.

Sarah just rolled her eyes and watched her go, thinking she must have not heard her properly. Monster in the garden? She thought. It must be some kind of new game she had made up; Nicole did that a lot. Nicole sat down on the edge of her bed, a fork in one hand to eat her pie, the phone in the other hand.

"Hey girl, can you talk?" Nicole asked.

"Sure! So what happened today? Did you see him?"

"Oh my goodness girl, he was simply dreamy. He is so different from anyone else I have ever met before. He is a real gentleman; great to laugh with and to talk to. And get this – he's studying to become a doctor."

"Cool bonus girlfriend. Since you're in nursing school now, you'll have lots in common to talk about with him. But what will your family say when they meet him? How are you going to tell them?"

"Well... I've been thinking about that old movie "Who's *coming to dinner with Sidney Poitier and Katherine Hepburn*, and I think I'll just do the same thing. I'll simply invite him home to Sunday dinner when the time comes. But really I just met him, and there's time yet. But I think Grand is on to me already; she had her eyes on me all through dinner tonight. I think she suspects something – she always knows somehow. I swear I can't get a thing over on her."

"Well good luck with that one honey. Keep me posted on what's happening. I'll call you in a few days. Goodnight."

***

The next two months passed quickly, and Nicole decided it was time for Samuel to meet her family. They had talked and managed to meet each day for an hour or two. They were getting to know each other well enough, and knew they wanted something more serious in the future. They sat having coffee at their favorite coffee shop late one evening.

"Samuel I was wondering if you would like to come by and meet my family, maybe have dinner one night?"

"Dinner ....you know lady we may very well, get a big surprise if your family disapprove of me. Are you ready for that?"

"As long as I have you by my side, then yes I think I am." He always walked her almost home, and she walked the rest of the way home alone.

"Sam why are you so quiet tonight?"

"I guess I am a bit nervous about meeting your family, I don't want to lose you. If they reject our relationship then it will be difficult for us to continue on?" He looked down at her, and kissed her softly on the lips, and pulled her into his arms. His desire for her growing stronger every time they touched. He knew she had not experience a man yet and he couldn't wait to make her his.

"I know you're afraid but I am not, just trust me on this one. I know my mother and family very well, I think most of them will give you a chance. It may be a shock in the beginning for them, but once they get to know you the why I do, I think they'll love you just like me."

"You love me, did I hear you say that?" he looked down at her beaming from ear to ear.

"Yes... I love you, I adore you."

"Oh my sweetheart I love you too. More than you know."

"Then let's just trust that everyone else around us will see this love of ours, and want us to be happy."

"If only life was that simple. But I am willing to meet your family whenever you decide the time is right." He kissed her goodnight, and watched her until she had reached her doorstep.

There was a family Thanksgiving dinner planned at her home, with all of her aunts and uncles. She thought she might as well get it over with, and let everyone meet him all at once. She smiled to herself; she could just hear her mother already in her head saying, "Couldn't you have let me meet him first, him being a foreigner and all? And you know being in a relationship with a black man will not be easy for you here."

But she believed in her family, and knew they were fair-minded people, and that they would give him a chance – or at least she hoped so.

"Mom is it ok if I bring one of my friends home for Thanksgiving dinner? His family is far away, and I'm hoping we can keep him from being too home sick."

"Yes sure dear. We always have room for one more."

Nicole ran to her room. She had to prepare Samuel for tonight's dinner. She picked up the phone and called him.

"Hello Babe I think tonight is the night. It's Thanksgiving, and I want you to come by for dinner tonight. I told my Mother and she is fine with me bringing you home. So ... what do you say, will you come?" They was a long silence on the phone.

"Yes... of course I will come my sweetheart, for you I will go anywhere. But just be prepared in your heart for anything."

"You worry way too much babe, just relax and be yourself, they're going to love you too."

Back in the kitchen Sarah got busy preparing the turkey with all the side dishes, she realized that Nicole had said 'him'. Him she thought. I guess it must be a new friend from college. That's funny she thought, Nicole never mentioned a new boy from school before.

Nicole took a shower and put on a simple, red-flowered A-line dress. Her aunts and uncles arrived on time, and they were all having a glass of wine before dinner when the doorbell rang. Nicole knew that it would be Samuel. Her stomach did a slow turn. She was anxious to get this over with.

She took a deep breath, smiled at her grandmother and whispered in her ear. "He's here. Back me up on this one, please Grand." She kissed her on her cheek and ran to the door.

Her grandmother knew something unexpected was coming, because she never asked her for backup, unless she was about to get into a heap of hot water. She shook her head. "This child will be the death of me yet," she muttered under her breath. She stared at the door to see what was coming next, and prayed that it wouldn't be too bad.

Nicole answers the door, and there stood Samuel in a dark green suit looking so very handsome. He took her breath away. "Oh wow they are going to love you. Please come in." They walked into the dining room where everyone was seated now for dinner.

"Hello everyone please let me introduce Samuel to you. He's in university here and we're kind of dating. He's from Africa originally."

Nicole held her breath and looked at her grandmother, hoping she'd say something. There was silence, and then Millie finally spoke up and said "Well then Samuel…. you come and sit over here by me son." She looked around the table with a face which absolutely defied anyone to say anything disapproving.

Sarah finally found her voice after the first shock had worn off a bit. "Yes… dear take a seat. Hope you like turkey; that's what we serve here for our Thanksgiving dinners."

"Oh yes Mrs. Butler, I love it. We serve goat at home, but I love turkey dinner too, especially when it is served by such a lovely woman as yourself."

Sarah eyed him, with her intense dark eyes. This one is a real charmer she thought. Well he can't fool me, too old and too wise for that nonsense. At least he's well-mannered; thank God for small mercies she thought.

Sarah stood up when everyone had finished the main course. "I guess I'll get dessert served up. I'll just be a minute." Sarah went out to the kitchen, her sister followed her.

"Let me help you," Ruby said. "Sis for heaven's sake, what is Nicole thinking with that man? You should send her to live with us. She'll be in a different city, and that will put a stop to this nonsense."

"Ruby I will do no such thing. If this is what my daughter wants, then I support her, and I expect you to do the same thing. I do not want to hear another word about it." She looked her sister in the eye, and Ruby knew that when Sarah had her mind made up, there was no changing it.

"Well I just hope you and Nicole know what you're doing. It is such a shame, a beautiful girl like her wasting her life on a man like that."

Sarah glared at her with her dark piercing eyes. "Just what Ruby do you mean? A 'man like that? Because he's black?"

"Yes. That's what I mean, and you very well know it."

"Look Ruby if her father was still alive today, he would have welcomed him at our table, if he thought he was a good and decent man. And so far he seems to be, so he *is* welcome here, got it? Color is not issue in this house. Now for heaven sake get the pot of coffee while I serve up this cheesecake." She went back to the dining room, hoping the desert would sweet everyone's mood up a bit.

Ruby came behind her with the coffee pot and a pitcher of cream, with a face that would have cracked had she smiled. Her husband sat beside her with his disapproving eyes glaring at Samuel all through dinner. Nicole's brothers were both concerned by her choice in men as well. But they had been bought up to be more opened minded. So they kept their fears to themselves. Nicole's old Grandmother had an uneasiness in the pit of her stomach, but knew she had to support Nicole in this, even those she had many reservations about this man. She knew Nicole was depending on her, to be on their side in this, and she wasn't about to let her down.

After dinner everyone went to the living room to play the piano and sing. They had always been a musical family, and they loved to have sing-along. Samuel went over to Sarah and Nicole's Grandma. "I just wanted to thank you both for making me feel welcome here; it really means a lot. I want you to know I love your daughter, and will try my best to be good to her."

Sarah looked at him. "That's good enough for me for now. You make sure that you do just that." She walked away, to join the others in the sing-along.

"Just a minute there now son," Millie said. "Samuel you do anything to my granddaughter and I will know it, do you hear me? I believe for the most part you love her, and she loves you. So for now, I will say nothing, but please treat this innocent girl well. If any harm comes to her, the person that hurts her will never find peace on this earth, and that's my promise to you". The look she gave him, make a chill run up his spine. Little did he know that there was some truth to that feeling he had, Millie had a special connection to the world of spirits. Some said she was an old witch, which always made her laugh. She was just a woman who loved her family, and would always watch over them in body and in spirit, even from the grave when the time came. She needed to keep Nicole close, so she could have a good sense of her wellbeing. Closeness was necessary for that special connection that told her of danger, it was a feeling she got inside her gut, whenever any of the people she loved happened to be in any kind of trouble

Chapter Two

Samuel sat on the bench in front of his university's library. It was the last day of class for this school year. It had been a year now since he first met Nicole; she was never very far from his thoughts or side. He had been lucky with her. Her family had been surprised in the beginning, but in a very short time they too had welcomed him into their family with open arms. His plan was coming together nicely. All he needed now was his acceptance letter into medical school here, and his dreams would be closer to coming true.

"Samuel my man. How are you? Where have you been hiding for the last few days?" Ben asked. He was Samuel's closest African friend in Nova Scotia, and they shared the same dream of becoming doctors. They totally trusted one another, and thought of each other as brothers. Ben often teases Samuel and called him an old man, but they were both in their late twenties; Ben was older than Samuel by a few months. When Ben was around, it was like having a part of home close by for Samuel, someone who spoke his language, and knew how to cook their African food. They often cooked and hung out together; they understood each other and faced the same difficulties. They shared a handshake, and Samuel welcomed him with his big smile, offering him a seat beside him. "Ben my friend how is it going? Have you heard yet? Did you get your letter of acceptance into med school here?

"Well okay I might just as well say it. I did hear back. I got my letter. But I wasn't accepted into medical school here."

Sam looked at his friend with a heavy heart. "I am so sorry to hear that."

"Have you heard anything yet Sam?"

"No nothing yet, but I have to say I am concerned, everyone else I have talked to, have so far."

"I have come up with a backup plan, which is why I dropped by today to see you Sam. I want to talk to you about my new medical school, and I want you to think about it for yourself. Your marks are excellent, but I have a feeling they are just tossing you around until the last minute. Then they will give you a letter, which will tell you the same thing I was told: apply again next year. Like we have another year to just waste in our lives."

"I know, that has been my fear for us both for some time now too, the good old boys club is alive and well here in Nova Scotia. They think if too many of us become professionals, then the tables will turn and they will lose control. They don't want the competition. But here is the thing Ben, I need to go to medical school. It's all I have ever wanted to do, and my family is counting on me to do it. So tell me my friend. What is your backup plan?"

"I got us both applications for a medical school in the Dominican Republic, in Santo Domingo. With our grades we will get accepted with no problem. I already spoke with the Dean of the university down there. He is waiting for our applications, school transcripts, and school fees, and then we will be good to go for this September."

"Wow Ben. Just the thought of leaving here makes me frustrated. What happens when we graduate? Can we come back and practice medicine here in Canada again?"

"I checked with the Ministry of Health, and they say we will have to write the Canadian medical exams here when we return, and with a one year internship, we will be able to set up practice, or go on to a specialty program here in Canada ."

"Really... but I wonder if we can trust that. The rules change all the time, and why would they let foreign medical graduates back in here again, when they will not even give us a chance to study medicine here in the first place with excellent grades?"

"Simple Sam they need the doctors here. They don't produce enough to serve the population, and some of their own graduates leave and go to the US to practice."

"Yes I guess that is true. I guess we have no other choice really do we?

"No there is no other way without wasting a year or two here, and still we will have no guarantees that after the wait, that we would actually get accepted. Now here take this application and send it out, and do it fast old man."

"But how can I just leave her?' He felt like he had the weight of the world sitting on his shoulders.

"I know how you feel, my brother, but you cannot let Nicole stand in the way of your dreams, and the other responsibilities you have. This is the dream, you have had ever since you were ten years old remember?"

"Yes I remember. How could I ever forget?" Samuel said looking down at the ground in total defeat.

"Look you know what the answer will be here. I don't want to leave you behind.

You have to leave! You have people back home counting on you!" Ben looked at him with nothing but kindness in his eyes for his brother.

"Yes I know. But one day my brother…. one day we shall overcome. Just wait – in another ten years or so things will slowly change. There are many black men in the US on the rise now, and here too for that matter. They are all working towards a better education and life. Things will change, but until then, we will just have to leave to get our education, and return with a skill set that no man can take away from us." As Samuel spoke sorrow washed over his face. There were years of suffering buried in his dark eyes. All that he had been through to get this far had left him tired – but even more determined not to give up. The next day Samuel sent off his application by express mail, and then called the Dean there as well. He was on his way, and the rest he had to just leave in the good Lord's hands. The following week Samuel headed over to the emigration department of Canada. His Canadian visa was due to be renewed. He had entered the country with a student visa, and it was about to expire. He knew he was headed for trouble with his current emigration officer, Mrs. Miller. Without proof on paper of his next school year in hand, she would not renew the visa. Many other students in this type of situation, were granted thirty days of grace, but this woman was heartless. She'd had it in for him ever since she'd found out his intention of becoming a doctor.

He sat in the outer office with a heavy heart; he was dreading this meeting with this cold detached woman. She had tried many times to get him kicked out of the country over the past year. Her distaste for him was obvious, because she wasn't smart enough to hide it away. There was no way he was becoming a doctor on her watch in her country she vowed.

Mrs. Miller looked out her door, and saw Samuel waiting there for her. The utter thought of this black man becoming a doctor, was totally unacceptable in her mind. Why her own husband was just a postman, a good job she thought, and he was a hardworking man. He'd been at the same job for over twenty years now, and he provided well for her and her two sons. Just who did this boy think he was anyway? She needed to get prepared, so she picked up the phone and dialed the registrar's office at Samuel's university.

"Hello. May I speak with your medical registrar please? This is Emigration calling regarding one of your students: Samuel Emeka." There was a pause as she was transferred.

"This is the medical registrar. What can I do for you?"

"I need to know if Samuel Emeka has been accepted into Medical School for the coming September semester. You see his visa is up for renewal, and I can't renew it without an acceptance letter. Has the decision been made yet?" She held her breath praying the answer would be no.

"We do not give out that information to anyone but the students first, and to my knowledge Samuel's letter has not gone out yet. It was held back for more consideration by the board of directors."

"So no decision has been made yet? Nothing in the file at all then, to say his application has been approved or denied?" she persisted.

"There was a decision in the file, but really I cannot say over the phone."

"I hope you understand the difficult circumstances I am in here. I cannot renew a student visa if he is not a student now can I?"

"Can you not give him a fifteen to thirty day grace period, long enough for him to receive his letter, and I will let the board know about this situation?"

"Yes… but why prolong the time if the boy did not get accepted?" Mrs. Miller demanded.

"I will check the list of people who will be entering our school in September. Just one moment please."

The Medical Registrar knew Samuel and liked him. She also knew that Mrs. Miller was out to get him. She had helped Samuel in the past, but this time she didn't know what she could do. He had not been accepted, and she had already sent the application back for reconsideration on Samuel's behalf, with a good reference from her. She had a feeling no one would listen to her, and as it stood his application had been denied once, but she hated to tell this dreadful woman that. But it looked like she had no choice now.

"I'm sorry to say that Samuel's name does not appear on the list at this time. But that doesn't mean it won't later; his file is still under consideration. I hope you give him another thirty days of grace in this country. Please try to do that Mrs. Miller."

Well I am not sorry, Mrs. Miller thought to herself. "If he is not on the list, he is not a student and that is that. So you just leave emigration decisions up to me Miss. That is my department not yours, but thanks for the information today, and have a wonderful day." She was so happy she finally had him right where she wanted him: on a plane and out of her country. Mrs. Miller sat at her desk with obvious glee in her eyes; she could not wait to give him the bad news, as she stared out her door at him.

Samuel sat in the outer office and pulled out his prayer book. It was worn around the edges. It had been a gift from his mother, she had given it to him the day he left their country. He could still hear her voice saying, "My dearest son remember God's word, and that he loves you, and so do I. Your faith my son can move mountains."

His heart ached as he thought of her. She had passed away last year while he was in Canada. He had never gotten to say goodbye. He was dreading the conversation with Mrs. Miller, he looked up and saw her standing in front of him.

Mrs. Miller opened her door with a big smile on her face. "Samuel you may come in now. How are you today?"

"I am okay Mrs. Miller. How are you?" He knew he was dealing with a devil in disguise of a woman, and ruthlessly she was about to eat him alive.

"Have you your student papers to show me please? As you know Samuel your student visa is up for renewal, and expires in less than three days." She looked at him over the top of her glasses with a smile playing on her face.

"I have not heard anything yet. I cannot say yes or no." He looked her straight in the eye; he knew she finally had him just where she had wanted him for the last few years.

"Well that's really too bad because as you know Samuel, the emigration laws are very clear about such things, so I have no choice but to decline your request for a student visa. Be prepared to leave this country in three days." She smiled thinking she had finally won – victory was hers at last.

"Mrs. Miller... can you not just extend it for at least thirty days until I hear something? What is the harm? It will give me time to make alternative arrangements somewhere else."

"No way Samuel; not this time. You cannot manipulate the system to suit your situation, no matter how much you may like to. I do not make the rules, I only follow them. So be prepared to leave in three days. That is my last word to you."

He knew his request was falling on deaf ears. "Well Mrs. Miller never let it be said that you do not enjoy your job, especially on the days when you get to kick black men like me out of your country. I get the feeling that is your favorite part of this job."

"Young man I assure you I do not take any pleasure in this. I do not know what you are referring to." She was getting slightly red; he had hit a nerve.

"Let me say just one thing, and please try to remember this. I will become a doctor and return to Canada, and who knows one day you may wish you had been a little more human to me. My mother always told me this one thing: treat people well, because what goes around eventually comes back around to you, and you wouldn't want anything to bite you in the ass when you're not looking." Samuel smiled at her and then stood up, and with all the grace and strength he had left. He walked out of her office and never looked back.

Mrs. Miller just stared at him as he left, a little twinge of guilt spread across her face. She knew she could have helped him had she wanted too. But why should she? Why her own sons were only bookkeepers and store clerks. No why should she help this black man – this foreigner – get ahead in her city?

***

Nicole sat in her cozy rocking chair in her apartment, staring out her window. She was watching and patiently waiting for her Samuel to come by for dinner. He was later than usual this evening, and she was getting worried; she didn't like the look of the dark clouds in the sky tonight. It looked like a rip-roaring thunderstorm was headed their way, and she was hoping Samuel would get there before it let loose.

He always called if he was going to be late. He had never made her worry in the past. It was Friday evening, and they always spent time together at her place on the weekends. She had graduated from nursing school, and had a job now at one of the hospitals. She had talked her mother into letting her get her own little place – a place where she and Samuel could be alone.

Her little apartment was warm and comfortable. She had learned to cook his African food, and had prepared his favorite food tonight – stewed chicken and rice with beans. The phone rang and she ran to grab it, thinking it must be him. "Hello?" she said anxiously.

"Oh hello dear. It's Grandma. Is anything wrong? I haven't heard from you today."

"Hi Grand. I'm okay thanks. Just busy cooking dinner for Samuel... but he's awfully late tonight, and I haven't heard a word from him. I'm getting worried Grand!"

"Maybe he's just busy with school business this evening." Millie had a feeling now that something was up. She'd hadn't just been calling tonight because she missed the girl underfoot at home. Millie had a strange feeling in her gut all this week that something bad was going to happen. And here it is she thought. It was something with Samuel and Nicole.

"No need to worry dear, Samuel will be along soon." At least she hoped so, but she knew he had trouble on the way; she just didn't want to worry her precious child any further with her suspicions quite yet.

"Grand he's really late, and you know there's a storm coming isn't there?"

"Yes there is one coming, but don't worry yourself about the storm. It will pass by, and no harm will come to him."

"It's just that I hate for him to drive in the storm, and it's going to be a bad one. I can feel it in my bones. The sky is so black outside, the wind is so intense. I swear Grand the roof is about to blow off."

"Now just stop with your worrying. I told you no harm will come – not from the storm." She hung her head; she knew she was in for a world of hurt. If only she could stop it, but she couldn't. She felt Samuel would go away soon. She didn't know why, and that worried her, because she knew how much her Nicole loved this man, and that she would suffer greatly when he disappeared. "He will be home soon. Call if you need me dear. "Millie had a sixth sense about these things, it had run through generations of her family, and now ran through Nicole. They both knew something was up, and she needed to prepare her mind for it. Nicole paced the floor, looking at her watch. She stood by the window wondering what had happen to him. The wind rattled her window panes in fury, and the tree twisted in anger, yelling out to her soul, screaming their alarm in the blackness of the night. She called Samuel's home number again, but still no answer. She couldn't imagine what the trouble must be. "Surely he must know how worried I am!" she said to the wind and rain as it lashed upon her window.

She decided to light some candles in case the power went out. She turned off the overhead lights, and let her spirit rest in the candle light. Then she got down on her knees and began to pray.

"Father God please bring him home to me, whatever the trouble is. Please be our solution, our comfort, and our joy as only you can be. She prayed with a childlike faithfulness that came from her heart. She laid down on her sofa and curled up like a wounded animal, waiting for his return.

***

The waves were smashing the shoreline now. The ocean carried a frosty white foam washing away the once-sandy beach, that had existed only hours before. The summer's air had cooled off, and fall was coming in with a raging force, bringing hurricane winds and rain. Samuel sat in his car at the edge of the cliff. He watched the raging sea, the rain and wind battering his car like it was about to toss him over the edge and down into the sea. He was feeling so discouraged, that he almost wished it would just take him away from all his worries. The rage of the storm made his soul feel peaceful, like Mother Nature was angry tonight just for him. Her rain lashed down on his windshield, and the flash of her thunder bolts streaked through the sky for all the injustice his soul felt.

The storm was helping him to release all the fury he felt inside, for all he had endured for so many years. Those prejudiced and unkind people, who had hurt and wounded him just because he was different, and because they could. He was worried for his future, and he was worried for Nicole's future too. The wind whistled around the door cracks, sending a chill up his spine.

Samuel knew he would soon have to deal with his life and situation; he would have to return to Nicole and tell her the dreadful news of his impending deportation. Looking out the window now, he noticed that the road up ahead was starting to wash away. He had lost track of time – it was almost midnight.

"Oh my goodness," he said out loud to himself. "Nicole must be worried out of her mind." Samuel rarely let his emotions get the best of him, but tonight had been too much. He had needed time to think, to cry, and to plan for his future, without the burden of her wellbeing in his hands too. He wiped the tears from his cheeks, knowing he needed to turn his car around, and get back quickly before the roads were impassable and completely washed away.

He started the engine and turned on his lights, only to see a river of water washing over the bridge, which he needed to cross to get back to the main road. The water had risen up to the rim of his tires; he would have to just drive as fast as he could across the bridge, and pray the good Lord didn't want to take him just yet. He needed to get back to Nicole; she was all that he thought of now. As he drove towards the bridge, it had now become more ocean than land. He just needed to get to the main road and then he would be fine he thought.

He slowly began to drive across the bridge, but when he hit the middle of it, the car engine died. Too much water had gotten into the engine hood. He knew he had been foolish to stay out in the storm for so long, and now he was in a heap of trouble, and all he could do was pray.

He bowed his head. "Well God if this is your will for me to die here on this road tonight, then may your will be done, but if it's not then I guess I need you to start this car again and get me home. Father God, please help me to find my way home to her, back to Nicole."

He turned the key again but the engine remained silent. He couldn't open the door now; the water was too high. He closed his eyes, then opened them and took his bible with the ragged edges out of his pocket. These are words he read: "The Lord is my shepherd; I shall not want... Yea though I walk through the valley of the shadow of death, I will not be fearful, for thou art with me." His heart was beating fast as fear crept in.

***

Millie had fallen asleep in her chair, and when a loud bolt of thunder jolted her awake, she had a panicked feeling in her heart immediately. He was not safe anymore; Samuel needed her help. She needed to pray now and focus her thoughts as intensely as she could. She stood by the window as the storm raged outside, and in the darkness of the night she prayed. "Save him dear Lord, please save him," she said over and over again until it was a single thought in her consciousness. She repeated the words in a chant-like melody, which only the energy of the universe could understand.

Nicole lay still and closed her eyes. She focused on Sam and his well-being. Soon the same words came to her mind: save him Father save him. She didn't know where these words came from, but she repeated them over, and over again, until they were a single thought in her mind. Her grandmother had channeled her thoughts with Nicole's for more power and strength, for when more than one of God's children pray together, so it shall be done. Millie knew this absolutely in her own heart and mind. She knew her methods were sound, and had never failed in the past. She focused even harder now, channeling all her strength to make one complete thought with her granddaughter. "Save him Father, save him Father, I know you are able." She kept chanting out loud, until her voice and thoughts were one. Nicole found herself saying the same words. "Save him Father, save him now." She didn't even realize she was now saying them out loud. Nor did she question the fact.

***

Samuel put down the book and tried the key again, and this time the engine started but died soon after. He tried again and once more it started, only to die again within seconds. He tried one last time and this time he put his foot to the metal and drove as fast as he could, with as much force as the car still had left, and off the bridge he came, and out to the main road. "Father I thank you," he cried out loud.

He took a deep breath and turned the car around, and drove in the direction of Nicole's apartment. He got out of his car and climbed up the staircase to Nicole's door. He didn't know how to tell her that she may lose him for years. He never wanted to hurt her, nor did he want to burden her with his troubles. In his country it was the man's job to provide for his family, not to burden down the woman he loved. But how could he do that now with all that had happened to him? No visa, no job, and no medical school in sight anywhere.

Nicole leaped to her feet as soon as she heard his footsteps on her porch. She opened the door, and there Samuel stood soaking wet. He could see the fear in her eyes; they told him everything he needed to know. "Oh Sam! You're soaked to the skin. Whatever happened to you to keep you so late? Come in and take that shirt off. Here take this towel and dry off. I've been out of my mind with worry." She looked like a scared little girl looking up at him; he looked terrible like someone had beaten him down somehow tonight.

Samuel dried off with the towel. He didn't take his eyes off Nicole. She was so young and beautiful, yet so fragile – all he wanted to do was to take her in his arms and make love to her.

He held her with all the passion and emotion of a man in love, who was about to lose the woman he adored. When they finished, he took her in his arms and pulled her naked body next to his. Swallowing hard he began. "You're been crying lady. You must not worry so."

"Worry so? You're six hours late; what was I to think? There's a terrible storm out there."

"Yes I know my sweetheart. Believe me I know. And I also know what will make you feel better." He smiled.

"You do?"

"Yes I do. That hot cocoa stuff you make. You stay here I will go make us some." Samuel went to the kitchen, made two cups of hot chocolate, and got two of her grandma's buttermilk biscuits, loaded them with butter and jam, and came back to bed. "There now. Sip on this, and let's eat."

They sat there for a few minutes, enjoying the comfort of her warm bed and listened to the rain on the roof, and in that moment they realized just how lucky they were to have each other. He held her close to his heart all night long as they slept.

The next morning dawned bright with sunshine. No one would have ever known there had been such a storm the night before, until they looked outside and saw all the trees that had fallen. The evidence of the flood damage was everywhere. But the sun was strong, and soon all would be back to normal.

"Nicole I made breakfast. Get up sleepy head. We have shopping to do for dinner; my friend Ben is coming over remember?"

"Yes I remember."

"But first we need to talk. Listen lady... I was late last night for a reason. I had an appointment with Mrs. Miller from the emigration department... she is deporting me because I am no longer a student here. I have not been accepted into medical school. I am so sorry." He looked at her with a deep sadness in his eyes.

"WHAT? That can't be possible! Oh dear God… that's terrible! What are we going to do? I don't get it. Your marks were so good, and you were at the top of your class here – what went wrong?"

"Things are not always fair plain and simple."

"There is no way I'll let them do this to you! This is my country too; they cannot do this to us." She felt like someone had just slapped her in the face, she couldn't believe what was happening to them, and in her beloved city. These were not the people she knew and had grown up with. They couldn't act this way. In her mind, fair was fair, and people here respected that.

She stood up, and looked at Samuel with her big brown eyes and said, "Let's get married. Then they can't do anything; they'll have no right."

There was a long pause, then dead silence. She knew she wasn't going to like the answer. Her heart began to pound. "Sam look at me please … answer me?"

Samuel smiled rather surprised by her solution, but it made him feel so loved just knowing she wanted to marry him. "Lady… listen to me please. You know I love you, but I couldn't let you do that for me. When we do get married one day, I want it to be for the right reasons, and not because we had to in order for me to stay in this country. You would always wonder if I married you just to stay here. And there is more – even if we did get married, they would still make me leave the country anyway, and reapply outside of Canada for a visa before I could come back again."

"I don't care. I will not let you leave this place without me. I don't want to lose you. What are we going to do?" She started to cry.

"Now calm down my sweetheart. I will go to England and stay with my sister Kate for a few weeks. I have applied to a medical school in Santo Domingo, and have been accepted. I will have to go there and study for a few years.

"A few years! Are you kidding me? Without me?" Her questioning eyes killed him; he didn't have an answer for her on that one.

"I don't know what else I can do. You have a job here, and a life with your family – you will need to work, you need money too. I cannot provide for us both in medical school." He looked defeated.

Nicole sat quietly beside him, her heart slowly sinking. Her chest was so tight it felt like she could hardly breathe.

"I know it sounds bad now, but we will work it out somehow. You can come and visit, I will come here and visit you whenever I can too."

"But you'll be gone for four years. How will we be able to survive that?" She put her head on his shoulder. She knew he had no answers. "I just can't believe that this is all happening to us. I feel so helpless." She hung her head in disbelief that the place she loved so much was now breaking her heart.

"There are many good people here; it's just that sometimes the ones who make these kinds of decisions are not so good. They are very protective of these professions."

"Be that as it may, they still have no right to make such bad decisions for those who live here. We all paid taxes and we don't deserve this. This situation has just changed our whole lives. And what is worse, I work in the hospital with all of them." She couldn't believe that her whole world was in such a mess in just twenty-four hours.

"I know. This is why I have to get my education and come back here for us, for my family, and for myself."

"I don't want to hear that you're going away." She started to cry again.

Two days later, Nicole stood in front of the gate at the Halifax airport, holding Samuel's hand as tightly as she could. She wanted to remember how his hand felt next hers. She was trying her best not to break down and sob uncontrollably in front of him. She didn't want Samuel to worry about her when he was gone. He had to now deal with various governments, and visa issues. So she promised herself she would be strong in front of him.

"I have to go up to the gate to board my plane now. Lady… promise me you will be all right. Think good thoughts until I return back to you."

She swallowed hard to keep from crying. She looked at him and smiled the best she could. "Yes I promise." She crushed her face into his chest and prayed silently to keep it all together for just a little while longer. He pulled her close one more time to his body; he wanted to remember how her body felt in his arms.

"My sweetheart," he whispered in her ear, "I will call you in about eight hours when I get into England, and I am at my sister Kate's house okay. No need to panic, I'll be back as soon as I can." She nodded her head yes with her face still buried into his chest.

"I got to go up now. Have faith I love you very much, and I 'll be back soon." His voice broke as he spoke to her. He wanted to cry his heart out. They announced his flight number; it was time for him to board. He hated so much to leave her, because he knew she was still so young in many ways. They had become so close over the last year; he had become her whole world, and she was everything to him now too. He had left so many people behind in his life that he had loved before. But she had not, and this was all new to her. She held him tight one last time, and then she just turned and walked away. She only turned and looked back once, when she was far enough way so he could not see her tears. He waved at her as he went up the stairs to catch his flight with a lump in his throat.

"Sam!" she yelled out, and he turned around. "I love you. You come back soon to me you hear?"

"I will I promise." They were both bursting with tears now, and then in only moments he was gone, through the gate and out to his plane.

Nicole stood at the window and watched his plane taxi out, and in a few minutes it was airborne, disappearing off into the white clouds like it had never existed. She couldn't believe it. They had taken her Samuel away from her. As she stood there staring out the window, a bitterness she had never known before started to creep inside her heart, from that day forward she never thought of her city in the same way again.

She slowly walked out to her car, and quietly drove herself home. She walked into her once-cozy apartment, which now felt cold and empty. Immediately she felt his absence. She fell onto her bed, as she laid there curled up into a little ball, she prayed for Samuel's safe return. And as she laid there in the darkness, she wondered how for so many years that she had lived in this place, why she had never realized the cruel heartless things, some did to people of color. They had taken away her restless night. It was already six in the morning. She quickly grabbed the phone, knowing it would be Samuel voice on the other end. "Good morning! Time to get up for work sleepy head," his voice said in her drowsy ear.

"Oh baby you made it. Are you at Kate's already?"

"Yes she was there waiting for me. It's good to have some of my own family around me right now."

"Yes I am sure that is very comforting. At least I know she'll feed you well." She laughed for the first time in days. "Don't get fat on me okay?"

"It's good to hear that laugh of yours. You looked so sad at the airport, I was afraid to leave you there."

"I'll get stronger; I promised you that didn't I? Now that I know what I'm dealing with, I'll find a way to cope.

"I am counting on you to do just that. I will call soon again. Remember you are my light at the end of this dark tunnel. "

"If that's true then I'm going to let this light shine so brightly, that you cannot help but find your way back home to me."

And that was it, he was gone again. She knew she had to get used to that.

Samuel sat down at his sister's table staring off into space, trying to plan his next move. He was trying to focus, to push Nicole's voice out of his head. He just picked at his food while Kate stood in the doorway looking at him.

Kate had studied hard and had become a lawyer, she was very observant. She was a big woman, with a motherly touch and good instincts, and she would do anything for her little brother. She hated to see him so depressed and out of sorts.

"Samuel are you too tired to eat my brother? Why not go to your room and sleep for a while? Things will seem better when you are more rested." She knew a little of his problem from their phone conversations.

"I think I do need to sleep. And thanks; it's so good to see you Kate." He hugged her and then he left her to take a shower. He laid down on top of the bed and fell fast asleep.

He was up at the crack of dawn. He sat at the table with some coffee, planning out his day. He needed to go out to the Canadian Embassy, and get a tourist visa to visit Nicole on his way to the Dominican Republic next month in September. He wanted two weeks with Nicole, before he left for his medical school in Santo Domingo.

A good night's sleep did help put things in perspective. Not getting into Canada's medical school was only a setback, not the end of the road by any means he thought. It would not stop him from achieving his goals. Nicole was the problem. How could he ask her to wait for him for so long, or to ask her to leave her career and home, to come there and live for years just to be by his side?

He had other responsibilities to his family as well, and one day he would have to deal with them. There was also the issue of money; it would be costly for them both to live there. His family had put aside only enough money for him and his medical school needs. There simply wasn't enough money for two. She wouldn't be able to work there; she didn't speak Spanish and she'd need a working visa. He would be studying long hours, leaving her all alone most of the time. He thought of everything, except how he was going to be able to let her go, and live down there without her. The fairest thing to do would be to simply let her go now, and let her have a new beginning with someone else – in his heart he knew that. But the heart wants what the heart wants. And all his heart wanted was her.

Samuel met with the Canadian officials, and received his visa for Canada. He was in a better mood by the time he got back to Kate's house. "Hello Sis." He went over and kissed her cheek. "I got everything done, but will be sticking around for a few more days if that's ok?"

"You silly boy, we're Africans remember? Family is everything to us. I think you have been living in North America for too long." Kate was doing Samuel's soul a good service, and he was becoming a little less stressed, with each passing day they had with each other.

***

A week later Nicole stood at the gate in the Halifax airport. She was so excited; all she wanted to do was throw her arms around Samuel as soon as she laid her eyes on him. In only minutes, she would be able to actually reach out and touch him. She spotted him coming in the distance. She couldn't wait, so she started to run towards him, she kissed him passionately, craving his arms around her.

"Hey lady. Do I know you?"

"You had better know me, or I am about to cheat on my one and only true love," she whispered in his ear. She threw her arms around him again and gave him a long hard kiss.

"I'm so glad to see you my sweetheart. Let me look at you," Samuel said beaming. She turned around in a circle for him.

"You look so lovely." He never took his eyes off of her, every part of him was yearning to be reunited with her again.

Nicole knew they had only two weeks together this time, so she had taken some vacation time off at work to spend more time with him. They arrived home to her little apartment, and she slipped into a long black shear nightgown. When he saw her, he had only one thing on his mind, and that was how fast he could slip his hands up under it, and into her haven of love. Soft music and the glow of the candlelight danced as they made passionate love. The fire and hunger between them was thriving, and growing stronger every time their bodies connected.

"I missed you lady. You feel so good in my arms."

"Oh God, "she moaned. " Don't stop let me feel you again."

"I can't stop thinking of you when I am away, you belong to me and no one else." He whispered.

When he entered her, their passion grew higher, as they moved their bodies in rhythm. Finally exhausted and content they both fell fast asleep in each other's arms. He gently held her naked body, in his muscular arms. Claiming her as his own.

She gently got out of bed, and went to her little kitchen to make coffee the next morning. Samuel was not far behind her. He stretched his strong arms, and wrapped them around her and kissed her lips. "Good morning sexy. It looks like you have been busy this morning, breakfast looks good and I am starving. I guess I worked up an appetite last night." He grinned at her.

"Yes you certainly did, and let me know when you're hungry again. I do believe we still have some of that food you love on the menu still left. Let's just enjoy this time together.

Like we have the rest of our lives to share. Let's pretend that everything is all right for just a little while. "Nicole looked at him with her child-like eyes. Her face was glowing from their love making. She was strong in many ways, but she hated being away from him. Her world was never happy when he was far away; that much she had learned in

36

the last few weeks.

"All right … it's a deal. We still do have the rest of our lives together, we don't have to pretend. If that's what we really want, we can make it happen my sweetheart."

"Yes I know we can, but sometimes things just happen beyond our control, like you going away to school for a few years. And these kinds of things can be really challenging for us, for any couple to survive. Sam how would you like to go out on a special date with me tonight?"

"Well… let me see if I'm free." He was ready to play with her.

"I would love that. What should we do my sweetheart?"

"Well I thought we could get all dressed up, and go out for dinner, and do some dancing at the same place we first met. It's Saturday night!"

"That sounds like fun; I get to dirty dance with you. That definitely works for me." That night she made a special effort to look her best; she wanted him to remember this night for a long time. She showered and dressed in a form-fitting little black dress with an open back. She wore sparkling crystal earrings with a matching bracelet, they were vintage from her mother's jewelry collection. Nicole pulled her hair up high on top of her head in a soft, simple knot. When she looked in the mirror, she saw a sexy grown woman. She was in the mood to turn some heads, and get her groove on with her man. But in Nicole's heart and mind, the only head she really ever wanted to turn was Samuel's. His eyes were the only eyes that she cared about.

Samuel appeared at the door in a dark green suit, they made a handsome couple.

"Wow you look beautiful tonight! You almost make a guy feel sorry he's leaving town."

"Well that's why I decided I had better give you something to remember, and give you a very good reason why you should always come back home to me."

"I'll always come home to you." He pulled her close and they danced the night away in each other's arms. Later that night they entered her little apartment, Nicole slowly undressed in front of him. She laughed as he pulled her down onto the bed.

"So you wants to play tonight I see, wow you look so sweet and sexy, I can't wait to feel you again."

"I hope it will always be this easy between us, I just want to feel your energy, and love you every day. Just take me, make love to me again." She moaned as he entered her, and soon there was nothing separating them. They slept peacefully wrapped up in each other's arms, every night until he was gone.

***

Samuel sat looking out the plane's window at the island, he was about to land on. He was thankful that he had not let Nicole come to the airport this time. Goodbyes there seemed to be harder, and he worried about her driving back home upset. So they had said their farewells in the comfort of her little apartment.

The flight attendant announced for them to fasten their seatbelts as they were about to land, and in only minutes he was safely on the ground and going through customs. When Samuel finished picking up his bags, he went outside to an overwhelming heat that slapped him in the face. "Oh dear God it's hot," he muttered.

He looked up and saw his old friend Ben standing there waiting for him, and his heart lightened. "Thanks for meeting me! Ben my friend, it's good to see you! Is this the heat we are going to live with for the next few years brother?"

Samuel had never liked the heat; even in his own country, he was always hiding from the sun. He pulled a white handkerchief from his pocket and wiped the sweat off his forehead.

"Oh yes old man. I'm afraid so. This is our car." Ben looked at him with a boyish grin on his face. The car was about ten years old, and had no air-conditioning, and windows that only half opened. It was all they could afford. They put Samuel's suitcases in the car, and off they drove into the crowded streets of their new city.

"Ben all I can hope is that our living quarters are a bit better than this car." Samuel almost regretted that he had let Ben handle these things on his own.

"Relax old man. Here it's every man for himself. I have gotten used to driving here already. You'll have gray hair before we ever get started here if you don't learn to relax." He grinned at Samuel, rather enjoying his old friend's discomfort.

"Wow, thanks for that Ben. That's just great news." Samuel shook his head and laughed, because at this point there was nothing else left to do but to have a good laugh.

They made it to their new apartment, and to Samuel's great relief, the place was actually nice. It was bright and had lots of space in the living room and bedrooms. The rents in the city were good, so they were able to afford a two bedroom flat with a large balcony that overlooked a lovely flower garden. The apartment already had furniture in it, so that took care of a lot of cost for both of them.

Sam got settled into his bedroom, unpacked his things and took a deep breath; he had to get used to the heat again. He took out his Spanish language book, and went out to the balcony of their apartment, he sat in a big comfortable chair with a cup of coffee. He had to review his Spanish language book, he needed to be able to communicate here if he was going to survive the next few years.

Samuel's mind kept wandering back to Nicole, he hoped she was coping without him ok. He wanted to call her, but knew he could only call once a week. And once a week in return, she would call him. That's all their budget would allow.

The first morning of school was both exciting and nerve-wracking for Samuel. With a coffee and a bagged lunch, they were ready for their day. They both wore white cotton T-shirts and lightweight cotton pants with sandals. The heat in the classroom was hard to take, no air-conditioning or fans – only windows wide open, blowing in hot air. They took a break at noon and went outside, the hot sun was penetrating through their clothes.

"My God man! This heat is killing me. I need some cold water Ben. Let's go to the vending machine.

"Okay, we have about twenty minutes I guess. They gave us so much information in three hours, my hand hurts from writing. I still didn't get most of it – did you old man?" Ben looked exhausted already.

"Yes, I did. Don't worry Ben; you can get my notes later on at home."

They suffered through the day, and by the end of it, they both knew that they had their work cut out for them. There would be many sleepless nights ahead of them.

The next day they needed to pay the registrar their fees for school. They entered the hallway only to find a huge lineup. They stood in line for an hour and a half. That was their first lesson as foreigners in the Dominican Republic: when you have to do anything bureaucratic, give yourself at least two hours of extra time.

After all that, they both still had to pay off the receptionist for their timetables: she said she had just run out of paper and needed more, so to get her last copies it would cost them both twenty pesos. They looked at each other and knew they had been taken.

"It is unreal how they rip you off here Ben. She knew what she was doing."
"Yes, she did. They nickel and dime all the students to make a little extra money on the side for themselves, because they are not paid well." Ben just laughed and nodded his head yes. "Look, Sam; just forget about all the bullshit, and remember why we are here. It will be better once we get used to it. Just kept walking old man."

"That's a frightening thought – it would mean that we have become just like them?"

"Bite your tongue. We just have to rise to the challenges and accept the terms of our stay here that's all."

Their afternoon classes started on time, their classroom was full of mostly Americans, a few Canadians, and a few African students. Samuel was surprised to learn that most of his professors had studied in the United States of America. Their classes and textbooks were all in English – in fact, they were the standard books used all over North America. The country itself may be a little slow, but there was going to be nothing slow about their studies, or how hard they were going to have to work. After a grueling six hours with only a thirty minute break for lunch, their day was finally over. They both came out walking in slow motion, suffering from heat exhaustion, hungry and brain-overload.

"My God man they are trying to kill us in our first week," Samuel said as he wiped his forehead.
"Oh without a doubt... most probably that's their plan bro, kill us off and keep our money!"

They both laughed at the thought. By the time they got home, the sun had hidden itself for another day. A much cooler breeze came in at night, making it more comfortable to sleep or study. After a cool shower, Samuel made them dinner. They ate, and then started studying again, until they couldn't keep their eyes open any longer. They slept on average only six hours a night. Both of their alarms went off at eight o'clock. Their first class this morning started at nine thirty.

Ben took the coffee that was handed to him. "Wow Bro. What time did you sleep? You look worse than me, or at least I hope you do." He smiled.

"It was late, but I finished the last chapter we had to read. I will tell you about it as we drive to class. We will get through this Ben, we just need to keep our backs to the wall, and our minds clear to learn." Samuel had decided to be optimistic. He'd made up his mind that he was going to be successful, no matter what the cost. His family had sacrificed a lot to get him there, and was sending money every six months so he could live, and pay his school fees. It was in fact, double the cost it would have been back in Canada. He owed it to them to succeed, and he could not afford to lament on the Halifax issue anymore. He knew one day he would return to Nicole, and he'd be ready for the next battle, whatever it was.

They walked into the classroom, and just as they sat down there was a dull roaring sound in the distance. The windows began to shake slightly.

Ben looked at Samuel with fear in his eyes. "What the hell is happening here? What the hell is happening?" He yelled again.

The shaking became more intense now. The vibrations started to rattle the desks and windows, and all the books fell off the tables, and onto the ground. Samuel looked out the window at the sky, it looked pitch black, like it was getting ready to explode with a thunderous downpour of rain.

"Take cover under this desk. I think this is an earthquake!" Samuel yelled.

"HOLY MOTHER OF GOD!" Ben shouted.

They both crawled under the desks, the other students did the same thing. The room began to violently tremble. The wind blew the doors and windows wide open. The rain, and the shaking felt like a whirlpool of water twisting all around them. They were totally disoriented. All they could do now was hold onto the wall, and the table they were under. Another fierce flash of lightning brightens up the skies. The rain was torrential. The roof slightly ripped off, and the rain beat down on the table they were sheltering under.

"Ben don't let go! Keep your feet against the wall and hold onto the table legs. The tables are fastened to the floor with large steel bolts."

"Oh my God man! We are going to die here!" Ben shouted.

"Hold on brother! It will pass soon, just keep your feet firmly against the wall and don't panic."

Sam stared at Ben with fear in his eyes, he grabbed his arm to hold him down. The shaking worsened; the whole roof was now gone, and they only had walls and the tabletops, for protection against the violent rain and wind. No one knew what to do, including the teacher who had just returned from America.

***

Nicole stopped in her tracks, as she was walking home from work. She felt something that made her uneasy. She could feel fear somewhere inside of her, right in the pit of her gut. She began to run home – she needed to talk to her grandmother. She would know, she would feel it too.

When she got home, she called her grandmother immediately. Millie answered, "Yes dear, I know."

"What is it Grand? What is it? I feel something bad is happening, and I think it's Samuel. Oh Grand what should we do?" She was out of breath with panic.

"Close your eyes dear, and see with me clear skies, no rain, only sunshine, and a calm land."

"Calm land? What does that mean Grand?"

"Just do as I say. See the sunshine with me, see the calmness of the land that surrounds our Samuel now, concentrate as hard as you can, see with me clearly, and see Samuel surrounded by calm land and sunshine. Can you see it, dear? Close your eyes, and just believe me when I tell you – you need to see it, and believe it with me. Now let's pray."

"Oh Grand I see shaking and rain. I don't see sunshine."

Her grandmother began to pray. "Father in heaven who sees all and knows all, keep your hands on our Samuel. Keep him safe from the wrath of mother nature, as she rages down on him."

Nicole puts her hand over her mouth, as she listened to her grandmother's prayers on the phone. She wanted to scream save him, just save him now, but she didn't. She obeyed her grandmother, and prayed with her until it became a chant.

Calmness, sunshine, all around Sam. Calmness, sunshine, all around Sam. Tears rolled down Nicole's cheeks, as she chanted with her grandmother. She couldn't even think what if this doesn't work; she knew she must believe absolutely. There must be no doubt, for doubt creates confusion in the universe, and she needed the universe to be very sure, in order to bring about what she, and her grandmother were seeing in their mind's eye. They met each other in midair in their mind's eyes; the laws of attraction were strong between Millie and Nicole. They both knew beyond a shadow of a doubt, that Sam was now safe, and the earth was now calm. They had seen it, and believed it to be true, with an absolute knowing. Nicole got on her knees, and gave thanks to her creator, for giving back safety to her Samuel.

***

"Are you all right brother?" Ben asked Samuel as the room settled down. The vibrations were only slight now, and when they looked out the windows that had been shattered, they could hardly believe their eyes. Trees had fallen, and roof had ripped off, but the entire house was still standing somehow. Everyone started to stand up and walk outside. The rain had all but stopped, and the earth was now calm once again.

"My dear God Sam. I thought we were goners." Ben's body was still shaking from the earthquake, and tornado that had just moved through.

Everyone started picking up the mess. They all knew they were lucky to be alive. All Samuel wanted to do was run home, and call Nicole. He knew she would have felt something; he had been with her long enough to know, that she had a special gift just like her grandmother, and he needed to reassure her that he was fine. What he didn't realize was, that these two had worked together, each and every time he'd been in danger, to save him from whatever was in his path. As the universal laws of attraction ebbed and flowed, so did their thoughts which prevailed against all evil, and brought about peace, and safety to those they loved. The secret was buried inside their mind's eye, to protect and keep them all out of harm's way. It was a special gift that was bestowed on Nicole, and her grandmother from their creator, and they gladly used it to offer protection, and guidance to all they loved.

Samuel entered his apartment and dialed Nicole.

"Hello?" She answered with a soft voice on the first ring.

"Hello Lady. I miss you so much. How are you my sweetheart?"

"The question is how you are? Was the weather very bad there today?"

"We had what they called a slight earthquake and tornado. It was very scary. Did you know that?"

"Yes, I knew that something bad was happening around you. I just miss you so much baby. I feel sad all the time without you. I try to keep busy, but there is no joy for me here without you."

"My sweetheart, you have to be strong. Remember we talked about this?"

"Yes I know, but after today I'm fearful that if anything were to happen to you, I wouldn't be able to breathe again."

"Nothing is going to happen except us growing old together, with many children, and grandchildren all around us." The thought of that, made him smile.

"You promise?"

"Yes. I promise." As he said it, the knot in his stomach grew bigger; he only hoped it was a promise he would be able to keep.

After they had hung up, Nicole felt something nagging inside, about forever. Like there was no forever. She didn't mention it to her grandmother, and never knew Millie held the same fear. They never spoke of it, for fear it would come true, if they gave it energy with words.

The next week of classes, were held outside due to the storm, it took another week for their classroom to get back to normal. It was finally Friday evening, and Samuel and Ben, couldn't wait to catch up on some much needed sleep. They left their classroom, and went outside to find the shade of a big palm tree. Two other Africans students, who were in their class, came over and sat down with them.

"How's it going guys? I am Tony, and this is Fred," said a little stout man with a heavy accent, who appeared to be in his mid-thirties.

"Hello guys. This is Samuel and I am Ben."

They all knew they were from Nigeria – it went without saying. They chatted, and then left to head home for the weekend.

As soon as Samuel reached home he laid down to sleep, but the sleep wouldn't come. He tossed and turned. He kept seeing Nicole's lovely face in his mind. He finally gave in and dialed her number.

"Hello?" Nicole answered in a sleepy voice.

"Hi Lady. Did I wake you up? It's still so early; why were you sleeping already?"

"Hello baby. I was just catching up on some sleep. It's my weekend to work, so I'm up at six remember?"

"I remember. I haven't been gone that long you know."

"It feels like forever." She sighed. "How was your week?"

"It was pretty crazy. Not enough sleep, and too many things to read and remember. I miss you terrible Lady."

"My poor baby. I know it must be terrible for you. But you're doing what you love, so just hang in there."

"I wish you were here".

"I know. I miss you more. You sound like you're a million miles away."

"No, I am not a million miles away – just a few thousand or so."

Then he asked her the question that had been on his mind ever since he had arrived there. "Nicole.... do you think you could live here with me on this island?'

"I don't know Sam. But... I think I could live anywhere, as long as you were there by my side."

"You know.... I am coming back to Canada this Christmas to see you." There was a long pause on the line; then Sam cleared his throat, he had finally made up his mind.

"Nicole, will you marry me then, and come back here with me to live?"

Sam knew he was asking a lot of this innocent girl. It was a purely selfish request on his part, because he had everything to gain, and she had everything to lose.

Nicole's eyes flew wide open now as she sat up straight in bed. She shook her head, to make sure she was not still half-asleep. She then broke the silence on the phone, with a simple, "YES!"

At just twenty years of age, she was much too young to imagine what her life would be like there. All she could think of was being near him again. She was so happy she thought she was going to burst. She wasn't thinking of her family, or of money at all.

Her thoughts were those of any young girl who was about to get married: how soon she could get the wedding arranged for Christmas, which was just two months away. How soon Samuel, would be back in Canada, and back in her arms.

"Now Lady I want you to think about this, because it will not be easy for you here. You will need to learn Spanish, and it's very hot here. I will be studying most of the time, and you will be on your own for long hours each day. I know it's really selfish of me to even ask you, but the truth is, I need you here with me. I need to see you every day, even if it's only for a short while." He knew it was impossible to let her know how everyday life would be there with him. She was not well-travelled, and had no idea what living in a country like the Dominican Republic would be like.

Nicole started to laugh. "Hey baby, I said yes already. Because no matter how hard it will be, there's still no place I'd rather be than by your side, wherever that is. Now may God help us both, when I tell my family! I have just a few months to plan a wedding, and get ready to move." She thought for a moment. "How about December twenty-sixth? It's my Mom's birthday, and the church will still be decorated for Christmas with all the pretty lights, I think it will be perfect."

"Okay. If that's the date you want, I am fine with that. And Lady... I love you," Sam whispered.

"It's settled then. I love you too," she said in a soft voice that spoke volumes.

"Sleep well my sweetheart, and I will call again in a few days to see how your family feels about everything." He knew they would be concerned; he only hoped they didn't talk her out of it.

***

The next few months flew by quickly. Nicole's family had accepted her wedding plans. Both her mother and grandmother, hated the idea of her going to another country so far away. It worried them, but they wanted her to be happy, and this was her life, and her choice to make.

Nicole was busy planning her wedding. She had finally picked out a dress that both she and her mother liked. The wedding was to be held in the small chapel, they all attended for church every Sunday, and the wedding reception would be at a nearby hotel, which sat on a pretty little hill that overlooked the city.

Nicole gave her two weeks' notice at the hospital, much to their disappointment. They had wanted to train her further, and offered her a promotion if she would stay. But Nicole had turned them down – all she wanted was to marry Samuel, and go away with him. She never told anyone about the offer at the hospital. She made her own decisions, and she believed she knew what was right for her – or so she thought at her young age.

She packed up her little apartment, and moved back home for the last month to save extra money. She had to save as much as she could; she knew they would need extra cash, so she intended to take all her savings with her.

Chapter Three

Samuel and Ben arrived on the morning of the twenty-fourth of December. They checked into a pretty little bed and breakfast. Ben was Samuel's best man at his wedding. Samuel was so happy; he couldn't believe his luck in marrying such a sweet girl, who would also one day make him Canadian citizen. He had picked up a lovely wedding ring set. The engagement ring he would give her for Christmas, and the next day he would put the matching wedding ring on her finger.

Nicole's house was bustling. Sarah had so much to do, with a Christmas dinner for the whole family, and Nicole's wedding the next day, which was Sarah's birthday too. She appreciated the child wanting to get married on her birthday, but it made everything so hectic.

"Nicole, honey what time did you tell Samuel and Ben to come for dinner tomorrow?"

"I told him around five. Is that ok?"

"Yes, I guess so. Have you seen your sister dear?"

"Yes, mom. She's in our room, trying on her dress for the wedding again."

Her younger sister was one of the three attendants, who would be standing with her at the wedding. She'd picked out a pretty pink dress for her, with lovely pink and white flowers. Her brother's girlfriend and Cathy her best Friend, were the other people who would stand with her on her special day.

Millie had a troubled feeling inside her heart, which she couldn't explain. She knew that the road ahead would not be easy for Nicole. She was an easy target for someone to take advantage of her. But the heart wants what the heart wants, and she must support her sweet child no matter what the outcome may be. For now they were celebrating the love of these two people, and they could only hope it was a true and lasting one.

***

It was late afternoon of the twenty-sixth of December: Nicole's wedding day.

"Happy birthday Mommy! I hope you like the dress I made you." Nicole had been sewing since she was ten years old and did beautiful work, she'd made her mother a lovely silk rose-colored dress to wear at her wedding. It fit her slim figure perfectly.

Nicole had always been a designer at heart.

"Yes dear, I love it. Thank you; you did a beautiful job. It fits perfectly.

"Are you ready to get into your dress? It's nearly six o'clock, and the all of the guests are at the church." It was a small guest list of family and close friends, only about fifty people, which was just right for the small chapel.

"Yes, Mommy I'm ready, but did you see how much snow is out there? I hope it's not a bad omen."

"Now Nicole. Don't be silly dear. It's no omen; it's just winter that's all." Sarah had never believed in omens, or such things.

But Nicole's grandmother sat in her rocking chai,r and looked out the window thinking. That Mother Nature was unfortunately not giving these two her blessing today – by the looks of the weather tonight, Mother Nature was angry as hell. It was snowing heavily, and the skies were gray. It was such a shame she thought, but what could she do? It was too late now.

Nicole got dressed, and put on the little pearl earrings her grandmother had given her. This was the only jewelry she wore.

Once again, she looked out the window.

"Wow, what a night. But it doesn't matter. This is the day I marry my Samuel." Nicole believed God's blessings would fall on them no matter what. She had faith like a child, looking up to her Father in Heaven; she believed that all good things, flowed from him into her life.

Samuel stood at the altar with Ben by his side. They both looked tall, dark and handsome, in their black suits. The little chapel's aisles were lined with red poinsettias, and bright red Christmas lights, and standing in the far corner was a huge Christmas tree, glowing with lights of every color.

The Christmas lights were the only lights left on in the chapel that evening. They created a warm, almost magical glow in the little church. It may have been snowing and overcast outside, but inside it was warm and radiant with love. The people that gathered in the church that night, could feel the love between these two people, who were about to commit their lives to each other.

The church organist began to play the wedding march, and then Marilyn slowly came out in her pink dress. Cathy came after her, then her brother's girlfriend Lorna. The music intensified, and the congregation stood up and turned to look at the little chapel doorway.

There stood Nicole. Her long golden hair done in soft curls, off to one side with a big flowing hat. Her dress was made of simple white lace with long sleeves, and a sweetheart neckline. She carried pink roses in a basket. Elegantly she began to walk slowly towards Samuel. His face was lit with the biggest smile she'd ever seen. He looked at his bride with pride in his heart. He knew he was marrying the love of his life tonight.

As Nicole walked towards him, her Grandmother put her hand out, and Nicole squeezed it and smiled as she walked by. She knew what a gift she had been given, what a blessing Samuel, and her whole family were. It was a night she would remember for as long as she lived.

She stood beside him, holding his hand as they said their vows. When Nicole looked around the little chapel that night, she knew that no matter what happened in their lives, they would always have these loving memories, of their very special wedding night. She could feel the overwhelming warmth, and love that surrounded them. For no amount of snow or stormy weather, would ever take away the fact that she loved this man, and that they would always be together now, in her mind and in her heart. They walked down the aisle as husband and wife, and the beaming look on their faces, was something that no one in the room could argue with – they belonged together. They enter the reception in the hotel, and were announced as husband and wife, then stood in the lobby as everyone took pictures. The guests lined up to congratulate them and wish them well.

Their wedding cake was simple and sweet. They ate, drank, and danced the night away. Joy surrounded them, and as Nicole's Grandmother watched them dance, she hoped they would continue to be as happy as they were tonight. Let them be happy she prayed silently to herself.

***

In less than a week they were packed up, and on their way to Santo Domingo to start their married life. It would not be in the best of circumstances they knew, but it would be okay as long as they had each other. They had no time or money for a honeymoon, and it was back to school for Samuel and Ben. Ben had moved out, and was now sharing a bigger place with Fred and Tony, and Samuel had found a smaller apartment for him and Nicole. It was clean and was on the top floor of a three-story building. They had rooftop access, with enough space for a small table and chair set outside, where they could relax and eat outside most nights. Nicole had her savings, and Samuel's family would send money every six months, for his school fees and living allowance. Nicole knew she had to try to find some kind of work. They would have many things to buy, like Samuel's medical books, food, and much more.

Nicole studied Spanish for the first few weeks outside on the rooftop, she was becoming a golden-tanned beauty from sitting in the sun for hours. Now with a little Spanish under her belt, she headed out to the local shopping plaza, to explore the work situation there. She could walk there, it wasn't far from their place. As she walked along the streets, she saw little boys around five years old, begging and trying to help adults carry bags of grocery to their cars for money. They looked dirty and tired. These little boys are just babies, she thought. Her heart broke a thousand times over to see them out on the street, trying to fend for themselves. She swallowed hard and kept moving. This is not a gentle country, she thought to herself. It seemed to her that it was a country where there were the very rich, and the very poor – and not much in between.

She entered the shopping plaza. There were many beautiful stores inside, but she was not there to shop, she was there to look for a job. When she entered the stores, she soon realized that her Spanish was poor, and she could hardly understand what the people were saying to her. She became very discouraged, and sat down on a bench with a cup of coffee she had purchased. She sat for a minute, and then she began to silently pray. "Father God in heaven, you have never let me down yet. Can you please supply me with a job? You know just how much we need it. Please help me Father." She was hoping for some inspiration to keep moving on through the shopping mall.

She stood up from the bench and began to walk further along. Something above her head caught her eye – it was a sign that said HELP WANTED in bold red letters. Wait a minute, she thought. I can read that. It's English!

The sign was posted in front of a medical bookstore. She went inside and said, "Hello?"

"Hello can I help you Miss?"

"I see you have a sign for help wanted in your window sir, I would like to apply for the job if I may?"

"My name is Gray, and this is my store, I am looking for an English speaking person to assist the medical students, when they come in looking for books, is that something you feel Miss you can do?"

"Oh yes, I'm sure I can, you see my husband is a medical student here, I have a nursing background, and my English is perfect."

"Wow that is a good fit for here I must say, how long will you be in this country?"

"For a few years at least."

"Well, in that case I would love to offer you the job, I will file the correct papers, and get your work permit, leave that to me. Your salary will be eight hundred a month, and you will work Monday to Friday with the weekends off. How does that sound, sorry Miss what is your name?"

"Nicole, and its Mrs. My last name is Emeka, my husband is from Africa."

"Very interesting last name, you can start tomorrow if that works for you okay. I have only one girl here at the moment, and she could use a hand right away, we can get pretty busy here at times. Her name is Phyllis she is an American girl, I think the two of you will get along just fine. So come back tomorrow for ten o'clock. Your hours will be ten to one, and then we close for a two hours for lunch, and then open again from three until six in the evening."

"That sound just wonderful. Thank you so much Gary. I will be here at ten in the morning." Nicole filled out all the papers, that Gary has asked her too, and then she walked home very pleased with herself, she could hardly wait to tell Samuel the good news.

She cooked dinner for Samuel, and set the little table up with candles and wine. When the food was ready, she sat outside waiting for him, but he was late, the food was getting cold, and she was hungry so she ate alone.

Sam came home around nine that night.

"Hi Lady. Sorry I am so late, I just had too much work, and I needed to go to the library to do some research. I am so hungry. What's for dinner?"

"I'll make your food hot again. I baked some fish and pasta for you." She got up from bed to prepare his meal, and sat at the table with him while he ate.

"So how was your day? What did you do today?'

"Well I got a job, believe it or not," she said looking very pleased with herself.

"A job... wow, that's great! Where did you get one so soon?"

"At the local shopping plaza in the medical bookstore, selling books to all the medical students here on the Island."

"Well, I bet you'll be great at that." He grinned at her.

"Yes, I think so. I know I am way over qualified, but it's a job for now to help us pay the bills. It's owned by an American man his name is Gary, and he needed an English-speaking person to help with the English-speaking medical students. What luck for us, don't you think? We'll now have a little extra cash. They are going to pay me about eight hundred dollars a month, and I get your medical books at half price."

"Unbelievable Lady!" He smiled, pleased that she would be helping them with some money, and relieved that she wouldn't be so bored anymore.

***

Nicole's walked to work the next morning it was only ten minutes away. She was wearing a cream linen dress and flat shoes. She was prepared to be on her feet all day.

"Hello I'm Nicole. I'm the new the girl." She beamed

"Yes, I know. I've been expecting you. I'm Phyllis and I'm from Montana in the US, but my husband is going to medical school here so that's why I'm here." She smiled. Phyllis was a tall, thin blonde woman in her mid-forties. Her husband had started his studies later in his life. Nicole sensed that she was a talker who was glad to finally have someone to talk to.

"Really my husband is going to Utesa Medical School here too. I'm from Canada –Nova Scotia to be exact."

"No shit! That's the same school as my husband, I guess he will be in the same class as yours. So how long have you been here Nicole?

"I just got here a month ago, and it's all been so hectic. But I am ready to learn all about the book business with you today." She said happily.

"It's great to have you here Nicole. I'll show you how to work the cash register, and then how the medical books are laid out, so you know how to assist the students when they come in. They usually all come in at the same time for some reason; I guess it's when they all get breaks. We can get pretty busy here sometimes."

They worked hard all day, and before Nicole even knew it, it was time to go home. Samuel made sure to come home on time tonight; he wanted to know how Nicole's first day at work had gone. They sat outside under the big round moon, and ate dinner.

"So how was your first day on the job my sweetheart?" Samuel asked, taking a long drink of water.

"It was really busy. Phyllis is the woman who is training me, I like her a lot, and I just know we are going to be great friends."

"That's great news. I'm so happy to hear that." He paused. "I have to stay up late tonight and study. Exam day tomorrow. So you will have to amuse yourself tonight my dear."

"I have been almost every night since I've been here. I know you need to study. I'm here when you have time for me." She kissed him, and went inside to take a long hot bath.

She got into bed alone, and read for a while before she fell asleep. The truth was she slept alone almost every night, Samuel studied until two in the morning, and then often fell asleep on their living room couch. She was in fact starting to feel lonely.

***

As time passed Nicole slowly adjusted to life in Santo Domingo. She was glad to have a job to get her out in the daytime, but at night she missed her family desperately. She knew when she'd agreed to come that Samuel wouldn't be around much, but she hadn't thought it would be quite so hard on her.

She was doing her best to make whatever money they had to go around. But with meals and all the other bills, they were just making ends meet. There was nothing in the budget for her needs. Occasionally she wished they had more time to just be newlyweds, and to have a little fun together. But the truth was that nothing about being there, was fun for her or for him. It was always about his career. She only hoped that when they finally got to go back home to Nova Scotia, things would be easier and kinder for them and their marriage.

It was the night of December twenty-fourth. Nicole and Samuel sat outside at their little table together. It was Christmas Eve already, and it would soon be their first wedding anniversary.

It was a warm night. They sat fanning themselves with paper fans, and for the first time in a long time, Samuel actually noticed his wife. He looked at Nicole closely, and couldn't help but detect the faraway look in her eyes. He felt her sadness now as she just sat there and rocked in the chair, looking up at the sky. She was wondering if someone at home might be looking at the same bright star tonight. Her heart was so homesick for her mother, sister, and grandmother. It felt like years since her brothers had teased her, and she wished with all her heart, that she was with them all tonight. She imagined in her mind the Christmas scene back home.

***

Sarah was busy in the kitchen as usual, preparing the stuffing for her turkey dinner tomorrow, but as she was doing so, she looked out her little kitchen window to see big snowflakes falling down. She looked up in the sky, and noticed that it was unusually clear tonight. She could see one bright star, and she somehow knew her daughter was looking up at that same star too. She was missing one of her children this Christmas, and for her things were just not the same.

Everyone was missing, Nicole in their own way, especially her little sister. They'd always done things together at Christmas, like shop, wrap presents, and help with the Christmas cookies. But this year Nicole was missing, and so there was a big empty space in her family's hearts. Millie looked up at their big sparkling Christmas tree thinking of Nicole, she knew just how much she loved the Christmas tree lights. Millie moved to look out their big front window and up into the sky. She could see one star brightly twinkling up in the clear winter sky.

Marilyn was sitting by the tree, thinking of Nicole too. "Grand what do you think

Nicole is doing tonight? I miss her don't you?"

"She's looking at this star. Come and have a look. She misses you too dear. Believe me, she misses every one of us tonight." She could feel in her gut just how homesick Nicole was.

"Oh Grand, how do you know that?" Marilyn asked.

"I just know dear. Why don't we give her a call? Go get your mother, and we'll call her. Hearing her voice will cheer us all up."

"Ok, but Mommy is making peanut butter fudge; I can smell it. How about I go get us a few pieces?"

Marilyn ran into the kitchen.

"Mom, Grand wants to call Nicole now. Can we please? I am taking some fudge into Grand too"

"Okay dear, yes let's go make that call now."

Sarah and Marilyn hurried back into the living room, and dialed Nicole's number.

Nicole came back to the present when she heard the phone ringing. She got up and ran to the phone with a feeling it would be her family.

"Merry Christmas!" Nicole said.

"Hi dear! How's my girl tonight? Missing all our snow yet?" Her mother joked. "We really miss you, dear; it's not the same without you this Christmas." Sarah smiled when she heard her daughter's voice.

"Oh Mommy, I miss all of you too. I wish I was home. How is everyone? What are you all doing tonight?" Nicole asked in a small, sad voice that broke Sarah's heart.

"Well dear, I just made peanut butter fudge, and your sister is already eating it with Grand. The boys are outside cleaning up the snow. Your sisters wants to say hello now."

"Okay, Mommy. I love you."

"I love you too dear."

"Hi Nick! What are you doing over there, and when are you coming back home? It's so boring here without you. Is it very warm there? We got so much snow here!" Marilyn said with her mouth full of fudge.

"I'll be coming home real soon Sis. I miss you guys too. How's the fudge this year?"

"Yummy, and I am going to get another piece! Grand wants to say hi," Nicole laughed.

"Hello child. How are you tonight? A little homesick no doubt," Millie said.

"Yes Grand. Very much. I really miss being home for Christmas this year, and... well, it's just that things here are kind of lonely, with Samuel being so busy with school and everything." Nicole wiped the tears from her eyes; she did not want her family to know she was crying. That would have made them feel even worse, so she tried her best to talk normally.

"I know, dear. Just hang in there. If you want to come home any time soon, you just say the word, and I will send you a ticket. I bet your cooking a big turkey dinner tomorrow?"

"Yes, I'm going to try. We've invited a few friends over to dinner, so I'll be busy cooking. At least that will keep my mind off of home for a little while. I'm even going to bake an apple pie."

"Wow, my sweet child has grown up. Now try not to be sad? We are never really too far away, and you can call me collect anytime you feel like it. You know I feel it when you're homesick dear."

"Yes, I know you do. I love all of you so much. Give my brothers a big kiss too. I will try my best to make the best of this Christmas, for all our friends tomorrow I promise. Merry Christmas and I love you Grand."

"We love you more, say hello and Merry Christmas to Samuel for us, and good luck with your turkey tomorrow dear."

As Nicole hung up the phone, she couldn't help but cry. She missed them all so much. But this year, Samuel and their new friend were her Christmas, and it was up to her to make sure they all had a merry one.

Samuel came in, and put his arms around his wife. "Lady just try to hang in there with me it will get better."

"Sure I will. Let's go to bed. I'm tired and I have a lot of cooking to do tomorrow." She smiled up at him, as he wiped away her tears.

He stayed with her all night long and held her close. He knew her heart was breaking, and that it was all for him – she had sacrificed Christmas with her own family to be by his side. He had been away from his family for quite some time, and he had gotten used to the fact that he never got to see them on the holidays. But for Nicole it was all so new, he could feel that she felt it so much more than she said.

The next day she prepared her first Christmas dinner for Samuel and their friends. They ate and drank together. Ben, Tony, and Fred had brought Nicole flowers and wine. They loved her turkey dinner, and ate all her apple pie. Nicole joked and laughed with everyone. She put on Christmas music, and offered everyone a cup hot chocolate before they left at midnight. She wanted them all to have a great Christmas in her little home. Samuel stood back and admired the woman he had married. He walked over to Nicole, and put his arms around her waist.

"Lady... thank you for making us such a wonderful Christmas this year. I know how hard it is for you."

"As long as you're here with me, I am okay, you're my home away from home." Ben and the other finally got up to leave, and Nicole and Samuel walked them all to their door. "Thank you so much Samuel. You are so lucky to have this wife of yours, Merry Christmas." Ben and the others said as they left.

"You're welcome any time guys. Merry Christmas." Samuel said as they stood in their doorway, waving goodbye.

"Thank you, for this wonderful Christmas. But I have a little surprise for you."

"You do? What is it?" She smiled looking amazed, that he had time to shop.

"Here lady. Open it."

It was a little blue box, and when she opened it, she found a pair of beautiful blue topaz earrings, which are her birthstone. "Oh wow! They're so lovely baby. Thank you so much.

"Now it's your turn." She smiled and handed him a larger box.

"Wow, I like Christmas," he laughed as he opened the box. She had gotten him the medical books he'd wanted but hadn't been able to afford. She had gotten a special discount from her boss.

"Wow I really needed these. Thank you so much for thinking of me." He looked into her eyes. "I saved the best for last tonight Mrs. Emeka."

"Oh? Dare I ask what that is?" She grinned.

"Yes, you may. It's me." He picked her up and carried her off to bed, and this time sleeping wasn't on his mind. He slowly undresses her, and they made passionate love. He wanted her to remember why she was his wife, and why she belonged to him no one else.

***

With the holidays behind them now, and a new semester beginning for Samuel, he was busier than ever before. He began to study longer, and harder for his January exams.

Nicole was busy at the store, but the money was barely enough to put food on the table, and pay their rent. Both she and Sam kept a watchful eye on their bank account, but with each school semester their account got lower and lower. Sam's books and school fees cost them dearly. They were anxiously waiting for Samuel's money from home to come in – it was later than usual. Samuel had called home and talked to his older brother, he told him that Nigeria had suffered a military takeover, and the central banks were not allowing any money to be transferred out of the country at the moment. His brother had promised that he would try his best to find a way to get him some money soon. A few more months passed, and Samuel's money from home still hadn't arrived. He tried calling home many times, and was always given the same answer. Their funds had all but run out now, leaving only Nicole's salary at the store to support them. It was only enough to put food on the table, and pay their rent, and phone bill. Sam was sitting outside one evening, he was anxious and upset. Nicole walked over to him and put her hands on his shoulders.

"I know it's money worrying you Sam," she said in a quiet voice.

"I don't know how I am going to pay my school fees this semester. They are due in 4 weeks, and I need two thousand dollars to pay them." He put his head in his hands. He had a terrible headache from all the stress.

"Don't worry Sam. We'll think of something, and hopefully your money will come soon." She walked away and went inside. She knew she had to do it – she had to call home. She hated to, but she had no other choice. She dialed her home number, and her grandmother answered on the first ring.

"Hello?" Millie said.

"Hi Grand. How are you?" Nicole's voice said that everything was wrong, to her old grandmother.

"Hello dear. The question is, how are you?"

"Not so good Grand. We haven't received Samuel's money yet from his home. His school fees are due in a few weeks. I don't know what to do. We need about two thousand dollars to pay for everything. There's still trouble in his country, and his brother can't seem to get the money to us. I guess we need a loan until his money comes in, and then we can pay you back."

"Yes, I guess you do... I'll put the money in the mail to you today. Everything will be okay, dear."

"I feel so bad about having to ask you for the money, but I didn't know what else to do. We've come so far; it would be a shame for him not to be able to continue with his studies." "You have no choice, you had to ask. You need help, and I am that help for now. So stop your fretting, and stop those tears. You knew it wasn't going to be easy over there. I know it's his career, and not yours that you're suffering for. But hopefully when he finishes, he'll provide a good life for you, and your children one day."

"Yes, I hope so Grandmother, thank you so much for your help today. Do you know how much I love you?"

"Yes but how much?" She smiled.

"More than I can possibly tell you, ten thousand great big kisses and hugs. You are a lifesaver. I love you, and will talk to you soon Grand bye for now. "

"I love you too, and take care of yourself dear."

Her grandmother's heart broke, she knew her too well; Nicole had never complained about the things that bothered her, even as a young girl. She just suffered in silence until someone she loved figured it out and fixed it for her. Millie knew this was one of those times. But how much more would there be to fix before it got better? Millie felt troubled because she just knew in her gut, that this was only the beginning of Nicole's grief.

She sometimes felt that maybe it would be better for her to come back home now, while she was still young enough, and had time to get over him, and move on with her life. But to even suggest that to Nicole would break her heart, and she would never be the one to do that. Nicole slowly walked outside to where Sam was still sitting. She sat down beside him, and took his hands in hers.

"Sam... I just called Grand, and asked for the money we need to get us through until your money comes in from home. She's going to send it to us tomorrow. We'll pay her back later once your money arrives... okay? So stop worrying, and go back to your studies before you get behind. "When she looked at Samuel, the degree of sadness in her eyes spoke volumes. She walked back inside to get ready for bed. Sam continued to sit outside. He was relieved, but unhappy. It hurt his pride for his wife to have to deal with money matters. He could see the strain when she looked at him, dealing with their day to day stress, was starting to show in her.

He went inside, looked at his wife sleeping, and gently sat down on the bed beside her. He felt sick inside – he could see how unhappy she looked even in her sleep. He knew he had to be strong and keep going, or he would never get them through it all and out of this place. So he pulled himself off the bed. All he really wanted to do was fall asleep beside her, and hold her all night, but instead he walked out to his desk sat down, and burned the midnight oil.

As the days passed and turned into weeks, and the weeks passed into months, it became very clear they were in trouble once again. Samuel became even more anxious. Still no money had come from home. In just a few more weeks they would need even more money to pay his finial school fee again. School break was about to start in a few days. He knew what he needed to do during this time. He went into the travel agency at the mall where Nicole worked and booked a ticket. He paid for it on the credit card he'd been saving for emergencies. Nicole never knew about the card, Samuel had kept it from her. He had to travel home, and bring back money for them. He needed to ease some of the stress on his wife's shoulders, and leave his own mind free to study. He was in his last semester of medical school. He hated to leave her in this country on her own, but he had no choice now. He booked everything and picked up his ticket, and then went by the bookstore. She would be closing soon, and he wanted to walk her home, and stop for dinner at the pizza place along the way.

"Hello. How is my sweetheart this evening?"

"I'm fine Sam. What brings you here tonight?" She asked curiously, thinking something was up. He rarely came by to walk her home. In fact, most nights he was late for dinner.

"How about we grab dinner out tonight? It's been a long week for you, and you deserve a break from cooking. Let's get a pizza. "

"Okay, that sounds good."

They walked down the street and took a seat at the restaurant, they ordered beer and pizza.

"So how was your day? I am surprised to see you so early this evening."

"Lady... I have to tell you something. I booked an airplane ticket home today. I have to go and get money. I hope you understand. I shouldn't be any longer than two weeks. I need you to be ok on your own here for a short while. "

"Well, I kind of thought that was going to happen, so I'm okay with it. I'll be fine here on my own. But how did you pay for the ticket?"

"I had a credit card, put away for emergencies, and I figured that this was it. Sorry I didn't tell you about it. It was a last resort kind of thing. I just hope I get the money when I'm home, so I can pay off the credit card and your grandmother, and have enough left to finish out school."

"Thank God you had it. I thought I was going to have to call home again, and that would have killed me Sam. I guess we are both weary these days from all that has been thrown at us here."

He looked tired too, she thought, he needed more rest and less worry, so going home will be a good thing for him, and hopefully it will solve their money problems for a while. She always tried to understand everything. The fact was she was so tired too, tired of living on this island, where there was nothing for her but work and worry. Even though he was there with her, he was never really there, not for her in many ways. She felt the burden of everything that was always being thrown at her. She wanted to go home too, it had been a long time since she had seen her family. But she knew that wouldn't be possible, she couldn't leave the book store, they needed the money, so she had to stay and work until he came back.

They finished eating and walked slowly home. She got ready for bed and when he came in and sat on their bed, she climbed on his lap like a small child would. He put his arms around her. He knew she was disappointed in how their life had been so far. But soon he would be finished, and they could move back to Canada. At least there they would have a chance to lead a happier, and a better life.

"I will hurry back as soon as I can. You know I hate to leave you here all alone."

"I know baby. We both hate a lot of things about living here, but we can't quit now. We're in the homestretch, we've come a long way, and both of us have worked very hard for your degree. So all we can do is keep going, until we are finished." He kissed her and made love to her, and slept beside her all night, knowing he was leaving the next morning.

***

Samuel hadn't been home since his mother had passed away four years before, and he wondered if anything would have changed. He tried to talk to his brother on a regular basis, but due to a shortage of money and time, that was limited. His brother Clem was expecting him; he had made a quick call, and told him he would be coming home with a time and date, so they could pick him up at the Lagos airport.

***

Each day that Sam was away seemed like an eternity to Nicole. But when two weeks went by, and Nicole didn't hear from him, she started to become concerned. Soon three weeks had passed since he'd been gone.

She knew it could be hard to call out of Nigeria sometimes, so she hadn't expected many calls from him. But she really thought that by now, he would be at least back in England, and he would have called her from there. His classes would be starting again in just a few days.

She was starting to get an unpleasant feeling that something was wrong. That dreaded feeling deep inside her gut, was warning her of some kind of trouble. When she slept at night, she had bad dreams of him, and his family being surrounded by armed guards. But how could that be? She thought. He was only visiting his family, and the central bank. So where do the guards come into play in my dream? She probed her mind for answers. He had been gone for too long with no contact. If everything had been fine, he would have called her by now – that much she knew for sure. If she didn't hear anything soon, she would have to call the Canadian Embassy, and ask them for help.

Nicole slowly walked to work the next morning.

"My God Nicole. You look so tired! No sleep again?" Phyllis was starting to get worried about Nicole. She thought maybe Sam had just taken off, and was never coming back. "No news yet?"

"No. Nothing at all. And I keep having the same dream with the armed guards. What am I going to do if I don't hear from him?"

"Well, like I mention before, we'll have to contact the Canadian embassy, and get them to look for him... I guess." Phyllis was equally unsure of how to handle a situation like this.

"Do they even do that kind of thing?" Nicole asked.

"I'm not sure. But we can try. The man loves you to death; he would never leave you over here. Something must be wrong Nicole, and we need to find out what?"

"Yes, I guess you're right."

Nicole walked home and got ready for bed. She made a cup of soup and slowly drank it. She'd lost several pounds in the last two weeks – enough so that all her clothes seemed too big for her now. She just drank soup and lots of coffee, and often walked the floors at night, worrying about the same recurring bad dream.

The moment she fell asleep, she would see armed guards all around Samuel's brother's house. She often tried to call his brother, but the operator would say the same thing, that the phone would not ring in that area right now. That there was trouble with their line.

"Why aren't you calling me by now Sam? Why?" She cried in the dead of night. She was so anxious and tired of it all; she just wanted to know he was all right.

The next morning, her phone rang. She jumped out of bed to get it. "Hello?"

"Hello child. How are you doing over there all by yourself? We're all worried about you, dear." Millie was feeling the same jumpy feeling inside her gut now too. "Have you heard from Sam yet?"

"Not a word. What am I going to do? I have the same dream every night now, with armed guards all around his brother's house. What do you see Grand?"

Millie hesitated. "I think it's time we contacted someone dear. You need to call the Canadian Embassy, and let them know that he's missing, and tell them he is now a Canadian citizen, or they won't do anything. I know there's some kind of trouble. I can feel it too, and we need to find out what it is. Does Ben know anything at all?"

"No. He's worried too." Nicole sighed.

"I'll call you later tonight dear. Your mother is worried sick too, but I'm trying to downplay it so she doesn't get too upset, and demand that you come home."

"Thanks Grand. I'll contact the Canadian Embassy this morning."

Once they'd said their goodbyes and hung up, she picked up the phone book, looked up the number, and called the Canadian Embassy. "Hello. May I please speak with whoever is in charge of foreign affairs Countries like Nigeria?"

"Just one moment please." There was a pause as Nicole was transferred.

"Hello. How may I help you? "An older man's voice asked.

"Hello. My name is Nicole Emeka, and my husband has travelled to Nigeria to visit his family there. It's been three and half weeks now, and I haven't heard a word from him. I'm terribly worried that something bad has happened. Here's the address of his family and his full name." She read him the information. "Is there anything you can do to help me find out what has happened to him?" She sounded very young to the man on the other end of the line.

"Is your husband a Nigerian?"

"Yes, he was born there, but he is now a Canadian citizen."

"I see. Let me look into it Mrs. Emeka. But I have to tell you that many of them go home, and leave their Canadian wives behind when they're finished studying, because they already have a wife back home. We've seen it happen many times. They marry a Canadian woman to get their citizenship here, and then bring their African wives back with them. But I'll check to see if there is any unrest in the country with our Embassy there in Logos."

"Sorry, what is your name, please sir?" Nicole asked.

"Sorry Mrs. Emeka. My name is Jason Lovett. I should have told you that before."

"I'm a bit shocked by what you've just said Mr. Lovett. I believe my Samuel loves me, and wants to come home to me. He hasn't finished his studies here yet. So whatever the situation may be with others, I don't believe that it's anywhere near the same for us. I know he loves me, and would never leave me here on my own. I would really appreciate your help. I'm living here on my own, away from my own family in Canada, and Samuel was all the family I had here. I am terribly worried, and I need to find out what is really going on. I know that something bad must have happened, to keep him away from me for so long."

The man at the embassy felt sorry for her. She sounded like she could have very easily been his daughter. He kind of wished now he hadn't told her all that he had, and he hoped for her sake that this man who was missing really did love her. "I will do whatever I can Mrs. Emeka. I'll call you back as soon as I hear anything. It should be a day or so, before I get any news from over there, so just hang in there."

She thanked him and hung up, feeling very disappointed. She had hoped for a more encouraging reply, but at least he would look into it. His words played in her mind all night, but she didn't believe for even one minute that Samuel would do such a thing to her. She trusted him with her life and her love, and she knew there was more to this story, than what the man at the embassy was thinking.

She called back two days later, and talked with Jason again. "Hello Mr. Lovett. This is Nicole Emeka calling back. Have you found anything out yet regarding my husband?"

"Yes, I have. There was a military overrule in the country last week. Samuel's oldest brother is an advisor to the government that was overruled by the military, and the whole family has been under house arrest while they question his brother. It is my understanding that they will soon be released, but with these kinds of things one never really knows how long they might take."

"Oh dear God! What can we do? Is he safe?"

"First of all, stop panicking Mrs. Emeka. When I talked with the government official, he said that they should be able to call out soon. Just sit tight until things calm down over there. It shouldn't be long now – maybe a day or so."

"Okay. That's easier said than done, but thank you for all your help."

"Call me again if you don't hear anything in the next week, and we'll check on things again for you."

"I'll do that. Thank you so much for all your help sir." Nicole hung up the phone, still stunned by the news she had just been given.

She sat down on her bed. "That's what my dreams mean," she said out loud to herself. "He's under house arrest. Well, at least I'm not crazy." She needed to call her Grandmother and tell her the news. She'd know what to do. She picked up the phone again.

"Hello Grand. It's Nicole. How are you?"

"We're all fine dear. How is everything there? What news do you have for us?"

"It's not too good Grand. His whole family is under house arrest. The government was overthrown by the military, his oldest brother was an advisor to them, and so they're holding the whole family for questioning. They don't know how much longer it'll last. It must be dreadful for Samuel and his family. What can we do? How can we fix it?"

"My dear child not everything is in our power to fix. You must understand that. But what we can do is pray. Remember, he never gives us more than we can handle at any given time. Just believe he is preparing a special grace to help us accomplish all that we must do in this situation."

"Yes of course I believe. But how can that help Sam right now?"

"Well, let's repeat this for him, every hour of every day, until he comes home: 'Free as a bird you will soon be, flying safely back to me, free as a bird come sing to me, free as a bird come home to me.' I know it doesn't seem like much, but it's a powerful thought dear. Implant it firmly in your mind until it becomes so"

"But Grandmother, will he be safe? Do you see anything terrible? You must tell me. Please... I need to know."

"You can see as well as me dear, if you try hard enough. You tell me this time. You need to learn to trust your own visions. What do you see sweet child, in your mind's eye?"

"I don't see anything past the armed guards, but I can feel him panicking, because he isn't able to contact me. How can I let him know, I know what's happening to him, and that I'm okay here."

"Just look up at the brightest star each and every night, concentrating as hard as you can, until you see his eyes looking at you from the star. Then say, 'I am all right, and so are you. I know and see all that they do. Repeat this until you believe it to be true."

"That's it? Just that?" Nicole asked.

"Yes. The energy of the stars, and the universal law of attraction are powerful dear, it will connect our energy with his energy. I promise you that. Never voice your doubts, for once spoken, they can become your realities. Only voice the positive things you expect to happen, and have faith and believe that they have already come to pass. When we both do this together, the force of our energy is greater. Remember: 'he who is in me, is greater than he who is in the world.' That means energy, my dear girl."

"Okay... I'll do it with all the energy I have. Will you do it with me Grandmother?"

"Of course, dear. We'll do it together, starting tonight at eight o'clock, when the stars are shining bright. We'll do it tonight and every night until we hear back from him."

"Thanks so much Grand. How is Mommy doing?"

"I think you'd better talk to her dear. She's worried too."

"Okay... let me talk to her then please." There was a pause as the phone was handed over.

"Hello dear. How have you been holding up over there with Samuel being gone for so long? Have you heard anything yet?"

Nicole explained the situation that Sam and his family were in.

"I think it's time you came home now. You shouldn't stay there any longer on your own. We'll send you a ticket – I want you home where you belong."

"I can't leave here Mommy; not without Samuel. He wouldn't know where I am when he returns."

"*If* he returns dear. You must face the facts. It could take months if the situation doesn't get better over there. And why should you be suffering on your own, when we're all here to support you and take care of you? My dear girl, please be reasonable. I want you to come home now." Sarah was supportive with her daughter, but she was afraid for her, and wanted her near in case the worst happened. She didn't want her daughter to go through that kind of thing all alone.

"Mommy, I simply cannot leave yet. Please understand; I have to stay for at least a little while longer."

"Fine. Then we'll give it another week. If there's no news by then, I want you on a plane and headed for home. Do you understand me Nicole?"

"Please give me at least another two weeks, and then we'll talk about this again okay?"

"Okay dear. But no longer than that. You are the most stubborn child I have; you're just as stubborn as your old Grandmother. But I love you dear, and you know I only want the best for you. Call us as soon as you hear anything please."

"I love you too Mommy, and I'll call soon. And please don't worry. I'll be just fine over here, I promise."

Sarah hung up the phone and looked at Millie. "Now please don't encourage her to stay over there. We don't know what will happen with Samuel, and she won't be able to handle it on her own if it goes sour, so please talk some sense into her head, and get her to come home now," Sarah pleaded.

"We can't control that girl and you know it. When she makes up her mind to do something, there's no stopping her. I will support you as you wish, but give her another few weeks."

Millie knew that if she, and Nicole concentrated hard enough, Samuel might be back by then, but she also knew it was going to take a lot from both of them to accomplish this because he was so far away.

At eight o'clock that night, Nicole sat outside in her rocking chair and looked up at the sky. She spotted the brightest star, and started to repeat the words her grandmother had shared with her. Her voice became a chant which whispered out into the night's energy. She repeated the words, until she could finally see his eyes looking back at her in her mind's eye.

She and Millie repeated this for three evenings, and on the third night she knew that he could somehow hear her, somehow she had reached him, and then her mind and heart were suddenly calmed. She knew he was fine, and he knew she was bravely waiting for him to come back home to her. Peace settled in her soul, as she patiently waited for his call.

***

Samuel had been terribly restless for the last few weeks, being kept in the house with no outside contact, was making him a bit crazy. He would never live in this country again, he vowed to his brother. As soon as he could return back to Canada and get established, he wanted to bring his family there to live. He was only thankful that they'd been able to get the money transferred to his Canadian bank account, before all this mess happened. He was so upset for Nicole, and for what she must be thinking.

Tonight he just sat looking hopelessly out the window. After a while a twinkling, dancing star caught his eye. He gazed at it for a long time. It was so odd, he thought. It was like it was talking to him. He couldn't take his eyes off of it; he felt like it was capturing his energy. Eventually he closed his eyes. He was so tired. When he did, he could see Nicole smiling and saying, "I am all right, and so are you." He felt more peaceful, and he hoped it was Nicole sending him the twinkling star. He knew she was able to do magical things sometimes, things he didn't understand, and he truly hoped this was a sign from her that she was okay.

Samuel's brother Clement came into the room, and noticed how miserable his little brother was looking. "Samuel no need to worry. They will soon release us. There is nothing they can find. I have done nothing wrong, and soon you will be able to get back to your studies, my brother."

"It's not just my studies that has me so worried Clement."

"I know my brother. But you must remember, you have many responsibilities here too, and someone who you have promised your future to."

"Yes, I remember all that. How can I forget? You never let me. But you must understand that I love Nicole too. She is just not a doll I am using, and will then throw away when I am finished playing with her."

"Love is something that one gets over. You do not give up your culture for just any love. You must remember that when the time comes. As long as she is useful to you now, that's all that matters. I understand that a man has needs, and having a good woman around makes life easier. I know that my brother. You must remember that she is not your future." Clement left the room. He didn't want to hear too much about Samuel's Canadian woman. He didn't really approve. Clement was a stern man with conservative beliefs, and he believed that Samuel's place was with his own kind. He knew he may love this woman, but he also knew that when the time came, Samuel would do the right thing – he would choose his own blood.

Samuel put his head into his hands. What had he done? No one would ever know or understand, especially his own family, what Nicole really meant to him. To them, she has been just a meal ticket until he finished his studies, someone to make life easier for the time being. But to him she was everything, and he loved her. He hoped he did not disappoint everyone – Nicole, her family, or his own family. Sometimes he felt the burden of all of them on his shoulders. He just wanted to finish his studies so he could decide what was best for his future. Nicole was the only one in his life, that didn't expect anything other than his love, and whatever time he could give her. She was completely undemanding, and did everything she could to support him. She was so lovely and kind, yet she never seemed to realize just how special she was. There was no ego involved for her, no jealousy and no hatred. And she had chosen him, with all his troubles and difficulties. He was the man she'd picked to be her husband.

***

A few more days passed, and then finally they were all released from house arrest. Clem took Samuel to the airport straightaway. "My brother study hard, and come back soon. There is much to be done here, and remember you have a family that needs and loves you here. I know you love this white woman, but that is not why we sent you to Canada. We have supported you there for years, and you owe us respect. I want your word that when the time comes, you will do the right thing." He looked Samuel in the eye.

"I will do my best, but what you feel is the right thing, and what I feel is the right thing, may be different in the future. But I will never turn my back on our family. That I promise you."

"Samuel my brother, we all love you, and the right thing is living with and progressing with your own kind. Believe me, one day you will see that. Safe travels… my brother. I love you."

They hugged and Samuel boarded his plane back to England.

***

Nicole was still not sleeping well, and she paced the floor most nights. She spoke only with her grandmother, because her mother was pressuring her, and wanted her to

71

come home as soon as they could arrange things.

 Her grandmother would simply listen, pray, and not press her on anything. She knew this girl couldn't handle extra pressure right now, and she also knew that Nicole would not leave there without Samuel by her side. She knew Sarah was just afraid for her, and wanted her close by. And no one could blame her for that. It was Millie's job to support both her daughter-in-law, and granddaughter, and that was just what she did.

It was six o'clock Sunday night, when Nicole's phone rang. She ran to pick it up. "Hello?"

"Hello Lady. Did you think I got lost over here?"

"Oh Samuel it's you! Oh, thank God! I am so glad to hear your voice baby. Where are you?"

"I am in England at Kate's place. Lady I am so very sorry. I know you must have been going crazy over there."

"Crazy is not the word. How about worried sick out of my mind? It was so awful. Not hearing your voice, and then when you didn't return on time, I was so scared for you and your family, that I called the Canadian Embassy. They told me what was happening. Thank God you are finally free to come home."

"I am glad you at least knew what was happening. I was so worried you thought that maybe I left you."

"Left me! No… not for one moment did I ever think that. Not for one single moment did I ever." She was so absolute in her words; there was no doubt as she spoke the words in a soft, steady voice. "No… not ever," she said again.

"I am on my way home. I will be there by tomorrow night, and back in your arms. I will make all of this up to you I promise."

He had tears in his eyes as he spoke. He couldn't believe she never doubted him through it all. She'd just patiently waited for him to return. No matter what anyone said, this was a woman to be treasured.

She slept soundly for the first time in weeks, and could hardly wait for Monday evening to arrive. She got up and ate a huge breakfast. All of sudden she was famished. After work she planned a special dinner, with candles and wine for his homecoming. She showered, and put on a soft flowery scent perfume. She picked a flowing silk lavender dress out, and put it on. Her long golden curly hair fell down her back. She lit the candles and put on soft music, and then sat outside in the moonlight, waiting for Samuel to return.

Very soon she heard his footsteps outside the door, and as she stood up and turned around, there he was standing at the top of the staircase staring at her. Nicole looked radiant in the moonlight, she took his breath away and made his heart beat faster. He ran to her and pulled her into his arms.

"Oh Lady, I missed you so much. How wonderfully sweet you smell. Let me look at you. Whenever I leave you and come back, I am so taken back by you."

She smiled and kissed him. "Well, I guess you'll just have to stop leaving me then."

"Yes, I promise I will try to stop doing that."

Samuel picked her up and carried her to bed. He slowly unzipped her dress and let it fall to the floor, and there she stood in all her beauty and innocence. At that moment, there was no one else but them. And when they made love, it was tender, gentle, and loving.

"You are just the inspiration my weary heart needed," he whispered.

"Promise you will never leave me again."

"I promise." In his heart, he knew he would keep her forever. Samuel went back to school and things got back to normal. He was on the homestretch now .He would graduate with his medical degree soon, and they would head back to Canada. They had both worked so hard for his degree. She worked every day to put food on their table, and he had studied hard in order to provide them both a better life in the future. They were a team. Their married life had started out with many struggles Sam knew, but he hoped one day to make it all up to Nicole. He wanted to give her everything; it was because of her that he'd been able to survive the last few years. She had been his heart and soul, and it was her support that had gotten him through it all. Nicole's home was now his home, no matter what his family thought. He knew in his heart that he was where he belonged, right beside his loving wife. When the time came, and his family could see how well everything was working out for them back in Canada, they would understand his choice.

Nicole came home from a long day of work and shopping with Phyllis. She arrived home just after four in the afternoon. Her stomach had been a little upset since lunch, and she was feeling very tired.

She started to feel very ill very quickly. Her head was pounding and her stomach was in serious pain, like someone was tearing her insides out. Her heart was beating so fast that she could hear it in her chest. She ran to the bathroom, where she vomited so violently she almost passed out.

Samuel was sitting at his desk studying. When he heard her in the bathroom, he came running in. He quickly got a wet towel and put it on her forehead. "Lady what's wrong? How do you feel?"

"Terrible. I need the toilet now. Sorry." She sat there and everything just ran out of her like a river. She held her stomach in agonizing pain.

"Oh my God. I think I have food poisoning. Maybe I got some bad water today in my coffee. I feel awful."

She began vomiting again, harder than before. Soon she was lying on the floor of the bathroom, looking pale and washed out.

"I think we need a doctor to come here and look at you." Samuel helped her up and laid her down on the bed, with a pan in front of her in case she had to vomit again. He ran over to the phone, and called his professor who was also a doctor with his own clinic. He agreed to come at once.

He arrived within an hour. "Hello Nicole. Let me take a look at you. I need to take your blood pressure and your temperature."

"My stomach is feeling pretty bad," she croaked.

He took her blood pressure, which was way too high. He knew she could be in real trouble. "I think we should keep you in my clinic for tonight my dear. What do you say?"

"No. I want to stay here. Please just give me something to settle my stomach down and stop the diarrhea. Then I'll be okay to stay here."

"Your blood pressure is very high, and I think it would be best if we keep you in the clinic tonight," he suggested again.

"I said no. Please just give me the medication. Sam is here to take my blood pressure and watch over me. I'll be fine."

"Lady, why not listen to him? They have everything you will need there."

"No Sam. I have everything I need here. Please do as I ask." She struggled to sit up, but couldn't.

Nicole could be very stubborn; she knew her own body and how to heal it. With the medication inside of her, she knew she would get better.

"Okay. I will give you the medication for your stomach, and something to bring down your blood pressure, which may make you a little dizzy. Keep an eye on her Samuel, and take her blood pressure every four hours. I am also giving you an antibiotic to get rid of the stomach infection, I think you have picked this up from bad water somewhere." He gave her a needle so it would work faster.

"I'll watch over her doctor, and thank you for coming out here. If she is no better tomorrow, I will make sure she comes into the clinic."

"Ok Samuel see that you do that, her system is very weak, she needs to be closely observed."

Samuel watched over her all night. She was getting very dehydrated; every time she drank something, she vomited. She wasn't getting any better – the medication wasn't working.

"Lady you need to go to the clinic, and maybe have an IV for a while. You're getting so dehydrated, and your blood pressure is still high. Please let me take you there."

"No. Just give me a little time to settle down. My system will come back to normal once all the poisoning is gone."

"But you're not even keeping water down. You need to listen to me on this Nicole please." Sam pleaded with her.

"No! Let me sleep, please." She was being unusually stubborn, but she knew her own body better than them, so she insisted on staying at home.

"Okay. I am right here if you need me." He walked the floor for hours, wondering if he should call her mother. Maybe she could talk to Nicole. But he didn't want to alarm them either. Not yet.

Nicole continued to vomit until there was nothing left in her stomach, and then she began dry heaving. Samuel was fearful of a possible cardiac arrest if her system didn't settle down soon, so he called his professor again. He came back, changed the medication, and upped the blood pressure medication to a higher dosage.

"Samuel if this does not work in the next few hours, and she does not start to at least keep water down, then I want her in my clinic. Understood?"

"Yes doc, I hear you. I will bring her in."

But the medication slowly began to work in her system, settling her back down. She was so weak she just slept. In her dreams Nicole, called out to her Grandmother for help.

It was just past midnight when Millie woke up from her sleep, and sat straight up in her bed. Her gut was unusually jumpy; she knew something was wrong with Nicole. She picked up the phone at once and called their home.

Samuel grabbed the phone on the first ring. "Hello its Sam."

"Sam... what's wrong with my girl? And why didn't you call us at once? She's our family!"

"Hi Grand. She's had a case of bad food poising, and has been very ill. She is sleeping now. She will not listen to me, or the doctor who is taking care of her. We both want her to go to the clinic, but she's refused to go. I am worried for her if she doesn't get better soon."

"Is she sleeping now?"

"Yes, she is; she appears to be settling down a bit better, but I am not sure yet how well she will keep down food, or even clear fluids."

"Just let her sleep for now. I'll call you tomorrow and speak with her when she's awake. Stay by her side Sam. Promise you will not leave her alone, not even for an hour."

"I am sitting by her side all night reading. She is right here beside me."

They hung up, and Millie laid back down. She closed her eyes and concentrated until she saw Nicole lying in bed. She talked to her and comforted her in her mind's eye.

"Nicole my sweet child, I heard you calling me. It's me sweetheart, it's your old Grand. Listen to me now. Calm and still your body stays, calm and still your heart remains, calm and still your stomach is, calm and still your body heals." She chanted until she could see Nicole's breathing get stronger and steadier, she could see her heart beating a strong regular beat now, and she could feel her body settle. Millie prayed for her precious child. "Father in heaven, from whom all blessings flow, I know she is one of your angels, and maybe you need her up there. But please... Father God, not yet. We need her down here more. So please be her healer, her comfort and her joy. Please awaken her tomorrow with the blessing of your healing hands. I ask you with the faith of a child, and believe with all my heart it will be so." She made a cross over her chest and fell asleep, knowing her sweet girl would soon be well.

***

The sun was shining through Nicole's bedroom window when she woke up. She felt hungry for the first time in days.

"Morning Sam." She smiled.

"Good morning. How are you feeling today?"

"I feel hungry."

"That's wonderful! Let's try some dry toast, and see how you keep that down, with some clear coconut water, and maybe some weak tea."

"Sounds good. I am so thirsty."

She had lost almost ten pounds, over the last few days and was very weak, but she knew her stomach had settled down, and had healed overnight. She ate her toast and drank two glasses of coconut water, and everything stayed down. She got up slowly from bed and had a shower with Samuel's help. She went outside, sat in her rocking chair, and looked up at the sun. She felt the warm rays on her face; it felt so good to be outside. She was smiling for the first time in days.

The phone rang, and she reached down and picked it up from the table.

"Hello?"

"Hello dear. How are you this morning?" Millie asked.

"Much better! I ate today and kept everything down, and my blood pressure is much lower now. I think I will be just fine in a few days. I'm just a little weak. Samuel told me you called last night." She paused for a moment. "Grand?"

"Yes, dear?"

"I saw you last night, didn't I? You were there on the side of my bed with me weren't you?"

Tears rolled down Millie's cheeks. She was so relieved Nicole was better. "Yes Nicole. I was there in my mind's eye with you all night long. I heard you calling out to me."

"Thank you so much Grandmother. I want to come home now please." She started to cry. She had been to hell and back in the last few days, and all she wanted now was her home, and her family around her. "Bring me home now please."

"Yes, I will do that, it's time. I'll send a ticket for you as soon as you're strong enough to travel. What about Samuel? Should I send him one too?"

"Yes, please. He'll graduate in a few days, we just want to come home so badly now." She couldn't stop crying, she had held everything inside for the last few years, and now it was all coming out. She wanted her family's arms around her. She needed them to get stronger again.

"Stop crying Nicole. We all love you very much dear. We can't wait to see you again too. We'll all be together in no time you'll see." Her voice broke in a sob. She had missed her too. "Now you go get some rest, and eat as much as you can. The tickets will be there by the end of the day."

"I love you so much, Grandmother. I really do. Tell Mommy that I love her too, and we'll be coming home very soon."

"I will my dear, get well fast."

Nicole hung up the phone. Samuel couldn't help but overhear their conversation. He went over and held her hand. He knew what a sacrifice she'd made, and what a toll the last few years had taken on his now fragile wife.

"Lady… you have to fight to get stronger. Don't let this thing get you down. I can't live without you. If anything ever happened to you, I would die. It was so good to see your beautiful brown eyes this morning. I think they're getting their sparkle back." His voice broke as he spoke. He knew down deep in his heart that she had always been the strong one, that it had never been him.

He would never take her for granted again; he would be a man and take control from now on. Samuel nursed Nicole back to her to radiant self, and only left her side to take his final exam. It had taken another two weeks, for Nicole to get back on her feet again, with lots of rest and good nutrition. She was much thinner than before, but she was healthy.

It was finally the day of Samuel's graduation, the day they had both suffered for and dreamed of. It was a day to celebrate and give thanks, for it was by the grace of God, that he was about to receive this degree, and they both knew that.

Nicole stood in the front row of the audience. She was so proud of Samuel, as she watched him come out on stage in his black robe. He eyed the crowd to find his lovely wife smiling up at him. This was a day he was always going to remember. He walked over and stood by Ben in the front row.

"Well... old man we did it. Can you believe it? We finally did it," Ben said with a huge smile.

"By the grace of God's hands, my brother." Samuel held out his hand to shake Ben's, for he was a true brother – not by blood, but by love, and he had no truer friend than him.

After the ceremony was over, they all went out to the reception in the front hall of the university. Samuel walked over to Nicole and gave her a single red rose. "Thanks for being here through it all. I hope I made you proud." He kissed her on the cheek.

"You have always made me proud. There's no place else I would have rather been than here with you. Even though it was difficult, we finally did it, and no one can ever take it away from us."

"Lady... you stood by me through it all, and that means everything to me. I will never forget that."

"You bet your sweet ass you won't, because I plan to be around and remind you if you forget. And I plan on telling our children. just how hard we suffered to be great for them too," she laughed.

He kissed her passionately. They held hands as they walked out into the courtyard of the university, the party and celebration were starting to get underway. They walked over to their group of friends. Ben, Tony, Fred, and Phyllis and her husband, they were all finally going home. They would all be going in different directions: Ben, Phyllis and her husband were heading back to the United States, Nicole and Samuel back to Canada, and Fred and Tony home to Nigeria.

"Congrats to all of us." Ben held up a glass of champagne and toasted the whole group.

"May I?" Nicole held up her glass. "I would like to make a toast to all of our dear friends, and say congratulations for all that you have achieved here on this little island. Here's to all the bonds, and friendships we've been lucky enough to share with each other. I love you all so much, and may God go with you all as you start your careers. And may you all be blessed with the luck of love, children, good health, and lots and lots of money honey." She laughed.

"Hear, hear! I drink to that!" Fred yelled.

"Thanks Nick," Phyllis said. "I'm going to miss you so much. You've been such a good friend to me here. We're going to always keep in touch, no matter what you hear." They hugged and toasted each other. Sam walked over to where Ben was standing.

"Well Ben, I guess you'll be heading out tomorrow as well. Let me know how Chicago treats you brother, and good luck with the next step of your career." Samuel hugged his old friend goodbye. Ben had decided to try his luck in the US. He had a sister in Chicago, and he could stay with her while he was getting settled.

"Yes I will, I'm leaving tomorrow afternoon too. My sister is picking me up at the airport in Chicago. She said she has my room all ready for me, so I can't wait to get started. Hopefully I'll pass the US exam, and get an internship there. I cannot believe that we are finally parting ways."

"I know brother. I shall miss you as well, but we will call each other often. And who knows, maybe one day I'll end up there too. Depending on how things go back in Nova Scotia. I am going to do the Canadian medical exam in two months, and hopefully apply for an internship. But whether or not I get one remains to be seen; you know the good old boys club there. I am sure this next step of integrating back into the Canadian system is not going to be an easy one."

"I know what you mean. That is the exact reason why I am going to Chicago. The boys in our class from the US, say it is easier to integrate back into the US system. So if things do not go well for you back in Canada, you let me know and I will set things up for you in Chicago."

"I will do that Ben, but I at least owe it to Nicole to try the Canadian system first.

She has no idea that there could even be any problems. She has been away from home long enough. There are a lot of great people there, and yes, lots of discrimination too, but I hope they will at least give me a chance this time. I will always fight the good fight my brother – this time for both of us." Samuel smiled and shook hands with his old friend.

"Yes and I wish you luck. But remember one thing: at some point that good fight has to be won." Ben winked and walked off to get another drink. Samuel spotted Nicole standing looking up at the sun that was now setting, he walked over to her and handed her a glass of wine.

"Pretty Lady may I have this dance?"

"Just when I thought you hadn't noticed, you show up with a glass of wine to sweep a girl right off her feet."

"Just you wait until I get you behind closed doors, and off your feet and onto my bed."

"Promises, promises," she teased. "Just think Sam; tomorrow morning we'll be boarding a plane and heading for home. I can't believe it. I'm so excited to see Mommy, Grandmother, and my little sis – she must be so mature now. I even think I missed my brothers. Mommy, and Grand are picking us up at the airport."

"I know just how you feel. Your family will spoil you for a while, and that's just what you need."

"Mommy is happy we're staying with them, until we find an apartment of our own. I guess it will be kind of nice to have her home cooking again. I'll go back to work for a while I guess, until you settle in, so we can afford our own place again. But I've been thinking I don't want to go back to nursing. I think I want to work in business; maybe manage one of some kind. I'll do some business courses at the university when we get back."

"Really? If that's what you want, then I think you should do it. I know you will be very good at it."

"Yes, I think so. But first things first. I need to get a job for a little while, and maybe study part time. To be honest, I think I want a totally new career path. So let's hope it all goes well for you, so I can have the time to pursue my dreams this time around.

But for tonight my husband, all we have to do is say our goodbyes, go home and relax for a while. We're all packed, and I have a taxi booked to pick us up at eleven in the morning. We should arrive back home in Nova Scotia by seven in the evening. We did it babe, we really did it. There were a few days, I have to admit, that I thought I was going to go crazy here, but it all turned out okay after all. Thank God!"

"Yes, let's start to say our goodbyes to everyone here, and get out of this place. I want some alone time with my very sexy wife this evening. There is one other thing I happen to think, that you're very good as well." He winked

"Oh really? How can a girl argue with that?" She laughed.

They walked through the crowd of students, found each of their friends, and said their farewells to each of them.

Samuel and Nicole slowly walked back to their little apartment for one last time.

"Wow… it seems like I have walked down this road so many times in the last few years, I think I am actually going to miss it a little," Samuel said as he looked around.

"Bite your tongue. We're going to be so happy, and so busy back home that we aren't going to miss anything! Okay… maybe the beautiful beaches, the aqua water, and the sweet pineapple, but that's it." She laughed.

They entered their little apartment for one last time, and he grabbed her as soon as they reach their bedroom. He kissed her passionately with a hungry that only she could satisfy. He pulled down on the floor, and then up on the bed. They made love over, and over again, until they were both exhausted. They fell fast asleep in each other's arm.

Their alarm went off at ten o'clock in the morning. They were running late, and the taxi cab had been already outside waiting for them. They took one more look around the little place they'd called home for the last few years, left the keys on the table, got in the taxi, and never looked back.

As they drove to the airport, they were so excited to finally be going back home, that they didn't notice the dark, heavy clouds that hung just overhead in the sky. They checked their luggage in as fast as they could, their aircraft had already started to board. The two walked on the plane, hand in hand and found their seats, they were feeling incredibly blessed, and full of joy to be going home at last.

As they fastened their seatbelts, Nicole began to get a panicked feeling inside her gut. Something told her that this wasn't going to be an easy flight. She looked out the window, and finally noticed how dark the sky had become. "Oh my *goodness*, Sam!" She clutched his arm. "Look at how black it is outside! It looks like a bad storm is almost on top of us!"

"It does look kind of threatening out there. But they wouldn't let us take off without knowing the weather was going to be okay, so just relax and think good thoughts. You know how nervous you get when you fly; just hold my hand and put your head on my shoulder. We'll be okay."

"Hello?" She waved to the flight attendant, ignoring what Samuel had said.

"Yes? How can I help you Miss?" The flight attendant asked.

"It looks so black outside. Are we okay to fly with the bad storm that's coming our way?"

"There's no need to worry Miss. We'll fly above the storm. Our captain and traffic controllers have it all figured out. It'll just be a bit bumpy going up. We have a very experienced captain flying today. Just relax and we'll be up and over this in no time. "

"But I think I also heard a noise like an engine that wouldn't start. What was that noise?"

"There is no problem with the engines. I guess flying makes you very nervous, but really we are very safe. There's no need to worry." She smiled down at Nicole, trying to get her to relax.

"But I really did hear a noise, so please tell the Captain to recheck all the engines. Please just tell him, I beg you." Nicole was becoming very distressed now.

"Very well, Miss. I'll tell him."

"Please come back and let me know as soon as you check," Nicole shouted to her as she walked away.

The flight attendant headed up to the captain's cabin and knocked on the door.

"Hello Captain. We have a very nervous passenger on board today, who said she heard a noise like an engine that wouldn't start. Is everything okay? All routine maintenance was done, and everything is good to go... right?"

"Yes, all engines were reported as working just fine," he said.

"How about the storm? What is the air traffic report saying?"

"It says it's a few hundred miles southeast of us, so we should be up and out of here before it hits in this location. There's nothing to worry about; just some turbulence on the way up. It may be a bit rocky for the first twenty minutes or so."

"Thanks, Captain. I'll let the passenger know."

She walked back down to where Nicole was sitting, and could see she was still very anxious. "Miss I spoke with our captain. All regular maintenance was okay, and we'll miss the storm, it's still a few hundred miles southeast of us. It'll just be a bit rocky going up. Please relax and fasten your seatbelts. We are about to take off now." She walked away to check on other passengers, getting them settled down for takeoff.

"Oh my dear Sam, I hate to tell you this, but I think they're all wrong. In fact, I know they are. So prepare yourself for a rough ride my love."

"What? How do you know this? Lady... what are you saying?" Samuel was starting to get anxious now too; he knew his wife's intuitions were usually right.

"The same way I know everything. Just a bad feeling inside my gut. I would take us off this plane right now if I could." But they were already taxing out, and gaining speed for takeoff – there was no way off the plane now.

"Oh my God! Are we going to die?" Samuel was panicking. He knew her gut was not often wrong.

"I sure hope not baby. Oh dear God, please save us," she said out loud.

The airplane gained speed, and very soon they were airborne and gaining altitude. They began to speed toward the black clouds. The plane remained calm as it slowly gained altitude.

The captain's voice comes over the speaker. "Hello and welcome aboard. This is your captain speaking. We are going to be heading for a bit of rough turbulence, but we should be up and over it in about twenty minutes. Fasten your seatbelt and please stay in your seats. We'll be serving you refreshments in about twenty minutes or so, just sit back and relax folks."

"Sam... I'll need you to repeat some words with me very soon. Just repeat my words with me as I say them okay?"

"What are you talking about?" He looked at her strangely; he had never seen this side of her before. He'd never known how the mind's eye worked.

"Just repeat the same words as I do when I do it. Please trust me." She had that look in her eyes that said not to argue with her.

Sam didn't know how she, and her grandmother, had communicated over the years, with their higher power and even sometimes with each other, through their mind's eye. This was really their powerful subconscious mind, working with the laws of attraction. Most people never developed, or knew how to harness these powerful laws of attraction that existed in the universe, but for Millie and Nicole it came naturally. They'd always been one with Mother Nature. And they knew how to attract what they needed most. Somehow they just knew when someone they loved was in trouble. It was like an energy that reached out to them, and stayed somewhere inside their gut troubling them. They also knew that they had to believe with an absolute knowing that whatever, they could see in their mind's eye was true – there was no room for any doubt whatsoever. It was a kind of knowing, a reality that was there to be created through the powers of their subconscious minds. Whatever they believed became their reality; it would be the same if the beliefs were negative. That was why there was no room for any kind of doubt.

***

"OH MY DEAR GOD IN HEAVEN!" Millie screamed.

She stopped in her tracks and looked up at the sky. Even though it was sunny where she was, she had an awful feeling now that Nicole was in the middle of a storm.

"What's the matter Grand?" Sarah asked.

"Turn on the weather report! What's the weather like where Nicole is flying? She's flying right now isn't she?"

"Yes, I do believe they are. But why are you so worried all of a sudden?" Sarah thought maybe Grand was losing her mind again. She sometimes was a bit off, and as much as Sarah tried she never could understand her most times.

They turned on the TV to the weather channel, listening impatiently through all the weather reports for Canada. Then the US weather report came on. Just off the coast, there was a tropical storm headed for Florida. It had suddenly changed direction, as storms sometimes do, in that area during hurricane season.

"Oh no! That's where they'll be flying – right over the coast of Florida Sarah"

"Maybe, but how do you know that?" Sarah asked.

"It's a feeling I have. I think it's going to be very bad weather for them."

"You're scaring me. What are you talking about?" Sarah never believed in what she referred to as 'that nonsense.' She sometimes thought that Nicole's grandmother was slowly becoming more and more confused; she was getting a bit worse every day now.

"Now stop that, you're not sure of anything, so don't get so upset Grand. I'm sure they wouldn't have taken off if there was any possible chance, they would run into a big bad storm. Would they?" Sarah held her breath; she hoped with all her heart that this old woman was just worried for nothing. Millie said nothing, she just closed her eyes.

"I'm going to go make us some tea, dear." Sarah said as she went out to the kitchen.

She needed time to pray in silence for her daughter's safe return. As she made a fresh pot of tea, Nicole was sharply on her mind. She was due home in a few short hours. Sarah had made her an apple pie and all her favorite treats; she wanted her homecoming to be special. Nicole had been gone for the last few years, and she needed to see her child now more than ever. She rocked in the chair, and prayed intensely for Nicole's safe return to them. She refused to believe that God would let anything bad happen to her child; not this one, she was far too special. Sarah knew that God would never be that unkind to take her daughter away from them, just when she was about to return home after years away. Even the thought of such a thing terrified Sarah.

Millie needed to be completely alone so she could concentrate on Nicole with all of her thoughts. She needed to find her in her mind's eye.

Millie decided to go outside. Their house sat high on the edge of a hill, overlooking the ocean. She ran out to the edge of the bank. She would be able to see her for sure from here, being closer to God's clear blue sky and to Mother Nature.

Millie looked out to the rolling ocean, and then up to the sunny sky. She asked

Mother Nature to hear her words and fly to where her precious child was.

She chanted "Clear blue sky spread your wings and fly to Nicole, clear blue sky spread your wings and fly."

Next she chanted, "Angel wings from heaven be present; wrap your loving arms all around her plane." She chanted louder. "God in heaven be present; save our child." She chanted these phrases over and over, closing her eyes and tilting her face up towards the sun. She could now see Nicole in her mind's eye. Millie was in a deep trance now. She felt a panic down deep in her soul now, and she knew it was Nicole's heart beating faster. She could feel that Nicole was scared to death. She must reach Nicole in her mind's eye. She kept chanting, but more slowly now, taking deep breaths, reaching out to Nicole with her mind's eye. Millie needed to calm Nicole, and help her with the powerful laws of the universe. She needed to concentrate like she never had before. There was a force which was so great that it could destroy all in its way, and that was the deadly storm Nicole was now flying through. It was raging all its fury down on Nicole's and Samuel's plane.

***

Nicole gripped Samuel's hand as she looked out the window. Blackness surrounded the plane. It started rocking heavily with turbulence. They climbed steadily gaining altitude. Then the sky opened up and torrential rain started lashing the aircraft. It rocked from side to side, like a toy piece of paper in the wind. Nicole leaned into Samuel. "My God Sam; it's a raging storm out there. We're flying straight through it. Oh dear God help us."

They hit a huge bump and flew up in the air; with only their seatbelts to hold them in place. Then all of a sudden they started dropping through the air, falling down into an empty sky they were losing altitude. Inside the cockpit, the Captain was fighting to find a steadier place to put them, where there wasn't so much stormy weather. He kept readjusting their levels of altitude, and each time, he tried they were tossed about like toys.

"Air traffic control, this is the Captain of Canadian Airlines 2014. Please give me a location and altitude free of this weather. This storm is ripping us apart up here over."

"This is air traffic control, to Air Canadian 2014. Your location is surrounded by this storm. You're about twenty minutes out, and this storm just changed direction on us. What is your current altitude?"

"We are at 30,000 feet. What altitude should we proceed at please? Over."

"There's nowhere to go at the moment. Try to hold that altitude for another five minutes, Captain. Just try to hold on, and then drop her to 25,000 feet you should be steadier at that level."

"Roger that," the captain said. Sweat poured down the back of his neck.

All the passengers were starting to get very jumpy now.

"Oh my God Lady! We are going to die!" Samuel looked like he was going to pass out.

"Oh no we are not! Look at me now and repeat these words." She looked like she was going into some kind of a trance as she softly said, "Clear blue sky please find me wherever you are, angel wings wrap your arms all around us, and steady this plane." She repeated the words over and over. Again, where the words came from she wasn't sure. They just seem to be planted firmly in her brain, and when she closed her eyes, she could see her grandmother smiling down at her, gently holding her hand and chanting the same words. In their minds' eyes, they could see each other, and they held hands to gain a stronger connection with the laws of the universe. Their concentration needed to be strong and lack any doubt; they knew it would prove to be their reality. There was no room now for hesitation – their lives depended on it.

"It's okay child. Just hang on a little while longer. Clear blue skies will be yours."

Nicole could see Millie smiling in her mind's eye. She felt comfort in her heart as it started to beat slower, and with that came a peace – she knew that God's arms were wrapped around the plane.

Samuel looked confused, but repeated the words as he'd been told. "Clear blue skies, find me wherever you are." He repeated this with his wife ever so softly, so anyone near them would have thought they were just having a conversation.

They held hands. After some time, Nicole changed her words to the 23rd Psalm. "Yea, though I walk through the valley of the shadow of death, I will not be afraid, for the Lord my God is with me." She was ever faithful and kept remarkably calm.

Samuel had always appreciated Nicole's faith, but he was especially thankful for it now. As he looked around at all the other passengers, he could see the fear lurking in their eyes as they wondered if they were going to make it. He prayed that God wouldn't be unkind enough to take them now, just when they had finished medical school, and were about to begin their lives again in Canada. And his poor wife. He had taken her away from her family for all those years; was she never to return? Oh God, he thought, please do not let this happen.

Then all of a sudden the plane took a drop. It felt like they were falling from the sky again. Some of the passengers yelled out with fear. It was beginning to look like they were all in real trouble now; everyone thought they were goners.

Suddenly the plane began to calm down and slowly level off. The rain had all but stopped. Nicole could see the sun just over the wing of the plane to her left. They had made it through the storm, and the wings were settling down to a nice even glide.

The captain came on the speakers. "Sorry for all that folks, but it looks like we're finally out of the storm. We're just running a few minutes late." The seatbelt sign was finally turned off, and the flight attendants began serving lunch.

Nicole's grandmother was still jumpy. She knew Nicole and Samuel were not out of the woods yet; something else was wrong. But it wasn't the storm this time, it was something the storm had done to the plane. She began to chant again. "Safe landing, Father God, safely land her plane, bring her safely back down to mother earth. Oh dear God, please bring our child, your child home to us, please I beg of you. Father you have never let me down ever, please hear me now." Nicole's Grandmother was still standing on the edge of the hill, looking up at the sky.

Sarah was looking out the window at her, wondering what the devil she was doing out there so long. She looked like she was talking to someone, but there was no one out there. Surely she is losing her mind, Sarah thought.

She stepped outside. "Grand! Come inside and have some nice hot tea dear. Who are you talking to out there?" Millie looked at her confused.

"I'll be right there Sarah. Just getting some sun." She didn't want Sarah to see how concerned, she was. She already thought she was crazy most of the time.

***

Samuel was sweating with fear. "Oh my God, Nick. I thought we were goners."

Nicole cut his words off. "Don't say those words. Just don't say it, you hear me? Not a word. Only good thoughts now."

"What's wrong? The plane is out of the storm. Aren't we past it now?"

"I'm just a little upset still. God is too good to let anything bad happen to us, so keep that in your mind. But I have a feeling the storm did something to the plane. I heard that noise again."

"But Nicole... I didn't hear anything, and I am sitting right here beside you. Maybe you are just still nervous." But he knew better, over the years that he had been with her, he had learned that there was always something behind those feelings. He started to feel uneasy again. He hoped they were just both overreacting due to what had just happened to them.

The aircraft was quiet now, most passengers had fallen asleep after their meal. Samuel was starting to doze off as well. Nicole kept a watchful eye, as the evening approached, and the plane glided smoothly along for Nova Scotia.

The pilot and co-pilot continued to check all systems to make sure everything was okay for landing, and that nothing had gotten harmed during the course of the storm. "Sir, I see a red light flicking on and off on the rear engine," the co-pilot alerted the captain.

"Check all systems again. That was one of the worst storms I've ever flown in, and I hope nothing was damaged. Radio air traffic control and alert them."

"Yes, sir. Air traffic control, this is co-pilot Smith speaking onboard Air Canada Flight 2014. We are experiencing a red light that is going on and off on our rear engine. Please have your computers check all systems on board for us."

"Roger that, Flight 2014. Sit tight and let's see what's happening." There was a pause. "All systems are reporting as okay. There appears to be a slight short in the rear engine, but you should be able to land her okay. You're due on the ground in 20 minutes."

"Roger that air traffic control, but I'm noticing that the red light of the rear engine is starting to flicker more and more now. I'm hoping our luck holds out and we don't lose

90

that engine. If we do, our landing gear may not come out." Co-pilot Smith stated.

The captain wiped the sweat from his forehead. He knew there could be trouble landing the plane, and started to think of possible ways to land in case they lost the rear engine. They would still have three other engines, but would lose altitude rapidly. If that were to happen, he could lose control of the aircraft, so he called back to air traffic control.

"Air traffic control, permission requested to bring Flight 2014 in early. I'm picking up speed and will be at the airport in 13 minutes. I think our rear engine is about to stall or possibly die on us up here."

"You now have our permission for an emergency landing Flight 2014. Begin to bring her in at 20,000 feet and counting. We will stay with you now. We'll guide you in Captain. God speed."

Back in the cabin Nicole found herself wide awake, and starting to get an overwhelming ominous feeling in her gut again. It was screaming at her. Just stay calm, she said to herself, we'll be okay. She looked over at Samuel, who was still asleep. She knew how much he hated to fly; this whole flight must have been his worst nightmare come true, she thought. As Nicole looked around the cabin, most of the passengers were getting set to land. They could all feel the large aircraft slowly lowering its altitude again. Nicole saw a little boy around 4 years of age, who smiled and waved his hand at her.

She smiled and said, "God always protects his children."

"What was that you said Nick?" Samuel was waking up.

"Oh, nothing. How are you feeling babe?'

"A little better. I can't wait to get on the ground."

Just then they heard an ever-so-gentle noise in the background; a mechanical noise that filled Nicole with dread.

"You awake now Sam? Fasten your seat belt sweetheart. Quickly please."

"What's wrong? You look pale again."

Her gut was yelling at her again. "Something's wrong. I heard that noise again, like an engine that wouldn't start."

"You keep saying that, but I still did not hear anything."

Back in the cockpit, they could see that they had just lost their rear engine. "Open the speakers and put me on the airways. I need to talk with all the passengers, and flight attendants," the captain said to his co-pilot.

"Right away, sir."

"Ladies and gentlemen, this is your captain speaking. Some of you may have heard our rear engine go out on us just now. Please stay calm; we still have three other engines working on this aircraft. We are going to attempt a landing in 10 minutes; we are now circling the airport and dumping all our fuel, with just enough left to land us. Fasten your seatbelt and prepare for a bit of a rough landing I'm afraid. There are emergency vehicles on the ground waiting to bring us in if need be. Do not panic, I repeat, do not panic. Stay calm. We are about to lose all power within the cabin now, as we glide down for a landing."

Just then, all electrical systems shut down, and the plane was completely black with only a dusting of light from the backup lights to guide them. There was a complete, dead silence in the aircraft, as the passengers looked around at each other with the look of sheer horror in their eyes.

"Captain waiting for your orders, sir?" The co-pilot announced.

"Let's sit this bird on the ground as softly as we can. Lowering altitude to 9000 feet and dropping." He was an experienced pilot who had flown for years, and he'd had a few close calls in his career, but this whole flight had been a huge challenge.

"5000 feet and dropping, sir."

"Drop the landing gear back and then front," he ordered his co-pilot.

"Back gear out, sir; preparing front landing gear... There's a problem with the front landing gear. It hasn't dropped out yet, sir."

"Damn it. Try again."

"Still not working sir. 4000 feet and dropping. Waiting for your orders."

The captain was sweating now. What the hell I am going to do? He thought. "Air traffic control, this is Flight 2014. Rear landing gear has dropped down. But a problem with the front landing gear they are not coming down for our landing. Prepare and clear all runways to the left and right of us."

"All runways clear, Captain. Keep your nose up and bring her in as softly as possible, then drop the nose. You will drag and drop with a heavy hit, but we'll get to you on the ground within minutes. You don't have much fuel, so hopefully there will be no fire."

The huge jumbo jet was slowly sinking to the ground, her lost engine moaning with the effort of trying to release the landing gear. She was about to drop out of the sky and hit the ground with only the back wheels to guide them along.

Nicole squeezed Samuel's hands much harder than before, and he knew it was bad.

"Sam I love you so much."

Oh my God. We have had it now, he thought. "I love you too Lady." He looked like he was going to pass out.

The aircraft slowly made a slight turn in the air. The grinding noise could be heard by all in the cabin, as the enormous machine started to echo her sounds of alarm. Samuel looked over at his wife, his heart about to leap out of his chest.

"Nicole, use whatever you can to help save us Lady."

She had a fear inside of her too now. To her right was a man with a briefcase on his lap, looking very tense. On her left was an older couple holding hands, staring straight ahead as if they were in shock. Just in front of her sat a woman who was travelling alone with a small baby on her lap. With tears rolling down her cheeks, she held her baby boy close to her body. It was so still in the plane now, they could have heard a pin drop.

The aircraft was completely dark now, as its power and life had all but been drained from her. When Nicole looked out the window, she could see a sea of red flashing lights from all the emergency vehicles, which lay in wait for them on the ground. The airplane now swayed, and rocked as it came through the night's clouds. She did the only thing she knew how to do, and that was to pray. In the dark cabin of this enormous aircraft, and in the stillness of life or death, there was only her soft and steady voice, which could be heard as she prayed out loud for all to hear. "Dearest Father in heaven, save us now. With your arms resting on our plane, land us on your sweet earth. Save us, Jesus, save us now. I pray as your child, and for all of the souls of your children on board, save us now." She ever so slightly raised her voice. "Believe with me now that

Jesus saves, for when all God's children believe, so shall it be done. Jesus can save us." And in the far back of the aircraft, another voice said, "Yes, I believe Jesus saves." Soon another voice joined her in prayer.

In the cockpit, the captain was praying his back landing gear would hold out, and they would not catch fire as they landed. He was thinking about his wife. He hadn't told her how much he loved her in such a long time. What if he was never going to get the chance to do that again? He had to land this bird safely.

"It's okay. Just stay calm; we will bring this baby in. Seven minutes to impact. Try the gears one more time, please," he ordered his co-pilot.

He tried. Still nothing came down. "Stay calm, and try again," the captain ordered with sweat pouring down the palms of his hands as he held the back gears in place.

Nicole looked at the small child in front of her, still holding his teddy bear. She once again raised her voice for all to hear. "Jesus, save us now. I know you are able to set us down with the grace of your hand safely upon your earth. Please, my father in heaven, set us softly down now. Please show us that surely goodness and mercy will follow us all the days of our lives. This is your promise Father, and I am now standing on your promise." Nicole believed with every ounce of energy she had left in her body and mind, that her God was a God of mercy and loved her, and her God would never let her down. He had brought them this far, and he would not leave them in their time of need. This much she knew for sure.

Nicole's grandmother and mother were waiting at the airport, and could not believe their eyes as they watched Nicole's aircraft sway and rock as it came down. They had already heard there was a problem on board their flight.

"Oh dear God Grand. Let us pray now," Sarah said as she eyed Nicole's airplane on the horizon.

Millie raised her hands towards the air and aircraft. "Father in Heaven from whom all blessings flow, bring our girl safely down as only you can now, bring the wheels of the plane out to land and bring them softly down. I believe you can and I know you will. This I know for sure. I declare it to be true, by the son of my most high God in heaven." Millie shouted up to the heavens. She shouted it with such a power, that it banished all doubt.

They sat and looked helplessly on as the plane came within only minutes of landing.

"Pull the gears again," the captain ordered. It was their last chance. "Please God, bring the gears down now," The Captain muttered.

All of a sudden, all they could hear was the gears, slowly grinding their way out, and when they hit the ground with full impact, all their wheels were gliding them along. Within only minutes the plane had all but stopped; there was no fuel left to carry them further. There they stood out in the middle of the runway, safe and all in one piece solidly on the ground. The life had all but drained from the enormous machine as it stood there lifeless. It had held the souls of two hundred people on broad that day. By the grace of God, they had all been delivered back to mother earth safely. The flashing red lights grew close as they came in to gather the passengers off the plane safely, and carry them out to the terminals.

There was a loud clapping for the brave captain who had saved their lives – or had he really? For him there was no doubt, that there had been a powerful force with him on board tonight, for only the hand of God could have lowered those wheels just in time to ground them safely. He walked away with a new outlook, vowing never again to leave his family without telling them how much they meant to him. He knew now that the most important thing in life were the people who you loved, and loved you in return.

As the passengers stumbled off one by one, they looked at Nicole and knew they would hear her voice, and remember her words for as long as they lived. For her voice had been the voice of an angel to many that evening; she had been their comfort in the darkness of a dying aircraft. When all power had died, and the blackness of the night's sky had fallen upon them all, they could hear the sound of a woman's voice that was soft, steady, and believable. So much so, that they all believed in their hearts with her.

The ground crew took a look underneath the jet, and shook their heads in confusion. One spoke up and said, "You know guys, they must have had angel on board, because this landing gear should have never have worked, with that broken axial up there. It's broken in two spots. I can't even explain how the front wheels ever got out." They looked at each other in absolute amazement.

Chapter Four

Nicole could see her Mother and Grandmother standing in the distance, waiting for her, looking like they'd just won a million dollars. They both smiled delightedly as they saw their tired child coming toward them. Nicole dropped her bags, and ran straight into her mother's arms.

"Oh Mommy, I'm so happy to see you. I love you so much," she cried.

"Oh my girl, I'm so relieved to see you too dear. Let me look at you. Why you have lost so much weight over there? I guess I'm going to have to fatten you up a bit. I know it was terrible up there this evening, but you're safe now, you're back home with your Mother, baby girl." Sarah cried as she hugged Nicole.

Nicole looked over her Mother's shoulder then, and in the background stood Millie looking exhausted and fragile. She couldn't help but notice how much her Grandmother had aged in her absence. She moved away from her mother, and stood looking at her Grandmother for a minute.

"Oh my sweet Grand, it's so good to see you. How are you? Are you well?" She hugged her and kissed her cheek.

"Well, my girl, I'd be a lot better if you'd keep your ass on the ground," she laughed.

"It was so awful. I don't know how we made it without dying of fear up there."

"You're stronger than you think Nicole, and you should know how you made it through. That one took a lot out of me my dear. I mean a lot." Her grandmother looked even more tired because of all the efforts she'd had to put into getting the landing gear down. She'd had to envision the wheels coming down one by one in her mind's eye, and turning around as they landed. She'd had to keep her vision strong, and that took a lot of energy, it was a difficult task for a woman of her age. Her head ached with the stress of the day, and she just wanted to take her precious child and go home.

"I can see that Grand. I saw your smile and I could feel you there with me, just like always. And these words just popped into my mind –"

"Clear blue skies find me, angel wings all around me." The old woman repeated the words before Nicole could and just smiled. One day the child would get it; she just hoped it would be before her time was finished on this earth. She still had a lot to teach her.

"What was that, Grand? How did you know the words too?"

"I gave the words to you my dear, to reach out to the laws of the universe, to the infinite Intelligence, to bring the thing we were asking for, to be a realization in our present lives. If we ask together without any doubt, with an absolute knowing, then it becomes our reality. It becomes so."

"But what if …"

Millie cut her off. "That's the thing, dear child. There's no room for what if's, because they are nothing but doubts. It must be a burning desire and an absolute knowing. That is the secret. We can't afford doubts. They are much too costly; always remember that. Now give your old grandmother a hug." She hugged her Nicole and whispered in her ear.

"You know the good Lord was always up there with you, and he would never let any of his angels come to any harm. But sometimes he lets his angels suffer to be great, and to get stronger."

"I always remember everything you tell me Grand. I knew he was there all along, I just had to make everyone else believe that with me." She smiled because in her own mind and heart, God had always been sitting in the empty seat right beside her, teaching her how to pray, so the others would hear her on broad and believe too.

Samuel greeted Nicole's family, giving both her mother and grandmother a hug, and then he collected their luggage and got into the car to head home.

Nicole stood in her living room, and looked at her little sister. "Sis, you've gotten so tall, and wow so beautiful, since I've been gone. Give me a hug."

"I missed you too; so glad you're home, Nick. Mommy made all your favorite foods for supper."

"That's sounds just great! I'm so hungry. Samuel my love, just put all our things in my old room, and we'll get settled in after supper." Nicole went out to the kitchen to see all the comforting things that she had grown up with. "I'll help you in the kitchen for a while," Nicole said to her mother as she hugged her again.

"Okay, dear. That would be so nice."

She just wanted to be near her mother; she had missed her so much. "Now we won't be under foot for too long. I plan to get a job, and as soon as Sam has done all his exams, and he gets a paid internship. We'll look for a place as soon as we can afford one okay?"

"Now my girl, stop worrying about all that. Let me spoil you for a little while. After all, I haven't seen you for the past few years – and you are way too thin. Why is that, Nicole?" Sarah never asked a lot of questions, but she wanted to know why Nicole had gotten so thin, and looked so fragile.

"I guess it happened when I was sick with food poisoning, and I just haven't regained the weight yet, but I'm fine now."

"Nonetheless, you need to gain a few pounds and get healthy again, and that means giving your mind a rest too. So no more talk of a job for at least a few weeks. I want you to rest and eat. Just pretend you're on vacation, only at home." She laughed.

"That sounds wonderful." She smiled at her. She had missed being mothered.

They all sat down at the supper table, which was full of everything Nicole loved. Roasted chicken, sweet potatoes, homemade brown bread, and warm apple pie fresh from the oven. Nicole and Samuel ate until their stomachs felt like they were going to burst.

"Wow, Mom. That was all so good. Thank you for all this." She had come to be so grateful for the little things in life over the last few years. She had seen so many children suffer while they were at medical school with not enough to eat, that she knew she would never again take any of this for granted.

"Yes, thanks so much for everything. I really appreciate it too." Samuel said as he helped himself to seconds.

Nicole's mother sat there with a smile on her face, as she silently thanked God for bringing her girl back safe and sound. Yes, there was one more at the table Samuel, but that was okay with her. Just as long as all her children were together and well, there would always be room for one more at her table.

"I guess you missed your old mother's cooking after all," Sarah teased.

"Oh Mommy I missed so many things about home, but mostly I missed all of you."

Nicole and Samuel took the next few weeks off. It was their time to be together at home, and they were able to enjoy a little of what a normal marriage was like.

Sarah watched as Nicole gained a few pounds; she was starting to look rested and healthy again. And much to Sarah's joy, her daughter was a radiant beauty once again. She knew the last few years of living away from home had not been very kind to her. Nicole was her child and it was her job, no matter how old her children became, to always take of them when she thought they needed it.

Nicole went over to the university, and signed up for some business and writing courses. Samuel registered for the Canadian medical exam, and was now spending most of his time in the library studying. The Canadian Medical exams were in two months, and he had a lot of material to review for it. Sarah packed a lunch for him every day, and off he went to the library, not returning most nights until eight or nine o'clock. Sarah always kept his dinner warm for him until he got home; to her he was her son now too, and she treated him just like her own sons, taking just as good care of him as she could.

A few months later Nicole and Samuel moved to the big city of Halifax. It was a two hour drive from her little hometown. Nicole found a job as a store manager, in a very prestigious menswear company in the heart of Halifax. She was the first female store manager the little company had ever had, and with that came many challenges. The former store manager was an older man who was near retirement now, and he did not really have what it took to manage the staff, or the store anymore. So she was hired to slowly replace him, but he would still remain on staff to take care of his own client base, that he had developed over the years. He was still a great salesman, but he had issues with her being a woman, and refused to speak to her on many occasions. The salesmen that currently worked there saw her as a blonde beauty with probably no brains or talent to sell, let alone actually manage the business. And maybe Richard, the old man who owned the company, was just interested in her beauty, and that's why he had hired her. They resented her being called their boss, partly because Richard had overlooked one of them for the job. But Richard felt Nicole brought new energy, and he could see she had a very talented eye for fashion, colors and style. She had done business management courses and had finished them, so she was qualified in his eyes, to run his business. Ever since his first wife, who had been the heart and soul of the

99

business had died, he had kind of lost interest in running things. Richard's late wife had worked with him in the buying department for years, and he had depended on her for everything. She'd died of cancer a few years ago. Since then all he thought of was retiring and getting away from the business, because everything still reminded him of her. His sales in the store had gone downhill, and his staff had lost interest. He was now remarried to a woman who was trying her best to take his first wife's place, but she just did not have the gift of retail or the good taste in the buying department that his first wife had.

Richards's current wife Helen's talents, were really in the kitchen. She was a great cook and homemaker. Nonetheless, Helen was doing her best to keep the business together, and keep her new husband as happy as she could. Richard knew that he needed this bright, talented young woman to run his business. She could bring the business back to life long enough for him to make enough money, so that he could retire in style. Nicole now had lots on her work plate, and was busy making his business successful again. She reminded Richard of his late wife. Richard handed over all the buying department to Nicole. She was just what his poor heart needed to get interested in his business again, and very soon they were making lots of money together.

"Gentlemen, can we please have a meeting this Saturday morning before we open? I think it is a good idea to do this every Saturday, so we can brainstorm about new business ideas, and how we can make this store even better." Nicole was polite, but firm with the men. She knew they did not respect her yet. One salesman muttered under his breath. "I have a great idea. Let's get rid of you."

"I heard that Jim. Why don't you like me for heaven's sake?" Nicole asked.

"Well, for one thing, you haven't earned this job. I've been here for years, and the old man just completely overlooked me, and handed you this job instead."

"Why do you think that was Jim?" Nicole asked, staring him straight in the eye. She never backed down from any of them.

"That's easy. You're much prettier than me."

"Really Jim, why thank you. But I think it's much more than just that. And if you really feel that way, then talk to Richard yourself, and let him explain why he hired me and believes in me. Let him tell you why our profits are increasing every week, since

I've been here, and let him go over the sales figures with you. I am working very hard here, and I think it's time you take that chip off your shoulders, and work with me. I am sick and tired of hearing you all talk behind my back. Work with me please; I want to make this a better place for all of you to work in. It's time to get rid of the old ideas, that a woman can't run a menswear company, because we *are* running it, and we are profitable again for goodness sake. She walked out of the store. She needed a coffee to calm down; she was just so sick and tired of all the bullshit from these guys, who were constantly trying to undermine her work, and she wasn't going to take it anymore. She was getting to be a much stronger woman now. That was why she was so successful with the customer base; they loved to talk with her. She made people feel special, and comfortable around her. She always remembered the names of her customers, and asked about their jobs and families. She was good at building relationships with people, and really cared about their needs. Some days she wanted to complain, about how hard she was working. But then she would remember, their life back on the Island, and was grateful for the job. She loved working there, and got great satisfaction of the success, she was making of the place.

To add fuel to the fire, the owner's current wife always took notice of her, and was a little bit jealous of Nicole. Nicole was able to do, what she herself could not do with the business, and that was to bring it back to life again. She felt threatened by Nicole's beauty, and was even more envious of the natural talents, she brought to her husband's store. She criticized Nicole from time to time, but her husband just let it go in one ear and out the other – he was a wise man, and knew women well. He could see all the professional men in the city coming back to shop again in his store, because they liked the modern-cut suits Nicole ordered, and beautiful colored ties, and shirts. Richard once again was making a healthy profit. Nicole knew she had no ally in Helen, so she always treaded carefully around her, she was just a devil in disguise to Nicole. Richard was in his early sixties, with gray hair and a warm smile. He was still a good-looking man for his age. He was slightly overweight, and he loved to tell stories of the early days of his business, when his late wife still worked with him. He felt comfortable talking to Nicole, because she never judged him, and she was a great sounding board for many issues for him. His new wife always took offense whenever he mentioned his late wife; it was almost like she was jealous of a ghost. Helen felt inadequate for all the skills she lacked in running his business. She wanted to move and open a bed and breakfast out in the country. That had always been her dream, and she was trying hard to make Richard think it was his dream too. All in due time, he thought. Let me make a bit more profit before I commit bankruptcy. He had fired his accountant just last week, so he could now do his own creative bookkeeping. This way it would be a lot easier for him to take the money out, and put it where creditors, and suppliers could not find it – in his wife's private account. He now started paying his wife, like a very expensive private consultant for his business. It wasn't illegal, just not a great business decision for someone who actually wanted to stay in business. He took all the profits, and most of the cash flow, and paid it all to Helen now, leaving many of his suppliers unpaid for the products they had received, and had already sold. Nicole was not aware of any of his business plans; she was just working hard to make the profit, and in good faith build back the business he had lost over the last few years. She knew they were making lots of money again, and was proud of herself for bringing back customers, who had all but abandoned the store years ago.

"Good morning Nicole. Helen wants to sit in on our meeting this morning," Richard said as he eyed her lovely long legs.

"Sure, that's fine," Nicole said. The meeting was for Richard to give Nicole her financial goals for the upcoming month, and to set up buying meetings with suppliers for the winter season. Richard would travel with her, and he was looking forward to it. Traveling with her out on the markets, gave him a much needed break from his nagging wife. Most of their buying was now done in Montreal, and Toronto.

"Hello Nicole," Helen said. She had a sour look on her face as usual. For some reason Helen, was always in a bad mood.

"Does anyone want coffee before we get started?" Nicole asked.

"No. Let's just get to the business." Helen said in a cold voice. She didn't want Nicole running off with her husband, so she had better keep a close eye on them.

"Your sales goal this month is fifty five thousand. This is a slight increase over last year," Helen said.

"Yes, it's about a twenty five percent increase over last year."

"Yes... well you should be able to reach that, if we go on sales, and advertise the sales." Richard said, trying to make Helen believe he was on her side.

"Yes we can, but there goes the profit if we do that Richard. I'd rather make a quick trip to Montreal, to buy off-price goods, and then advertise, that we have a limited-time special with new merchandise, for one week only. Our customers will come, and see what's new, and what's on special. That way we make cash flow and profit. I think I can negotiate with Rafael Loin for his shirts, at thirty percent off wholesale."

"I knew there was a good reason why I hired you young lady. That's a great idea. But can we get the supplier to give us that discount? That's just like what my wife would have done back in the day. She had a natural gift for this kind of thing, just like you Nicole." Richard smiled in admiration, forgetting that Helen was at the meeting.

"Why thank you Richard. They had better give us a deal, or I won't give them anymore regular price business, and it just so happens that we are their biggest customers here in Nova Scotia. You've been doing business with them for many years. So I guess I'll have to play a bit of hardball with them, if you're willing to go along with it."

"Yes, I'll play along." Richard was always happy when someone else was willing to do his dirty work, or bargaining. He then noticed that his wife Helen was upset. "Helen... what's got you so upset my dear?" Richard asked, totally unaware of why she would be so unhappy.

"Well, for starters Nicole is not your dead wife, and I am sitting right here, your very much current alive wife. I just hated when you always talk about her like that, and you know it! Dame it!"

"Well, Helen, that's why I don't ask you to sit in on these meetings, because I can't help myself. And frankly, there's no need for you to be a part of these meetings, why don't you go shopping, and cook us a wonderful dinner for tonight? That's something I would appreciate very much from you, and you enjoy doing that."

"I'll do that for you after the meeting. I want to hear what you're doing these days with this business."

Nicole interjected, trying to get the meeting back on track, and to keep them from arguing.

"I'd like to go this following week to the market to make the buy, if that's okay Richard," Nicole said.

"Yes. Book it for both of us, and we'll stay at the Sheridan hotel there. We can leave on Monday, and return on the Wednesday evening. That should give us enough time I think."

"Okay, I'll make the arrangements," Nicole said.

"Are you serious Richard? Tuesday is our anniversary!" Helen said. "Can't she go by herself?" She looked livid.

"Yes of course I can. I'm so sorry; I didn't know it was your anniversary Helen."

"No Helen, she can't go alone. I need to be there to write the checks, and I always go to the market with my buyers. You know that. I'll make it up to you when I get back. We'll just celebrate one day later."

Helen got up, and walked out of the meeting without another word.

"Maybe we should put the trip off until the following week, so you can be there for your anniversary?" Nicole suggested.

"No. Business is business, and she has to get used to that. What's one day anyway? We can go to dinner the next night when I get back. I don't see what all the fuss is about." Richard just wanted the date to pass on by, so he wasn't reminded of how many years, he had put up this woman, and her selfish ways. Working closely with Nicole, had made his wife's faults stand out even more to him.

***

Samuel studied seven days a week now, with only two weeks to go before the Canadian medical exam. He needed to pass this exam, in order to get on with his career. After that he'd get a one year paid internship, and then write a few more exams to get his licenses, to set up a practice in medicine in Canada. He was devoting every waking minute, in reaching his career goals. All he needed was just one more chance in this country, and he knew he'd be a great doctor.

Nicole booked the trip for the following Monday. The weekend flew by. Samuel took a few hours off on Sunday evening, to have a meal with Nicole, and make love to her before she left the next morning.

"You know lady, soon I will have more time for us. After the exam I will try to find a part-time job to help you with the bills. It will get easier my sweetheart, I promise you that." Samuel said as he held her close.

"That would be wonderful. Hopefully soon you can work as a doctor, and we can start to have a real life. Maybe have some time for a little more fun. These are our young years, and so far I can't say I am enjoying them"

"I know it's still very difficult for you. But you are my world, don't ever forget that." He pulled her close one more time, and passionately explored her body. His desire never seem to fade for her, and there were moments when she wondered, if he ever really saw her. Once his yearning was satisfied, he fell asleep beside her.

Monday morning she headed to the airport alone. She boarded the airplane, and waited for Richard, who was always running late, barely catching most of their flights. He came running on board with a smile, as soon as he saw Nicole.

"Good morning my girl. Hope you had a good weekend with that husband of yours."

"Yes, we did. How was yours? How's Helen today?"

"Still sleeping. It's six in the morning you know." He smiled.

"No kidding," she laughed.

They took off, and were in Montreal in just two hours. Nicole was always a little more nervous, and she prayed every flight, and was always so happy, when the plane landed safely. Richard was in deep thought thinking about all the unpaid bills he had, they were starting to pile up. He was undeniably running up their bills with all their suppliers, and keeping the money for himself. He only paid them little bits at a time, just enough to get more product, but never paying off the bill completely. He was thousands of dollars in debt, with all his suppliers. Helen knew his plan, and was of course delighted at the idea of them moving soon, and opening a bed and breakfast, out in the country. She had already started looking at different locations, and planning their menus. She was so happy he was finally seeing their future life the same way she did: living peacefully out in the country, and away from all the stuff she hated like Nicole, the retail store, and all the memories of his dead wife.

Richard knew Nicole would never understand his plans, and would never support his ideas. After all, he was betraying all the men who'd worked for him for years, and ripping off all his suppliers. He was really doing something he had never done in his whole life, but Helen had thought of the idea, and he'd agreed to do it. He didn't even feel guilty; he felt he had paid his dues over the years, and now all he wanted was to get out of the business world.

The plane landed on time in Montreal. They checked into their hotel, and then got a taxi to their first appointment.

"Hello Richard. Nice to see you again. And Nicole how are you today?

Mark, the man who owned the menswear company, was always pleasant to his customers, and Richard was one of his best ones.

"I guess we need to get started now; we have another appointment in a few hours," Nicole said as she got up, and headed to the showroom.

They followed her out to Mark's showroom, where all the sample clothing was hanging, she and Richard began their ordering. They choose several new designs, and then Nicole stopped, and looked at Mark.

"We need to run a sale next week, and we'd like to run it on your classic shirt in the Rachel Lion collection. We need to get a discount of about thirty percent off wholesale prices from you for that. I need about one hundred units in assorted colors, solids and stripes. I know we've never asked for a deal in the past, but I also know you've been discounting, some of these styles to a place in the valley in Nova Scotia, so we need that same deal. I hope that's not a problem for you today Mark?"

"Well, you know we never discount these shirts, and that store in the valley only bought discounted pieces, that were discontinued from the line – colors and styles, that the company is not producing anymore."

"It's the same brand name, and customers don't know the difference. And you should have offered us that deal first, we've been loyal to you for so many years, and purchase a great deal from you." Nicole stared him down and held her ground.

"I really don't think I can do what you're asking me too. I'm sorry we may not have the stock, and really we don't discount regular items like that." Mark was getting slightly angry at her demands, turning slightly red in the face.

"Richard." He was starting to fall asleep. He looked up when Nicole called out his name. "Yes Nicole?"

"I've been thinking we should really wait awhile for this order. I want to see what Tommy Hills has in their showroom, and that's our next appointment. I hear their merchant has been selling everywhere like crazy." She knew this was Mark's competitor.

"If that's what you think, I guess we can do that." Richard was no fool. He knew how to play the game too; he'd just never had the guts to do it on his own.

"We're sorry to have wasted so much of your time today, but I think we are going to pass on your line this season." They both stood up, and started to walk towards the door.

"Now just hold on Nicole; I need to check and see what's in our warehouse. Just give me a minute." Mark left the room, realizing that this woman meant business, and he had no choice but to meet her demands, if he wanted to keep them as a customer. He hated being backed into a corner like this, but he knew he would lose a longtime customer, if he didn't give in and meet her demands.

"Wow Nicole. You sure told him. Let's see what he does." Richard looked impressed.

Mark came back into the room after a few minutes. "It looks like we can give you this discount this time Richard, but it's a one-time only deal okay?"

"I appreciate that Mark. It will help us out a lot. Thank you," Richard said.

Mark spoke to Richard, and completely ignored Nicole, because he was so upset with her for backing him into a corner.

"Well Nicole? What do you think?" Richard asked, inviting her back into the conversation. He was making a point to Mark, that Nicole was running the show, and what she said mattered a great deal to him.

"I think that would be just fine. Thank you Mark. I also appreciate your cooperation with this special buy. I already have the details of the sizes, colors, and styles, I would like shipped out. Here's the printout; all you have to do is ship it to us. I guess we're done here for today. We're running a little late for our next appointment, so we should be off now."

"Well, that's done for another few months. I think we'll have a very successful sale Nicole, thanks to all the great deals you made."

They headed back to the hotel. It was after nine, and they had an early flight the next morning. They grabbed a bite at the hotel bar.

"I'm going to call it a night. I'm beat. See you at five in the morning. We have a seven o'clock flight home Richard – do you need a wakeup call?" Nicole asked him.

"Yes, I guess I'd better have, or I might miss the flight. I think I'm going to have a second drink down here in the lounge".

Nicole went up to her room, put on a big soft white T-shirt, crawled into bed and called Samuel.

"Hello?" Samuel said. He was still sitting at his desk studying.

"Hi baby. How's life back there in Nova Scotia without me these days?" She laughed.

"Way too quiet and lonely. How was your day in Montreal?"

"Very busy. I'm so tired, and even more tired of hearing about Richard's late wife."

"That's going to be us one day. Together for the next twenty years, with children and a house, and we are going to be very happy."

"Just twenty years? What happens after twenty years?"

"We have grandchildren, and retire to some beautiful beach house somewhere."

"Now you're speaking my language," she laughed. She was a sun baby, and loved the beach, that was her happy place in life.

He loved the sound of her voice, and loved to hear her laugh. He knew she wasn't laughing often enough, mostly because of all the burdens she had on her shoulders.

"Hurry home. I hate living alone."

"Wow, really? Most of the time we aren't together anyway. I'm surprised you actually even know I'm gone, or miss me."

"Lady... I know I am not here enough for you, but you're always on my mind, and I am working hard for a better future for us. Just hang in there with me baby."

"Always...you know that. Just don't forget to show me that you love me from time to time okay, make time for us a little more?"

"I'll never forget to do that. I can forget many things in life, but you're not one of them. Goodnight my sweetheart, and safe trip home. I love you."

"I love you more, good night." She hung the phone up, crawled into bed, and prayed for Samuel's success with his exam, that he was writing in just a few days. She couldn't wait to get home, and sleep in her own bed; she liked going away, but loved coming home more. They flew home the next day, and Samuel was waiting at the airport with flowers for her when she arrived.

"Wow, what a nice surprise to see you here, are these for me?"

"Yes, they are, I just missed you, and want to meet you here, to let you know how much you matter."

"Well, I hope you can show me that behind closed doors later." She winked.

"That would be my great pleasure." He whispered in her ear, and kissed her.

After dinner that night they curled up on their sofa, and talked.

"You know, I can see us, with at least two children, and a house with a back yard one day."

"Yes, I can see that as well Lady, maybe even that little dog you like so much."

"Oh, you mean a golden lab?" She laughed.

"Yes, you know the golden one, every time you see one you always say how much you love them, and wish you had one."

"Wow I am surprised you even remember that, with everything you have in your head these days."

"It's true, I have a lot on my mind with my studies, but remembering your dreams, are important to me too. Now if I remembered correctly, you wanted some special loving tonight." He reached over and pulled her into his arms.

"Oh, I thought you had totally forgotten that promise." He wrapped his hands around her long ponytail, and gently pulled her down on the rug. She moaned as he enters her, and soon they were completely one again. His hunger for her body as he took her, made him feel weak, and vulnerable in many ways. His restraint and self-control were always lost when she touched him. She never questioned his passion, it was that connection that had kept them strong, through all their struggles.

Nicole was back at work early the next morning. She had called a store meeting to explain their new clothing lines to all the salesmen.

"By tomorrow we will receive about twenty boxes of new items. Some will be for our special week of sales, and some will be brand new lines of clothing, we haven't carried before. So when our customers come in for the sale items, we can show them some of the new clothing items as well, and I'm sure they'll want to buy those items too. I'll be completely remerchandising the whole store. I know it will be a long day for all of us, but it will only be for one day, so please know that I so appreciate your time. and you will be paid for the overtime."

"I sure hope your new ideas pay off, because I am going to miss my night out with the boys," Jim muttered.

"Wow Jim. Really? That's what you have to say? Come on everyone. Let's get to work; we need to take everything down and start cleaning. We'll work around the customers for today, but tomorrow I'll close our doors for one day, and then the next day we'll reopen for the start of our sale, and to show off our new clothing lines. I've put ads in the newspapers, so I do expect we will be very busy."

They all worked hard, and the staff talked among themselves, still debating about their new manager's ideas. They decided in the end, to take a wait and see attitude. If the sale was a success, and they all made lots of commission, then she was a good guy with them, but if they worked hard for nothing, then she was just a pretty face with impractical ideas. Nicole knew this about her staff. She was no fool, but was sure the sale would be a success, so she only smiled to herself.

The next day everything arrived on time at the store, and everyone was busy opening the boxes of new product. It was nearly seven o'clock in the evening when they finished, and everyone was tired. Richard finally walked in the door from playing two rounds of golf with his buddies. He was stunned when he looked around the store. He couldn't believe how great it looked; Nicole had done an amazing job with both the buying, and the merchandising. Every display was perfectly coordinated, looking new and fresh. He called Nicole over, as she was putting on her coat to finally go home.

"Nicole, you did a wonderful job in here. Well done my girl." He said with a big smile, he knew he was about to make a lot of money this week.

"Thank you Richard, but all the staff worked very hard right along with me. I do hope, you'll thank them tomorrow too."

"Sure I will Nicole, but that's so like you."

"Like me? What do you mean?"

"You always give other people more credit than is due."

"No, they really worked very hard this time. Believe me, I couldn't have done this without them." She was just happy, she was finally winning them over.

Jim was standing in the background, and he'd overheard her reply to Richard. It warmed his heart that she'd given the credit to the staff, because he knew how hard she'd worked all day. It had been many years in the store, since anyone had thanked the staff for anything, or even noticed the work they did. Maybe we can learn from this woman after all he thought.

Nicole headed home, and walked through the door of her little apartment, feeling totally exhausted.

"Wow that was a long day. How do you feel?" Samuel asked, reading his papers.

"So tired. Did you eat supper yet?'

"No. I was waiting for you. My big exam is tomorrow, so I haven't taken the time to eat yet."

"Oh dear. Well, let's see what I can make us for supper then."

"Look it's late, and you're tired. Let's just make a sandwich, or something easy. I can help you."

"Okay. That sounds good. I am so beat. How was your day? Are you ready for the exam?"

"Yes, I think so, or at least I hope so. You never know what kinds of questions are on these exams, so I had to review everything again."

"Don't worry darling. You'll do just fine. Now sit down at the table with me and eat."

"I hope so Nick, because everything rides on this one exam."

"I know, but it'll do no good to worry all night about it. You need a good night's sleep, so you'll be able to concentrate better tomorrow."

"Okay. Makes good sense. Let's have a shower together." He smiled and winked at her.

"Wow, really? Sex after the day I've had?" She laughed because she never denied him.

"I know you're tired. Let me give you a nice backrub, after our shower instead. You'll feel better." Sam knew she loved his backrubs.

"As long as you don't mind if I fall asleep, then I would love that."

"Just relax. You need to rest, I know that. We both have a busy day tomorrow."

They fell asleep early that night in each other's arms. The alarm went off at five, and they slowly got up. She hugged him as they made breakfast in the kitchen together. She made a point to hug him every morning, before she left him to start her day. They ate and got dressed quickly; he wanted to get there early so he could take his time, and relax a little before the exam.

Nicole dressed for a busy day. When she arrived at work, she couldn't believe her eyes. There was already a lineup at their door, waiting for the store to open. She went inside and looked at her staff; she could see they were impressed at the crowd waiting outside. That had never happened to them before; it had been years since they'd had that kind of turnout to one of their sales.

"Good morning everyone. Are you ready for a busy day?" She asked, feeling excited.

"Great job Nicole. You really came through this time for us, and I'm glad to have you as our manager," Jim said so all the others would hear him.

"Thank you Jim. I appreciate that. Now let's open the doors and start the selling games."

***

Samuel entered the classroom of the building, where he would write the Canadian medical exam. They handed out the first section of the exam. They would write for four hours straight, then have an hour break for lunch. The second half of the exam would be handed out in the afternoon, and they would write for another four hours. He prayed for knowledge and strength, as he began to write the exam. He started answering the questions as fast as he could, so he would have enough time for the hard questions. So far so good, he thought as he completed the first section of the exam.

***

Back at the store, Nicole was so busy with the customers, wanting her attention, she couldn't even think straight. Richard finally came in around one in the afternoon, and couldn't believe his eyes. They were all so busy, he decided to roll up his sleeves and help too, he didn't want a lot of theft in the store today. Nicole never left the floor at all that day; she worked nonstop until they closed at six. She felt the hunger pains hit her, as she was counting the cash from their busy day.

"Oh my God, I thought I would die today," Richard said.

"I know! It was so busy. But guess how much money we brought in today?' Nicole said, looking very proud of herself.

"How much?" He asked greedily as he stared at her.

"Over twenty thousand in just the first day. And we still have four more days. I think we'll meet our budget and then some." Nicole felt great relief that her plan had worked.

"Really? That's wonderful my girl. Well done." He was starting to feel a little guilty now, because she was making such a success of everything, and he was only going to destroy it all, and leave them all unemployed by the end of the year.

"'I'll tell you what Nicole. If we make our goals this week, I'll give you an extra bonus." He wanted to ease his mind of some guilt.

"I would very much appreciated that Richard, thank you. But could we also include a bonus for the staff as well?" She looked hopefully into his eyes.

"Well... I guess we can do that. But let's not say anything until the week is over, and then we can give it to them on the final day. Maybe Saturday okay?"

"Okay, I think that's fair. I'm off now. I am so beat, and I need to get home to Samuel and feed him." She put on her coat and walked out the door. She couldn't wait to see Sam, and find out how his exam had gone that day.

Samuel's day, however, hadn't gone as well as he'd hoped it would. He'd had his lunch break, and then came the afternoon section of the exams. He began to read the questions, but he couldn't understand what the hell they were asking. They weren't direct questions, like they'd been in the morning session; they were true or false questions, and the question could apply to many of the answers to the list. They were supposed to answer which one was the *most* right.

"These are such stupid questions," he said under his breath. No wonder the foreign medical graduates, write a different exam than the Canadian medical graduates. The whole last half of the exam, was made up of trick questions. The sweat was rolling down Samuel's forehead, and his heart was slowly sinking. He knew he wasn't going to pass this exam. He was spending too much time just reading the questions over and over again, because most of them made no sense. It didn't test his knowledge of medicine at all, just how good of a guessing game he might be able to play. This exam was just a matter of luck not skill. This whole exam had been designed to working hand-in-hand with the government, and licensing bodies, to keep most of the foreigners out of the medical profession. There would be no other reason why they should write a completely separate exam from the Canadian medical graduates. After all, they all needed to know the same material at the end of the day, in order to be able to take care of patients. Samuel wondered what else they did to stop them from proceeding on with their medical careers there. Maybe Ben was right after all, to have gone to the United States to write his medical exams. The teacher announced that the time was up, and to put down their pens, and stop writing. He was slowly coming around to collect the papers.

Samuel put his forehead in his hands. There was still a whole page he hadn't gotten to yet. He knew he was in trouble, and maybe would not pass this exam. In his heart he knew he didn't stand a chance, he had spent too much time rereading the questions, trying to make some sense of them.

They all stood up and left the room. The foreign medical graduates all gathered together outside the classroom; Samuel stood and silently listened as the others talked.

"Oh man, what a hell of an exam that was. The questions were completely ridiculous. So many things could have applied – you just had to guess as to which answers they were looking for," said an Indian doctor who had studied in India.

"This is my third time doing this exam. I did not pass the first two exams, because they do not test basic knowledge. They are asking impossible questions," said another man from South Africa.

"I can't believe it either. I am a heart specialist from Pakistan, and I have practiced for over ten years in my own country, but here I am writing this exam now for the fourth time. I can't seem to pass." He was speaking directly to Samuel.

"You see Samuel? This is directly designed to keep us out of practicing medicine in this country. I know you have just gotten back from medical school abroad, but this is what's going on here now. They do not ever want us to compete with their graduates in any way. You're just back in Canada, and you haven't yet realized what's really going on here."

"I guess not, but I sure do know what you mean about the exam. Why hasn't anyone ever complained about this to anyone?" Samuel asked.

"Who is going to listen to us? Think about it, Samuel. We will be complaining to the people who designed the exam, so do you really think they are going to change it, or even listen to what we have to say? Their little conspiracy to keep us out of the medical profession is working for heaven's sake. They do not care about us, they are happy to see us drive taxis, or do pizza delivery for a living. As sad as that is Samuel, that's what most of us have to do to feed our families here in this country, while we are trying to read and pass this exam. But the worst thing is that emigration picked us, and allowed us to enter this country, based on our qualifications." The poor Indian man stood there heartbroken, and looking exhausted.

"Oh man. I had no idea what was happening here," Samuel said.

"No you wouldn't, because when you first come back, you are in isolation from all the other foreign graduates, and all you're doing is studying as hard as you can to write the exam," the Indian doctor whispered in a low voice so the teacher couldn't overhear him.

"But why are they so protective anyway? There is more than enough need in this country. Over half of the small towns in this country do not have doctors to fill the community's needs. They do not even train enough Canadian graduates, to cover the needs of this country. In my wife's hometown, the women can't even have their babies at home anymore; they have a big new hospital, with no qualified doctors to deliver them there. So they drive miles to get to another town to have their babies. And most of the Canadian graduates, will only set up practice in the big cities. Then some of them leave, and go to the United Stated to practice, because they make more money over there. Now tell me: is that right, or is that just fucked up?"

Samuel was getting more discouraged as he talked about everything with the other doctors, so he decided to head home, and pray that maybe God would somehow give him a miracle, and a pass mark, but he knew it was very unlikely. He knew he would have to start to make other arrangements of some kind, and God only knows what they might be. Samuel walked away with a sense of hopelessness in his heart, weariness slowly creeping into his tired bones. He couldn't believe the events of the day. He had studied so hard for this; he had stayed up night and day to pass the exam, and he never even thought it would be an exam that did not test his true knowledge, or skills in medicine. What a shame he thought, for us, and all the small communities, that need us. The government knew that they would need a yearlong internship, in order to qualify for a medical license, which was set up by the government, with the licensing bodies, as a criteria in order to practice medicine in Canada. So they had total control over all the necessary steps, each foreign medical graduate, needed to do, in order to practice medicine in Canada. Much of this, the general public, would never know; they would just think there was a shortage of trained doctors in Canada, and that's why they couldn't find family doctors, anymore when they needed one. They would never know the real reason, why they had to drive so far away for treatments, like having babies, and surgeries. But the real truth was that most of the qualified foreign medical doctors that lived in Canada, were handicapped from practicing medicine, because of the unfair systems, that the government allowed to be in place. They were unable to contribute to society, in the way they should: caring for an aging population, and taking care of families where they lived. Samuel's head hurt from all the thoughts that were going through his mind. He knew the story very well now, but most of the citizens that lived there, would never believe the truth. It would be too hard for them to believe, that they'd allowed their government to mishandle the system so badly. It didn't serve the public well, and it didn't serve the foreign graduates who were Canadian citizens at all. All he could do now was to pray for a break, for a door to open, for just one chance. He knew that many people, would never be able to understand what he'd gone through, because most believe that if you work hard enough, success comes at the end of the day. That equal opportunity exists for all, and that one is judged on his merits, and not on where he was born, or the color of his skin, or where he studied. Once you are a Canadian citizen, born or emigrated, then the same opportunities should exist for all. In his heart he knew this, but unfortunately many people did not.

What a joke, he thought to himself, for there is the real true travesty of justice: that no one cares, or is willing to fight for that simple right. Or even examine the possibility that equal opportunity only really exists for those Canadians, who studied here. And not for those Canadians, who have the same knowledge and skills, but acquired their knowledge somewhere else in the world. Samuel just couldn't understand, why there was no fair way to access this better.

He had to find a way to beat them at their own game, if he was going to stay here in Canada with his wife. He would have to try, and explain things to his hardworking wife too. She still thought her country was blessed with plenty of everything, and in her mind, there was always room for one more. Most Canadians would never realize, what it was like to have worked incredibly hard, and still have doors closed in your face, and access denied to your profession.

He felt defeated all over again, because he still had too many obstacles in his way. It was heartbreaking to live in a country that was so close-minded. But how was he going to cope, with this situation if he couldn't pass the medical exams. Well, at least he knew he'd have another chance in two months to write it again. He made a vow to himself to study even harder, if that was possible.

He slowly walked into their little apartment, and there was Nicole after her long day of hard work, with a hot meal already prepared, and on the table for them both. She was ready to sit, and eat with him.

"Hi babe, come and sit down here at the table. You look totally exhausted," As she looked closer at him, she could see the sadness behind his eyes.

"I am just so tired of it all."

"What do you mean? How was the exam today?" She asked as she sat quietly by his side.

"It was just awful. The first half was okay, but the second half was full of trick questions, that did not test our knowledge at all. They just set us all up, to fall down in failure." He put his head in his hands.

"How is that possible? How can a whole government, and licensing body just do that, without anyone challenging the system?"

"That's a great question, but I have no answers for you, I am sorry to say. I may have to rewrite the exam again in two months if I fail this time. The thing is I am not sure how to even prepare for the exam so I will pass. There were so many other graduates there who have written the exam up to four times, and not passed yet, and most of them were older doctors with lots of experience. It was unbelievable and very sad, and I feel so discouraged, that I have to ask you to wait even longer for the life you deserve."

"Now stop that. Do you hear me? You will just keep trying and you will pass next time, or maybe even this time. Just hang in there, and wait and see what happens. When do you get the results back from this exam?"

"In a few days they'll let us know. But it wasn't a good one, so I am sure I will have to write it again," he said miserably.

"Now just calm down for now. Try and eat your supper, and let your mind just be at peace for one night. After a good night's sleep, you can plan your way better tomorrow babe?"

"I'll try." He ate slowly and very little, but she had worked so hard at making a nice supper, that he ate without hunger tonight, just to please her.

He had a shower, and decided he wanted to go for a walk alone to think for a little while. She stood there helplessly as he left for his walk. She sat down in her big chair to get off her feet. She'd been up for over ten hours on them, and she was exhausted too. And deep inside her soul, she was so disappointed to hear Samuel's news about the exam; there seemed to be no end to their troubles with his career. She couldn't even think about her own; she was so busy just trying to put food on the table, and keep a roof over their heads, that she never let herself think of what her life would have been like without him. Because he was her life, and marriage was forever to her, the same way it had been for her mother and father.

The tears rolled down her cheeks out of pure exhaustion. She couldn't believe that a place where she'd grown up could be so unfair. How was it even possible? She wondered. Most people she knew would never have believed it either. Most of the people she knew were loving, kindhearted, everyday people, who lived their lives as God-fearing people. They always believed that hard work paid off, and opportunity was offered to the most qualified candidates. But what they would have never known was that it was only true in certain jobs, and in certain professions, and not in the ones that needed licenses from the licensing bodies, which government officials controlled, those jobs, and professions were very protected. It was hitting her hard now, as she realized that her Samuel may never be able to work in Canada. And then what would happen to them? Where would they go if she couldn't come home again? She started to cry like her heart was breaking; she was tired and weary of the whole life they were leading. It was like a cage without a door – you could see the outside, but there was really no way to get out. Unless someone, somewhere changed the rules, they were totally screwed, she thought. She made a vow to not let this unjust situation get the best of them. She would fight the system if she had to. She could feel her husband's despair, because it matched her own. What they did to him, they did doubly to her. Tears rolled down her cheeks because this was her country, and they were stealing away all her hopes and dreams. The dream she had to start a family, and have a home with the man she loved. He was working as hard as he could, and so was she, but all their hard work was just hitting a brick wall, and somehow she needed to find a way to knock it down, to get past all the obstacles in front of them. Shame runs deep among those who should know better, she thought, wishing someone could hear her and just help.

The next morning over breakfast they talked about their future. Samuel had more time to think and do some research online, and he was feeling a little better about the whole situation. A good night's rest, and the much needed hope in his heart was slowly returning.

"So where does this whole situation leave us now Sam? After all the hardships we've faced in other countries to even get us this far, only to come home, and hit a brick wall again." Nicole sounded discouraged and tired. She was in need of a vacation; she'd been working too hard at her job, and the stress of his career was getting to her.

"Let's not give up just yet. Let's see what happens with the next exam, and I hear they are giving out temporary licenses at the hospitals if you work with another doctor, and he co-signs all your orders. So I am going today to apply for that position at the hospital's job bank. I will put in an application for a job, called a clinical assistant there. You need a week off. You're tired; I can see that. That store is working you too hard.

Can you ask your boss for a little time off soon?"

"It's not possible for a while. We have this big sale running right now, and we're crazy busy. Maybe in a week or two I'll ask."

She kissed him goodbye, and they headed out in different directions. He dropped her off at the store, and just as she had expected, they were lined up at the door again. Nicole knew it was going to be another hellish day, with people looking for bargains.

"Good morning everyone. I hope you're all ready to run again today." She said with a smile. But today her smile wasn't as bright as usual. Sam's news had put a great deal of sadness in her heart and eyes, for everyone to see. Her staff had grown to actually respect her now. They all noticed today, that she wasn't herself.

"Nicole? Is everything okay with you?" Jim asked. He had grown to like her, and he wanted to help her if he could.

"Oh sure... Jim. Just a little tired, that's all. I'll be in the back room getting more shirts to put out if you need me," she said. But really she just wanted a little time to think without the customers demanding all her attention. Today she didn't have the energy in her to be kind, nice or polite. She just wanted to hide, curse and swear at her life. She knew she had to be strong, and carry on with business, because someone had to pay the bills. And the more the store made, the more money she made. She emerged from the back room, and started to mingle with the customers. Three more days to go, and she knew she would be way over her financial goals for the store.

Richard finally showed up around two o'clock to help out a bit. "That was another busy day Nicole. How did we do?" He asked, staring at her with greedy eyes.

"Another twelve grand today Richard," she said barely making eye contact with him. She was so tired, and all she wanted to do was go home, and go to bed. She hadn't slept well the night before, worrying about Sam's exams.

"Nicole, are you all right, my girl? What's wrong?" He didn't want her so unhappy. It would cost him too much money if she quits on him before it was time.

"I'm just tired."

He looked at her and knew it was more than that. Maybe she was working too hard, he thought. Maybe he needed to help her more. "I see. Well, I promise I'll be in earlier tomorrow to help you. Why don't you come in a little later? Say by noon. Sleep in a bit," he offered.

"No, that's okay. We'll be very busy tomorrow. It's Friday and the staff will need me. But after the sale I'd like a week off, if that's okay. I just need a little break."

"Sure, that would be fine. I can handle things while you're gone. But... you will be back. Right?" He was getting worried. She did not look happy at all today.

"Yes, I'll be back Richard. No worries okay? I just need a little break. You have a good night." She walked slowly out of the store with her head down like she was depressed. That was what worried him the most.

He had no idea of what she was facing with Samuel and his career. She was always very private about her personal life, and he never asked questions about it either. Most of the time he spent with her, she was either talking about his business, or he was talking about his dead wife. Samuel was always pleasant when he came in most nights to pick her up, but Richard didn't really know him either. He made a note to himself to pay more attention; he wanted to make sure she was happy working for him. And in his own selfish way, he liked the girl. But mostly he liked her talent for his business, and he wished he had met her years ago. She would have made such a difference for him in his life, especially after his wife had died. Somehow Nicole had made him feel young again.

***

Samuel entered the biggest training hospital in Halifax and went straight to the Human Resources department. He met with the doctor in charge of hiring temporary doctors, who helped out as clinical assistants, while they waited to get their license to practice medicine in Canada.

"Hello. I am Dr. Samuel Emeka, and I am here to apply for a temporary position as a doctor's assistant. I am doing the exam within the next two months, and I would love to work here if that is possible please." Samuel held out his hand.

They shook hands. "Hello Samuel. I am Dr. Rogers, and yes, we do have some openings here for that. These positions we have created here, are really to take a lot of the workload off our residents in training. Fill out this application, and tell me about yourself Samuel."

"Well... I studied in the Dominican Republic, and I am a Canadian citizen, married to a Nova Scotia girl. I would love a chance to help take care of my family, and hopefully learn more about the Canadian system here. I graduated with honors from medical school over there, and I did my premed here in Nova Scotia. I am just asking for a chance to show you what I can do. To prove that my skill set is a good one. My goals are to get a paid internship, and get my medical license here."

"Well Samuel your English is good, and I love the fact you want to still learn, so let me see what I can do. I'll call you tomorrow." Dr. Rogers was a smart man, and he could see that Samuel was a good fellow. He looked better than the last two doctors who had applied for the job. At least his English was good, and he seemed to be a very likable kind of person. Too bad he was African he thought, and married to a Nova Scotia woman – that would mean he would stay, and practice medicine here after his internship.

"Thank you Dr. Rogers that would be great. I would so much appreciate this opportunity if that is possible sir." Samuel left feeling better; maybe he would be given a chance after all.

"Hello lady. What smells so good?" He was happier tonight; he had a much lighter spirit about him.

"Supper I hope." She smiled. "How was your day? What happened at the hospital today?"

"I met Dr. Rogers, who said he would call me tomorrow, and maybe they can hire me as an assistant with a temporary license. Let's hope that happens baby. We are due for some good news around here.

"I am so hungry. Can we eat now, please?" As he sat across the table from his wife, he couldn't help but notice how sad and tired she looked again.

"How are you doing? You look tired tonight."

"Yes, I am. I asked my boss for a week off after the sale and he agreed, so I think I'll go home and see Mom, and Grand for a while next week, if that's okay with you."

"Sure. If I get this job, then I can at least start to help pay some of the bills again, and take a little of the workload off your shoulders."

"That would be great. But let's wait and see what happens tomorrow." Nicole was so tired of getting her hopes up, only to be told another sad tale at the end of her day, of

122

how the situation was not what they had hoped it would be. Sometimes there seemed to be no end in sight for her disappointments, and she was just so tired now, she felt like she could sleep for a week straight. She always knew it was not her husband's fault, so she encouraged him the best she could. But most days there was no one to encourage her about anything, no one to notice how unhappy she was. No one to tell her that it was all going to be okay.

Chapter Five

The next day the phone rang. "Hello?" Samuel answered.

"Samuel this is Dr. Rogers. How are you today?"

"I am fine, thanks. And thank you sir for calling back."

"Can you come back in today, and see me again around noon? I'd like to talk with you a little further about the job here."

"Yes, I would love to. See you then." Samuel hung up the phone, his heart was filling up with hope.

He arrived at Dr. Rogers's office at noon on the dot, well-dressed in a dark green suit with a fresh white shirt and tie, looking very professional. He was excited to see Dr. Rogers again, and hear what he would say.

"Come on in Samuel, and take a seat. I've spoken to the powers that be here at the hospital, and this is what we can do for you. We'd like you to come in and act as an observer. You'll go through all the motions, just like your one of our interns, letting us test your knowledge as we do in our normal morning rounds. You'll sit in on various prognostic procedures, and assist with the diagnosis of the patients under the supervision of our trained doctors. We normally ask that you do this for at least three months; then if we like what we see in you, we'll put you on the payroll as a doctor's assistant, where all your work would be co-signed by another doctor on staff here. How does that sound to you?"

"It sounds like an opportunity for you to see my skills and knowledge. But I do have a question. When I pass the medical exams, will this position help me get an actual internship for a year here in this hospital with you? Dr. Rogers I am a qualified doctor, and I would like to be working as one. I would like to be able to set up practice at some point; my goal is to get my medical license. How is this position viewed here at this training hospital? I know you give out many internships every year; will this help me get one here?"

"I'll be honest with you, Samuel. Getting an internship here is very hard. We get so many applications every year. This position will help you get to know all the right people, and let them see what you are capable of, but there are no guarantees that we'll

124

give you an internship. You'll need to apply for that after you pass the medical exam, like everyone else. But you will get to work with the woman who is in charge of the internship program over here, so you will need to impress her, and then she may match you to this hospital for an internship."

"I see... I will take the observer position here then, Dr. Rogers. Thank you for the opportunity. I will do a good job for you. When do I start?"

"Come in tomorrow morning. Rounds are at eight, and I will introduce you to everyone then." They stood up and shook hands again, and Samuel went to the library to continue studying for the next exam. He was not sure if the position at the hospital was anything or not, but it was a chance to meet the right people, and to show them his skills. They wanted him to work for free for three months to prove himself, for a job that was beneath his qualifications. But if that's what it took, then he was willing to do it. He just hoped Nicole would understand what he was trying to do. He would now have to manage his time even better, because he would be at the hospital for eight hours, and then studying again at night for the exam, which left no time again for his wife.

Later that night over dinner, he talked to Nicole about his new position at the hospital.

"Well at least it gets your foot in the door as Grand would say, even if you are working for free. I thought those days were over, but I guess people still get taken advantage of, even in this profession. They know you have no other choice but to take this chance, so they'll take full advantage of your free labor." Nicole's soft, sad voice said how disappointed she was with their situation.

"Yes, I know. But time will tell. I have a feeling there is more here, that meets the eye at first glance.

"How was your sale today? I know it seems like I never ask anymore; it's just that I have so much on my mind these days." Samuel reached over the table for her hand.

"I know you do darling. It seems like for our whole married life, we both have had a lot on our minds. The sale is going very well; I'm making lots of money for the old guy, so he's happy. The staff are all coming around now too. Richard's wife... I have a feeling, is a storm waiting to happen. She's never happy about anything. She always finds things to complain about, that are simply not important. To be honest I am damn tired too of it all."

"As soon as I am settled you will quit that job and go back to school and study whatever you like. Maybe have a baby even?" He looked at her hopefully.

"A baby. That would be nice, but not now. If I got pregnant, who would work and pay the bills." The look on her face told him she meant business. It was hard enough just to keep the bills paid. A baby was something they just could not afford – but inside she wished they could.

Samuel's soul ached with what Nicole had just said. They couldn't afford a baby. Back where he came from, babies just happened, and they made do. But he didn't want to pressure her with more than she could handle. There was time for all that; they were both still young, and he knew that maybe a baby would just complicate things for later.

"It's time for bed… come to bed with me tonight. I don't want to sleep alone." Her eyes pleaded with him.

"You know I need to study."

"Yes I know, but I feel lonely, and I just want one night with my husband in bed beside me. Is that so much to ask for?" Her eyes were gentle, and kind as she spoke to him.

"No my wife it's not." He took her hand, and walked into their bedroom. She slowly undressed in front of him. He took her into his arms, and pulled her down onto their bed.

"You are so sweet, I just want to hold you all night long."

"Just hold me. Is that all you want?" Her lips begging to be kissed.

"No that's never all I want." His hands and lips fervently exploring her body.

"Oh Sam don't stop, I need to feel you inside of me."

He passionately embraced her curves, and soon they were climbing to a place where only they could go. They hadn't made love in days, and she was reminding him again of why he was fighting so hard to stay in Canada. He was staying for his loving wife.

The next morning, Samuel was at the hospital by seven forty-five for the early morning rounds, with the other doctors.

"Morning Samuel and welcome," Dr. Rogers said.

"Good morning sir. I am happy to be here with you today," Samuel said with a beaming smile.

"Everyone, this Dr. Samuel Emeka. He will be observing with us, and helping out for the next three months. Please make him feel welcome, and take him along on whatever procedures you are doing." They all looked him over, and many of them decided he was no competition for them, so they ignored him. The rounds begun, and of course Dr. Rogers wanted to test Samuel's knowledge, so they asked him question after question, about the patients they were visiting during the rounds. Samuel was at a disadvantage, because he'd had no time to read the patient history, or the treatment plans. But in spite of it all, he did wonderfully well; he got most of the patient diagnoses correct, and also recommended the correct treatments. He could see the impressed looks on most of the doctor's faces. He had given them confidence, to take him along on their various medical procedures.

"You did very well Samuel. Keep up the good work, and I'll see you tomorrow morning. You'll work the rest of the day with Dr. Adrian. You can go with him to check in new patients, and do their histories and physicals. Under his supervision of course."

"Thanks Dr. Rogers. I had a lot of fun today, and I realize how much I love being a doctor."

"It shows Samuel." Dr. Rogers walked away. He felt sorry for Samuel. He could see he was there for all the right reasons, and generally loved medicine. Samuel had a special way with the patients. He noticed he made them feel comfortable, and relaxed when he was talking to them, and about them. He was careful not to make them more anxious, he talked in a way they could understand, and he treated them with respect. Dr. Rogers liked that very much; he was old-school in his way of thinking, and near retirement himself. And most of the new medical doctors coming through his rounds, just didn't have that kind of bedside matter anymore.

"Nice job today Samuel. I'll see you tomorrow." Dr. Adrian said as he walked away, impressed for once by what he had seen today with this new clinical assistance. This one would be beneficial, and safe to work with. Dr. Adrian was a senior resident, and was happy to just have some good help for a change; most of the working doctors were already feeling the shortage of help in their departments, and often they were overworked themselves. Samuel's day finally came to an end, and he was pleased that everything had gone so well. He went over to pick Nicole up at the store, and decided to take her out for dinner.

"Ready to go home?" Sam asked cheerfully.

"Yes, I am. How was your day babe?"

"Let's go out and eat. You're too tired to cook its Friday, and you need a break. What do you feel like eating tonight?"

"Oh, I don't know Sam. Maybe some kind of shrimp or fish I guess."

"Great. Let's go to the seafood restaurant on the corner. They make great fish and chips there. They enter the place and took a seat, and order a plate of seafood with two glasses of white wine.

"So do you really think these people at the hospital will give you fair chance this time, or are you working for free for nothing?" Nicole asked, looking skeptical.

"Well... who knows with these people? You know they always have hidden agendas of some kind. But I can tell you this much. I think they were all very impressed with my work today. They told me how well I performed with all the patients. So I hope they will play fair, and give me a paid position after the three months is up."

"So after three months of free labor Sam, you'll get paid as a doctor under a temporary license? Did they even say what the salary was for that job?"

"No... not really. They want to know how committed you are as a doctor. The salary is unimportant to them."

"Oh really. It's unimportant to them, because they all have their big cars, and homes, and don't have to live paycheck to paycheck like us." Nicole was tired and getting annoyed by the whole conversation.

"That's true. But what other choice do I really have?"

"It's just so unfair that they can do this. It makes me so damn angry."

"Well they have said that this position may lead to a fully-paid internship, and that's what I need, so I guess we just have to play the game for a while, and see what happens. I write the next exam in just a few weeks, and hopefully this time I will be more ready for their so-called medical exam, I really need to pass this time. I have gotten some past papers from some of the other foreign graduates, who have written the exam and have been successful. I have studied some of the trick questions, so this time I am more prepared. God knows I am trying lady."

"What a shame that this is the way you have to study for the Canadian medical exam. It's just crazy that we have such a system in place. You'd think they would really want to test your knowledge so that we have better doctors here, and for the wellbeing and safety of our general public. My God... it's just unbelievable to me," she was feeling more frustrated than ever.

"Sometimes I feel like we're being treated like second-class citizens, but when it comes to paying taxes, I'm considered a first-class citizen, because they sure do take a big chunk out of my paycheck every month. And I resent that. This is my country too, so why shouldn't we have the same opportunities as everyone else?"

"I know it's a difficult thing to understand, but these are the rules we have to play by for now. So let's just hope that we are playing with some fair-minded people, because they hold all the control."

"Yes. The same fair-minded people who kept you out of medical school here in the first place. Somehow that doesn't give me much hope. Why would they play fair now, when they didn't then?" She was totally discouraged, and she just knew they were going to get screwed over again by the so-called system. She could feel it in her heart and in the pit of her stomach, but she never said a word of that to Sam. But that was the real reason why she was so thin and tired-looking, because she knew there was no end in sight, only a false sense of security for the time being while they used her husband for free labor. Within a few weeks they would be able to tell at the hospital that his skills and qualifications were good enough for the temporary license, so why would they still use him for three more months? They did it just because they could.

Sam was at the hospital, faithfully putting his skills to work every day. The nursing staff admired the way in which he treated the patients. He was always smiling and singing, although they all knew he had little to sing about, considering he was working long hours, and not getting paid a penny for his labor. Most of the nursing staff wondered just how many promises were made that would be actually kept. They had seen it all before with foreign graduates who worked hard, only to be turned away at the last hour, and not receive an internship as promised. But they hoped for his sake that this time would be different, because he was different. Samuel was a good doctor, and it was obvious how much he loved medicine. Many of his patients looked forward to his visits. They often kept their questions just for him, because he explained the answers to them in a way that they could understand. He always greeted them with a smile, and a joked to get them to relax. But of course it was those same patients, who would have never known, that Samuel was working for free. Like most people in Canada, they had no idea how the medical system actually worked in their own country. It was only those who had developed the system, and those who unfortunately had to go up against the system and try to penetrate it, who actually knew how unfair it was.

***

Nicole's hard work had paid off at the store, and the sale had been a huge success. She was looking forward to her week off. She had called her mother, and said she would be home late Friday evening, and that she would stay with them for a week.

"I left lots of cooked food for you in the icebox Sam. So please make sure you eat while I'm gone, and I'll call you when I get there."

"Yes I will eat, please drive safe." He pulled her into his arms and kissed her goodbye, she got into the car and drove off .In only minutes she was on the open highway, heading for home. Nicole was happy to get away from it all for a while. She listened to her music, and sang her heart out, it felt good to sing while no one was listening. In a couple of hours, she pulled the car up into the driveway and got out. Millie and Sarah came to the front door as soon as they heard her car door open; they stood at the front door with big smiles on their faces waiting for her.

"Wow Grand! The garden looks great. So many lovely flowers this year." She ran up and gave both a big hugs and kisses.

"Let me look at you dear," her mother said.
"Why on earth are you so thin again? What's happened to you in the last few months?"

She looked her daughter over like a mother does, and couldn't believe that she had lost more weight.

"Come in dear. We've just finished all your favorite food. You probably haven't even had lunch yet."

"I'm okay Mommy. Where is everyone? Where is little Sis?"

"She'll be home soon. She's still at school, and the boys are inside at the table waiting to see you."

"Hi everyone. How's life in the fast lane guys?" She joked with them.

"Doing okay Sis. How about you? You look like you haven't eaten in weeks. Isn't that husband of yours feeding you?" Her brothers always spoke their minds directly.

"No, he beats and starves me. Really guys, I eat when I'm hungry, so don't you worry about it." She made a funny face at them, like she always did when they were small children. She was somewhat defensive regarding Samuel; she knew they would never be able to understand how hard he was working, and what kind of people he was up against, so she just joked with them instead of trying to explain.

"Now stop that, you two. What do you want to eat dear?' her mother asked.

"Some pie and coffee would be great."

"Nonsense. That's not food. Put some chicken, and vegetables on that plate, and sit down here and eat while we talk. Now don't argue with your old grandmother. Just eat for heaven's sake." Millie said and Nicole did not dare disagree, she never won anyway. She obey them as she had when she was a child living under their roof.

"Okay Grandmother."

Sarah served her food and she ate like she was starving. The food tasted so good to her that she ate seconds and then apple pie too.

"Wow, thanks Mommy. That was so good, I'm so full I think I could burst."

Her little sister came running in. "Nick! How the hell are you?" She said with a sparkle in her eye.

"What did you say, Young Lady?" Millie looked at her over her glass.

"Sorry Grandmother." She gave Nicole a kiss and a hug, and then hugged her grandmother too. She sat down and ate with the family, and they all chatted about school, Nicole's job, and life in the city. It was nearly eight o'clock when they left the table.

"May I please be excused? I'm so tired after my drive, I just want to sleep early tonight Mommy."

"Why of course, dear. You look like you need a good night's sleep. I'll be up shortly to make sure you have everything you need. Just go on up to your old room; your bed is already turned down. Nothing has changed; it's just the same way you left it dear."

She went up the stairs, and laid down on her old bed. Within minutes, she had fallen off to sleep. Still fully clothed.

Her grandmother looked in on her. She wanted to have a talk with her, but instead found her fast asleep. She put a blanket over her, and sat quietly beside her. She just knew something was slowly killing her – she could feel it now as she sat silently beside her. No matter how old Nicole became, Millie always thought of her as an innocent child, and often refer to her as a child, in her heart it made Nicole feel closer.

She walked downstairs and out into the kitchen, where Sarah was finishing up the dinner dishes. "I tell you Sarah, something is bothering that girl. Just look at her, so thin and pale again. I know it's Samuel career. You mark my words – he'll leave her alone and frail." She cared for Sam, but she also knew that this road was much too hard for Nicole, and she wished she didn't have to be on it.

"Now stop that talk Grand. She's just tired. We need to make sure she eats, and sleeps as much as she can while she's here with us."

Nicole woke up early the next day and came downstairs in her night dress, like she always had when she was a small child, and sat down at the breakfast table. Her sister and brothers had already eaten, and were off somewhere with friends. Only her grandmother, and mother were still there eating breakfast.

"Good morning dear. How did you sleep? Help yourself to some coffee." Sarah said.

Nicole poured a cup of coffee, picked up a blueberry muffin from the counter, and came over to sit beside her Grandmother.

"Good morning. Hope I didn't sleep too late. I'm just so tired these days. Mmm… good muffins Grand."

"I want to know what's going on with you. Why are you so thin and unhappy these days my child?"

"Oh Grand… its Samuel's career. It never seems to be going well, and I'm always picking up the pieces, and trying to put them together. The whole system to integrate back in Canada is messed up and very unfair. He's working as hard as he can, but really who knows what will happen? They now have him working for free for three months, to show them his skills, with a hint of a promise that it will lead to an internship. But I don't trust them to follow through, and I know in my gut that they won't. And I am

132

so saddened by it that most nights, I can't eat and rarely sleep well. Then there's my job. I'm working my ass off to get the store functioning again, and to make a profit. Because it's my job that's paying all the bills Grand, so I guess I'm just stressed out a bit." She smiled up at her old Grandmother.

"A bit? I would say more than a bit. You will need this week to just rest and take better care of yourself. You see Nicole, trouble will always be all around us, but it's how we handle these situations that will either make or break us. Not eating or sleeping only makes you weak, and you need to be strong enough to fight the system. And if it's unfair, then tell someone. Hell, child, tell everyone until someone changes it. You can always fight back. There is no need to feel helpless, but you can't fight back if you're not strong enough. Taking care of yourself has to be a priority, so you can help Samuel with his fight to get an internship here. And if that doesn't happen, then make an appointment to speak with our Minister of Health. They should see and hear you both out regarding this situation."

"Oh Grandmother you are so right, how did you get to be so wise. I love you so much. I never thought about that, but it's a great idea. But first I guess we have to wait and see what happens for a little while longer. I'll try to eat better – it's just that I get so tired, and upset with things that I can't most times."

"Oh, but you must my child. Just pray and believe that things will change for the better, and they will, they most surely will dear. Now tell me, have you been going to church on Sunday dear?"

"No… Grand. I'm so tired, and it's one of the few days I have to sleep in. Then I have to do housework, cook, and all that kind of stuff."

"I understand that too. But here's the thing: get up anyway, and go at least once in a while. You need that dear; your soul needs that. How can you be strong without hearing God's words, and being around the people who believe in him and love him?"

"I know you're right. I'll start to go again. I'll try harder, I promise." She never wanted to disappoint anyone, especially not her Grandmother.

"Promise what?" Sarah asked as she walked in. "Here are your eggs honey. Eat them before they get cold, and then maybe we can go for a little walk together and pick some fresh flowers in the garden. It's so lovely this time of year."

"That would be so nice! I would love to Mommy."

Sarah knew how much Nicole loved flowers, and walking quietly along the water's edge next to the ocean. When she'd been much younger, she would sometimes fall asleep on a blanket outside by the ocean, getting a sun tan. Sarah hoped today's walk would help her daughter to relax and to feel more rested, and maybe open up a bit and talk to her.

Sarah and Nicole walked along the ocean bank, and picked some flowers from the garden. They sat on the bench out on the porch, and Sarah eyed her daughter, and then decided to speak her mind.

"You know Honey, I don't like seeing you so stressed and thin again. What's happening with Samuel these days to upset you so much?" Sarah was no fool when it came to her children. She knew what her daughter's trouble was, but she didn't want to discourage her more than she already was. She just wanted to encourage Nicole to talk to her about the situation.

"It's just work, and then Samuel's career has been slow to take off, so I'm just tired of it all. That's really what it is. I love him so much, but it's all such a burden all the time. There's no fun or laugher for either of us most times, and I just feel like all my young years are passing me by in sadness."

"I know honey. You have to find a way to put those things back into your life somehow. It can't always just be about his career while you suffer and wait. He can't expect that of you. Most of the time you're all alone when I call, and he's busy studying at some library. I know he's trying his best, but my dear child, life is too short to be saddled with unhappiness at such a young age."

"I know Mommy. But what can I do? I have all the bills to pay, and most nights I'm just so tired, then I have grocery shopping, cleaning, and then cooking to do too."

"You can take a day just for you; go get your hair and nails done. Then go to dinner once a week; that won't break the bank. Go dancing, go see a movie – you love movies dear. Do some things that make you happy too – just for pure fun. You know fun in your life is not forbidden just because Samuel's career isn't working at the moment. It's not the end of your life or his; you just have to make time to enjoy the things you love a little bit more. It will help ease away some of your stress, and his once in a while."

"You know Mom, you're so right. I'm going to do that. Thanks for the talk. It makes me realize, that I do need to have some fun, and to laugh more often."

She slept soundly that night, and over the course of the week, she ate better than she had in months. Being around her grandmother, and mother had made her realize that she needed to stay positive, and be kinder to herself. She was determined to do that, and change the way she and Samuel were living.

Before she knew it, the week was over. She'd been eating like a pig, and had a nice golden tan, and the sparkle was back in her eyes again. She looked healthy again, and all the stress was gone from her face for now.

"I can't believe this is my last breakfast with you guys. The week has gone by so fast." Nicole looked sadly at her mother.

"Yes, it has honey. I packed a lunch for you to take on the drive back. Just a tin of blueberry muffins, some for Samuel too, and a chicken sandwich, which you'd better eat along the way. Just stop halfway there, get some tea, eat your sandwich and then continue on again. Call me when you're having a break, and let me know how the sandwich and the muffins are." The real truth was that it scared Sarah to see her daughter so thin and frail-looking, and she was worried Nicole wouldn't continue to take care of herself, after she went back home to Samuel.

"I will, I promise. I love you." She kissed her on the cheek. "Grandmother, I love you so much; take good care of yourself okay?"

"Yes child, I will, if you promise to do the same. You know Nicole I have a longing to see the city again, so I think your mother and sister and I, will come and visit for the weekend real soon."

"That would be so lovely Grand. I hope you do."

Sarah walked Nicole to her car. They put her suitcase in the trunk, and slowly opened the door. She turned and looked at her mother like she was lost. "I love you Mommy, and I'll call in an hour or so."

"I love you too dear, I be waiting for your call." Sarah hugged her daughter and watched her drive off. She walked back inside and sat quietly at the table, she felt sad for her daughter, and the life she had chosen.

"Sarah, she's okay. She just needs to start taking better care of herself. I just wish Samuel could get that career of his on track so she could get some rest," Millie said as she rocked in the chair beside the window. But deep inside her gut, she knew just like Nicole, that it was never going to happen. Not in their country.

Nicole pulled the car over to a coffee shop, and got a cup of tea. She sat outside at a table under a tree, and ate her sandwich with one of the muffins her mother had packed for her, and then as she had promised to do, she called her mother.

The phone rang only once, and her mother grabbed it. She'd been waiting for Nicole's call, and hadn't moved all morning until she heard the phone ring.

"Hello dear," she said.

"Hi Mommy! The sandwich was so good and so was the muffin. Thank you so much. I just finished them both, and now I'm off on the road again. I'll call in an hour or so when I've reached home. I love you."

"Love you too dear." They hung up the phone, ending the conversation the same way they always did. Sarah knew that life was short, so she never missed a chance to tell one of her children that she loved them.

Nicole drove home, and stopped off at the market to get groceries. Samuel would be home in a few hours, and she wanted to cook a special dinner for them. Hopefully they could just relax together for one night. She was determined to change the way they were living their life. They needed to make changes so they would be less stressed, and find more joy out of their lives.

Sam walked into his last treatment room, took a few more histories, and did some physicals, with the last two remaining patients. At last his day was finally done. All he wanted to do now, was to run home and see his wife. He knew she would be patiently waiting at home for him. "I am off now. Have a good night," Sam said with a smile for the nurses, at the nursing station.

He got into his car and drove straight home. Nicole was in the kitchen, taking a roasted chicken out of the oven, just as he walked in the door.

"Hello beautiful lady. Come give me a hug my sweetheart." Samuel stood at the door and looked at his wife.

Nicole put the chicken on the table and walked over to him. "I missed you so much all week." She hugged him as tightly as she could.

"Nice table. I see you have been working hard since you got home. How is your family, and how was your trip my love?" He noticed how lovely she looks tonight. She'd taken the time to put on a soft pink sweater with a pair of comfortable pants, and she looked so beautiful to him.

"My trip was relaxing, it was just what I needed. It made me realize that we need to make more time for each other. We need to start, to have a little more fun in our marriage. I know things are not what we want them to be, but life is passing us by, and these are our young years. We need to make a little more time to be with each other." She spoke softly and loving, her words made him feel guilty all over again.

"I know... we will try to do that. Believe me, I am happy to have you by my side through this, and I am sorry that I leave you alone too much. But I am just one man, and most times I am so tired. Tired of studying all the time, tired of trying to find a way out of this whole situation, that I find myself in. Some days I can see the end in sight, and other days I can't." He was so exhausted from studying for the next exam, and working a full eight hour day at the hospital, that all he really wanted to do was sleep – sleep forever if he could. That night they lay in each other's arms, and fell asleep.

The alarm went off at seven, and they were both up and off to start another week.

"Lady do you want a ride to work with me today? I need to leave by eight."

She poured his coffee and handed him breakfast, and then gave him a big hug.

"Yes, I'll drive with you. I need to go in early, and see what kind of state the store is in." She drank her coffee, and ate one of the muffins her mother had sent with her. She got up to go shower and changed for work. Nicole was at her desk, reviewing the last week's sales, and writing up the timetable her staff for the following week. Richard came in, and he noticed that Nicole had the sunshine back in her eyes again.

He smiled up at her. "How was your trip? You are looking well."

"It was restful, and it was so good to see my family. Thanks for asking Richards. How are things here?"

"Ok, but not as good, as when you are here my girl, glad to have you back." He walked off his office.

It was exam time again, and Sam was burning the midnight oil as he always did leading up to exams. He kept his Bible in hand and read it often. He knew just how much was riding on this exam. If he didn't pass, that would give them a perfect excuse not to hire him, and then he wouldn't get an internship program. He also knew the pressure Nicole was feeling at her job. She rarely said anything to him about it, but he could see it in her eyes when she looked at him. She never seemed to laugh anymore, she had a lot more headaches than usual, and she rarely ate much. It was all just too much stress on her. His career battles were making them both so exhausted. If they just got just one chance, most of their worries would be over.

He went over to their bed where Nicole was asleep, kissed her cheek, and then out the door he went, with a coffee in hand, and a good frame of mind to write for his life.

Nicole stirred but fell back asleep. It was still dark outside. She woke up at eight o'clock, made coffee, picked up a biscuit, and curled up in her big chair. She was praying for Samuel's success today. She knew it was their turn for a break, and she hoped God granted them one today.

Sam got out of his car, and went inside the exam hall. He saw many of the same faces from last time. He greeted them and wished them all good luck, then moved away and took a seat. He wanted to stay positive, and focus on the task at hand. The papers were handed out and they started to write. This time he had one belief in his heart: if God was on his side, it simply did not matter if no one else was. He wrote fast, and this time he knew he would conquer this beast. He knew most of the answers, and he finished them all in good time.

At lunch, Nicole took out her little Bible and prayed. "Father God... please help Sam today. I believe you will give him your passing grace this time, and for that, I give you thanks." She went on with her day, knowing in her heart he would pass. Of this she had no doubt. She envisioned his handwriting quickly in her mind's eye. All she wished for, was that this nightmare would have a happy ending. All she wanted was a normal life, where they could live happily together and start a family. She couldn't remember the last time her head hadn't been full of worries and problems. She had the burdens of a lifetime on her shoulders, and these were supposed to be the best years of her life. She hoped they weren't. They had worked so hard. Yet success was still not in their hands; it had eluded them.

Sam stood up. His exam was over, and he knew he'd done well. He got in his car and headed home to Nicole. She was already at home, and had prepared an evening meal for them. She wanted him to forget all the troubles, and stresses of the day, at least for one evening. They deserved to relax.

"Hi Lady." He came through the door, looking exhausted.

"Wow. You look like you need some tender loving care tonight. Dare I ask how the exam was this time?"

"It wasn't too bad. I think I stand a very good chance at a pass mark."

"Really?" Relief flooded her face. "Oh, that would be great. Let's keep our fingers crossed. How long before we know?"

"They will send out the marks by next week." He looked relieved that the exam was over, and she could tell that he was feeling more positive tonight.

"Well, I think you need a little R&R, darling." She handed him tea and some homemade apple pie. He had learned to love apple pie as much as she did. It was their comfort food when they were extra-stressed.

"I'm going take tomorrow off from the hospital. I just need to sleep all day and relax my head."

"Things will get better. Come to bed with me and let me take your mind off of all that stuff." She held out her hand for him to follow her to bed. She just held his hand and let him sleep. She curled up beside him and listened to his heartbeat, she knew how exhausted he was. In no time at all, they were both asleep, in each other's arms.

He checked the mail almost every day now. A week had already passed by, and he was extremely anxious to hear back from his exam. It was the end of the week, Sam got out of bed, and ran down to the mail. He opened it and found his results. He read them, and then returned back to Nicole, who was standing in the kitchen getting breakfast ready. She poured them both coffee and put oatmeal on the table, with a bowl of fruit.

"Come and sit for breakfast. Was there anything in the mail this morning?"

"Yes, there was."

"Well, for heaven's sake Sam... what was it?"

"My results," he said in a soft voice.

"How did you do?" She looked anxious as she studied his face.

"I guess I am going to have to celebrate tonight, because I passed that damn exam." He was so happy he laughed out loud, and danced around in front of her. He ran over, gave her a big hug, and picked her up. He was like a little boy who'd just won first prize.

"Oh that's so wonderful! I am so proud of you." She hadn't seen him this happy since his graduation day; it felt good to see him happy again.

He got dressed, went to the hospital, and presented his exam papers to Dr. Rogers. "Here you go Dr. Rogers. I passed the exam," he said proudly.

"Very good news Samuel. I'm so glad to hear that. Now I can transfer you to another department, under Dr. Jane Hays. She's in internal medicine, and now we can put you on the payroll. You will be paid as a Clinical Assistant, and the pay is thirty thousand a year. You can do that until the next round of internships are out in about six months. Then let's just see which hospital you get matched to for an internship. Dr. Hays, has a lot to do with picking the new internship, for this hospital and across Canada, so be good to her Sam. She will play a big role in you getting into the internship program. Dr. Hays does the actual matching for this hospital, so it's good for you to get to know her, and show her your skill set, which are very good, I must say. You've been doing very well here with us. I am hearing good things about you from the nursing staff and residents. But for now your career will be in her hands, so make the most of it. And good luck, Samuel."

They shook hands, and Sam left on cloud nine. Finally, he was going to get paid, with the hopes of getting an internship. "I finally have good news to tell Nicole tonight," he said out loud to himself.

He picked her up at the store after she'd cashed out for the day. "How was your day?" He asked cheerfully.

"Pretty good. And you? You sound happy tonight."

"My day was great. I will tell you all about it over dinner. We are going out to eat tonight," he said with a grin. "How about that fish and chip place on the corner?"

"Okay babe. That sounds good." She smiled; it made her feel good to see him so happy for a change.

They went to the restaurant and ordered a bottle of champagne. They both had fish and chips and cheesecake for dessert. It was a very special occasion, and he wanted to celebrate this next step in his career with her tonight.

"Okay Sam, tell me what's up. What are they saying at the hospital?"

"I am now a paid clinical assistant, and I am officially on staff now. I am being transferred to a new department, called Internal Medicine, under Dr. Jane Hays. She is the one who actually picks the new interns for this hospital, and many others in Canada. She is in charge of the matching system for the internship program. I'm going to work hard and impress her, and hopefully secure an internship here in this hospital. Working alongside of her should give me a better opportunity to get it here I think, or at least that's what Dr. Rogers said to me today. After one year, I can apply for my full medical license, and set up my own practice right here in Nova Scotia. Isn't that great news, my love?" He reached over and took her hands in his.

"Dear heavens Sam! That's great news for a change. Yes indeed it is. But the whole system is so complicated. Can't these people do anything simply?" She was so relieved that they'd actually kept their word, and had given him a paid position.

"Yes, I know. The fact that we are all Canadian citizens' means very little – in fact, it means nothing at all."

"But the really sad part is, that they don't even graduate enough doctors to fill the needs of the communities, especially in the rural areas. Just look at my hometown Shelburne, for example. The women there now have to go to Bridgewater to have their babies, for heaven's sake, and that's an hour and a half drive away."

"That's because the Canadian graduates do not want to go there. Would you be willing to go home for a while if we got the chance to?"

"Of course I would. I think it would be a great place for us to start our own family." She smiled at the thought of it.

"Let's see how Dr. Hays responds to me. Hopefully it will lead to good things."

Nicole seemed happier now, and actually started to sing again. Sam noticed as she cooked dinner at night; he could hear her singing in the kitchen. It made his heart feel proud that he was able to contribute money to their household. He could see less stress in his wife's face, and noticed that she actually was eating dinner again in the evening. She was starting to look like her old self – radiant and beautiful.

On Samuel's first morning working with Dr. Hays, he arrived before any of the others. He was standing at the front desk with a smile on his face, waiting to do morning rounds.

"Hello Dr. Hays. I am Samuel and I will be your clinical assistant. I was assigned by Dr. Rogers."

"Yes… I've heard good things about you." Dr. Hays looked him over.

"Thank you for this opportunity."

"This is Dr. Glen and Dr. Vincent from Poland. We'll all be working together as a team," Dr. Hays said

"Hello. I am Samuel." He shook the hands of the other two doctors.

"My name Glen from Poland, we come here one year now. How long you are here now?" Glen said in his broken English.

"I have been here for more than ten years. I did my premed here. I left for medical school, and studied outside of Canada, which is how I ended up here in this system, but I am a Canadian citizen, and my wife is a born Canadian citizen right here from Nova Scotia."

"We just come one year now, we get an internship and go to the big city and make lots of money. I hope to get an internship this year," Glen said.

"Me too, but I want to stay here, and work in the small town where my wife was born, and help the community there." He smiled as they started to walk towards the patients.

"But why waste time? Get more money in bigger city Sam," Vincent said in his broken English and heavy accent.

"Because it's not all about the money for me and my wife. It's about the people, and the community and family." He shook his head, wondering how these two had managed to get this far. He only hoped they knew some medicine; otherwise he'd be doing a lot more work to cover for them than he'd bargained for.

"Let's start our round's doctors?" Dr. Hays said in a businesslike tone. She was a small woman in her late fifties, with gray hair and hardly any personality. Dr. Hays stood at the foot of a patient's bed, and handed Glen the report. "Can you please read that, Dr. Glen? And then let me know what you think we should do."

"Sorry doctor. I don't know how report read yet?" His face looked totally blank.

"I see. Samuel, can you please read it for us? And can you let me know what we should do next for him please." She sounded irritated as she spoke now.

"Yes of course I can." He scanned the paper. "His blood report indicates that the WBC blood count is high, and because of this I think there is possibly an infection in the kidney. Let's start a course of antibiotics, and do further testing of the kidney functions. He is running a fever, and we need to watch his urine output. Let's give him lots of fluids, and see how the next 24 hours are for him." Samuel moved beside the patient and addressed him.

"Sir, we are going to start some new medication today. It's really important that you try your best to drink everything you are given today for fluids." He smiled to help the patient feel more at ease.

"Sure thing, doc. I will. What do you think the trouble is?

"I think you have an infection in your kidneys. Don't worry, we will get you fixed up in no time." Samuel smiled.

The patient smiled back. Finally someone was actually acknowledging him as a person and not a chart, the old man thought.

They moved on to the next patient. This time it was an older woman in her late seventies, suffering from a high fever with reasons unknown.

Dr. Hays asked Dr. Vincent to read her report. After Sam had explained the last one, he should be able to read this one, Dr. Hays thought.

"Sorry Dr. Hays. I still unsure what reports says." He just stood there, and looked at her.

"Dr. Emeka, please read this one as well." She was getting visibly upset now.

Samuel reads the report, and then moved over to the patient. "Hello Mrs. Adrian. I am Dr. Emeka. Samuel is my first name." He gave her his wonderful smile, so she would relax.

"Okay son. How about I call you Dr. Sam? Your last name is too hard for me, sonny boy."

"Sure thing Mrs. Adrian. How do you feel today?"

"I have chills and a stomach ache, and I feel very tired."

"I see. Have you been out of the country lately my dear?"

"Yes. I just got back from Costa Rica."

"Wow! Lucky you. Were you bitten by many mosquitoes down there?"

"Yes. One night I got some bites on me. Quite a few actually," she said.

"Here's what I think is happening to you. Your tests indicate that you have a touch of malaria. We need to get you started on some medication. To get you better. If Dr. Hays agrees, I would like to start a full course of IV antibiotics, and give you something to settle your stomach down. Then we'll give you some further tests for parasites, and see what is happening in a few hours with you. Do you agree with that, Dr. Hays?"

"Very good Sam. I do agree. How did you diagnose her like that so soon?"

"Studying infectious diseases was a big part of our medical school training down on the islands, as the patients there are often sick with this kind of thing. And if I may be honest, I also grew up with these kinds of diseases, back in Africa."

The patient reached out and grabbed Samuel's hand. "Where are you from son?"

"I was born in Africa, but I am married to a Nova Scotia lady, so this has been my home for many years now." He smiled at her kindly.

"Will I see you again tomorrow?" She looked hopeful.

"Yes my dear. I will see you tomorrow, and if you have any more pain this evening, tell the nurse. She will page me, and I will come back at once okay? Don't worry Mrs. Adrian. We treat this kind of thing all the time. You'll be fine in a few days."

"You're a nice man Dr. Sam. I'm glad you're my doctor."

Samuel smiled at her, and walked away with Dr. Hays.

"Excellent Samuel." Dr. Hays smiled in spite of herself.

Dr. Hays usually didn't smile much, and stuck to business. She was a hard woman to read in most cases. But he could tell that she knew her stuff in the medicine department very well.

"That's all for the rounds today. Dr. Glen and Dr. Vincent, I suggest you go to the laboratory, and learn how to read our reports by tomorrow's rounds, understood? Samuel you will have to do all the histories, and physicals of my new patients coming in today. I think there are about eight of them. You'll have to fill in until Dr. Glen and Dr. Vincent are up to speed."

She walked off, wondering why in hell she was sent such idiots as Glen and Vincent. They hardly even spoke English she thought. At least she had gotten one good one with Samuel. He was as impressive as Dr. Rogers had said he'd be. He was going to be a big help to her, of that she had no doubt. The other two Doctors should be helping, but they still had a lot to learn before they would be of any use at all. She realized it was unfair to Samuel, but what could she do? She had no choice but to leave him with the work. She had other patients she had to see back in her office.

She walked off the floor and went into her office. She picked up the phone and called Dr. Rogers. "Hello Dr. Rogers. It's Jane Hays. May I ask one simple question? Just where on *earth,* did you get those two Polish doctors from? They can't even read a report, either of them! And they barely speak English!"

"Now calm down Jane. It was either them or two more black Africans, and I thought Samuel was enough. The Polish doctors will leave here after their internships and go to bigger cities, but the African doctors will stay here, and before you know it, they'll take over. Just look at how good Samuel is – the patients love him. We have to protect this profession as best we can. We want to train foreign doctors who will leave, because if they stay, before you know it, they will change the system, and we both know how that works right? When internship time comes around, just give it to the Polish, and then they will leave. Save Samuel until next year. He's a good Clinical Assistant, and we can use him for another year here. It makes all our lives so much easier. For God's sake, Jane, just get Samuel to train them. He knows the system very well now."

"Just how much work do you think one doctor can do? If Samuel has to do all the new incoming patients, then he has no time left to show these Polish Doctors anything. I'll have to be the one to do that, and you know it. Damn you Dick; you should have trained them before you sent them to me. You know how busy this department is. Samuel will now have to do the job for three doctors instead of one, and that's just not right. And besides, Samuel is smart. He'll want to get on with his own career, and not be our assistant."

"Look Jane, he's just happy to have a chance for now. He'll manage. He's fast and he knows his stuff. Samuel is too damn smart, and that's dangerous. He could move up the ladder fast, so damn it Jane; just follow my instructions for once. Send back the other doctors to me for a week, and I'll train them on the lab work and hospital procedures. I'll send them back to you next week okay? Happy now Jane?"

"Fine. But hurry up with those two for God's sake. Samuel will be living in the hospital for the next little while." Not that she really cared about Samuel; she just didn't want any unfair complaints on her watch. They were often nightmares to deal with, and she knew this one would be hard to refute. But Samuel seemed like such an easygoing man; Dr. Rogers was most likely right that he would manage fine for a while. Sometimes she hated the good old boys' club herself, but it was just the way the medical community worked there. Always afraid of the newcomers, always saving positions for sons and daughters who were about to graduate. She knew this plan was unfair to Samuel, but she had to follow it. Otherwise the club would blackball her, and that she did not want. She needed all her connections. She washed their hands, and then they washed hers. If someone got blackballed, all referrals stopped, and that would add up to a loss of income for her. She had no other choice; she would have to delay this poor young man's career for a while, as ordered by Dr. Rogers.

If he did well and was made head of any department, then he would have a voice to change things, and that would be no good. She didn't know if he was the type to fight for change, or if he would just be happy to make a living, and care for his family. That was yet to be determined, so she had to play it safe for now.

Samuel worked long, hard hours in the hospital, the Polish doctors hadn't returned yet to his department, to help him with the workload. Samuel came to work each morning full of joy and enthusiasm. It was obvious to all that worked beside him that he loved what he did. They loved his attitude, the nurses liked how down to earth he was, and the patients loved how comfortable he made them feel. On Samuel's second week of working eighteen hour days, Dr. Hays could see the fatigue in his eyes, but he was still there working hard and smiling.

He hadn't seen his wife in days, and had barely seen his own bed to sleep, but he was happy to have the opportunity, so he never complained. He just hoped that soon he would get some much-needed help, and maybe a day off to rest.

The weekend finally came around, and Samuel was given three days off. He couldn't wait to sleep, and spend some time with Nicole. He picked her up at the store on Friday night.

"How are you Lady? I feel like I haven't seen you in days my sweetheart."

"That's because you haven't," she said with a smile. She knew he was overworked, but he was also happy, and seeing him smiling again was good enough for her.

"I promise I make it up to you this weekend," Samuel said laughing.

"Oh really? That sounds promising. Just how do you plan to do that, Doctor?"

"Let me see. How about we start with dinner out tonight at the steakhouse? We can go dancing tomorrow night, and Sunday we will sleep all day in each other's arms. Will that please you my sweet lady?"

"Sounds lovely. Except for one thing."

"What's that?"

"We'll need energy to do all that, and I'm so damn tired that all I want to do is sleep all weekend."

He laughed. "You will feel better after dinner, and a good night's sleep tonight. Then we will find the energy for the rest." He smiled at her as they walked into the steakhouse. It felt good to be able to take his wife out to dinner, and to know he was finally a working man making a salary.

The next night, Nicole dressed up in a little gold evening dress, and put on her high heels. Her long golden hair hung in curls around her shoulders. She and Samuel had not been out dancing in such a long time, so tonight she wanted to look extra special for him. She knew how hard he'd been working, and she just wanted him to have some fun, and enjoy his evening for once. Samuel put on a pair of black dress pants, and a fresh white shirt, with a dark blue jacket. They made a handsome couple. In fact, most people stared at them when they were together, because they looked so in love. Those same people would have never known the hardships the two of them had faced, and we're still facing. To the outside world, they just looked like a couple having fun, lucky to be in love with each other.

They held each other tight on the dance floor; Samuel stared into Nicole's eyes as they danced, he was always the most happy, when he was close to her. She had become his family; she was his safe heaven and now his home.

***

Samuel was back at the hospital early Tuesday morning, feeling rested from his days off. Finally the two Polish doctors, Dr. Glen and Dr. Vincent, had been returned to his department. They were at early-morning rounds again – ready to start working.

Dr. Hays looked at them, knowing she had to test their knowledge again. "So... Dr. Vincent. Tell me about this patient, please?"

"I think this patient will require surgery today. I think she has a kidney stone which we need to remove."

The patient became visibly alarmed by Dr. Vincent's words.

Samuel picked up the report and read it, then looked at Dr. Hays. "May I suggest Dr. Hays something?"

"Yes Samuel. What do you think?"

"I think the diagnosis is right, but the treatment I disagree with. I would like to try and dissolve the stones with medication, and force fluids as a first recourse, and leave the surgery as a last recourse. If I may, I would like to start this patient on an IV within the hour, and see how she does over the next few hours."

"I agree with that Doctor. Very well done. You may take this patient over." Dr. Hays walked away, without a second glance at any of their direction.

Samuel walked over to the patient. "Mrs. Smith no need to worry, just yet about any kind of surgery. Let's see how the meds do first. Often the meds will break up the stones. If you wish to see me, or you have too much pain, just have the nurse page me and I will come running." He smiled as he held her hand, and took her pulse at the same time.

"Thank you doctor. I'll let them know." The woman looked slightly relieved.

Dr. Hays had been working with Glen and Vincent for about a week now, and she knew she couldn't trust any of their diagnoses or treatments; she had to watch everything they did. She couldn't wait to get rid of these two, but she had to talk to Dr. Rogers. There was just no way she could she put these two ahead of Samuel, who had been working his heart out and doing a great job. She picked up the phone again and called Dr. Rogers.

"Dr. Rogers, this is Dr. Hays. We need to talk. I simply cannot push these two Polish doctors ahead of Samuel. He'll be heartbroken, and it's just not right. Those two fools don't know anything, and Samuel is still doing most of the work. For God's sake, let me do the right thing here."

"Look Jane. I have told you what has to be done and why, so you're just going to have to close your eyes for this one and do it. I know he's good, but that's not the point and you know it. So if you know what's good for your own career, you'll play ball with me. I hope you've got that in your head. Now let's not speak of this again."

"You know what Dick? Sometimes you *are* a dick." She hung the phone up in his ear.

Dr. Rogers looked out his window and thought to himself, this is what we get for putting a woman with a soft heart in charge of the internship program. She wants to do the right thing, but she doesn't realize, that the right thing is keeping control over the system. Dr. Hays hung up the phone, and pulled out the Internship Matching System papers. She put the two Polish doctors at the top of the list to be matched first, and she put Samuel's name at the bottom of the list. She knew full well that he would not get matched at all anywhere in the country. The few positions that were available countrywide were always full midway through the list, and those at the bottom rolled over to the following year for another chance. She closed her eyes and dropped the list in the mail. She didn't know how she was going to face Samuel, when he finally found out what she had done. He had worked so hard to please her, and did such a great job with all his patients. She felt guilty and ashamed of herself, but she had no choice, but to do what Dr. Rogers demanded.

Later that night at home as Dr. Hays stood in front of the mirror, she could hardly look at herself. "How am I going to look this honest, hard-working young man in the eye tomorrow?" She said to herself. "But really what choice did I have anyway?" She sat down in her big expensive armchair, and looked out the window of her million dollar home. She wondered for just a brief moment, what it would be like to be in Samuel's situation, totally at the mercy of such an unfair system, and working with men like Dr. Rogers. Who set up their iron-tight systems, and that let no one enter, that was any kind of threat to life as they knew it. She knew it must be heartbreaking, and it saddened her that she wasn't strong enough to just say no to them all.

However, better Samuel's heart break than hers. She had a family to look after, and her husband only made half her salary, so all the burden of a good lifestyle was on her shoulders. She walked upstairs, and turned out the lights to sleep. Her husband had long been in bed, so she was careful not to wake him. She tossed and turned that night. She lay awake, wondering just when it was, that she'd started putting money first, and everything that should matter last. She looked at her beautiful silk dressing gown, knowing full well, it cost her more than she cared to admit. All the costly, pretty things that surrounded her, weren't worth her morals and self-respect, this she was beginning to realize.

The next day and every day after, Dr. Hays went to work and worked beside Samuel, like nothing had ever happened. He worked hard and covered like always, for the two Polish doctors. But any day now, the results of the internship positions would be out. Each day Samuel went to the mailbox, faithfully expecting to see the papers with the results of the internship program.

"Still nothing today. Well... maybe tomorrow I will get good news," he said out loud to himself as he closed the mailbox. For no matter what had happened to him in the past, Samuel always lived with hope that he would achieve his goal of becoming a practicing doctor in Canada. Nicole was slowly getting ready for work this morning, but in the pit of her stomach, she could feel that something bad was coming. There was a dark cloud hanging over them, and it made her feel deeply sad inside. She couldn't shake the feeling all day.

"They are devils in disguise; they are not what they say they are. They won't do what they say either." She could hear her old grandmother's words still in her heads, when she warned her the last time they had spoken on the phone. She could feel it now, in the pit of her stomach, those words coming true, and it scared the hell out of her.

Nicole went off to work, but she was more confused than ever now. She knew she had to prepare for the worst, as her Grandmother had warned her. "Devils in disguise. Just what does that mean?" She said out loud to herself.

"Nicole! Are you calling me a devil?" Helen asked as she passed her in the hallway.

"No, of course not, I was just trying to solve an issue in my mind. How are you today Helen?"

"I've been better. Shouldn't you be out on the floor working?" She said spitefully.

"I'm always working very hard; I can assure you of that Helen. Just look at the dollar figures of this business since I've been working here. That really says it all... now doesn't it?" Nicole mockingly smiled at Helen, she was getting very tired of being bullied by this woman. She knew that Richard knew the truth, and at the end of the day that's all she cared about. But a devil was exactly what this woman was, and no one had to tell Nicole that twice. But just who were the other devils in Samuel's life? She wondered as she walked around the store and merchandised the clothing. One thing was for sure; they would show their faces soon enough.

The next morning, Samuel ran down to the mailbox, like he had for the last two weeks. But this morning there was a big brown letter inside. He quickly grabbed it and ran back to Nicole at the breakfast table, where he ripped it open.

"Oh Sam, is it finally here then?" Nicole looked at him as he opened the letter.

"Yes, it's here." His voice trailed off as he read the words in big bold letters:

"NOT MATCHED"

"How can that be Nick? They told me I would have the best chance to be matched working with Dr. Hays, and I have done everything she has asked of me." Sam couldn't believe what he was reading. Not matched with bold black letters was written at the top of the letter." How could this be?" He asked himself again.

Sam stood up mad as hell, and grabbed his coat. He headed straight for Dr. Hays' office. With tears in his eyes, he mumbled, "Damn them. They will not get away with this again, not this time."

He knocked on the door, but didn't even brother for her answer. He stormed in.

"Samuel? What's wrong? What can I do for you?" Dr. Hays asked, knowing full well what was wrong. The look in Samuel's eyes told her he had received the notice of the internship matching program. It was lucky that Dr. Rogers had just dropped in her office for a moment.

"I would like you both to tell me, just what the hell happened here with the matching program for the internship, tell why I wasn't matched. You both told me not to worry, that I would get a position, and be matched to an internship, if I worked hard and proved myself. And to make matters worse Dr. Hays, I ran into Dr. Glen on the way in here. He had a big smile on his face. It seems that both of my Polish colleagues got matched. You matched them over me! You know full well I have been doing their work for months now. Dr. Hays you gave me an excellent job review, and said my work and job performance were above average, and that you were lucky to have me! And Dr. Rogers, you said if Dr. Hays gave me a good review then there should be no problem with receiving an internship. Those are all your own words doctors. Now stand behind them." Sam stared at them, shaking with anger and frustration. Both doctors put their heads down for a moment. They couldn't look him in the eye.

"Look... Sam. I had your name on the list," Dr. Hays said softly. "I never know where the cutoff point will be, because I never know just how many positions we have left for foreign graduates, and I guess this year there weren't many positions open. I had your name on the list, and I put it where I thought you would be safely matched to a hospital. Samuel I am so sorry." Her voice got even softer, as she looked up for the first time, and saw the tears in Samuel's eyes, as he just stood there and stared at her in total disbelief. All the hurt and mistrust in his eyes now looked Dr. Hays, full on in her face. It was so great, that she felt sick inside for him.

"Just where did you place my name on the list? At the bottom? Because Dr. Glen and Dr. Vincent's names, had to be placed higher than mine to get ahead of me. You know damn well they are dangerous. They don't know what the hell they are doing, they cannot speak English, well enough to even understand the patients, and the patients, do not understand them either. They cannot read the lab reports correctly; I still do that for them, and they cannot even write English properly on the charts – I do that for them too. That's the reason, and you both know it, that I live in this damn place most nights. And if you don't watch over them carefully, they are going to kill someone, and that will be on your conscience. That is, if either of you actually have one." Samuel stood his ground and stared them down, shock was written all over his face.

Dr. Hays looked over at Dr. Rogers, and he quickly interjected, he could see Dr. Hays was weakening under the pressure.

"Look Samuel. You still have your clinical assistant job here. Just apply again next year, and you have our word that you'll be matched. You'll get in next year, I promise you that. Just hang in there with us for one more year," Dr. Rogers said like it was no big deal – and for him it wasn't.

"Dr. Rogers... let me tell you something. I've been through a lot. I have been hungry, I have been so tired I couldn't see straight, I have been sick, and yes I am poor. For the last four years I've been struggling, and working my ass off to get my career going, to be able to work as a qualified doctor – which I am – for the sake of my wife and family. You see... my poor wife has stood by my side through it all, every step of the way she has been there, and she has been suffering through all this right beside me. She is a born Canadian woman who deserves everything good in her life, because she is good. So tell me, just tell me please, how do I go back home to her, and tell her that we need to wait just one more year? Just one more year of struggling and uncertainty, because next year I will get into the program. That I now have the word of a man who has lied to my face, and screwed me over with absolutely no remorse. You see, doctors! I studied the same bullshit psychology as you both did, and guilt is written all over both of your faces. I am not a stupid man; my trouble is that I just trusted the wrong people. But then again, what real choice did I have but to trust you both? I had to put my career in your hands, because you designed this system so well, that foreign graduates do not even have a chance, no matter how good of a doctor we are. We do not get treated fairly in this system you designed. You both have deceived me, and I cannot trust you."

"Samuel! Please try to understand; your best chance to get in is still here with us, where you've established your skill set. The same system exists all over Canada," Dr. Hays said. She felt so sorry for Samuel.

"Oh, indeed, Dr. Hays. I have established myself as being a good doctor. The nursing staff respect me, the patients all praise me. But the doctors, the ones who just gave me an excellent job evaluation, have also just stabbed me in the back. What is that old saying you all have here? Better the devil you know, than the devil you don't. Heartless, that's what I call it. Someday I hope someone treats both of you the same way." Samuel stood up, stared at them a moment more, and then walked out. He knew they had no concept of what fairness was, or equal opportunity. They only cared about themselves; he could clearly see that now.

Dr. Rogers was worried. They had never seen Samuel speak in such a way, or so strongly, about what they both knew was the truth.

"See we got through that, Dr. Hays. I told you we would," Dr. Rogers said as he wiped the sweat off his forehead.

"Don't say another word to me. Because if you think we've heard the last of this, then you are a very stupid man." Dr. Hays stood up.

"He'll calm down and come back to work, you'll see. He has a wife to support and he can't prove anything."

"Oh really Dick! You forget he has a very high evaluation report from me, and a very low evaluation report I wrote for the other two doctors that just got matched. How do we explain that one? This is a mess, and it will all come back to haunt us, you just wait and see. And I am not going down alone Dick. That I can promise you."

"We'll have to change the others' evaluations. Why didn't you give them a good one to begin with? You knew the plan."

"Because they are stupid and terrible at what they do, and Sam's right – they're going to kill someone if we aren't careful. You think he'll still cover for them now? Just how stupid are you?" She was yelling now. She couldn't believe that she was involved in this whole situation to begin with, and she was even more upset with herself for being a coward, and not standing up to Dr. Rogers in the first place. "Listen to me you asshole. That is one very angry young man. He'll most likely go to the human rights commission with all this, and put in a complaint. And who could really blame him?"

"You might be right about that, Dr. Hays. If that's the case, then I guess we'd better change the fact that the two Polish doctors got paid five thousand dollars more than Samuel too," Dr. Rogers said.

"What! You paid them more than Samuel, when he's doing all the work? Are you

154

crazy? The nursing staff can verify that Dick. They see him here late almost every night; they all know the Polish doctors have gone home without their chart work done, and they see Samuel doing it for them. You idiot!" She couldn't believe what she was hearing.

"I know it looks bad, but maybe we can offer Sam a raise in salary if he comes back, so at least the pay would be equal." Dr. Rogers looked surprised that Dr. Hays was so upset.

"Just leave me alone Dick. Go away." Dr. Hays walked out of her office. She couldn't stand to look at him for another minute. She could only imagine how poor Samuel must be feeling. She would have to call him in a few hours, after he calmed down a bit, and try to get him to return back to his job. She had to avoid trouble at all cost. This whole situation could turn out very badly, if she didn't do something quickly.

Nicole picked up the paper that Sam had thrown on the floor and read it: "NOT MATCHED." She let herself slowly sink down to the floor by their big armchair, she sat and cried as if her heart would break. Her whole body shook with pain and bitter disappointment. She felt sick inside. There they are, the devils in disguise, she thought. "They're the ones Grand was talking about," she said out loud. She didn't want to be in this place anymore. She was so tired of all the stress of everything: her job, Sam's never-ending career problems, and all the racism she faced next to Sam's side every day. She didn't understand them, she wasn't like them, and she hated everything they stood for. Whatever they did to Sam, they did doubly to her, because this was her country, the place where she'd been born and raised. But she sure wasn't raised like them, so unkind, so hateful, and so fearful of any kind of change.

"Why, Father, why? Haven't we suffered enough? How could you let these devils win again? I just don't understand." She sobbed desperately. Her heart was full of disillusions of what her country was all about. Sam came home, and found her on the floor in tears. He sat down beside her and pulled her into his arms, and they sat together and cried. They were both brokenhearted, left to deal with nothing but broken promise

Chapter Six

The next morning was a difficult one. Neither one of them knew what to do next; they could barely face the reality of their lives anymore. The phone rang, and Samuel picked it up.

"Hello?"

"Samuel? It's Dr. Hays." She spoke quickly before he could hang up. "Listen... Sam I know you're disappointed, and I don't blame you one bit, but please come back to work at the hospital and don't give up. We're going to give you a five thousand dollar raise if you come back to work, and I promise it will be better. We have new doctors coming in from Saudi Arabia, and hopefully they'll be a lot better for you to work with. Please just calm down, and come back into work. You need to work to support your family, and it might as well be here with us until next year. I am so sorry about all this. You're a good doctor, and you deserve an internship. I'll make sure Dr. Rogers keeps his promise next time around. Please just come back in to work," she pleaded.

"You mean I am a lot better than Dr. Glen and Dr. Vincent, the ones you just gave an internship to over me?"

"Samuel like I said before, I didn't give them anything. I simply had their names on the list just like yours."

"Yes, but way ahead of mine. And no matter what you say, I know that's what happened, but why did you do it? I just cannot understand that. I did everything you asked of me and more. You have not even explained that to me yet Doctor."

"Samuel I can't explain it, just come back to work, and like we said, next year you'll get in. Please think about what I said. I'm sure you and your wife can use the extra five thousand dollars in income, so be smart and return back in with us tomorrow." Dr. Hays hung up before Samuel could answer. She just hoped that after he calmed down, he would return back to work.

Nicole and Sam looked at each other, all the bad memories of the day before came to their minds. Nicole's eyes held a thousand words that only he could hear. Those big brown eyes held so much despair, that it hurt him to look at her without feeling like he had let her down. When they sat down at the breakfast table and talked, they both knew it was time to start fighting back.

"Sam baby, I think we need to file a complaint with the Human Rights Commission. We both know you were overlooked because you're black. The Polish doctors are not better Doctors then you."

"But how do we prove it? It will be very difficult to do, almost impossible." Sam was miserable, and just hearing the voice of the woman who had just strewed him over royally, made him fall even further into a depression.

"There's the evaluation report that says you're excellent, and there's no way the Polish doctors' reports were as good. Those job reports should prove that you were more competent, yet they were chosen over you. You had to read their evaluations to them yourself, because they couldn't read it remember?"

"Of course I remember. But I do not have any copies of their reports, and I bet their evaluations have been changed by now, to work in their favor, and to support the fact that they have internships. In fact, they will probably try to label me as a troublemaker."

"How can they do that? The nurses love you, and so do the patients."

"I just don't know any more, what I should do! I guess I should just go back to work for another year. At least it's a bit more money, and we can see what happens next year. They are trying to cover up their mistakes by offering me more money I guess." Sam got up from the breakfast table. Neither of them had touched their food.

"I think I have to swallow my pride, and go back into work tomorrow. I have to keep them thinking I have accepted their dirty deeds, and that I am willing to play ball with them. Better the devil you know than the devil you don't... right?"

"I guess. But I think I'll try to get an appointment to speak with our representative in Parliament, and I'll also try to get an appointment with our Minister of Health. Let's just tell them our story, and see if there's anything they may be willing to do to help us. After all, they're supposed to be our voice, and represent equal opportunity for all Canadians. Not just the Canadians that studied here. Surely they can't turn a blind eye; they have to be objective in these matters."

"Don't count on it Lady. They are all working together in this. But do whatever you think may help us, and I will go along with it. I do not believe for one minute that they will follow through with their promise for next year either." Sam hugged his wife, and when outside to take a walk and clear his head.

The next day Sam got ready, and went into the hospital. When he walked in for early morning rounds, they were all startled to see him. Dr. Hays looked up from her chart, relieved to see him standing there. Maybe it would be all right after all she hoped. "Welcome back. I'm glad to see you this morning; that's a very good decision on your part."

"What other choice do I have Dr. Hays?" He raised his eyebrows, letting her know her dirty deeds were not forgotten.

"Dr. Emeka these are two new Clinical Assistants from Saudi Arabia. They'll be taking over from Dr. Glen and Dr. Vincent. Please show them around, and show them how our systems work, so tomorrow they can actually be of some use to us."

She left without another word; she couldn't really look Samuel in the eye for too long. She still felt ashamed for the part she'd played in the whole situation. She'd had no choice, but Sam had no way of knowing that she had been under duress by Dr. Rogers

Samuel just stood there and watched her leave. He wanted to reach out and put his hands around her neck, and slowly squeeze the truth out of her. But he knew she would never be worth it, so he just swallowed hard and decided to hang in there.

Samuel looked at the others doctors and said "Well follow me, and I will start by showing you the layout of the hospital, and then where the lab is, and how to read the reports."

***

Nicole stayed at home, and decided to call in sick. She wasn't able to deal with the stress at work today, she wanted to try to get the ball rolling with some of the government officials. She picked up the phone and dialed her MP's office.

"I am Nicole Emeka. I'd like an appointment to see our local Member of Parliament, please."

"I have one for Friday evening at seven, one week from now, is that's okay for you? That's the time he sees people from his constituency."

"That will be fine for us and thank you. We'll be there."

She hung up the phone, and then dialed the Minister of Health, Department for Nova Scotia.

"My name is Nicole Emeka. I'd like to make an appointment to meet with our Minister of Health please."

"Okay. What organization or company are you with?" The receptions asked.

"I'm not with any. I'm representing myself and my husband, and we'd like to meet with him regarding a situation that needs to be brought to his attention."

"Perhaps you could write him a letter first, you see he is very busy and really doesn't meet with individuals."

"Ok I will do that. May I have the address please?"

Nicole wrote down his address and then hung up. Another runaround she thought. But she very carefully typed out a two page letter with details explaining their situation. She also stated in her letter, that Samuel was willing to go anywhere in the country to train in the one-year internship program. She knew there was a shortage of doctors in most of the rural communities. She made copies, and sent them to her Member of Parliament, and to the Human Rights Commission, asking them to start an investigation into the internship system that was in place.

Sam walked to the nursing station. Dr. Hays looked up from the chart she was studying.

"I have to send you, and the two other clinical assistants down to the emergency department this week. They are very short-staffed down there. How are the two new ones doing?"

"It's not my job to evaluate them, and I obviously do not have your sound judgment, when it comes to these doctors and their capabilities. But in my opinion, they are both very slow, and that's your burden to bear not mine. I will not cover for these two like I did for the last two. I will do my own work, and then I will go home. I hope you understand that." He walked away and headed down to the emergency room.

Dr. Hays watched him leave. She knew she deserved his lack of respect; hell she didn't even respect herself for allowing Dr. Rogers to railroad her into this situation. Damn him, she thought. She was glad Sam would be working down in the emergency department this week; it was stressful for her to see the constant look of disappointment in his eyes. Dr. Hays just wanted to come into work, deal with the day, and go back to her beautiful home and family. She couldn't even imagine what it must be like to live Samuel and Nicole's life. She would never have been strong enough to deal with all the drama. She had been lucky when she was training – she'd studied there, and had been given a position right after she graduated. She'd worked her way up the ladder very quickly, playing the game the right way, never rocking the boat, and always being willing to go along with any unjust rules in place. But this was the first time she'd actually had to go against her own conscience, to please the good old boys' club, and it had a very bad effect on her. She wasn't sleeping well, and was thinking more about the situation than she cared to. It was because she knew, deep down in her heart, that Samuel was a good doctor, and she'd prevented him from proceeding with his career.

She felt bad for him and his wife, and knew it was going to come back to haunt her one day. Whenever she thought of Dr. Rogers now, she disliked him even more. She knew he was wrong in everything he stood for, but she also knew she wasn't strong enough to change anything on her own. She was almost fifty-five, and soon she would retire, a happy and wealthy woman. So why would she want to put herself in harm's way for a young man, whom she could do more for by working with the system? She hoped that next year she could do as she'd promised him, and put him at the top of the list to be matched. She walked out of the hospital feeling exhausted.

Samuel walked down to the emergency room, and introduced himself and his two colleagues to the nursing staff.

"Hello, I am Samuel and these are my colleagues. We are here to work with you as your clinical assistants for the next week." Samuel smiled at the two nurses who were on duty that evening.

"Hi. I'm Susan, the head nurse here. This is Mary, the other nurse on duty tonight. Just follow me and I'll show you around." She led them down the hall. "This is the doctors' rest room, where you can sleep whenever you have a little time, or eat something there too if you like." It was a small, clean room with a few single beds, a lamp, and a small television. Just off to the side was a small washroom with a shower. Sam looked around the room for a minute, but that was all he saw of it that night. As soon as Sam and the other two got back to the station, there were already several patients waiting to be seen.

Mary, a short redheaded nurse, announced that examination rooms one, two, and three had patients in them waiting to be seen. Samuel and his two colleagues, each took a room. It was their job to evaluate the patient, and recommend treatments, before the chief resident saw them. If the resident agreed with them, he or she would just sign off on the orders.

Sam got his patient's history and did their physical. He returned with his evaluation, and had the nurses arrange for an x-ray, before the resident on call that night came in to see him. He looked around for the other two clinical assistants, but couldn't find them. He hoped they could handle these patients tonight. He was sent off to another patient's room, but returned quickly.

"Susan, Mrs. Smith needs to be admitted. She needs blood work done ASAP. Can you make the arrangements please?"

"Sure thing doctor. But there are three more patients waiting to be seen. We haven't seen the other clinical assistants in a while; they finished with their patients and then left. They said they had to go and pray." She looked at Sam as if to say – what's up with those two?

"Pray? Great, just great." Samuel shook his head, picked up the chart, and headed off to see the next patient waiting for care. He returned twenty minutes later, and picked up another chart. There was still no sign of the other two.

"I might as well be working on my own tonight," he muttered to Mary.

She nodded as Samuel went off to see the next patient.

He came back within minutes. "Susan calls the senior resident right away. I need him to see the patient in room four immediately."

"No problem." She paged him and went to look in on the patient.

"Dr. Emeka! I need you right away! Code Blue! Possible cardiac arrest!" Susan yelled to him. She paged code blue as Samuel ran in, to assist until the cardiac team got there. He walked over to the patient, and saw that it was his former immigration officer Mrs. Miller. He stood there for a moment, knowing she could refuse him, but there was no time. He prayed the cardiac team, and senior resident would arrive soon, he started to work on her, giving orders to start an IV.

"Susan, maybe one of the others should take this one."

"What are you talking about Dr. Emeka? She needs you, and the others can't handle this! We can't even find them. What next doctor, give me your orders now!"

"She's not in cardiac failure yet. Let's get an EKG Stat, blood work, and give me her vitals."

"Right away."

The patient was waking up. "Mrs. Miller? It's Dr. Samuel Emeka. I am the clinical assistant on duty here tonight."

"Oh dear God." She muttered.

"Do you want me to treat you, or would you like to wait for the resident?"

"Mrs. Miller," Susan injected, "you should let Dr. Emeka treat you right away. The cardiac team is on the way, and should be here within a few minutes. We need to start treatment with Dr. Emeka right away."

"Fine. Okay." The pain in her chest was killing her, and she was in acute distress.

"How do you feel, Mrs. Miller?" Samuel asked her.

"Chest pain. Can't breathe well. Pain in my right arm," Mrs. Miller gasped.

"No need to worry, Mrs. Miller. I am going to take very good care of you. Just try and relax now." He wanted her to feel at ease with him. He could see her face was an ash white. Her heart was beating rapidly, her breathing was weak, and she was very ill.

Just then, her heart monitor went off.

"Code blue! Cardiac arrest, room four!" Susan called over the monitor again.

Samuel quickly hooked Mrs. Miller up to the crash cart. "Stand clear to shock."

"All clear," Susan said.

They shocked her.

"Still no heartbeat, doctor."

"Stand clear to shock again."

"All clear." They shocked her heart again.

"Come on Mrs. Miller! Fight back! You're not dying on my shift," Samuel yelled out to her.

"Still nothing on the monitor. No heart rate," Susan said.

"All clear to shock again."

"All clear, doctor."

The shock pulsed through chest again.

"We got her back doctor. There's a weak heartbeat."

Samuel quickly ordered the medication she needed to strengthen her heartbeat. He held her hand as Susan gave the injection. As her pulse got stronger, he gently put the oxygen mask on her face.

"She is slowly stabilizing doctor," Susan announced.

Finally the cardiac team came running in, and adjusted her medication, and the chief resident in charge took over. Samuel breathed a deep sigh of relief, and left the room.

Later that evening, the chief resident came over to Samuel to speak with him. "Good work Dr. Emeka. Have her transferred to ICU immediately," he ordered then walked away.

This was everyday life for him in the E.R. But for Samuel it wasn't, he was just getting used to the fast pace, and he couldn't believe he had just saved the life of a woman who had caused him such heartache and pain. But that was what he did. He was a doctor and he saved lives, no matter whose life it was. He assisted in getting her on the stretcher, and stayed by her side until they rolled her away. He knew he would see her again the next morning at early morning rounds. He was getting tired now; he hadn't eaten anything all night, and had been run off his feet. He headed back to Susan in the nursing station.

"Oh my Lord! Look at the backup of patients! Where are the other two clinical assistants?" Susan asked Mary.

"I paged them twice, but still no answer from either of them."

"I can't have this on my shift. Samuel is working all night without a break, and he can't keep up like that. Call Dr. Hays for me at once Mary. She's the one who sent the other two down here, and I want them off my floor now, and new replacements sent down here."

The senior resident had been listening. "I have to tell you Susan – I couldn't read the orders they wrote for the two patients they did see. I had to reassess the patients myself."

"Damn it! I am calling Dr. Hays myself right now. I am not having those two back, in this department tomorrow night." She picked up the phone and called her.

"Good morning, Susan. What can I do for you?"

"You can start by sending me two more clinical assistants for tonight. The two Saudis took most of the night off to pray. Poor Samuel worked his tail off here by himself all night."

"Yes... I already heard that from Mary, and our senior resident. I'll have a talk with them, but they're all we have at the moment, so we have to make do for now."

"I don't think so, Dr. Hays. Samuel can't handle the entire workload, and they're totally undependable. Where did you get them?" Susan's anger was coming through very clearly now.

"They were sent by Dr. Rogers. If you have complaints, call him. But they're what we've got for now. Just give most of the patients to Samuel – he can handle them. He's fast and good at what he does. He's been with me now for a while and I trust his judgment." Dr. Hays felt the guilt of her decision to hold him back, rise up again in her heart.

"Well, that is just downright unfair, and he'll make mistakes because he's overworked. So no, I will not do that Dr. Hays. I'll be speaking to the head of the department about this, you can be sure of that. You are not going to railroad me into keeping those two in this department. No way in hell Dr. Hays – you hear me?" She hung up the phone looking disgusted. They didn't know who they were messing with. She had been with this hospital for more than twenty years, and she wasn't about to let them get away with this kind of nonsense. Not on her floor.

Dr. Hays immediately called Dr. Rogers again.

"Hello Jane. What is it this time? "Sounding very annoyed.

"Dick! We have a problem with the Saudi Doctors."

"What's the matter now?"

"They prayed most of night, and no one could read their charts or orders. Where did you get them from?"

"They were sent to us from the Saudi Arabian Government. They're paying us for them to train here. They don't cost us anything, and I've used the money elsewhere in

164

the hospital."

"That's all well and good, but they can't function. They're just as bad as the Polish doctors you sent me. The nursing staff and senior residents want them gone, and so do I. Samuel ended up doing all the work last night, and dealt with a cardiac arrest too. He will not put up with it for long either; he's a lot braver than before, and the longer he works here, the more people will back up his good work habits. We aren't going to be able to be unfair to him any longer. You need to fix this, and fix it now. I'm not playing ball with you anymore either. You can do your own dirty work from now on Dick. I am simply done doing it for you, got it?" She hung up the phone.

Dr. Rogers should be the one to work with these people if he wanted to play these games. She sure wasn't going to. She could hardly sleep as it was, thinking about the situation she'd put Samuel in. She should have stood up against him long ago. He could take back the matching program position, and give it to someone else. She didn't need the hassle, and heartache of it all on her shoulders anymore. She was going to resign from that position, and just take care of her patients from now on.

Damn that weak woman, she can't handle anything, Dr. Rogers mumbled to himself. He'd have to replace her on the internship-matching committee. He needed a doctor that would play along, and not give him so much grief. He needed someone stronger than a woman in that position, someone like himself. In the meantime, he had to do something about the Saudi doctors, before all hell broke loose down in the emergency department. When Dr. Hays found out that he'd promised them both internships in this hospital over Samuel again for next year, she would have a meltdown for sure. She had to be replaced, and somehow Samuel would have to be placated. He'd give him more money – another few thousand to keep him quiet. He could take some of the money he'd received from the Saudi Government, and pay Samuel with it. At least it would be a little more for him. since he was doing all the work anyway.

Dr. Rogers' own conscience had started to bother him lately. He a bad feeling that if it was ever really investigated, he wouldn't be able to cover up his bad decisions, and would end up in a shitload of hot water. He'd better take the Saudi Doctors back into his department. There was one Indian doctor, he had just hired as a clinical assistant; he would send him down to Dr. Hays. He was a good doctor, and could communicate well. Although Dr. Rogers didn't like the color of his skin either, it didn't matter right now. He needed the backup down there.

The next morning the Saudi doctors were transferred back to Dr. Rogers, and Dr. Abdul from India took their place.

"Good morning. I am Dr. Abdul. I am here to work as your new clinical assistant," he said to Susan.

"Oh great. This is Dr. Samuel Emeka, our other clinical assistant. You'll be working with him tonight. This is Mary, our staff nurse, and I'm Susan, your head nurse. Welcome aboard, doctor. I hope you're fast as it gets pretty busy, and crazy around here. Dr. Hays is our senior doctor in charge, and she'll be here any minute to do rounds."

Just then Dr. Hays arrived. "Oh here you are doctor! This is Dr. Abdul, our new clinical assistant. He's replacing the other two from last night," Susan said.

"That was fast. Let's do the rounds. Samuel grabs the chart cart and let's go."

"Most of the patients from last night have been released, and booked to see you in your office next week Dr. Hays. The cardiac arrest is in ICU, and that's it for now," Samuel said. He walked away, and headed back to the nurses' station to get ready to go home. He was in need of some sleep, it had been a very long night.

"Oh… Samuel, well done last night. I hear good things from the nursing staff, and our senior resident." Dr. Hays said as she walked away. She'd had complaints from both the nurses, and the senior resident, about the Saudi doctors last night, but had not heard a single word of a complaint from Samuel, who'd had been left to do their work. That fact alone simply amazed her, and spoke volumes of Samuel good character.

"Dr. Emeka; drink this before you drive home." Susan handed him a cup of steaming coffee. "Well done last night. We can finally call it a night. Let's go home and sleep."

"Thanks Susan. And please just call me Sam."

"Okay, Sam. I was very impressed with your work last night. You're a good doctor. I like you."

"Thanks. It helps when you have great nurses by your side, like you and Mary. He turned around to head out the door when his pager went off. It was the ICU. He would check in quickly with them, to see what they wanted, on his way out.

"Hello I'm Dr. Emeka. You just paged me?"

"Oh yes doctor. Mrs. Miller requested to see you."

"How is she doing this morning?"

"She's doing better; she's stabilized and is a little stronger this morning."

"That's good news nurse." He was pleased to hear that. He knew he'd done a good job last night with her care, and felt proud of himself.

He walked over to Mrs. Miller's bed. He was so tired he couldn't even think straight, and this was the last thing he wanted to deal with – let alone see – this woman again, but here he was at her bedside at her request. She still had her eyes closed, and he didn't want to wake her up, so he was about to leave when she opened her eyes.

"Don't go Samuel please," she said in a weak voice. "I just wanted to say thank you, for saving my life last night."

"It's my job Mrs. Miller. No need for thanks. Get some rest." He started to walk away.

"Samuel! I was wrong all those years ago… just wrong. I'm deeply sorry for everything I did to prevent you from studying here. You've turned out to be a fine doctor, and I thank you again. I was a blind old fool Samuel .Please forgive me?"

"Mrs. Miller get some rest now. You need to get better, so you can get out of here, and back to your family. We all make mistakes in life, and if we are lucky enough, we learn from them." He could see the look of regret in her eyes. He then turned and walk away.

"Sam? Will I see you again?"

"No Mrs. Miller you won't. I am not assigned to the ICU department. You will be under the senior resident's care from here on out. He will take very good care of you. I do hope you feel better very soon." The look in his eyes told her he had forgiven her.

When he finally left the hospital, he couldn't remember when he had felt as weary as did now. He couldn't understand why some people, made such grave errors in judgment. Why they were so narrow-minded. And why it was usually not until it affected them personally, that they realized that maybe they should have done something better. Mrs. Miller's never did realize the pain, and suffering she'd caused him and Nicole.

Sometimes the wounds never heal, in fact, they last a lifetime for some people, like his poor wife. She'd lost her faith in her own country that day, she felt helpless, and that she was living among heartless people. Racism was something she'd never known existed until Sam met this woman, and since then she'd looked at life very differently.

He arrived home, unlocked the door, and went inside. It was quiet; Nicole had already left for work. He got ready for bed, and noticed a note on his pillow.

"My dearest husband," the note read, "I know your night was a long and hard one. Please eat something, and sleep with peace in your soul, as our God sees all things, and will one day be our champion. Prayers heal all wounds and so for now, God knows I am here with you, and we are both patiently waiting on him to answer. God's time is the best time, and he is never late. Sweet dreams my love. See you tonight. Nicole." She had sensed his hardship that night, and wanted to leave him words of encouragement to help him sleep.

He smiled for the first time all day. With everything that had happened to him in his life, the one thing God had given him, was the blessing of a good wife. Just when he thought he couldn't love her more, he knew he did.

***

Nicole decided to call the Minister of Health again on her lunch break. It had been one week since she'd written the letter to them, and she'd still had no reply.

"Good afternoon, this is Nicole Emeka; I spoke to you a week ago regarding an appointment to see the Minister of Health. You asked me to write a letter, which I did right after we spoke. I'm wondering if the letter was received, and may I now have an appointment, please?"

"Yes Mrs. Emeka, your letter was received. It was given to the Minister of Health Assistant, Miles Green."

"May I speak with him please?"

"Yes. Just one moment." There was a pause, and then the phone clicked over.

"Mr. Green speaking. How I can help you today?"

"Mr. Green this is Nicole Emeka, I gather you have read my letter regarding my husband's situation with his career in the medical profession. I'd like an appointment to see the Minister of Health, to discuss our situation and his future. I would like him to help with this problem."

"I read your letter, and you have suggested that Dr. Emeka could work in a rural area. I know he has passed the Canadian exam, but he won't qualify for a medical license without a one-year internship program, which he has not received yet."

"Trust me, I am very well aware of how the current system functions – or should I say malfunctions. That's my whole reason for wanting to meet with the Minister of Health."

"The Minister of Health doesn't have anything to with the administration of the internship program. That's handled by the department heads at the hospital. I believe Dr. Hays and Dr. Rogers are in charge of this program."

"I know all this as well, but please just try and listen for a moment. Those doctors administrating the program are not playing fair in my husband's case. The program only gives a few positions to foreign-trained Canadian citizens in the whole country. But the Canadian-trained citizens just go through, and on with their careers. That is totally unfair, because a citizen is a citizen, and we all pay taxes, so why should there be such a big gap in the system? Where is the equal opportunity in this profession? The few positions that are available, aren't being handed out fairly by Dr. Hays and Dr. Rogers."

"Those doctors have been in place for a few years now, and we've had no complaints about them. They make the decision on who gets matched with a matching system, based on who they feel is ready and best-qualified. We supply the money for the program, but leave it up to the administrators to make the selections."

"Yes, I understand that too, but my point is that they are making bad selections, and I would like to have the opportunity to prove that to the Minister of Health. Surely no one group of doctors can make decisions, without anyone doing the checks and balances on their work. After all Mr. Green, I do believe it would be part of my tax dollars, which would be paying for the program. And I am tired of paying for a system that is unfair, and does not offer equal opportunities for all Canadian citizens. So please set up an appointment for us to see our Minister of Health." Nicole was getting very impatient now with all the run-around.

"The Minister doesn't have time to deal with such matters. Unfortunately he will not be able to meet with you."

"Mr. Green, you do not seem to understand me very well. Perhaps if we all meet together, I would be better able to explain. I need an appointment to meet with the Minister of Health. You know, the person who we've put into a public position to represent all citizens who vote and pay taxes, like me and my husband. It's his job to serve the public. Not just a select group of people, but all the people. So please Mr. Green, let's not waste any more time. Can you give me a time when we can meet with him?"

"I don't make the appointments. His secretary does. I'll put you back on the line with her."

She waited on the line for another few minutes, and then the same female voice came back.

"How may I help you?"

"This is Mrs. Emeka again. I would like an appointment to see the Minister of Health, please."

"As I explained before, Mrs. Emeka, he really doesn't meet with individuals. His time is very limited, and he usually only meets with organizations and such."

"Be that as it may, I need to meet with him, so please give us an appointment. It is my right to meet with him just as much as any organization." Nicole had started to raise her voice slightly.

The secretary sighed. "He can't see you for long, he's completely booked solid. But on the Friday, one week from now he has about twenty minutes in between his other appointments, so I can book you in then."

"Fine, I'll take that. Thank you for your cooperation in this matter."

She hung up the phone feeling exhausted. She only hoped that when she finally did meet with him, he would have an open mind regarding their situation.

She now had two appointments set up: one at noon next Friday with the Minister of Health, and one later that same evening to see her Member of Parliament. She still had not heard back from the human rights commission. She hoped they would be able to comprehend the complexity of the situation.

But for now she had to go back to work. Richard walked in and went straight into his office. He started looking over the books for the store again. He just needed a few more months of good sales. Then he would add that money to the other money, he already had stored away in his wife's bank account. Then he could declare that he was bankrupt. He hadn't paid many of his suppliers in months now; he was amazed that they still shipped him anything anymore. But he knew it was because he had been dealing with most of them for many years, and they'd never suspect his plan to leave them all with thousands of dollars owing to them. He wasn't even concerned about leaving all the debt behind; he would never need those kinds of suppliers again. And after all, he'd given them all so much business over the years – so what if he screwed them over for one year of goods. He only felt bad about the people that had worked for him for years. But they all had lots of experience, and would find jobs elsewhere. Then there was poor Nicole, working so hard, building his business back to its former glory, or so she thought, only to have it fall to pieces after the holidays.

For her he did feel badly, because he knew she was an honest, hardworking person. He planned to give her a large Christmas bonus that would get her through most of the next year, or until she found another job, it would help him to ease his conscience. He had to be careful never to let his wife know about that plan. He needed to be careful not to piss his her off now, all the money was currently in her name, and sitting in her bank account.

***

The dates came around quickly to meet with the Minister of Health, and their Member of Parliament for Nicole and Samuel.

"Are you ready to plead our case today? I think it's best if you explain the hospital situation, and make sure you bring all your evaluations with you."

"Listen… Nicole, don't get your hopes up too high."

"I'm not, but at least we'll have tried."

"You're right lady. At least we are giving it a fighting chance."

Samuel had on a dark navy suit, with a simple white shirt and tie. Nicole dressed in a simple tailored black suit. She was a woman who stood out in a crowd, no matter how subdued her appearance was. She always commanded the room when she entered, and today was no exception. They were a striking couple to look at.

Nicole prayed that God would let them stand before men with kind hearts, and

171

open their minds to solutions. Samuel looked to his wife for emotional support, lately his faith had been fading fast, and was now almost gone. He didn't hold out much hope anymore for his career in Canada, but he still needed to try for her sake. But he knew this would be his last try.

They met at the Minister of Health office at noon. They looked to each other for encouragement, and held hands as they walked in.

"Hello. We are Dr. and Mrs. Emeka." Nicole told the secretary.

She looked Nicole over well. She wasn't at all what she'd thought she'd be after her persistence in making the appointment with the Minister.

She was a beautiful girl with a kind, lovely face, and Dr. Emeka was a handsome man with warm eyes, and a wonderful smile. She wanted to help them if she could. She had a daughter around Nicole's age, and she couldn't imagine her own child standing up for what she believed in the way this young woman was. She had read the letter, so she was familiar with their difficulties, and she knew it wasn't going to be easy for either of them to convince the Minister of Health to help.

"Just take a seat please. The Minister's last appointment is running a little a late but he'll be here shortly. "

"Thank you." Samuel said, and they took a seat next to her desk.

"I just want to wish you both good luck today with the Minister. There's only been one other case like yours presented to the administration where he actually helped." She wanted to let them know that there was an instance where a request similar to theirs was actually granted. They could use that to their advantage.

"Really? What year was that?" Nicole asked, knowing she would research it later.

"It was just last year; not long ago." She smiled. She had said all she could without getting herself in trouble. Just then two men in black business suits came rushing by, they walked into the office just beyond her desk, and closed the door.

"That was the Minister and his assistant. They'll see you in a few minutes." The secretary went into the office to tell them their next appointment was there. They asked her to send Nicole and Samuel in. She escorted them into a large office that was comfortably decorated, with six large black leather chairs that surrounded a large round oak table. They all took a seat. The Minister of Health and his assistant stood up to greet them. "Hello Dr. and Mrs. Emeka. This is my assistant, and Mr. Green, our legal counsel. Just what can I do for you today?" They sat back down.

"First sir, let me thank you for seeing us today. I know you are a very busy man." The Minister nodded.

"I know you have read our letter. We hope today for your intervention, and much needed help. You see Minister, I need help with some funding, for one more internship program for one year. I am hopelessly stuck in a system that does not function fairly. I feel the quality of my work is better, than that of the doctors, who were chosen for an internship this year over me. I am a very good doctor; here are my evaluation papers by Dr. Hays and Dr. Rogers, at the hospital where I'm a clinical assistant. They are also the administrators of the internship program." He handed them the papers, and they carefully read them over.

"As you can see, I am a very qualified doctor, but I cannot get on with my career if an internship, of one year is held back from me unfairly." Samuel looked at them with tears in his eyes. He couldn't help it; he just felt so helpless.

As the Minister's eyes met Samuel's, he quickly looked away. He was uncomfortable with open displays of emotion. "How can I help you? What is it you think I can do for you?"

"The administrators of the internship program claim that all the funds for the program are finished for this year. Please make an exception and grant them enough money for one more position for me. Please give me one chance, I have earned it. I know you have the power to do that sir." He looked very humbly at him.

"Dr. Emeka, if we do that for you, then that opens the doors for many others to ask for the same thing in the future. How can I justify that? As far as I know, we do supply enough funds to train, the supply of doctors for the public demand in this country."

"Sir... if I may?" Nicole stood up to speak, commanding their attention. "The so-called others you speak of, are not here knocking on your door today. We are. It's only us, so please do not judge us on anything other than our own merit. If the public demand is filled as you say, then why is there such a shortage of doctors in my hometown? There is also a shortage in most rural communities all over Nova Scotia, and Northern Canada. Here is a list of communities that currently have ads running for doctors to join their team. I spoke with most of them, and their ads have been running for months now with no response. The doctors that currently work in these small communities are overworked, and are burning out. Here is a written statement of some of the department heads of the rural hospitals, and outpatient clinics, stating that they're in need of more trained doctors. So I respectfully ask you sir: how can that statement of us training enough doctors, to supply public demand be true in any way?

Furthermore, I have been made aware recently that the very thing we are requesting today, has been granted in the past; in fact just last year. So you see gentlemen, I believe that you do have the power to grant this request, if you are willing to see, and understand our point of view. If you support our request, you will not only help Dr. Emeka, you will also help one more communities, get a doctor they need. This is a win-win situation for all involved. We are willing to train anywhere in the country. The problem is that our Canadian-trained doctors, all want to work in the bigger cities, and some then go over the border to work in the US, leaving our country with a shortage of trained doctors in the rural areas. Here are the latest stats on that, as well." She handed him more papers.

"Please sir, think with an open mind and heart, and grant our request." She looked at him with eyes that said she had no intention of ever backing down.

He could see the determination in her eyes, and hear it in her voice. He looked over at his legal counsel; he knew she had nicely backed him into a corner. In spite of the situation, he found himself admiring this young couple. They had done their homework well.

"Dr. Emeka, the minister is out of time for today. He has another appointment across town, so we have to go now," the Minister's assistant said, trying to get out of answering them right away.

"Dr. Emeka, the person that was funded for a position last year was not under my administration, I have just started with my term as Minister of Health," said the Minister.

Nicole stood up again. "Be that as it may, you still have the power to grant our request. If you have a full understanding of our situation, and the current situation in our country, then I simply cannot understand why you would ignore such a request that would benefit so many people. Sir, this is my country too, and I grew up believing in equal opportunities for all Canadian citizens. Not just the ones who choose to study here, but for all who are qualified and have merit for the job in consideration. We are just asking for a fair, and level playing field in this profession, which we all know does not currently exist." Her voice softened. "Please try to put yourself in our position; try to imagine working hard for years, only to be denied access to your profession, because of a discriminatory system. Try to imagine having every door closed in your face, with no reasonable excuse given. We are suffering here. Please help us, don't leave us at the mercy of this unfair system." She stared him in the eye.

He could see the despair buried in her big brown eyes. He felt sorry for her, and he knew the system was a difficult one. However, he also knew if he did this, he would be opening up a big can of worms, and that he did not care to deal with during his first year in office.

"Dr. and Mrs. Emeka, I'll look into the situation further, and talk with the administrators of the program, but I can't promise anything. Our office will get back to you in the near future with our decision." The Minister looked at his watch, held out his hand to Samuel and Nicole, and walked away. "Talk to Dr. Hays about Dr. Emeka. Ask if we give them more money, would Dr. Emeka be granted an internship this year. "The Minister told his assistance.

"I will but you know you're going to be opening up all kinds of problems with this request, this system has been in place for years now, and to try and change it will cost us all a lot of money and time."

"Maybe... but if her information is right then the system no longer serves our communities very well. I can't believe the amount of research the woman had, and I was surprised by some of the fact myself," the Minister said, feeling embarrassed.

"I was too, but you have to remember it's also the licensing bodies that are involved, and they have always worked hand-in-hand with the current system. Changing anything within this system isn't going to be easy. In fact, there are lots of staff doctors and department heads, that don't want anything changed."

He wanted the Minister to keep his eyes wide open, and be careful not to rock the good old boy's boat too hard. After all, many of them had helped put him in his position to begin with. They always chose men who they could count on to support their cause, who would play along with the system.

Samuel and Nicole went back to work for a few hours, and then Samuel picked Nicole up at the store after work. They drove to their M.P.'s Office for another appointment. They walked into the office of Mr. Steels, the M.P for their area of the city. His assistant offered them a seat and asked them to wait for a few minutes.

"I hope this one will at least listen. I could tell the Minister was very hesitant to get involved with our situation," Nicole was feeling discouraged, by their lack of understanding.

"I told you not to expect too much. It's all politics as usual for these people. I don't think any of them really care about our situation; they only care about causes that serve their own political careers." Samuel's own hope for his career in Canada was dwindling.

A middle-aged, slightly overweight man with a very kind face came through the door. "Hello! I am Mr. Steels, your M.P." He held out his hand to Samuel, and smiled at Nicole.

"Thank you for seeing us," Samuel said.

"I read your letter... folks, and I did some looking into the situation, but I must tell you this situation you find yourself in is not an easy one to solve. It's very complex, and it's just the kind of thing governments, like to sweep under the table whenever possible."

"So you are beginning to see that as well sir?" Nicole said.

"I do see it. I'm just not sure what I can really do for the two of you."

Samuel cleared his throat. "We need your support. The fact is that the current system no longer serves the best interests of the public. It also does not serve the best interest of people like me, who are trapped in the system. We would be very grateful if you could write a letter of support, to the Minister of Health on our behalf. It would also be good if you could put a phone call in to him, and follow up with our request for a paid internship with the Ministry."

"We know that these things are hard to prove, but we also know just how many racial issues exist in this place, and we know that the administrators of this program, are playing unfairly with our careers and wasting taxpayers' money, on doctors who do not deserve to train further, yet were chosen for internship programs over me. They were not better. I covered for them, and did most of their work. I know it may be hard for me to prove, but it's the truth." Samuel was getting upset; he knew he was sitting once again in front of a man, with little or no understanding of what it was like to be discriminated against. Mr. Steels was a white man, who lived in a world that had been handed to him on a silver platter. He may have good intentions, but it was impossible to understand the full impact of discrimination, until you'd lived through it. It was one thing for him to listen to complaints, but at the end of his day, he still had his career, and was able to take care of his family.

Mr. Steels was trying his best not to play politics. He could see that the two of them had been through a lot, and he truly did want to help them if he could. But he also knew he didn't have the influence they needed to get ahead of the system.

"Look... Dr. Emeka. I'll write a letter, and follow up with a phone call on your behalf. Let's see what kind of response I get. But to be honest, I really do not have a lot of pull in that office.

"Thank you sir. We do appreciate any assistance you can give us with this," Nicole said. They stood up and shook hands with Mr. Steels, and then they left his office and headed home.

"I guess that went as well as it could. What do you think?" Nicole asked as she eyed Sam.

"I guess so, but like he said, he has little to no influence." Sam's sounded miserable. They had a late dinner at home. Nicole baked some fish, and put it over pasta, followed by some leftover apple pie – comfort food was in order for this evening. She just wanted them to feel better somehow.

Why don't you stay up, and watch a movie for a while, since you are off tomorrow?" He knew how much she loved movies, and they helped her forget about their problems for a while." He kissed her and went off to bed.

Nicole cleaned up the dishes, and then took a hot bath, put on her big comfortable bathrobe, curled up in front of the TV, and watched the movies Samuel had picked up for her. For just a while, she forgot their worries and laughed, even if she was all laughing alone. She went to bed shortly after midnight, and it felt good to have her husband sleep beside her tonight. She lay quietly beside him, her eyes wide open, feeling stressed out again. Her life hadn't turned out the way she'd hoped. None of her dreams had materialized yet. And the saddest part of it was that it was all beyond their control. She didn't know what to do next, or where else to turn. Out of pure exhaustion, her eyes closed, and she finally fell off to sleep.

The morning came all too soon, Sam's alarm went off, and he quickly shut it off. He didn't want to wake Nicole up; he wanted her to sleep as long as she could. She was looking so thin and pale again; he worried about her now more than ever. It was becoming very apparent to him that he couldn't put off, the future of his career much longer; there was only so much time he had left to waste in Canada. She didn't know it, but Samuel's older brother, and most of his family was putting pressure on him to leave Canada behind, and get started in the US with his career. He had obligations to them, and the other people whom he'd left behind. He needed to get settled there, in order to do what he'd promised his family he would do. He stood looking at his beautiful wife sleeping.

Nicole had never discovered Samuel's secret, the one he'd been keeping for years. It broke his heart even more when he thought about having to leave her behind. He just didn't know how on earth he was going to be able to. The secret of his past mistakes, was one that he always carried with him every day, and he knew sooner or later it would come to light. He also knew that when he finally left, neither of their lives would ever be the same again, the guilty feelings were eating his heart away bit by bit.

He sat down at the table with a coffee in hand. He ate without appetite, just ingesting strength for the day. But in truth, all he wanted to do was cry. How had his life gotten so confusing? He loved a woman he shouldn't, and he lived in a country that refused to give him a fair chance. All the odds were against him now. Why on earth had he promised his family anything? He was trapped with no way out. He'd been so young when he had promised to marry a young African woman. Before he even knew what was happening, the African girl was pregnant, and he'd had to promise to marry her when he got his career on track, and was settled in America or Canada. He had first tried Canada, because he truly loved the country, and wanted to raise his family there. But then things became so messed up. He found Nicole and fell in love with her, and before he knew it, his life and heart were with her. Not back home with the girl who was now a woman, and lived with his older brother, and his young daughter. They were patiently waiting for him to return to them, and bring them back to live in the promised land of America. He didn't know how to turn his back on his own child, or a woman who was his own kind, from the land where he'd grown up, and was everything his culture stood for. And he didn't know how to leave a woman who had stood by him for so many years, fighting every step of the way for him and his career. She had loved him like no other woman he'd ever known. Nicole loved with a love that was so pure and true, and he knew he would never ever find, a love like hers again in his life. He loved her for all that she was, and for all that she stood for, but mostly because she loved him unconditionally, without fault or complaint. He felt so tired he wanted to just crawl back in bed beside her, and hold onto her for as long as he could. He knew he was running out of time.

He knew the truth would be devastating to Nicole; he only hoped she would be able to bear it when it came to light. Maybe if his career path had gone better in Canada, he could have made it work, but it hasn't, and now he had to make some hard choices. It was keeping him up at night, and making him horribly sad.

He was running out of excuses. His eldest brother was no longer happy to keep this young woman, and his daughter there. He wanted them all together to grow as a family. He needed Samuel to get his career in order, as soon as possible, and he was putting lots of pressure on him to relocate to the US. Their system was a lot easier for foreign medical graduates, and he would at least have a fighting chance. His friend Ben had gotten in, and he was promising to help him get settled as soon as he came over. Ben had never learned of Samuel's African woman and child, he would have been heartbroken for Nicole. The one thing that was holding Samuel here, was his love for Nicole. He knew that as soon as he made the move to the US, their life as they knew it would be over. He couldn't take her with him, not this time, and that was the thing that was killing him the most. It wasn't that he didn't like the young African woman – he didn't really know her well – but he had a responsibility to her, and to his child. His brother kept telling him that in time he would grow to love her, and he would become a good father to his child. Samuel knew only too well how his whole family felt, about the situation. Even his sister Kate in London agreed with his brother.

They knew nothing of the kind of love he had with Nicole, because they'd never had it in their own lives. They'd married people that were chosen for them, and they'd made it work. They had love, but not the kind he had. Not the kind that made your heart want to stop beating if that person wasn't at your side. Nor the kind of love that made it hard to breathe, when you thought of living without them in your life. That was the kind of love he had for Nicole, and he was struggling now, on how he could possibly turn his back on her. When he woke up in the morning, no matter how bad the day before had been, there she was smiling at him, lovingly giving him a hug, and making him breakfast with words of encouragement to get him through his day. Samuel grabbed his coffee cup and got into his car, and drove over to the hospital, to start another day, in hell with the devils he worked with. That was what he called them all now; they had no good intention, where he was concerned and he knew that. He guessed that same thing could be said about him, that maybe he had no good intentions concerning his wife. But they would be wrong; he was just in a bad place. His intentions were never to hurt her, only to love her the very best he could. He was not an unkind man by any means, it was just that things had not gone the way, he had hoped they would for him and Nicole. Instead, they had gone terribly wrong. There were too many people who didn't want him to succeed here. So he hated more and more the days he spent in the hospital, with the very people who had destroyed his career, and his ability to tell his family they were all wrong.

***

Sam walked back into the emergency department. He was on call for the next eight hours, and it made him tired just thinking about it.

"Hello Susan. How is everything today?"

Susan knew the situation that Samuel was dealing with, and that he'd been overlooked by the program this year. Word travelled fast in the hospital, especially when they all liked Samuel, and knew he was good at what he did, and they also knew he shouldn't have been overlooked. Susan noticed how stressed he looked, and that he never ate all day. She felt so sorry for him that she grabbed him a sandwich and coffee, and made him sit in the lunchroom and eat.

"Dr. Emeka, your lunch is in the lunchroom. Go sit and eat for ten minutes. I insist." She was like a mother telling her child to eat.

"Thank you Susan. I'll try." He went in and ate a bit of the sandwich and sipped his coffee. But with all that he had on his mind, it was hard to swallow food these days. The only time he actually felt like eating was when Nicole was sitting down at the table with him, and he could see her smile and she was close to him. Then he could breathe again. He couldn't wait for his day to finish so he could go home to her. The afternoon flew by and finally, his day was done. He got into his car and drove home. It was after dark. He was late as usual. But when he got home, and entered his little apartment he was amazed.

"Wow Lady you look so beautiful! And what smells so good?"

"That would be my chicken pot pie." She had the table all done up with candles, wine, and flowers. She had on a soft blue flowing dress. She always made a special effort to look as lovely as she could, just for Samuel. His eyes were the only eyes, she cared about. If he couldn't see how lovely she looked, then she didn't care what anyone else ever said to her. It was only his words that mattered.

"My sweetheart, I see you have worked hard all day. Thank you for all of this." He kissed her softly before he sat down beside her. He stared into her eyes, and held her hand for just a moment.

"How was your day?" She asked.

"Let's not talk about work tonight Lady. Let's just be together." He took a bite of the pot pie. "This is so good. How did you know I would be so hungry?"

"Because you worked all day silly, and you haven't been eating well lately. So tonight I want you to eat a lot, and then we'll dance to our favorite music, like we use to." They ate and then she cleared the dishes away.

When she came back into the living room, he had dimmed the lights, and put on their song: "Endless Love" by Diana Ross and Lionel Richie. They had it played at their wedding.

"Wow babe, interesting choice of song tonight. Why this one?"

"Let's just say I'm feeling sentimental tonight. May I have this dance please?"

She laughed. "I thought you'd never ask." After everything they'd been through, they still knew how to love each other.

They danced together, with his strong arms wrapped around her thin waist. He couldn't take his eyes off of her; she was so beautiful to him. He picked her up, carried her into their bedroom, and carefully unzipped her dress. He let it fall to the floor, revealing her soft white lacy bra and panties. "How did I get so lucky to have you in my life lady? I love you so much," he whispered in her ear.

He pulled her gently down onto their bed, and made passionate love to her, like she was a gift he had only borrowed, and would soon have to give back.

His heart was breaking, and he knew the best thing he could do for her now was prepare to leave. He didn't want to make her suffer anymore with the hardship of his career, or try to fight the government on an issue he knew was useless. He was giving up the fight. They had all won now. All the racism he had faced, and all the people who had never given him a fair chance, had now won. He was a broken man, without a career, and the woman he loved by his side. He knew it would be hard to start over in another country with a new family, but he knew he had to start preparing for the long journey ahead. He only hoped Nicole wouldn't be destroyed by his absence. He didn't want her to ever know the bitter truth about his child, or his promises to marry another woman. He just wanted her to remember him, and their love the way it was now, if that was at all possible. To know the truth would leave her a broken hearted woman, who would be afraid to trust or love again, and that was not what he wanted for his Nicole. He knew he would never be able to communicate with her again after he left. He wouldn't be able to hear that soft, sensual voice, on the phone saying his name, and he wouldn't be able to see her again, because he would only want her in his arms, and she would no longer be his to have. He wouldn't be a free man; he would be tied to a woman of his own culture, and the mother of his child. He knew his life without her would only be an existence, not the happy life he had always dreamed of. He was an honorable man when it came to his own kind; he knew his whole family would disown him if he didn't man up. He had no chance of changing anything, not his family's minds, or his own career situation in Canada. Nicole was everything any man could ever want for in a wife, and he was the fool who was about to leave her. But she wasn't African, and she didn't have his child, and that was the thing that bound him to the other woman.

The following week, Sam started to prepare his mind for what seemed like an inevitable separation. He had started to read for the US medical exam. Ben had sent him the past papers he needed to prepare with, so he was keeping long hours again when he returned home at night.

Nicole sat quiet early one evening, staring at her husband across the room, as he sat with mountains of papers at his desk. He was going through them over and over again. She knew this routine very well. He was studying for another exam. But what exam? She wondered. It had been almost two weeks now, and they hadn't heard a word from the Minister's office, or the human rights commission. Nothing at all from her M.P. She made herself a mental note to call them all in the morning.

After what seemed like forever, Samuel finally looked up from his papers. He was startled to see his wife staring intently at him.

"Lady, what is it?" He asked.

"You're studying again. For what?" She spoke ever so softly, with tears rolling down her cheeks. She could feel that something bad was coming, and she just wanted to stop it all any cost. He put down his papers, and went to Nicole's side. He bent down on his knees and held her hand.

"You're too smart for your own good my sweetheart."

"Why didn't you tell me? You've decided to go to the US, haven't you?" She was openly crying now.

"Now Lady, listen to me please. I can't waste any more time here. I need to get my career moving again. I need to practice medicine. That's why we suffered so hard for years in another country... remember?'

"Oh yes, I remember. I was right there suffering with you. I have suffered ever since. I think you need your career, much more than you need me." She'd never said that to him before.

"Nicole baby, that's not fair and you know it."

"Nothing is fair. Nothing at all. We never do anything together anymore; we are always sad, and suffering because of your career. We never lived our lives together, doing the things that normal couples do; we just lived for your career. That never took place, and its looks like it never will, not in this country. Everything is always on hold, just waiting for your career. We hardly laugh or make love anymore, and we don't spend

183

enough time together, because you're never here. I sleep alone most nights, because you're either working, or studying for some exam. Soon I'm so afraid there will be no us Sam, and I can't even breathe thinking about that. You need to be very careful now Sam, or we will be lost forever." She ran out of their apartment, got in their car and drove to the Oceanside.

She stopped the car and got out. Then she ran to the water's edge. She climbed up on top of a huge rock, just like she used to do when she was a little girl, and cried as if she was breaking. With each rolling crash of the waves, she cried for their unborn children they may never have. She cried for all the time she'd spent chasing empty promises, but most of all she cried because she was desperately lonely, with all the burdens of the world on her shoulders. She cried even harder for the husband she felt she was about to lose. She was so afraid she couldn't move. She just stayed on top of the rock, and stared out into the ocean that was rocking like a monster. She had never once complained to Samuel about anything, never asked for much at all, and now she realized that it may have all been for nothing. No matter what she did at this point, it was all out of her control. She'd done all she could do, and it wasn't enough so save her marriage.

Samuel walked the floor, wondering where on earth she could be. It was starting to get dark. "Where the devil could she be?" He said out loud to himself. He kept hearing her words over and over in his head. But he already knew in his heart, that he had lost. Maybe she went home, he thought. He picked up the phone and called her house.

"Hello?" Millie said.

"Hello, Grand. It's Samuel."

"Hello dear. How are you? Is everything okay?' Millie had been jumpy all day; she knew something was wrong.

"I don't know Grand. Nicole left a few hours ago, and hasn't come back home. It's getting dark, and I am worried. Did she call home?"

"No dear. We haven't heard a word. But why did she leave like that son?"

"I am studying for the US medical exam, and she just got upset and left, and to tell you the truth I am worried about her."

"I can see that." And there it was, she thought. He was getting ready to leave her precious child behind. She could feel it, and she was most likely panicking over it. The old woman's face suddenly clouded over. She could feel her granddaughter's heartache now more than before. But she said not a word about it Samuel.

"I am sure she will be home soon. Please have her call me when she gets in son. Please don't forget."

They hung up the phone. She was a funny old woman, he thought. She seemed to somehow know that Nicole was not in harm's way.

"Sarah, I'm going to take a little walk down by the ocean. I won't be long," Grand said, as she grabbed her coat, and walked quickly out.

She walked until she was standing by the ocean, and then she stared out into the crashing waves as they came to and from the shoreline. She could see the white frosty mouth of each wave, as they moved and rolled closer in the moonlight. She looked up at the nearly dark sky to the brightest star, she could find, then back to the rolling waves. She opened her mind, and had a fixed picture of her sweet child's face.

"Child listen now. You must be strong. Pick yourself up off that rock and come back home. It's getting dark. Hear me child, see me in the rolling waves, and in the brightest star. I am watching over you from afar."

Nicole looked up at the sky to the only star, she could see, and then down at the rolling sea. Just for a moment, she could see her old grandmother's face smiling back at her. She closed her eyes, and in the sound of the waves she could hear her voice. "Get up now child, and go back home. It's dark now, and you should not be alone. "Nicole could feel her presence in the wind that blew her hair away from her face; she could hear her words in the roaring of the ocean waves. She knew now she was no longer alone. She knew her grandmother, was standing on the other side of the shore.

"Oh Grand, it's so awful! I have no home here anymore!" She cried out in despair.

"I am here with you. It's cold and dark. Don't be foolish. Please go back to Sam. I am watching over you from afar. Go home child, go home now."

Nicole slowly picked herself up off the rock, which had become surrounded by water when the high tide came in. The waves crashed all around her; she knew she had to be careful when she climbed down. The mighty undertow of the waves could drag her off the shore, and out to sea if she lost her footing. She stepped down with a steady foot, and the water rolled up to her knees. Mother Nature was trying its best to pull her off her feet, and down into the blackness of the ocean bed. A part of Nicole just wanted to let herself go, to float off into the blackness of the night, and into the rolling ocean. She looked toward the shoreline, and there she was. Her Grandmother's face, smiling at her.

"Come to me, child. Just come back to me. I'm right here. Walk towards me now."

She could see her Grandmother's hands held out to her, as she walked closer to the shore. Nicole focused on her smiling image in the blackness of the night, and took slow steps. She was about ten feet from the shoreline. She knew she had been foolish coming out there at night. Peggy Cove was a dangerous spot to be when the ocean was at full tide, but she no longer cared. She just wanted to get away from the heartache of her situation, and all the stress, and disappointment of her life.

"That's it child. Just keep walking. Come to me, come to me now." The old woman's face smiled down on her from the shore.

Nicole looked like a lost little girl standing in a deep black ocean, that was about to swallow her up. She took one step at a time. She lost her footing and almost fell as the waves got stronger. She took another step, and a heavy, freezing wave hit her in the face. She struggled to regain her balance, wiping the salt water from her eyes. She placed her foot hold as strongly as she could, focusing only on the shoreline, and the image of her Grandmother's smiling face.

Finally, she was on the shore's bank. Her legs were wet, and she was frozen to the bone. Her Grandmother's image had disappeared. She slowly walked to her car and got in, and drove back home.

Samuel was sitting by the window. When he heard her footsteps at the door, he ran and opened it. There stood his wife, cold and soaking wet.

"My God Lady! Where have you been? I have been worried sick! You are so wet and you're shaking. What happened?"

"Sorry Sam," she said wearily. "I just needed to get away for a little while. I'm going to take a shower and warm up." She walked past him with such sadness in her eyes, that he put his head into his hands and cried too.

Nicole went to her bedroom and called her grandmother. She knew she was in big trouble with her.

"Hello?" Millie answered.

"Hi Grand. It's me."

"It's about time you called me child! What in heaven's name are you thinking, going to the ocean so late at night? Sam was worried sick and so was I."

"I am so sorry Grand. It's just that everything is starting to fall apart, and I am so scared. I just needed some time alone to think."

"I know child, but it's far too dangerous there at the shoreline. You must promise me you'll never do that again. If you're not careful, the devil of the night will come at you before you know it and catch you unaware, and you will be lost. You must always pray child. You are his, and he is always watching over you. He will help you overcome all obstacles in your way. You must not worry, you must not doubt him, and he will not let you down. Just remember to be faithful to his word. God has such good things in store for you. You are so creative, you haven't even begun to use your God-given gifts yet. When you start to realize these gifts, you will experience surpassing greatness with God's favor in your life. Sometimes your plans are just not his, and he has something better in mind for you. When his blessings come, they come in abundances. So just have faith and believe. No matter how bad things look now, just remember there is an abundance of blessings coming your way."

"How do you know Grand? How can all that be true, when nothing much has worked out for us?"

"Maybe there're not meant to, or maybe he's not meant to be here. Just be patient and stay in faith, and you'll see his blessings unfold in due time. Sometimes they unfold in such an explosive way, that you know they had to be from him, because it couldn't possibly happen any other way."

"You really think so Grand?"

"I know so. Would your old Grandmother tell you lies?"

'No... and thanks Grand." She smiled for the first time in days. "You're getting stronger. Keep up the good work, and remember you're special. You're very special, and I love you dear."

"I love you too Grandmother. Don't say anything to Mommy, okay?"

"I never do child. Sleep well."

"'Night Grand."

She walked out to where Samuel was sitting. They needed to talk.

"How are you feeling my sweetheart?" Samuel eyes were full of worry.

"I'm better now. I just talked to Grand, and she has a way of making me feel better. But we need to talk about what your plans are."

"I know, we do." He took a deep breath. "I am reading for the US medical exam, just in case I get passed over again here in the next few months, or if nothing happens with the Minister of Health's office. Believe me when I tell you this Nick: I don't want to leave you here. He knew he could never tell her the truth, so he told her a half-truth to soften the blow. When the final blow came, he knew he would not be there to pick up the pieces, and he also knew Nicole would have a long road back to regain her life again. He hoped she would find a way to come around to the other side of sadness, and regain her joy one day. He had to deceive all of them now, the same way they had deceived him – all but Nicole. Yes, he knew his wife well; it was sad that she'd never really known who she was married to. She'd never known the purpose she was supposed to serve in his life, though she had done it well. He couldn't have asked for a better woman by his side. She had gotten him this far, but the rest, he had to do on his own, with a different woman at his side. His African woman, and his child would be his concern after he got his career on track, and was making real money. He knew he was doing Nicole a great injustice. She had grown into a beautiful woman; she was no longer a girl, with little girl dreams. She was becoming a force on her own, and he knew any man would be lucky to have her at his side and in his future.

Nicole interrupted his thoughts. "Samuel? What are you thinking of my love? You look so far away. What is it that's really bothering you? Just tell me. Please."

"So sorry lady. I just have a lot on my mind these days, trying to figure out my next step."

"Don't you mean *our* next step?" She looked at him with suspicion in her eyes.

Yes of course. But here is the thing. I may have to leave you here for a while, until I get settled down over there and do the exam, and then I can send for you. I will stay with Ben. He said it would be okay with him, and I will have time to get settled in that way."

"Leave without me again, Sam? Really!" She looked stunned.

"Yes, lady. It would only be for a little while, until I got on my footing over there. You can't work there, so better you stay here, and continue to make money. We will still have bills to pay."

"I suppose so. And I am the one, as usual that will have to pay them. Right?"

"Yes, lady. I am afraid so. It will just be for a little while, I promise you that."

"Just a little while? I believe I've heard that a thousand times already in our married life. But when will it all get better? I'm nearly thirty years old, and we should be starting our family by now. How can we do that? Without you being settled, and living in the same country as me, that will never happen!"

"I Know but please just trust me. I will make it all right somehow."

"I've always trusted you Sam. Even when everyone else told me to leave, I've stayed right by your side all these years. So you have to know by now that trust has never been in question. I trust you with my life for heaven's sake. You're my husband, my family – you know how I was brought up. Family means everything."

"I know that my sweetheart, but sometimes in life we are forced to do things we wish we didn't have to."

'What does that mean? What are you trying to tell me?"

"I am just tired Nick. Can we talk another time, please? Let's just go to bed for now." He was weary, and he didn't have any answers to her questions.

"Okay. Just go to sleep. I'm going to stay up a little while longer."

He went off to bed and she sat in her big rocking chair, knowing in her heart that he wasn't telling her the truth about something. But never in her wildest dreams, would she have imagined what the real truth was. Eventually she got up, slipped into bed, and gently put her arms around Samuel. She was careful not to wake him up. She just liked the feel of his warm body lying beside hers, as she listened to him breathe. She thought of how many years they had shared together, and were still so in love.

She fell off to sleep, but it was uneasy. In her dreams, she kept seeing a short black woman and child who stood by her door, like they were waiting for something. She tossed and turned most of the night, wondering who these people were.

The sunlight came through their bedroom window as usual and woke them up, as it had done for the past two years. Nicole slowly got out of bed, and started making them their morning coffee. Samuel took a shower, and she put breakfast on the table with their coffee. Samuel came out to join her, dressed in his white shirt and pants for his hospital shift. He was doing a nine to five shift this week, so he would at least be home for dinner, and would be in bed with her each night. She was grateful for the little things now; each hour they got to spend together, felt like an opportunity for them to bond, and appreciate each other's love.

Samuel sat down at their breakfast table, and began to eat his breakfast. He noticed his wife staring at him.

"Lady? What is it my love? Why do you sit so quiet this morning?"

"I guess I just had a bad night. I kept having this weird dream every time I fell asleep, so I'm still tired."

"What kind of dream was it?"

"There was this short black woman and child. They just stood at the foot of our bed, waiting for something, but I couldn't tell what they were waiting for."

Samuel almost choked on his food. "What was that you just said?"

"Like I said, there was a woman and child standing at the foot of our bed, waiting for something. What could that possibly mean Sam?"

"I am not sure lady. Maybe it was someone back home, like my sister and her daughters, waiting for me to come home and visit. It has been a while now since I was there." He was amazed. He knew full well what it was, that she was seeing in her dream – it was his child with her mother, and he knew they were waiting for him to come through with his promise to them.

But how in the hell could Nicole be seeing that? This was no ordinary woman he had married, that much he knew for sure. His only saving grace was that Nicole refused to believe what her gut told her. Instead her heart overruled any mistrust, or negative thoughts where Samuel was concerned.

"Lady... I should be off to the hospital. Do you need a ride into the store today?"

"No, it's still too early for me. I'll take the bus to work soon, but thanks babe. Have a wonderful day." She stood up and walked over to him, putting her arms around his waist, and hugged him like he was about to disappear.

Chapter Seven

Nicole got herself ready for work, and on the ride to the store, she wondered incessantly about her dream, and Millie's advice to her on being prepared for anything. How on earth she thought, does anyone prepare for almost anything? She was beginning to understand that Samuel was hiding something, but just what it was she was still unsure. But she knew her grandmother well enough to know she had warned her of something imminent.

Samuel's day was flying by in the emergency department.

"Susan I think that's all for me today. It was a busy one, and I could eat a horse I am so hungry now," he laughed.

"No lunch again today doctor? He just nodded no and walk off.

After Sam had left, she picked up the phone and rang Dr. Hays' office.

"Hello Dr. Hays speaking."

"This is Susan from the emergency department. Listen Dr. Hays, I simply cannot have those two Saudi Arabian doctors down on my floor again. They are much too slow in this department, and poor Dr. Emeka is overworked again. What happen to the Indian Doctor we had once?"

"The problem is Susan, we don't have anyone else to send down there other than them, and the Indian Doctor quit, and moved on to the US I'm afraid."

"If that's the case, then I suggest you get yourself down here tomorrow and help. Because if you don't, I will report both you and Dr. Rogers to human resources, and file a complaint. You simply cannot overwork one doctor, because you both hired two inappropriate doctors, which are totally incapable of doing the work down here.

"I guess I'll see you tomorrow, or I'll be writing a lengthy report Dr. Hays." She hung up the phone without even giving Dr. Hays time to reply. She knew how to handle doctors like them. She'd seen many of them come and go over the years she'd worked as head nurse in this hospital, and when she filed a complaint, the hospital seniors listened. They all knew what a dedicated nurse she had been, and that her only concern was for her patients' care.

Dr. Hays picked up the phone and called Dr. Rogers. "Dr. Rogers, we have a problem again."

"What is it this time Jane?"

"It seems those two Saudi Arabian doctors are too slow down in the emergency department, and they want someone else again. That old bitch Susan is going to file a complaint with human resources, if I don't go down there myself and work tomorrow."

"So just go down and work for a bit; make it look like you're helping. Stay a few hours, for God's sake, just do it."

"Listen Dick: you go down and work. I have patients to see in my office all day tomorrow. I can't cancel those appointments."

"Then go down after you see them. Work overtime in the evening down there."

She laughed sarcastically. "Work overtime? I don't think so. I have a family at home. You got us into this mess, you get us out. I will not work there tomorrow. You go work there yourself Dick." She hung up the phone.

"God damn that woman," he shouted. "I have to do everything around here." He picked up the phone and called the emergency department.

"Hello Susan. This is Dr. Rogers. Listen... you'll get someone new down there in a few days, but neither Dr. Hays nor I can come down tomorrow. I'll get the Senior Resident to fill in tomorrow, until I get some new clinical assistants down there soon okay? You happy with that?"

"No! Dr. Rogers, I am not okay with that! You should have never hired these two doctors to begin with, especially after the disaster of the last two Polish doctors who you gave an internship to. I know full well that you purposely overlooked Dr. Emeka for them, and that is just shameful. I can testify to their lack of skill, and you know I can. Just what the hell are you doing over there in that department? I will not have you abuse your status here, and fuck up good doctors like Dr. Emeka, you hear me? You mark my words: you make this right, or you'll be in a shitload of trouble Dr. Rogers. You got that?"

She slammed the phone down. She didn't give a damn what they did to her. She was about ready to retire anyway. She was also the Godmother of the hospital's president, and he would most certainly listen to her when she spoke to him of just what was going around there.

Dr. Hays and Dr. Rogers were thicker than thieves, and she knew it. There was no damn way she was going to let this continue, there wasn't much they could do to her, but there was a whole lot she could do to them if she wanted to.

Samuel picked Nicole up at the store and they drove home together.

"How was your day Lady?"

"It was okay. A bit quiet today for sales."

"My day was busy as hell. I never even got lunch. I am so hungry, I could eat a cow." He smiled over at her.

"In that case, I guess we need to stop by the market, because I'm pretty sure we don't have a whole cow at home." She laughed in spite of all of her worries. She just loved being with Samuel at the end of her day.

"Ok, maybe not a whole cow."

"I do have dinner already in the oven; we just need to heat it up. I have chicken, sweet potatoes, and a fresh salad for us. Shouldn't take long to get it on the table my love."

They sat at the table, and Samuel ate like he was indeed starving. She just picked at her food as usual.

"Why are you not eating again Lady? Aren't you hungry?"

"I'm eating, don't worry. I just have a lot on my mind."

"I know you do, what can I do to help?"

"You can be straight with me Sam. I need to know what your plans are, and how soon you're planning on leaving me here alone again."

"I am not sure yet. We need to wait and see if the government here will help or not, and I still need a little time to study for the US medical exam. So I guess maybe another few months. Then I will start to plan my journey to the US. I will stay there with Ben for a while, until I get settled, and then you can come over to live with me."

"Really... then why don't I believe you on this one? I can't shake the feeling that something is off. And the dream of the black woman and child – who are they really?"

"How can I answer that? It was your dream. Stop worrying and go take a shower while I do up the dishes for you, and then I will meet you in our bedroom my sexy wife." He was trying his best to get her off the subject and on to something more fun, like making love.

He never missed a chance these days to make love to her. He knew he was living on borrowed time, and he was panicking inside, but he was trying hard not to show it. Nicole was sensing something was up. It was in the way he made love to her; there was a passion in his touch that she hadn't felt before with him. It was like he couldn't get enough of her. He was like a man who was desperate to hold on to something that belonged to him, but was slipping out of his grasp. She enjoyed his attention every evening, but wondered what was really behind it all. Usually Samuel would study most evenings, only coming to bed after she had already fallen asleep, but lately he'd made sure he was there loving her almost every night until she fell off to sleep. What she didn't know was that, he then got up and studied for a few more hours, then went back to sleep for a few hours until the alarm clock woke them both up together. She never saw him study, so she never really knew how hard he was working on his escape to the United States. He didn't want to upset her anymore, or have her worry every time she saw him open a book to read.

Nicole woke up each morning now with a feeling that somehow her whole world was about to fall apart. If only she could see what it was, and why was she feeling so lost these days. Nothing much had really changed – she went to work each day, and Sam was in bed beside her most nights. But it was like a false sense of security, and she knew down deep inside her gut that it wasn't real.

This morning she needed to make a call to her Minister of Health's office to see what the results were of their meeting, she needed to know if they were going to help out or not. So on her lunch break at work, she picked up the phone and called them.

"Ministers' Office, how many we help you today?"

"This is Mrs. Emeka; we had a meeting a month ago with the Minister. We haven't heard a thing back from this department in regards to whether or not, they are going to assist us with an internship program this year."

"Oh yes, I remember, let me transfer you to his assistant. Just one moment please." The phone went silent for a moment, and then she was put through.

"Good afternoon Mrs. Emeka; this is the Minister's assistant. We've come up against some problems. When we called Dr. Hays and Dr. Rogers, and asked if we presented them with the funds for one more internship, could it go to your husband, they said they couldn't guarantee it. It would go to the person who was next on the list of names on the matching program, and that wasn't your husband's name. So our hands are somewhat tied here."

"It is just unbelievable that they would say that, when it's my husband who's been doing most of the work for the incapable doctors they've hired. This is why we've asked you to help. Dr. Hays and Dr. Rogers are simply not playing fair, and they need to be questioned regarding the decisions they're making over there."

He sighed. "That's difficult for us to do, and it would involve a whole lot of unnecessary paperwork, time and extra money to do that, Mrs. Emeka."

"Tell me then sir: if you were in our situation, what would you do to get into the system, knowing what we have just told you to be true? Where would you go, what would you do, to move forward with your career?"

"I wish I had a simple answer for you, but I don't. I know it's an unfortunate situation your husband is in, but hopefully next year he'll be lucky enough to get in the program."

"That's the whole issues here. You see luck should have nothing to do with this situation. It should be based on skill and merit, and you know that as well as I do. Your department is choosing to overlook this whole situation, because of too much red tape and its inconvenience. The truth is that this system is unfair, and doesn't serve the doctors who deserve a fair chance to progress with their careers. It also doesn't serve the smaller rural communities that need doctors. I am only one person who sees the injustice of it all now, but in a few years there will be many people who will see the results of this system, and how poorly it's been managed by you and the Minister of Health. You'll have to deal with the consequences of this, and your names will be written all over it. When there's a shortage of family doctors, and our emergency room are overcrowded, you'll be the ones to blame for having turned a blind eye to this situation, because it was too much trouble for you both, to do your job.

"One day I will find a way to tell this story, and let everyone see the injustice in your department's decisions." She hung up the phone in tears. How could they just do nothing? She could hardly function anymore that day, so she decided to leave work.

She told her staff, she had a doctor's appointment, grabbed her coat and left the store. They could see she was upset, but had no idea why. They felt sorry for her. She worked so hard all the time, and her normally bright eyes were always sad these days.

She walked over to the public gardens, and as she looked around, the flowers were just as beautiful, the trees just as green, and the sky as blue as she remembered it being that day she meant Samuel. What had changed was her heart and soul. All her innocence was now gone, and with it her dreams and hopes. But not her faith. She would never give up fighting for what was right, and for what she believed in. One day she would tell the world the story of how a good doctor had been denied access to his profession, of how the good old boys' club had systematically destroyed equal opportunity in her province and her country. She would tell the story of how two people who loved each other, were driven from her country in order to survive. But she knew it wouldn't be today. Today she had to go home and tell her husband, that they wouldn't be receiving any help from their elected officials in the Ministries of Health department.

She would tell him to leave her country, and prepare for the exam in the United States. Maybe there he would stand a fair chance. She could no longer allow him to stay where he had no opportunity to succeed with his career. She knew he loved medicine as much as he loved her, and that he'd never be happy, until he was a practicing medical doctor. So she was going to do the only thing she had left to do, and that was to tell her heart to let him go, to tell him to go to another country where he would stand a chance of becoming what he deserved to be: a working medical doctor.

She hoped that it would include her one day. But for now, she had to be brave and let go of her childish dreams and beliefs. She had done all she could for him now. She was a grown woman, who looked at her world much differently than before. She now saw the world through the eyes of a black man trying to survive in a white man's world. Her heart was heavy as she thought about all the hardships they'd faced, and were still not able to overcome. She had no idea what her future would be now. She only hoped it would be with her Samuel, and that they would be able to one day be happy.

Samuel got in his car to drive home. His day had been long, and he was tired from being up most of the night studying. The emergency ward was horribly stressful, with hardly anyone to help him. Susan was furious that they hadn't done a damn thing to change the situation. She was about ready to file an official complaint with human resources. She had already arranged a meeting with her godson, the president of the hospital, to discuss the situation with her department. She was hoping to put in a good word for Samuel.

Samuel walked through the door of their apartment, and saw Nicole sitting in her big rocking chair with a cup of tea in her hand. Samuel dropped his briefcase on the floor, went over to her side, bent down and kissed her on the cheek. "Hello pretty lady. You look far away tonight."

"Hi baby. Dinner is almost ready; it'll just be a few more minutes. You have time to take a shower if you like."

"Okay. I think I'll do that."

She got up and took the roast out of the oven, cut it up put all the roasted vegetables beside it on a big plate, and sat in the middle of the table.

"Hope you're hungry." She plated him a big helping and set it in front of him.

He knew something was wrong. She was distant and unhappy looking this evening. "I called your work today, and they said you came home early. Is everything okay?"

"As okay as it's ever going to be. I called the Ministry of Health today, and they said they can't help us. Dr. Rogers and Dr. Hays said that even if they were given funds for one more internship, it wouldn't go to you, it would go to the person who was next on their so-called list. It appears you're at the bottom of that list."

"That does not surprise me Lady; it was a long shot. That's why I have been studying for the US medical exam. Now you can understand why I have to leave this place. I need to get settled somewhere else where I will have a fair chance."

"Yes... I see that now. Do what you have to. I get it." She just stared straight ahead as she spoke to him, like she was slowly removing her heart from him.

"Lady if I could have worked here, it would have all been so different for us. God knows we tried our best to make that happen. But it hasn't, and now I have no other choice but this one. You know that... right?"

"Yes, I know that. Like I said, do what you have to do. I'll manage on my own here for a while until you get settled. Then I'll join you there – right?" She looked him in the eye as she asked the question.

"That would be my greatest wish. You know I don't want to leave you here alone." He reached out and grabbed her hand. "I do love you. No matter what happens, I will always love you, and I have been damn lucky to have you in my life all these years. I hope you know that." He looked at her helplessly with tears in his eyes.

He could sense her distance and it bothered the hell out of him, but what else could he expect from her? Everyone had a breaking point. He'd never meant to hurt her, and he'd always wanted her for himself. She didn't belong to anyone else in his mind. But he was about to give all that up and leave her behind, for some other man to come into her life and lay claim on her. The very thought of it made him go crazy in his soul.

"How was your day at the hospital?"

"Pretty much the same, very busy. Poor Susan the head nurse there is so angry, they have not given her another good clinical assistant yet, and the senior resident there is also complaining he has to do too many long hours. When I leave, they will have no one that is any good in that department. The senior resident will be working even longer than he is now. But at least the money I am being paid has helped us out a lot, and allows me to put most of the money in the bank for my move. Will you keep this place, or look for something cheaper, and smaller for yourself after I go?'

"I haven't thought about that yet. I really won't need this two-bedroom apartment, I guess. I'll check with the landlord to see if they have something smaller in the building. It would be cheaper, and I could save more money for when I move over there with you. "I'm sorry, but we do have to discuss this. I will be leaving in a month, and you have to make serious plans on how you will live when I am gone."

"Well then I guess I'd better get started planning things out. I'll speak with the landlord tomorrow." The look on her face was one of disappointed.

"Why don't you do that, and see what he says. If there's a smaller apartment here, I will still be around to help you move. Otherwise, you will end up doing that all on your own."

"If I have to, I'll call home and ask my brothers to come in, and help me with the move. No need for you to worry yourself about that. Just worry about what you always do, your career." She got up from the table and went out to the kitchen to do the dishes. She was starting to resent his career choice, and wished he was anything else other a damn doctor, who couldn't work in her country. She knew that was unfair, but she was only human, and she was beginning to realize that she was going to be alone again for a long time to come.

She went to bed early that night, and was asleep when Samuel finally came to bed after studying. He looked at his sweet wife, sound asleep beside him, and he was suddenly hit with the reality of losing her. He closed his eyes and fell asleep out of pure exhaustion.

Nicole was already up and had breakfast made when the alarm clock rang out. Samuel turned over to find he was alone. He had better get used to that, he thought. He got up and went out to the kitchen, but she wasn't there either. He finally found her curled up in her rocking chair with a cup of coffee in her hand, just staring out the window.

"Oh there you are. Good morning."

"Morning. Would you like me to get you a cup of coffee and some muffins?"

"I can get them my sweetheart, and then I will come and join you here." He went out to the kitchen and got a cup of coffee and a muffin, then headed back into the living room and sat down beside her in the big chair.

"Lady... what's on your mind this morning? You're not usually up before me."

"I was awake so I just got up. I have a lot of planning to do, and I was just thinking about where to start."

"I know all this is hard on you again, but I know you will find a way to handle it."

"You think so?" She stared blankly at him.

"Yes, I do. And when I am gone, you can spend more time with some of your friends, and see your family more often."

"There is just one problem. They're not you Sam. I'm not married to my family, or my friends, or my job. I am married to you, remember?"

"I know that, but I will come back home to you as often as I can. I promise you that. Now let's get ready for work my dear. Do you want me to get you some food before we go?"

"No thanks, I'm not hungry. Just get some for yourself. I'm going to take a shower." She left him standing in the kitchen.

He knew that his leaving was starting to kill his wife inside. Slowly and quietly, she was disappearing right before him, and he was helpless to do anything about it. He'd already told Ben when he was coming, and he was about to give notice at work that he would leave in a few weeks. He had secretly told his brother to send his child, and his African woman to the US in a few weeks. He'd estimated that he'd be working within a year over there, according to his conversations with Ben. He hadn't yet told Ben about his plans, or that Nicole wouldn't be joining them, but that was something he couldn't even tell himself yet.

"Do you want a ride into work today?" He called from the kitchen door.

"No thank you. Go without me this morning. I'll see you later tonight. Have a good day." She yelled from their bedroom. She never came out to kiss him goodbye. He stood by the door for a few minutes, waiting for her and then he left.

She'd never done that before. All the years they'd been together, she'd always kissed him goodbye and greeted him with a kiss to say hello. But he couldn't blame her. He knew how very disappointed she was with their situation, and with him leaving her again.

She listened for the door to close, and then went and sat back down in her rocking chair. She had already told her work she wouldn't be in again today. She just needed some time to get her heart, and head around everything that was happening to her. She picked up the phone, and called home to speak with her mother.

"Hello?" Sarah answered.

"Hi… Mommy. How are you today?"

"I'm fine dear. How is my girl today?" Sarah asked, knowing her daughter wasn't so fine. She could hear it in her voice.

"Samuel is getting ready to leave for the US in a few weeks; he'll be trying to get into the medical system there. We haven't been very successful here, but we tried so hard. I promise you, we really did." She began to cry as she spoke.

Her mother's heart broke into a thousand pieces as she heard her girl crying her heart out. "Oh sweet girl, I know you've both worked very hard. Why all the tears today?"

"It's just that, I have to start to make plans to live on my own again with Samuel being gone. And I don't know where to start; it's all so hard for me. It's always been hard, but at least he's been here with me. Now he's leaving again, and I'm scared that it's for good this time, that we'll never be able to come home again and live here."

"What kind of plans do you need to make right away?"

"Well, this apartment is too big for me. And you know I hate living alone."

"Yes I know dear. I have an idea. How about Marilyn comes and lives with you for the summer? She wants a summer job anyway. That way you can take care of each other. What do you think of that idea?" Sarah was hopeful she'd agree.

"Really, you'd let her do that? I think that would be great if she wants to come. I know schools will be out next month, and I could put out some job applications for her for a summer job."

"Well then that's settled! I know she'll love the idea, so why don't you do that? We'll bring her down to you in a few weeks, right after Samuel leaves. You won't be alone, and you won't have to move. Marilyn can help with a little bit of money, and you can still stay in your apartment. And believe me, you will not be lonely with your sister around," she laughed.

"I think that's a wonderful idea. Thank you, Mommy. You and Grand can come and visit whenever you like too."

"Yes, we'll be there often dear. Now stop feeling so sad. I know all this is hard on you, but you are a strong girl and you can do this."

"Okay mom. I love you."

"I love you too. Goodbye dear."

They hung up, and Nicole was feeling slightly better now. At least she would have family close, and she wouldn't feel so alone.

Sarah walked into the kitchen and stood there, and looked at Millie, with a sour look on her face. "He's leaving her, isn't he?"

"Yes. He's getting ready to go to the US to write their medical exams over there."

"I told you he'd leave her all alone. That girl has done nothing but suffer in silence by his side all these years, and now he decides to leave her here and go away. And you know, Sarah, he's not coming back for her. He'll tell her he is, but I guarantee you he's hiding something from her, and he'll never have her live there with him."

"My goodness! What has gotten into you Grand? He told her she'd go over there with him once he's settled. Why do you think he isn't telling her the truth?"

"I just know, Sarah. I feel it. I can't explain it, but I see her tears for a long time to come, because of how he appears in my dreams." For the first time, she actually tried to explain to Sarah, but she knew she most likely wouldn't get it.

"Oh Grand, really! Are you mixing up your medications again? Dreams can't tell you anything. It's just your imagination, and you're imagining the very worst, so don't tell her that. She'll be even more upset than she already is. Now let me look at your medications. I want to make sure you're taking them correctly." She walked over to the medicine cabinet and took them out.

Nicole's Grandmother just went out to the living room, sat down in her old rocking chair, and looked out the window and smiled. She knew better than to try to explain any further to Sarah. But she also knew just why Nicole was so upset; it was because she could feel it coming too. She was still in denial and unsure of what exactly was coming, but she knew it wasn't good. She knew her Nicole would do nothing to retaliate against Samuel in the future, so she would do it for her.

***

Samuel went over to Susan at the front desk where she was reviewing the patient list for the day. "Good morning, Susan. How's the day looking so far?" Samuel smiled at the kind hearted older woman.

"Not too bad so far."

"Susan… I want to tell you I just gave my two weeks' notice. But I wanted you to know just how much I have appreciated all your support, while I was here in your department."

"Oh! Samuel, I'm so sorry to hear that. But I can't blame you. I know very well what's going on here with your situation; don't think for one moment that I don't. If it were up to me, I would have had your name at the very top of the list, doctor. You're one of the best we've ever had in this department. And it's a goddamn shame what Dr. Rogers and Dr. Hays have done to your career. I plan on telling the president of this hospital just that, when I have my meeting with him this afternoon."

"Susan it is very kind of you to say all that, but really it will do no good. They all know what they are doing. Yet there is no one with enough guts, or sense of justice to put a stop to it. So please don't put yourself in harm's way on my account – it will change nothing at this point." He kissed her on the cheek, grabbed the charts, and went off to see the first patient of the day.

Susan walked into the office of her godson, later that afternoon.
"Susan! How is my favorite godmother today?" Frank asked.

"To tell you the truth Frank, I'm as mad as hell at the situation down in the emergency department. I need you to listen to me and do something about it." She looked him in the eye as she spoke, wanting him to know that she meant business today.

"Calm down and tell me about the problem. You're going to get your blood pressure up again." He sat up and gave her his full attention.

"For starters, we're really overworked down there. The clinical assistants they've been sending me are completely incapable of the work. There's only one good clinical assistant, Dr. Samuel Emeka, and that poor man has been doing most of the work for months now, while the other clinical assistants disappear for half the day. I personally talked with Dr. Rogers and Dr. Hays, who is currently in charge of hiring and training the clinical assistants. I told them point blank that these four clinical assistants they'd sent me – two Polish and two Saudi Arabian – were simply dangerous, and that I didn't want them on my floor again. But that leaves us very short-staffed. They said the senior resident would help out more, but he's overworked too.

"Now the good clinical assistant I told you about, Dr. Emeka, just gave his two weeks' notice. I can't blame him either Frank. Dr. Hays put his name at the very bottom of the matching list this year, to make sure he didn't get into an internship program here, and gave the two Polish doctors an internship instead. They're up on the cardiac floor now, and they are damn dangerous. Dr. Emeka just wants to get on with his career and practice medicine, like all you doctors do, but they've stopped him from doing that here. They're just plain stupid, and they're thicker than thieves I tell you. Someone needs to look into exactly what they're doing over there in that department, Frank. You're in charge of this hospital, and it will be on your hands if those two polish doctors make a mistake and kill someone."

"Wow! That's a lot of stuff you just laid on me here Susan. I'll look into this right away, I promise you that. In the meantime, I'll see who else we can send down to your floor to work. Now stop worrying yourself silly; let me handle this you hear?"

"I hear you Frank, but it's a damn shame we're about to lose a good doctor like Dr. Emeka." She got up and left.

Frank picked up the phone and called Dr. Rogers at once. He was a man of principals who believed in fairness, and he wanted his hospital to be excellent in all matters regarding patient care.

"Dick, it's Frank. I want a meeting with you and Dr. Hays in one hour in my office please." He hung up without giving him a chance to say no.

Dr. Rogers immediately made a phone call of his own to Dr. Hays.

"Hello Dr. Hays"

"Yes Dick, what is it? I'm with patients." She was annoyed at being interrupted.

"Listen. Frank wants a meeting with you and me in one hour in his office."

"What is this all about? Damn it, what have you done now? I told you all this would come back to hurt us."

"Just relax. I'll do all the talking. You just go along with whatever I say."

"Whatever you say? That's what's gotten me into this mess in the first place. This time you're on your own. I will be there in one hour." She hung up the phone, her face turning red. What she had done was shameful and she knew it.

The doctors met outside Frank's office an hour later.

"What is this all about Dick?"

"He didn't say, so just relax."

A few moments later, his secretary showed them into Frank's office.

"Hello! Frank. How are you?" Dr. Rogers asked as he took a seat, looking rather tense.

"I'm good, Dr. Rogers, Dr. Hays. Thank you both for meeting with me on such short notice. I've just had some very disappointing news from our head nurse, Susan down in the emergency department. She tells me you've sent her four different clinical assistants who were under qualified for the position. And the one doctor who *was* qualified, Dr. Emeka, who is overworked and is now leaving us, mainly because you both blocked him from an internship program here, and gave it to two doctors who she claims are downright dangerous. What do you have to say for yourselves?" Frank had known Susan all his life, and knew she was not one to complain without just cause. He'd already checked the cardiac floor where the two polished Doctors, had been working, and he had gotten feedback from the nurses there too.

"Listen… Frank. We're doing the best job we can with this program. You know perfectly well that when it comes to these foreign medical graduates, it's not easy to get good ones. We just do our best with what we have." Dr. Rogers was starting to feel anxious.

"Then why Dr. Hays did put Dr. Emeka's name at the bottom of the list, when he's more skilled than the two doctors who you actually matched to our hospital?"

"It's plain and simple. I was following Dr. Rogers's orders."

Frank turned to Dr. Rogers. "Why in God's name would you tell her to do that?"

"We have enough African doctors in the system as it is. The two Polish doctors will leave and go to bigger cities to work. We needed Samuel for one more year to work as a clinical assistant; we needed someone to do the work!"

"Are you saying that you put the two under qualified doctors ahead of him, simply because they will leave us in a year? My God Man! We need good doctor's right here in this hospital. Good ones like Dr. Emeka. What kind of thinking is that?"

"If we let too many doctors like Samuel in, they'll change everything. You will have a son about to graduate next year from medical school, and you'll want him to have the first chance here. I'm just protecting those placements for our own children."

"My son doesn't even want to come back here and live, and even if he did, he'd want to earn his own way, not have it given to him just because I'm the president of this hospital. And besides that, I spoke with the nursing staff on the cardiac floor where the two Polish interns are working, and they are also very unhappy with their performance. What happens if someone dies because they can't do the work? That would be on my head as the president of this hospital, and on yours and Dr. Hays for having hired them in the first place. Now how are we going to fix this Dr. Rogers?"

"I'll have to think about it. The two interns only have three more months here with us, so that should take care of it, right?"

"Only if they don't kill someone in the meantime, and Dick we're about to lose a good doctor like Dr. Emeka."

"We can't stop him from leaving us. If he doesn't want to work here anymore, what can I do?"

"The reason he doesn't want to work here is because the poor man feels his career is hopeless here, and he's overworked. That's because of the two of you, and what you've done in misrepresenting the matching system."

"That's very hard to prove and you know it. Just let sleeping dogs lie. There's no reason to stir up this nasty business now Frank. I promise you that next time I'll be more careful in who we hire and train here. I'll keep a very close eye on the two interns until they're finished, and we'll just let Samuel go to the US if he wants to."

"That's your solution, Dick? Just let him go because you're afraid of change?"

"It's not only me that likes it this way. The licensing bodies and the Ministry of Health department do too. They helped put this whole system in place to begin with. It would cost the taxpayers a whole lot of money to change it. So just let it go this time."

"Doctors I am afraid I cannot do that. I'll be filling a report, and it will stand on the record that I disagree with the decisions that the two of you have made. As of this moment, the two Polish doctors are no longer interns here at this hospital. Regarding Dr. Emeka, I suggest you talk with him, and try to get him to stay on here. We need good doctors here too. Dr. Hays and Dr. Rogers I am very disappointed that the two of you have put this hospital, and our patience's in harm's way. If Dr. Emeka leaves us which I understand he is, just who will cover off down in the emergency department?"

"I have a few more applications. I can interview them, and see what they're like to replace Dr. Emeka."

"I want to see them personally, and speak with them before you offer anyone any kind of position. I hope I have made myself understood doctors. Dr. Hays if I were you, I would not be responsible any longer for the matching program, because I'm sure there will be further investigations into this whole mess. I recommend you just take care of your day-to-day patients. Let Dr. Rogers handle the fallout of his decisions. And next time, let me know if there are any problems with the doctors that are hired by his department right away. Don't let Susan be the one to inform me. You're both lucky that I'm not firing you today. It's unbelievable that such things are still happening in this day and age." He stared at them, clearly disgusted. "You're free to go." Frank stood up and left the room.

"Dick that's it. I'm done with the internship program. I don't want anything more to do with it, or you for that matter. You can speak with Samuel regarding him staying on; I don't want anything more to do with any of this mess."

"Can't you at least talk Samuel into staying for a while longer? It would give me a chance to find someone to replace him. Can't you do anything right woman?"

"No Dick I can't. I'm just going to take care of my own patients, and the department that I'm in charge of. And don't even think about sending me anymore unskilled doctors. If you do, I will report it immediately back to Frank. You're nothing more than a bully and a bigot, and you should be ashamed of yourself. I regret the day I ever let you intimidate me. Samuel deserved that internship and you know it, and now he's leaving because of it. And I don't blame him one bit. Who would want to actually stay and work, in this hospital with a racist fool like you in charge?" She stormed out.

Dr. Rogers went back to his office, and decided not to even bother, to talk to Samuel. It was best to just let him go; it would be better in the long run he thought. He would just cause further problems if he stayed on. He'd already promised the Saudi Arabian government, that their two doctors would be placed into an internship this year, and he'd accepted the money for them. So he knew there was no more positions available, and that Samuel would be left out in the cold for another year. The fact that Samuel was leaving was a relief. He'd never be able to explain two more bad clinical assistants getting in again over Samuel again.

Susan walked over to where Samuel was doing his charts for the day.

"Samuel may I interrupt you for a minute? I just wanted you to know I had my meeting with the president of this hospital today, and I told him exactly what's going on here. I didn't mince words with him either. I told him the truth!"

"That's very kind of you Susan. But it's too late for me here, I don't trust them anymore. I have no more time to waste. I need to move on with my career. I hope you know how much I appreciate, that you spoke up on the matter." Samuel walked into the office, took a bite of his sandwich, and sipped his coffee. He sat staring at the wall as he ate. Soon he'd be gone from this place, and it would all just be a bad memory. He wasn't really sure, what the hell had happened to prevent him from getting ahead at the hospital, because Dr. Rogers, and Dr. Hays had covered it all up so well. But he knew they were to blame for him having to leave his life in Canada behind.

***

Nicole couldn't shake the feeling that when Samuel left, he was never coming back. She told herself that it was just her fear talking, and it had nothing to do with reality. But with each day that passed, she could feel something dying inside of her. Maybe it was all her hopes, and dreams of a happy future with him, or maybe it was a warning from the universe.

She knew she needed to get dinner ready for when Samuel returned home. She got up and prepared their evening meal. She sat back down in her big rocking chair, and waited to hear Samuel's footsteps at the door. She closed her eyes. She felt so tired and weary. It was amazing how sadness, could take all your energy away she thought. She'd always had so much energy to get through her day, and now she could barely get through dinner. She knew she had to get her thinking right again, if she was ever going to regain back her joy. She couldn't let Sam see how apprehensive she was about everything. She needed to enjoy the time they had left. She wanted him to remember their last days together in Canada as happy ones. She'd decided to make the best of every day they had left in each other's life. She quickly got in the shower, and put on a long mint-green cotton dress, followed by her favorite perfume. Then she pulled her hair up on top of her head. She looked like a woman now, not a little girl. She was a woman who loved her husband, and wanted him to notice her for all the right reasons. Just as she was finishing her hair, she heard his footsteps at the door, and his keys in the lock. The door opened, and his familiar voice called her name.

"Nicole my sweetheart, I am home." He went to their bedroom, and there she stood.

"How was your day?" She walked over and greeted him with a kiss, and a warm hug. Just like she always had. She had willed herself back to him, even if it was only for a short time.

"That's better. I missed you all day. I am just glad my day is over, and I get to spend the rest of my evening with you. You look wonderful this evening, and smell even better."

"Thanks babe. You must be hungry. Meet you at the dinner table my handsome husband."

"That's the best offer I had all day." Samuel smiled down at her, and walked away to take a quick shower.

Nicole walked out and put the hot food on their plates. She poured a glass of wine for each of them, and sat down to wait for him. Soon she thought, he wouldn't be here anymore to eat dinner with, or to sleep beside, or to make love to. Her eyes clouded over with her tears, but she quickly wiped them away when she heard Samuel's footsteps coming.

"Wow! Everything looks great." Samuel sat down and began to eat.

"I called you at work they said you were not there; you didn't go in to work today again. Are you feeling okay?"

"I guess so. I just need some time to prepare myself for when you leave. I can't help but feel that this time it's different, that there's more than you're telling me. I feel like you're going to forget about me here, leave me behind. Why do I feel that way Sam?"

His heart could hardly bear her words. He was helpless to assure her that she was being fearful for nothing. He knew she was right to feel the way she did, but he still didn't have the courage to tell her the truth.

He held her hand in his, "I don't know why you are feeling that way, because I will only be one hour away by plane, and will return home as much as I possibly can."

"Really Sam, I hope you will?" Her eyes looked brighter for the first time in days.

"Of course I will. You are my wife. No matter how far away I am, you will be right in here." He put her hand on his heart.

"I'll wait patiently for you to get it all together over there, and then I'll join you. So you had better hurry that process up mister. I will not be ok again Sam, until I am by your side you know that, right?"

"I know that Nick, but you must be very strong when I go. Life goes on even when I'm not here you know. You will need to get out with friends and family, and make the best of life when I am away. I want you to promise me that Lady." His eyes pleaded with her.

"I'll try my best, but my life has always been with you. So when you not hear, my world feels empty." He hugged her as tight as he could, he had no more words left that he could say, which would give them both any further comfort.

When they'd finished dinner, she took him by the hand and walked him into their bedroom, where she slowly undressed in front of him. As he watched her, he still couldn't believe how beautiful she was, and how she was able to still take his breath away after all these years. He lifted her onto their bed and slowly made love to her, the passion between them strong. Soon they were only aware of the raw lust and emotion between their bodies. Their two bodies blended together until they felted like one. They slept peacefully together, like they had all their lives still ahead of them.

The next morning Nicole went in to work, only to find the whole store in a mess. "Why on earth does this place look like such disarray? What happened in the last two days?"

"Helen decided to change the store around, and then she began to realize she didn't know what she was doing, so she just walked out and left it." Jim said.

"What is wrong with that woman?" She said under her breath. She began to rearrange the clothing, setting the coordinating collections back up together. She worked hard at it all day, and by the end of the day the store looked suitable again. Richard came in around four o'clock, to check on things and was relieved to see Nicole there.

"Hello my girl. I am so glad you're back. How are you?"

"I'm okay. How have things been around here Richard?"

"Not as good as when you're here. I'm sorry that Helen ripped things apart when you were off, but sometimes I just can't stop her, when she gets an idea in her head." He rolled his eyes.

"I can see that. No worries, I fixed everything back. How does everything look now to you?"

"Simply wonderful. The store looks fresh and clean again, the way it always does when you're around." When he spoke to her, he noticed she still looked tired and pale. "Are you feeling okay Nicole?"

"Yes for sure. Just a bit of the stomach flu. Nothing to worry about." She smiled at him.

But he was no fool; there was no light in her eyes, or behind her smile. He had noticed when working with her over the last year, when she was really happy, her smile could light up a whole room. But today it was dim, and barely present in her eyes. "You sure you're okay, my girl?" The older man looked at her, with a thousand questions in his eyes.

"Well... no, not really Richard. I might as well tell you the truth. Samuel will be leaving soon to go and do the medical exams in the US. We haven't been very successful here in getting him back into the Canadian system, so in order for him to move forward with his career, we'll have to leave the country. I'm not going with him right away, it will be at least a year or so before I join him. So no need to worry; I'm not leaving the store any time soon. It's just that he's leaving, and I'll be here on my own for a while. Anytime I'm without my Samuel, I'm kind of not myself." She looked at him with so much sadness in her eyes, that it startled him to see her that way.

"Oh my girl, I'm so sorry to hear that. I had no idea Samuel was having any kind of difficulty here. You've never mentioned it before." Even though her own life was in shambles, she was always willing to listen to other people's sad stories, and offer words of encouragement. She'd never complained about all the times his wife had made her life difficult in the store, and when the staff were against her, she'd just loved them into loving her back. The more he thought about it, the guiltier he was starting to feel about his plan to go bankrupt in a few months, and leave her with nothing at all. He was only now beginning to realize what a kind woman, he had been working with, all these months.

"If you need anything, just talk to me. A little time off to go and visit him, or to rest – just take it okay?" He hugged her for the first time. He'd almost begun to think of her as the daughter he never had.

"Thank you Richard. That's very kind of you to offer me extra time off. And to be honest, I'll probably need it. I'd like to take the next week off to help Samuel pack, and get ready to leave for the US if that's okay."

"Yes of course my dear, we'll manage while you're gone. And I'll try my best to keep Helen from ripping the store apart again." He felt so sorry for her now.

"Thank you for that. Yes, please keep your wife out of this store." She smiled.

"Take very good care of yourself, and I'll see you in a week my girl." He walked away, feeling terrible. As he walked away from her, he couldn't help but think, what a strong woman she was. She'd managed to keep a big secret like that from all of them for such a long time. Yet he was giving up, running away to some little town, and opening a bed and breakfast for his wife to run. He was giving up on his dream, giving away his baby – the store – and his first wife's life's work. He really didn't like himself very much right now. He needed a good stiff drink.

Nicole left the store, and walked over to the lovely public gardens where she had first met Samuel. She couldn't control her thoughts, as she walked along. What had they done wrong? Why hadn't Samuel been able to break into the Canadian medical system? The matching system, and the people that ran it were like a big machine. One couldn't work well without the other. One was the gears, the other the wheels, and one did the steering. The machine knocked down anything in its path that didn't suit its purpose, destroying equal opportunities. Nicole's knew this in her heart, and with that her whole outlook on life had changed. This well-oiled machine of discrimination, had all but run over the both of them. There was no one to campaign the cause, no one strong enough to fight for change, and no one's shoulder to cry on.

Someday she'd write in all down in black and white on paper. She would let other people see, and feel what it was like to be a second class citizen in her own country. Maybe it would help others who found themselves in a similar place, to be courageous in the face of heartache. But for now she had to get through the next week of her Samuel leaving, she had to pack up all his things and let him go. She picked herself up and headed home, and prayed for the strength to do what she had to do.

It was finally Friday night, and she was grateful to have the whole next week off, so she could spend it with Samuel. Today was his last day at the hospital. She knew she needed to make it a good final week for them as a married couple, their future was unsure, and she wanted to create the best memories possible in the last week they were together.

Samuel said his goodbyes to Mary at the hospital, and then went over to Susan. "Susan my dear, it was a pleasure working here with you, and I wish you all the best in the future." Samuel gave the older woman a kiss on the cheek.
"Thank you Samuel, and I am so sorry we are losing you today, I am going to miss you."

Susan gave Samuel a hug, and then he walked out the hospital doors for the last time, got into his car, and drove home. He never looked back.

"I'm home, my sweetheart."

She stood up and gave him a warm hug. "I've been waiting for you." She smiled and then walked out to the kitchen to heat up the soup. She wore black silk pajamas which were very feminine and soft to the touch. Nicole set the table and put the salad in bowls. She poured a glass of wine and sipped it until he came out to join with her.

"Are you hungry tonight?"

"Just a little, but mostly relieved to be finished with that hospital. The situation there was slowly starting to kill me."

"I know it was baby. Let's hope the next one treats you better, for both of our sakes." She raised her glass of wine to make a toast. "Here's to a happier future for both of us, and hopefully it's together."

"Wow, why do you think it's not together?"

"I don't think that in my mind, but my heart feels somewhat out of sorts these days."

"Well then.... I will just have to make love to that heart of yours, until it's back in sorts." He smiled that big smile that had made her fall in love with him years ago.

"That works for me," she laughed.

"Soup's good tonight. What's the plan for the rest of the weekend for us?"

"Well... I guess we need to start, to get you packed up and ready to leave. I've taken next week off to be here with you, so we'll have time together our last week here as husband and wife." Her eyes dimmed as she spoke, and he could see that all this was killing her.

But as much as he wanted to stay back with her, he knew he had no choices left here. His African woman Jane, and his child Tracie had already landed at Ben's place, and he had phoned to say he'd found a small two-bedroom place for Samuel and Jane. Ben had been completely surprised when she showed up at his door with Samuel's little girl. Samuel hadn't warned him of anything. But Ben was an African man himself, and he knew all too well how these things worked back home with arranged marriages. Family bonds were strong. He also knew there was no way out for Samuel, but to live up to his family obligations. He felt so sorry for Nicole and Samuel. He'd been there with them most of their married life, and Nicole had opened her heart and home to him, and treated him like a brother. Samuel must be crying inside to leave such a woman behind. He worried about how Nicole would be on her own too. He knew Samuel was her whole life, and that she'd given up everything to be by his side for years. It was tragic, but they were African men, and they didn't turn their backs on their blood. Jane had Samuel's child who was his own flesh and blood; he had to do the right thing now. But who did the right thing for Nicole? He wondered. Who was going to be there for this special lady when she fell apart? He hated that part of their African customs, and that's why he'd never become involved with anyone in North America. He didn't want to hurt an unsuspecting good woman, who'd be ripped apart in the crossfire. Ben's family had already picked out a bride for him, and he knew he had to commit to that relationship soon and have children of his own.

***

Samuel sat staring at Nicole as they slowly ate dinner.

"Are you sure you want to take a whole week off? What did your boss say about that?"

"I told him the truth Sam, and he understood. I have over three weeks of vacation left that I haven't taken this year, so it's okay. And to be honest, I need some time with you. I mean... we don't even know when we'll see each other next. And then the following week Mommy, and Grand will be driving down with my sister. Marilyn will be moving in with me for the summer, so I won't be alone here."

"Really? I am glad to hear that lady. I was worried about you living here all alone."

"I guess I just forgot to mention it. I have lots on my mind these days."

Nicole went into their bedroom, and picked out the new dress she'd been saving for a special occasion. She guessed this was it; if she wanted Samuel to see her in it, she'd better put it on tonight. She stood in front of the long mirror, and turned around and looked at herself. The dress was red, and hugged her curves in all the right places. She put on high-heeled gold shoes, and long gold earrings.

Tonight she was going to create a night to remember, one with music, dancing, and lovemaking. They were going to celebrate their love, their bond and their life together. As she stepped out into the living room, Samuel couldn't believe how sexy, and alluring his wife looked tonight.

"Oh Wow lady, I am not even sure I want to leave this house. I think I need to take that dress off right now," he joked.

"All in due time, my love. Tonight we're going to dance and laugh, and have fun." She grabbed his hand, and pulled him out the door. As they enter the night club a special song started to play.

"I love this song. Let's dance!" She moved in perfect rhythm to the music, and he moved equally as well beside her. Most people in the club watched them because they looked so beautiful together. Samuel began to have an unpleasant feeling in his gut, when another man started looking at his wife. Soon she would become lonely, and some other man would take advantage of her loneliness. The very thought of it made him crazy. Jealousy was running through his veins, as he watched the other men stare at his wife.

"Babe... you look so far away. What's on your mind?" Nicole yelled over the music.

"I was just thinking of how many men, will be after my lovely wife when I am not here."

"Oh you're such a silly man! There will be no other men after me when you're gone; I'll just be working and taking care of my sister."

"I hope so." Maybe for a while he thought, but how long could he really expect that of a woman like her.

"How about we go home, and take this sexy little dress off?" He whispered in her ear.

"You naughty boy! But somehow I like that idea," she laughed. On the drive home, they were both sitting quietly in the car, lost their own worlds. Nicole looked over at Samuel once or twice; she knew he was worried about leaving her behind.

"Darling, you're so quiet tonight. What's really on your mind?" She asked.

"The same thing that's on your mind; we're just not talking about it."

"That's because we're pretending that it's not happening."

"But it is Lady, and we have to deal with it sooner or later. You know I will be coming back as often as I can."

"I know. We'll adjust, we always do right, its temporary?"

"Yes." He turned his head and looked away. It was that one look that told Nicole everything she needed to know. But she was still in denial. Samuel would never leave her like that, she told herself. He loved her. He would be back, that much she knew for sure. They crawled into bed that night and made passionate, fiery love. He couldn't get enough of her in this last week together, it felt like she would disappear if he let her go, and for all he knew she would soon disappear from his life. Soon after she was asleep, Samuel got up and called Ben. Samuel knew he'd still be awake; he was a night owl.

"Hello?" Ben said.

"It's me."

"You! My friend, must be hating yourself about now."

"I am brother. How are Jane and Tracie settling in there? Sorry I didn't tell you they were coming."

"Yes, that was quite a surprise old man! They are doing well, and your place is just across the street from mine, so I check in on them every day. When are you here?"

"I am leaving at the end of the week. I will be there on Friday morning. Can you pick me up at the airport? I have a few suitcases, so I hope your car is a big one."

"I am sure we can manage. How is Nicole handling everything? What did you tell her?"

"I just told her I was coming over to stay with you, until I get settled there with my career."

"Oh wow Sam. She doesn't even know what is going to hit her then? She is a good woman my man. This will destroy her."

"I know. I can't tell her Ben. I don't know how. So I am just leaving. I know it's heartless, but I will come back here, and see her as often as I can. I know it's not fair, but what in hell in this life is?"

"You know leading a double life will make you an old man fast, and it will catch up with you. You will not be able to keep that up for long."

"Maybe not. But for now, it's all I can figure out to do. I have to go. I will see you on Friday. Please tell Jane, that I am coming in on Friday, and will be there with them by Friday night."

"Will do my brother. Try to keep calm Sam. I know all this is killing you inside too."

"I am trying, but it's the hardest thing I have ever had to do, Goodnight Ben." Samuel hung the phone up, and went back to bed. He put his arms around Nicole, and watched her sleep. His heart was breaking. He knew he had taken the best years of her life from her, only to leave her behind, and that would haunt him forever in his mind and soul. The morning sunlight came through Nicole's window and woke her up. Samuel was still sleeping, so she gently slipped out of bed, and went out to the kitchen to make some coffee, and breakfast for them. She fried bacon and eggs, and made toast. As she puts the coffee pot on the table, she looked up and there was Samuel, standing in his pajama bottoms looking at her with a big smile. She was standing in her big white t-shirt, with her hair hanging down around her shoulders. He always thought she was the prettiest, first thing in the morning, natural and without makeup.

"Good morning, how did you sleep?" She walked over and wrapped her arms around him tightly, just like she always had every morning that they'd woken up together.

"I slept okay, thanks. You?"

"Good. You hungry? I just finished making breakfast. Come and eat."

"I know; the smell woke me up. Nothing smells as good in the morning as fried bacon, and fresh coffee."

"That's why I decided to make it for us. It's a treat, and I want you to have happy memories, of our life here together." She looked at him like she knew he may one day forget about her.

218

"I have nothing but happy memories of you my dear. But this place... well, that's a different story."

"I guess we need to get you packed up today. It's already Monday, so let's get started."

"Yes, I guess so. I don't want to, but I know I have to," he said looking down at his plate.

"Let's start with all your medical books. You decide which ones you are taking for now, and we'll pack them today. Tomorrow we'll pack your clothes."

"Okay. That sounds like a plan."

They packed all day, and by night, the realization had set in that he was really leaving. Nicole made dinner, while Samuel went to the store, he needed to just to get away and think. He picked up Nicole a bunch of red roses, and went back home. Nicole had made his favorite food, fish and rice with homemade raisin bran muffins. She took a shower, and put on a simple pair of jeans and a white cotton shirt. She thought maybe after dinner they could go walking together. In the beginning of their relationship, they'd walked together all the time, but lately they hadn't because of their limited amount of time together.

"I am back" he called from the kitchen.

She walked into the room, and there he stood with a huge bouquet of roses.

"Wow for me? They are so lovely! Thanks so much for thinking of me. How very sweet." Her smile beamed at him.

"It's nothing really. I just wanted you to know that you're the most special woman, I could ever meet in this life," he said in a sad voice.

"Thank you babe, are you hungry?" She said brightly. "Supper's ready, with all your favorites tonight." She tried her best to put on a happy face for him, but he knew her heart was breaking just as much as his.

"Nicole... baby, I just want you to know that this move, is not an easy one for me either. I don't want to leave you behind."

"I know, we've been over all this before. Why do you feel so guilty over everything?"

"I guess because you deserve so much better than what I have given you. It has

219

all been so hard on you, and now it seems like I am abandoning you, and you'll be alone here on top of everything else."

"It has been a lot. I won't tell you a lie – it's been very hard on me all these years. And I hate the fact that you have to go away again. I'm scared to death that our life will never be the same. But I understand the reason why you need to go, and I wouldn't hold you back for anything. I want you to be happy in this life, and I know you will never be happy until you can practice medicine, so you need to go. You have my blessing, and I will pray for your success every day that you are away from me my love. I am not that little girl you met years ago. I'm stronger and wiser now. And I won't be alone; Marilyn will be here with me. I'll have family around me a lot. So no need to worry yourself. Like you said, we'll see each other as much as we can, until we're living together again. The time will fly by; you'll see. Now let's eat before everything gets cold, and then let's go for a long walk like we used too. It's such a lovely evening."

"Okay. If that's what you want, we can do that." His words had no joy in them, because a part of him wanted her to need him, and miss him more, than she was letting on. He was afraid she'd meet someone else when he was gone. He was about to go live with Jane and his daughter, and that scared him to death too. He would be living his life with strangers for a while, until he bonded with them. He knew that would change him, and she would eventually come to see that change in him. There was only so much a man could hide.

They finished dinner, went out hand-in-hand, and walked for a long time, mostly in silence, just taking comfort in each other. When they came home later that night, Samuel drew a hot bath for Nicole, and let her soak a while. Then he gave her a long backrub.

"Thanks so much for that backrub my love, I am going to miss those. That helps a lot in getting me to relax."

"Well if that did not do the trick, I have other ways." He smiled at her.

"I know you do, and I think I want those ways too." They made love before falling asleep. The days passed by quickly, and the time had come. It was the day Samuel had to leave for the airport. His clothes and books were all packed; he'd only left a few things behind, like some clothing he would use whenever he returned to see her. A few old medical books he didn't really need any more, were all that remained of their life together. It all now fit into one small drawer in Nicole's bedroom, the same room that he'd shared with her for the last one year. He took one last look around, and then put everything into the car. Nicole drove him to the airport in silence; they looked over at each other every now and then. Twenty minutes later, they parked the car at the airport.

"Well we're here safe and sound. Let's get you inside and checked in."

"Let's say goodbye here. I want to go the rest of the way alone."

She knew that would be easier. "Okay. I understand." She fought back the tears. "I will call you in a few hours and let you know I am there, so no worrying my sweetheart."

"I can't believe you're leaving me again. I guess I didn't realize how hard this last goodbye, was going to be."

"Not goodbye Lady. Just so long for now. I will see you soon, I promise. Please no tears my dear, I can't bare to see you cry because of me."

"I am sorry. You be safe and call me as soon as you can," she said in a small voice that he could barely hear.

She got out of the car, and came around to where he was standing. She wrapped her arms around him, and held him as tightly as she could. She looked into his eyes, and kissed him with all her heart, to let him know how loved he was.

He never said another word to her. He took his suitcases and walked away. He couldn't even look back; he was too afraid of what he would see. He was scared that his own eyes would betray him, as he was betraying her.

She stood by the car and watched him leave, her eyes full of tears as she stood there and watched her heart walk away. After he disappeared inside, she got into her car and drove home. She entered their apartment, sat down in her rocking chair, and sipped her tea. The apartment was quiet, and she found herself restless. She got up and walked into the bedroom she'd shared with Samuel. She sat on the bed where they'd made love, and slept together only the night before. It's funny she thought, how twenty-four hours can change a home. How empty it now seemed with him gone. No one to cook for, or to dress up for. She undressed and put on one of the big shirts he'd left behind. Then she curled up in their bed and fell asleep.

The ringing of the phone later that evening, woke her up. "Hello?" She said sleepily.

"Hi, my sweetheart were you sleeping already? It's only seven o'clock."

"Yes I was, I guess I fell asleep for a while. How was your flight darling?"

"It was good. Ben picked me up, and I am just going to start to unpack, so I just wanted to touch base with you, and let you know I am here safe and sound, and missing you already."

"Right back at you Sam. Did you have dinner yet?"

"No not yet, but I will soon. What about you?"

"No I was sleeping. But I'll get up and make something now I guess. Is there a phone number there I can call you at? What's Ben's number?"

He had to think fast, because he wasn't even staying with Ben, and he couldn't give her his other contact number where he was staying.

"Just call me on my cell; I will always have that on me, and you can reach me easier."

"Okay... if you think that's best. I'll call you later, and say Goodnight after you unpack."

"Okay Lady, we will talk later. Go eat something now, please." He hoped he would be able to answer her call later. He was about to leave Ben and go to his new home, where his daughter Tracie, and Jane were waiting for him.

Nicole got up from her bed, went out to the kitchen and heated up some soup, and sat down in her rocking chair to eat alone. Her sister would arrive tomorrow, and her apartment would seem less empty then. She was looking forward to seeing her grandmother and mother tomorrow; they'll all stay with her for a few days.

Samuel picked up his suitcases, and headed for the door. "Come on Ben. Let's get this over with. Jane will be wondering where I am."

"How was Nicole tonight?"

"She seemed okay I guess. I just hope she eats. She doesn't when she is unhappy, and she gets way too thin. But her mother and family are arriving tomorrow. Her sister is moving in with her, so at least she will not be alone. They usually make sure, she is eating okay."

Ben drove Samuel over to his new little apartment, and he went to the door and knocked.

The door opened and there stood, a little girl about ten years old. He'd only seen her a few times in the last ten years. She was a little beauty with long curly dark hair, a sweet smile and big dark eyes just like his. Tracie had Samuel's smile too.

"Hello Daddy! Welcome home!" She smiled up at him, and wrapped her arms around his waist.

"Hello there. How's my girl?" He kissed her on the cheek, and smiled down at her. "I got something special for you my baby girl. A surprise."

"Really Daddy! What is it?" She looked very excited to have her father with her.

He handed her a small jewelry box. She quickly opened it and inside was a golden heart, which was surrounded by diamonds on a chain. It was small but suited her perfectly. She put it around her neck, and wore it proudly. It was her first gift from her father.

He looked across the room at the woman standing there.

"Jane! How are you? You are looking well my dear." He walked over, and gave her a kiss on the cheek. He pulled another jewelry box out of his pocket, and handed it to her. "I hope you like these."

She opened the box, and inside was a pair of blue topaz earrings. "Yes my husband, I like them very much. Thank you." She kissed him on his cheek in return. It was a very formal kiss, without any kind of passion. It was a kiss of respect.

"Come my husband, give me your suitcases. I will unpack them. Go to the table; I have food prepared for you." Jane was a woman of ceremony, and she knew her place very well. It was her job to make sure her husband was well cared for.

For the first time ever, they all sat at the same table and ate their first meal as a family. His little girl's eyes lit up at seeing them all together. That made him happy in his heart. She was his flesh and blood, and he knew he had a lifetime commitment to her. He was falling in love with her as he looked into her sweet eyes. He felt guilty for having left her so many years ago. He looked across the table and noticed Jane staring at him.

"Thank you for the food Jane. It is very nice."

"Do not thank me for food, my husband. It is my duty to you." She smiled. Jane was a tiny woman almost boyish like, but she had a pretty face, and lovely dark eyes. She was soft-spoken and very intelligent. She could sense Samuel's discomfort, and she wanted him to feel welcome in his new home. She wondered what his life had been like all those years in Canada, yet in many ways she didn't really want to know. She didn't want to know of other women her husband may have had, or of the one he was possibly leaving behind. She only wanted to make him hers, and she would do everything in her power to do just that.

It all felt so strange to Samuel now, to be sitting there with them, to hear another woman, call him her husband. Many years ago, they had done a ceremony which made them husband and wife. It would not have been legal in North America, but many times in Africa, that was what they did. In Jane's mind, Samuel had always been her husband. They were family, and she was going to make it work between them. She had been studying long hours herself for the medical exam. She had become a doctor back in Africa, and wanted to be able to work alongside her husband; they shared the same love of medicine. She would help him prepare for this exam, so he would be successful.

"You must be very tired, my husband. Why not take a shower and go sleep? I will sleep for this night with our daughter. You need time to adjust to everything. Just go and sleep, and do not worry. Everything will work out here for you." Jane got up from the table, went out to the kitchen, and cleaned up. Samuel's daughter gave him a kiss and hug, and then went off to bed.

Samuel undressed, and got in the shower. He put on clean pajama bottoms, and laid down on his bed. He looked around the small room. It had just a bed and dresser. It had none of Nicole's flare; she always knew how to make things look beautiful with very little money. But this room had none of that appeal. It felt cold and dark to him, as he lay there. It smelled like Jane, and he was so used to the sweet smell of his Nicole.

"My God! How am I going to do this?" He said out loud to himself.

His phone rang, and he quickly grabbed it. He didn't want to disrupt Jane.

"Hello?"

"Hi baby. Did you get unpacked yet? How was dinner?" Nicole was curled up in their big bed all alone.

"Yes I did my sweetheart. Dinner was fine. Ben has gotten to be a good cook over the last few years," he laughed.

"How very lucky for you! You must be very tired tonight?"

"Yes I am. How was your evening? Did you eat?"

"I had a bowl of soup, and some tea with a biscuit. Don't worry, I'm not starving over here."

"You had better not be. I miss you Lady, more than you know already."

"I miss you more. What's your plan for this week?"

"I am going to get set up to do the exam, and then start applying for some kind of job, I guess."

"Okay then. Get some rest tonight. We can talk soon. I love you."

"I love you too Lady." They hung up the phone, both beginning to realize that their life would be a lot of this for a long while.

She turned out the lights, but could still feel his presence in her bed, as she hugged her pillow tight, tears run down her cheeks until she finally fell asleep.

Samuel closed his eyes and when he did, he could still see Nicole's sad eyes as he fell off to sleep.

The next morning Samuel was up early. He went out to the kitchen to make some coffee. Jane and his daughter had not gotten up yet. He made a pot of coffee. It was strange to eat alone. Nicole was such a morning person, and she was always up, and had breakfast ready when he got up. But he could see that both Jane and his daughter, liked to sleep in late in the morning. There was a lot he needed to do today, and he wanted to call Nicole this morning as well.

He left a short note for Jane, explaining that he'd gone to Ben's, and would be back later that day. He rang Ben's doorbell at eight o'clock.

"Wow Samuel, you're up early this morning. What's up brother? How was your night?" Ben made some coffee for the two of them.

"It was fine. Let's talk about what I should do next, for this medical exam here brother."

"Jane has been studying herself for the same exam. I have given her all the special notes to study, so I suggest you get to know your new wife, and study with her. You can help each other a lot with that. The exam sits in two weeks. Then I will get you

225

on at my hospital. I have already spoken to them about you; you can go in for an interview, in a few weeks when the exam is over. In the meantime, how is your money situation?"

"I have been saving so I will be okay for a little while, but will I need to work soon."

"If you need some extra cash just ask my brother. I have good savings now, so you need not worry about money right now. You have many things on your mind to worry about."

"Thanks Ben, I am grateful for all your help. Can I use your phone to call Nicole? I will block the number, so she doesn't know it is not on my cell. I just need to hear her voice this morning."

"Sure brother, tell her I said good morning."

Samuel dialed the phone. "Good morning Lady."

"Good morning. How are you this morning?"

"I am doing well, and there is someone who would like to say hello." He handed the phone to Ben.

"Hello Nicole. How is my sister today?"

"Ben! It's so nice to hear your voice. I am managing okay, I guess. Just waiting for my family to arrive this morning. I hope you are taking good care of my husband over there."

"The very best of care my dear. You take care of yourself too Nick."

"I will. Many hugs to you my brother."

"Many hugs right back at you my dear."

He handed the phone back to Samuel.

"Ben is alive and well. You see my dear, we are going to start studying this morning for the exam, so say hello to your family for me and I will call you soon."

"Okay. Goodbye for now baby."

"You know brother, I know why you did that, but you can't do it forever. One day you will have to leave her for good."

"I guess so, but I can't right now. I need time to deal with everything, and get used to my new life." He knew he was being selfish, but he still wanted, and needed her in his life, and the saddest thing was that he couldn't imagine a time when he wouldn't. Samuel walked back to his new home, and new little family.

"Good morning my husbands. You got up so early! I made food for you. Come now sit and eat." Jane was studying his every move; she needed to try to understand this man, so she could be a good wife to him.

"Thank you Jane. Where is our daughter this morning?"

"Tracie has gone off to school. She is in the fourth grade now. You have missed a lot with this child. You need to try and get to know Tracie better now," Jane said with a warm smile.

"Yes, I know I do. I have missed a lot, and I guess you and I need to try and get to know each other better as well. Ben tells me you are studying for the medical exam too. He suggests we study together."

"Yes of course my husband. That is my plan, to assist you in achieving your goals here. I am your wife, and I am here to help you in whatever you need Samuel. You must leave your life in Canada behind you now. Your life is here with us."

He knew exactly what she meant. Jane was a smart woman, and she knew that Samuel would have had a woman back in Canada, to help him all those years he was there. She also knew he had been over there much too long, and would have formed a deep bond with whomever he had been with. She knew she had to gain his love and trust quickly, in order to keep him there with her and their child. Jane knew how their culture worked; she knew Samuel would remain present in their lives from now on, but she wanted more than that. She wanted the love of her husband. He was more attractive than she remembered him being years ago, and she already loved him. She'd never stopped. Even when he'd left her back in Africa, she'd remained faithful to him. And now she was ready to fight for his heart, and be the kind of wife he would fall in love with.

"Yes, I would like to study with you Jane. Where should we start first?"

"Let's set some time aside every day, from eleven to three for studying. When our daughter is back from school, you can spend time with her until bedtime, and then we can study for another few hours after that. We have much to do, and we have only a few weeks until we write the exam, so I have prepared notes on what we must cover

227

and in what time frame."

"Wow! I am impressed. That's good work. Let's get started then." Samuel looked at Jane with admiration. He was happy she was a woman he could rely on.

The time flew by and before they knew it, they heard the footsteps of their daughter as she entered their little apartment.

"Hello Father and Mother. Good afternoon to you both." She smiled and ran over, giving them both a hug.

"Are you hungry Tracie?" Jane asked.

"Yes, very much so Mother, what do we have to eat?"

"Come and sit with your father, and I will go and prepare food for both of you."

Samuel's daughter showed him her homework for the week, and they sat doing it together. He helped Tracie with her spelling, and made jokes with her to help her learn better.

"Come my family. The food is ready now."

They sat at the table, and ate the African food Jane had prepared. She was a good cook, and the food reminded Samuel of his mother's cooking. He was growing fond of Jane, and was starting to see her as a good light.

He didn't really know her yet, but he knew in his heart she would be a good wife for him. His family had chosen well for him after all. He felt sorry that he'd missed so much time with his child. She'd lived under the guidance of his eldest brother. He began to realize how much he owed his brother, for keeping them both happy and safe over the years.

"Now it is time for bed Tracie. Say Goodnight to your father please."

"Goodnight Daddy. Will you be here in the morning?" She looked at him with her lovely dark eyes.

"Yes of course I will. We can eat breakfast together, and I will walk with you to school." He smiled his big wonderful smile at her.

She hugged and kissed them both Goodnight, and went off to bed.

Jane looked at Samuel and smiled. "She loves you very much, and she is so happy you are finally here. When you were away, every night she would ask me, when is daddy coming home, and I would just say very soon. I am so glad you're here too my husband. Would you like to sleep in our bed tonight with me?" Jane asked with a warm smile that said he was welcome.

"Thank you for being such a good mother to our child. I am pleased with you Jane. But I would like just a little more time to get to know you, so I hope you don't mind, but I will sleep here on the couch tonight. And thank you for everything. Goodnight."

"As you wish, my husband." Jane left to go sleep alone in their bedroom. She was disappointed that he had refused her offer, but she knew he needed time to get over the woman from Canada, and get to know her better. It was all right by her; they had the rest of their lives to do just that.

Samuel lay on the couch. It was uncomfortable, and he couldn't sleep well at all. He kept seeing Nicole crying in his dreams. He knew now where he belonged, and he felt very guilty that he hadn't done his duty over the years to his child. He also still missed Nicole like crazy.

He couldn't help but compare the two women in his mind. They both were so giving of themselves, yet they were also very different in so many ways. Nicole was such a beauty, with great style and class, and had been courageous through all that she'd endured over the years by his side. She was a woman men only dreamed of, and he was so lucky to have had her all those years.

And now as he looked closely at Jane, he realized she was a gentle soul with a sweet smile, and who was very wise. She wasn't a beautiful woman, but she was attractive and she was his own kind. She knew her place in his life, and he knew she would be a good kind wife to him. He didn't feel love for her the way he did for Nicole, she made all his passions and senses come alive. But he knew in time he would grow to love Jane in a comfortable kind of way, just as his brother had said.

It amazed him now as he thought of his life in Canada, and how different his life would be in America. He finally fell asleep, and woke up when his phone started to ring. It was near seven in the morning.

He grabbed it as quickly he could, so it would not wake up Jane and his daughter. "Hello?"

"Good morning baby. Did I wake you up?" Nicole sat drinking her morning coffee in her rocking chair.

"Yes you did, but it's ok. How are you?"

"I am missing you this morning my love. When are you coming home again?" Her voice sounded lonely.

"Soon my love, very soon. I am writing the exam in a week, after that I will be back for a few days. Maybe I can come for a four-day weekend. Ben has a job lined up for me after that. Once I start working it will be harder to leave here for a while, so I will come by before I start."

"I hope so. Marilyn, Mom and Grand say hi. They arrived safely.

"Really? Just tell them I am fine, and I will be back home with you very soon. Now have a great day my sweetheart, and I will talk with you later tonight."

"Okay, you too." Nicole hung up the phone, but there was a small voice speaking to her somewhere inside her gut, saying that Samuel was distant in the way he'd spoken with her, and he'd kept the conversation very short. It sounded like he couldn't speak freely. Maybe it was just her own mind playing tricks on her, because she missed him so much already.

"Oh Grand there you are. You're up early this morning. Would you like some coffee? I just made some."

"Yes, please. Was that our Samuel you were talking with this morning?"

"Who else would I be talking to so early yes of course? He says he's doing fine, but I miss him so much already. How am I going to do this?" She looked at her with tears in her eyes.

"I know it's hard, but you'll just have to get used to it and build a life for a while without him. Let your sister and friends, all be a bigger part of your life now."

That was the best advice she could give her. She knew Samuel was never coming back, and that it was just a matter of time, before it all fell apart for good. She was an old woman, and she knew that this kind of deceit would wound, and maybe even totally destroy her. She only hoped, she would recover, and have a better life with someone else in the future. But she also knew this girl, and knew that when she loved, it ran deep.

Sarah sat quietly and thought to herself, that maybe the old woman was right this time, and it made her mad as hell. How could he just leave her beautiful girl like that, after all the years she stood by his side? Damn him to hell she thought, and may the good Lord, forgive me for my thoughts, but what kind of man acts like that she wondered.

Later that night as Nicole got ready for bed, she went over to her jewelry box to look at the gifts Samuel had given her over the years. When she opened it, she noticed that the blue topaz earrings she loved so much wasn't there. She must have misplaced them, she thought. It bothered her terribly to think that she may have lost them. They meant so much to her; they were the first Christmas gift Samuel had ever gotten her, and she'd always treasured them. She turned all her dresser drawers inside out, but she couldn't find them. What in the world could she have done with them? She wondered. They were her birthstone, and she only wore them on business trips or special occasions. As she thought about it, she was sure she'd put them back, exactly where she always did last time she'd worn them.

She lay in her bed, heartbroken at the loss. She didn't know how she would ever tell Samuel she'd lost them. She guessed that it was probably best not to mention them at all until she found them. She fell asleep, but was restless all night long. When she got up the next morning, it was all too obvious that she hadn't slept well. She had dark circles around her eyes. She went out to the kitchen to find her mother making breakfast. She'd prepared bacon, and eggs and toast, and had a fresh pot of coffee on the table for them.

"Good morning dear. It looks like you didn't sleep well at all last night."

"I didn't. I was looking for my blue topaz earrings, you know the ones Samuel gave me one year for Christmas? I can't seem to find them anywhere, and I'm so upset."

"Don't worry, we can look together after breakfast. Maybe your sister borrowed them for some reason." But she knew that was unlikely. Marilyn has never worn much jewelry.

"I guess we can ask her."

"Come and eat. They're only earrings; they can be replaced if need be."

But how do you replace a memory? Nicole thought. After breakfast, she stared out the living room window, remembering that Christmas. When she opened the box she'd been so surprised. She had admired the earrings in the window of a jewelry store one day when they were walking together, but never even bothered to check on the price – she knew they couldn't afford them. Samuel had gone back, bargained with the store owner, and purchased them for her. It was one of the rare happy memories she had with Samuel, and now they were gone, just like him.

Millie just wasn't sure why Nicole couldn't see what Samuel's game was about these days. She guessed that the love that Nicole felt for him, must be blocking the sight, and that maybe she was in denial that a man she loved so much, could betray her the same way the Nova Scotia politicians, and medical community had. But sooner or later, the truth would come to light, and she dreaded that day.

***

Night after night, Samuel continued to sleep alone on the couch. The day had finally come when he and Jane would write the exam. He felt fully prepared to write it, thanks mostly to Jane, who'd sat by his side, and assisted him every day with his studies. He was grateful to have her in his life now, but he still wasn't ready to accept her into his bed. He needed to visit Nicole after the exam was written, and he didn't want to start anything with Jane until after that visit home with Nicole. He knew he'd never be able to look her in the eye, and hold her the way he always had once he'd slept with Jane. He also knew he had no right to even see her again, but he had to. He longed to see her, and make love to her again.

"Come now. We will be late. Sit by me when we write, and just relax Samuel. You know all this information. Just write as quickly as you can."

"I will Jane. And good luck to you too."

They wrote for hours. It seemed to come easy for both of them, there were no trick questions. They were all straightforward, testing their medical knowledge the way it should, unlike the test he'd written in Canada. He knew he would pass this exam on the first try. He felt so relieved when he was done that he wanted to celebrate.

"How was the exam for you Jane?" He asked as they walked out.

"It was good. How was it for you?"

"Good as well. Let's go out and celebrate. Ben has offered to sit with our daughter tonight. Let me take you out to dinner, and maybe dancing. Do you like music?"

"That would be wonderful. I would like that very much." She smiled knowing, she was making process with him every day. Maybe tonight would be the night, they finally made love. She had waited for many years to be with him again.

Jane put on a flowered dress, with the blue topaz earrings Samuel had given her. She put on high heel shoes with socks, and came out to greet Samuel. As soon as he saw her, he laughed out loud.

"Why do you laugh?" Jane said, feeling shy.

"Because you do not wear socks with high heels, you wear pantyhose. Please go and change into them. We cannot go out like that." She walked away and did as he asked.

He knew Jane was more of a homebody, and did not dress with much flair. That was okay by him, because he would not go out with her the same way he had with Nicole. Their life together would be a very different one, than what he'd had with Nicole. Nicole was like a shining star on his arm for other men to admire. Jane was a woman most men would look right past; only a man who was married to her, would enjoy her comfort. And in some ways he was happy that no other man would want her, or tempt her. He had always been worried that some other man would capture Nicole's attention, and eventually get her in his bed. Samuel and Jane went to a nice dinner club. They ate dinner and danced to the slow songs. Jane wasn't much of a dancer, but she did feel good in his arms – it had been a while now, and he was missing female company. She was doing her best to turn on her husband, and she was hoping for a loving night with him.

"Let's go home my husband. I would like to have time alone with you tonight."

"Okay... I guess." He felt a little uncomfortable at first with the idea, but he knew it had to happen sometime, so why not tonight? After all, he was a man with needs, and she was his wife, and willing to meet those needs. He had another drink, and took Jane home.

They entered their little apartment, and Jane excused herself for a moment. She returned a few minutes later, dressed in a long black nightgown, which was only slightly revealing. She'd been saving it for the day that Samuel would finally want her in his bed. They still felt a little uncomfortable with each other, but she took Samuel by the hand, and led him into their tiny little bedroom, where she had only a dim light on and the bed turned down. She looked up at him with her beautiful dark eyes shining in the dim light, and Samuel could see how much this woman was longing for him. He closed his eyes, and gently lifted her onto the bed. He took off her gown, and touched her smooth dark skin. Jane had small breasts and a round behind. She was nice to look at, but she didn't stir his soul. Not the way he had hoped she would, or the way he was used to. He gently lowered himself on top of her, and slowly entered her. Jane gave a breathless moan, and he started to move slowly inside of her. He closed his eyes, and tried to forget that she wasn't Nicole, and after a little while they had finished. He lay quietly beside Jane, wishing he could bolt from the bed. Jane put her head on his strong shoulder.

"We will get better at this. Just give us a little time." It was as though she could sense his disappointment.

"Yes we will. Try to sleep now." His voice spoke volumes to his new lover.

She now knew that her husband's heart was still very far away. She wondered what the other woman was like. She must be very beautiful to have kept her husband away for so long, she thought. Samuel was awakened by his cell phone ringing. He looked at his watch. It was only eight in the morning, and he knew it would be Nicole. But Jane was beside him, and he couldn't answer the phone.

"Who is calling you so early? Should I get it for you?" She asked in a sleepy voice.

"No! You cannot get my phone. In fact, I prefer that you never answer my phone. It may be a job opportunity, and I should be the only one to answer it."

She knew he meant what he said, and that it was mostly like because of the woman in Canada, who would still be calling him, if he hadn't yet told her the truth of his situation. She hoped that wasn't the case, but she suspected that it was. Samuel got up and took a shower, and then came back out to the kitchen, and made coffee. Jane had fallen back to sleep; she loved to sleep late most mornings.

Samuel paced the floor, waiting for the right time to call Nicole back. He checked in on Jane, and found she was still asleep, so he guessed that he could call back now.

"Hello?" Nicole said.

"Hello Lady. Sorry I missed your call. I guess I was in the shower."

"I guess you had a very long shower. That was way over an hour ago babe. How is everything going for you?"

"It's going well. I wrote the exam, it was so easy here. Nothing like the one in Canada. Just straightforward questions that actually tested my medical knowledge."

"That's so great! When do you hear if you passed it?"

"In a week I think. Ben has set up a job interview for me today and after that, I will book a flight home to see you for four days this weekend. How does that sound?" He was so excited to tell her the good news.

"That sounds great! I can't wait to see you. This weekend we'll have our place all to ourselves, Marilyn has gone back home to visit Mom. So the timing is perfect." She smiled for the first time in days.

"Well good then. I have to go now, but I will see you soon." He hung up the phone as quickly as he could – he could hear Jane's footsteps coming out of their bedroom.

"Do you want food?" Jane asked. She hadn't bothered to brush her hair or wash her face, and she looked awful. Samuel just stared at her, somewhat startled to see her looking so unkempt.

"Sure, but maybe you should go clean up first before Ben, and our daughter come over."

"Yes, okay sorry I will." She left and took a shower and combed her hair, put on her face and then returned in a long African dress.

She went out to the kitchen, and prepared fried eggs and tomatoes, with bread for Samuel. He had started to put on a little weight around the middle, because most of her dishes were fried. He would eventually tell her to start cooking their meals a little more healthy, but for now he didn't want to upset her, or make her feel like she wasn't a good wife or mother. But he thought she should know better regarding their food; after all she was a medical doctor. Ben knocked at the door of Samuel and Jane's apartment, and within seconds their little girl came running in.

"Oh daddy! I'm so glad you're still here!" She looked up at him with eyes that said she adored him already.

"Of course I am still here. I told you I am not going away. Only on short little trip, and then I will return right back to you." He hugged her and gave her a big smile.

"Ben come in and sit down. Jane has made food for us. I was hoping to go do some errands with you after the interview, if that's okay?"

"Yes, sure old man we can do that." Ben grinned at him. He was so happy that his dear friend was back in his world again.

"Jane, I will be gone for a few hours today with Ben. Do you need anything done while I am out?"

"No. I will go to the store later and get food for us." She smiled at him as she spoke.

"Good. We will be off then." Samuel and Ben left and went to the hospital where Ben worked. He introduced Samuel to the chief of staff there, and explained Samuel's situation, and asked if he could help him with a job.

"Samuel it's good to meet you. Ben has told me many good things about you," said Chris Carlson, the chief of staff.

"Thank you sir. It's a pleasure to meet with you. Thank you for seeing us today." Samuel shook hands with him and took a seat.

"I see on your resume you were a clinical assistant in the emergency department back in Halifax, Nova Scotia for a while."

"Yes I was. I was hoping to gain an internship there, but was not successful, and so I moved here, hoping to proceed on with my career. My wife and daughter also lives here with me, so I need a job to support my family."

Chris Carlson was also a black man, who had managed to work his way up the ladder, he knew just how difficult it could be.

"Okay Samuel. I'll find you something. Please leave me some references, and I'll check them out, and then give you a call later on today."

"That would be great. Here is Dr. Hays' number, the one I worked directly for back in Halifax. Thank you Dr. Carlson; I really appreciate all your help today."

Samuel and Ben walked to a little coffee shop just outside the hospital, and sat down to chat.

"Samuel ordered a muffin and coffee, they were exactly like the one's Nicole made for him at home.

"Thank you for everything Ben. I hope to start working as soon as I can here. But I need to travel back to Canada this weekend. It's been almost four weeks now, and I need to visit with Nicole. I will only be gone for about four days. I need you to cover for me if Jane starts asking questions."

"You are playing with fire, running back and forth. It'll catch up with you, and you'll end up hurting Nicole even worse. Just tell her the truth now. You can never go back there for good, and she can never come here either. Do the right thing, and just end it with her, so she can get on with her life. Be fair brother. She is a wonderful woman; you can't keep doing this to her." Ben looked angry.

"I know. You're right, but I love her, and I can't say goodbye yet. I don't know how. Just the thought of another man touching her makes me crazy. It's like I am stuck between two different worlds, and I can't let either one go." Samuel looked helpless.

"I understand old man, but at some point you must! You can't live in two different worlds. One of them will catch on, and you had better hope it's not Nicole, because if it is, you will completely destroy all faith and trust she ever had in you.

"You cannot choose Nicole, because you have too much to lose. You will lose your child, your family will disown you, and you will end up having no medical career. But if you choose Jane, you will have your child and your family's blessing. You will have a medical career here; I will make sure of that. The choice is already made for you. You just have to accept it. It's Christmas in a few weeks, so file the divorce papers now, and by Christmas you will be free to marry, the mother of your child here in America, you need to get her papers here." Ben hated the thought of Nicole getting hurt so badly, but he also hated the thought of his own kind getting left behind, especially when there was a child in the picture. Ben knew Samuel's heart was still with Nicole. He knew how much he had grown to love his child, and that he was becoming very fond of Jane too.

Poor Nicole he thought, doesn't have a fighting chance, and she doesn't even have anyone to warn her, or pick up the pieces when she falls apart. Samuel would have Jane and his child, and Ben to get him through it, but she would have no one that would understand her pain. Samuel sat in the chair with his head in his hands, and tears in his eyes as he began to realize that Ben was right. This trip would be the last time he would ever see his Nicole. He went down to city hall and filed the divorce papers, but asked that they wait for a few more weeks, until they served her with them. That would give him a chance to return back to Nicole one last time, and say his goodbyes.

Samuel walked back to his apartment, where Jane and his daughter, were waiting for him to have their evening meal.

"Welcome back my husband. You have been long today. We are waiting to eat with you," Jane said, staring at him, wondering where he'd been.

"I was out preparing for my new job, and I spend the day with Ben."

He looked at his daughter. "Daddy is leaving you tomorrow for just a short while, but I will be back in four days, I promise you that my baby girl. Is that okay with you Tracie my sweet baby?" He asked her with a sparkle in his eye.

"You are going away again?" She looked sad.

"Yes I am, but just for a short while, and then I will not go away for a very long time, I promise. Ok baby?

"I guess it will be okay then. But don't forget to come back daddy."

"I will not forget I promise." He smiled down at her. He wanted to make sure she understood that he would be back soon, and that he wasn't leaving her for very long.

Jane sat at the table, and just looked at him. She waited until after their daughter had gone to bed, to ask him where he was going. "May I ask where you are going away to for four days, and why?" Jane's eyes were piercing.

"I am going back to Canada for four days, just to tie up some loose ends. I will be back on Monday night."

"What kind of loose ends?"

"Please don't ask me these kinds of questions, and I will tell you no lies."

She never said another word to him; she just went off to bed. She knew he was going off to see the other woman back in Canada. She just didn't know why she'd thought when he came over to be with her, that his life in Canada would be all behind him. Now she was beginning to wonder exactly what the real situation was. It bothered her to know that he may be going back, to be with whatever woman, he'd had a life with there. She was helpless to do anything about it for now. She would just be patient, and hope that it was the last visit. Maybe he just needed closure, she thought. She could feel that he was growing closer to her and their child. So she wasn't worried; she was playing all her cards exactly right with him, and she knew she would win his heart, and would go on to have even more of his children very soon. She was a patient woman, who knew exactly how to treat the men from her own country. No woman other than one from the same area, would be able to do that. The poor woman in Canada would be left behind – Jane almost felt sorry for her. She knew the woman may not know anything about, what the real truth was of Samuel's life back in Africa. That was a shame, but it was of no real concern to her. Her only concern was for her own child, her own husband and herself. She was going to do whatever she had to, to make sure they remained a family, and that one day soon they would grow closer and expand their family, just like all African families did.

Samuel had his suitcases packed, and he decided to sleep out in the living room tonight, so he wouldn't wake Jane up when he left early in the morning. He could tell that she was upset with him, but he had to do what he had to do. He slept half-heartedly, and in his dreams he kept seeing Nicole's face smiling at him. He could almost feel his arms around her slender waist, and yet his soul felt very heavy. He was beginning to feel the impact of what he'd done by filing the divorce papers. He couldn't even imagine, what it would do to her when she received them. In his dreams and in his own heart, what he had done was already starting to haunt him.

Nicole woke up very excited. Samuel would be in her arms by tonight. She got up, had her coffee and got in the shower. She put on a blue dress that was simple yet sexy. The dress had a V-neck, so she decided to go to her jewelry box, and put on the little diamond heart necklace, Samuel had given her one year for Valentine's Day. She went over to her jewelry box, but to her surprise she couldn't find it. She became frantic, looking everywhere for it. Yet another piece of her precious jewelry was missing. What in the world could be happening to them? She knew Marilyn would never have taken them, and there had been no one else in her bedroom except her and Samuel. She didn't know how she could have been so careless with her own jewelry. She must never let him know how careless she'd been. She found another necklace, and put it on. A golden teardrop with a small gold chain. She wondered what was happening to her, why she was being so irresponsible with these precious things, and why was her mind so preoccupied that she was losing stuff.

She looked at her watch, and realized she was running late. She parked the car, and quickly walked towards the arrival gate. Her smile brightened as she saw Samuel standing there with his suitcase, patiently waiting for her. She started to run towards him now, and as she reached him, he pulled her into his arms.

"Wow, if it isn't my lovely lady, how I have missed you my sweetheart," he whispered in her ear.

"I bet I missed you more," she laughed.

"Let me look at you my dear," he said.

She did a quick turnaround for him, and pulled him by his hands out to the car. They put his suitcase in the trunk.

"Wait Lady. There is something I need to do." He pulled her close, and gave her a long hard kiss, that told her everything she needed to know – or so she thought at that moment.

"I think we should finish that one at home. Shall I drive or you?"

"I'll drive; you can talk to me, and tell me everything I missed."

"Ok for starters, Marilyn has a new job as a chef. I am doing okay at work. Just the same old stuff, but it's very busy as always. Richards's wife has been staying out of my way, thank heavens. The only thing missing is you my darling. How are things going over there?"

"Pretty good actually. I wrote the exam and I think I have passed. I went on an interview for a job, so we will see when I get back if I got it or not."

"I am so glad to hear that. I will be able to visit you soon when you get the job right?" His face looked stunned by that comment; he needed to think fast.

"Sure… just give me time to get settled in, and then we can talk about it."

"I'm so happy you're home for a few days. I've missed you so much."

"I have missed you too." He parked the car and they went inside their apartment. He looked around. Everything was spotless as usual, and he couldn't help but notice how fresh the apartment smelled. The place he now lived in didn't have the same flare or comfort, as his apartment with Nicole did. Everything had its place, and was styled beautifully. "I forgot how lovely you keep everything."

"You forgot already? I hope there are some other things you want to be reminded of as well." She laughed.

"Oh yes there are!" He picked her up, and carried her to their bedroom. He unzipped her dress and let it fall to the floor, revealing pale blue lace panties and matching bra. She took his breath away, she made his heart beat faster, and she still gave him butterflies in his stomach when he looked at her. She made him feel alive when he was with her. They laughed and loved with such passion, in spite of all the troubles that life had thrown at them. They'd been each other's safe haven for so many years. As he looked at his wife, he knew he was making the biggest mistake of his life, by leaving her behind. But his hands were tied, and he had already filed the papers for his divorce. He had a child who was expecting him to come home soon, and another woman, one of his own kind, that was depending on him to do the right thing by her, and their child. She had been patient for so many years, and hadn't asked for anything in return, only his love and presence now in their lives. All she wanted was a chance for them to become a real family, and grow their family with the blessing of more children.

"Babe… are you all right? You seem a little distracted," she asked as she laid down beside him on the bed.

"I am so very fine with you by my side. You're so sexy tonight. Let me love you." He gently pulled her on top of him and entered her, and soon their passions for one another took over, and there was no one in the world but them. He loved her that night over and over again, hoping his lovemaking could take away what was to come.

He looked at her with tears in his eyes; he knew his betrayal would live with him for many years to come. It would haunt him when he slept, and every time he met a woman with her name, it would be her face he would see. After he'd left and she had the divorce papers in hand, he knew she would never forgive him, or understand why he'd done it. She would never know the truth, or the situation he had come to find himself in.

As looked down at her face, and felt her soft hair on his skin. In many ways now, he looked at life through her eyes; eyes of compassion, and understanding for the crazy world around him, and for the mother of his child, and his beloved daughter. He knew he would be a better husband and father, because of everything that Nicole had taught him, over the many years he had lived with her. He knew she would never be able to feel that way about him; she would live with regret and resentment for the loss of her young, which she had given only to him. For the loss of their children together, and for the loss of a life they would never have. Her only memories would be about the struggles and disappointments, he'd brought into her life for so many years. He only hoped that in time, she would let forgiveness, be a part of her memories of him. Nicole had a heart that was pure and kind to everyone she met, and he knew to hurt a woman like her was unforgiveable. He finally fell off to sleep, holding her in his arms.

The sun came through their window like it was just another day the next morning, waking Nicole up from a sound sleep. Samuel was still sleeping beside her. For a minute, she had almost forgotten he was back home, but as soon as she looked over, her smile brightened. There he was the love of her life, sleeping like a baby by her side. She quietly got out of bed, and went out to the kitchen to prepare their breakfast and make coffee. Samuel stood in the doorway, staring at his wife as she put the coffee and breakfast, on the dining table for them. He wanted to always remember what it was like to wake up to her, and how she looked first thing in the morning.

"Good morning darling. How did you sleep?" Nicole asked as she walked over to him, and wrapped her arms around him tight. She looked up at him, and in her eyes lay all the secrets she never talked about, all her fears, and all her private worries.

"I slept well because I was beside you, my sweetheart."

"That's exactly what I like to hear babe".

They sat down, and ate like they had the rest of their lives together, but little did Nicole know that the rest of their lives, was just two more days away.

That morning they took their showers together, and got dressed for the day, and went out Christmas shopping together. Christmas was just a week away. They walked through the mall and bought each other a gift, stopped for coffee and kissed, as they walked hand in hand through the shopping mall.

"That was fun today, and we got all our Christmas shopping done. Let's have a nap before we get ready to go out," Nicole whispered, knowing their nap would involve making love again.

"Best offer I had all day my love." Samuel grinned at her.

They made love, and napped for an hour. Nicole woke up before him, and got into a hot bath. She put a soft rose bubble bath into her water; it was fresh and she smelled divine when she got out. She put her hair up on top of her head, and put on a pair of long sparkling earrings. She pulled out a midnight blue dress, with a low V-neck. It had no sleeves, fitting her figure like a glove. When Samuel came out, and met her in the living room, he was wearing a dark navy suit, with a soft blue shirt and tie. She had bought it for him from her store as his Christmas gift, and she wanted him to wear it tonight so she could see him in it. This year, he wouldn't be home for Christmas. They'd be spending it apart. So tonight, they were making it their very own special Christmas. She took a camera along for some pictures, she would later put them into their photo album. Samuel wanted as many pictures as he could get in these last few days too, so he could remember her, being happy and beautiful. He wanted to take them back with him when he left.

They sat happily at the steakhouse they'd chosen for dinner, and their waiter took pictures of them, sitting together, laughing, and then some more pictures, when they were out on the dance floor. They moved slowly together when the band played their favorite song, "Let's Get It On" by Marvin Gaye. She always felt so good wrapped up in his arms. Tonight he pushed everything out of his mind except Nicole, they laughed, ate, and danced the night away. To everyone around them, they looked like a happy couple who were very much in love, and many who looked in their direction wished they had that special connection themselves, with the person sitting beside them. Looks can be so deceiving he thought, but that true sparkle of love, between two people was a hard thing hide. This he knew, but unfortunately it was mixed between two people now, who did not have the luck of time nor fate on their side. And no matter how much he wished he could change that, he knew he couldn't.

"I had such a great time tonight. I wish every night was this good," she said as she undressed, put on a pink soft nightdress, and crawled in bed beside him.

"That's why we appreciate nights like tonight; because they are rare. Just like you

243

my wife. Oh Lady here is your Christmas gift before I forget." He handed her a small blue box.

She opened the box, and inside was a blue topaz ring her birthstone. "Oh Samuel. I love it." She put it on her finger. It reminded her of the blue topaz earrings she couldn't find anymore. She knew Samuel probably gave the ring, to her to go with the earrings. She reached over and kissed him, and then climbed on top of him.

He pulled her close, and they made love passionately, the fire was burning hot tonight between them. They slept in late the next morning. It was almost noon, when Nicole finally opened her eyes and when she did, Samuel was standing by the bed with a fresh cup of coffee, and two of her homemade muffins in his hands for them. He climbed back in bed beside her, and they sat happily eating their muffins and sipping their coffee.

"These last few days have just flown by. Soon you'll be leaving again." Nicole was starting to feel sad again, because they had just one last night together before Samuel had to return back to the US.

"Let's make the best of our time then, shall we?" He took the cup out of her hand, pulled her into his arms, and made love to her. He was like a man desperate to hang on to something he knew he could no longer have. An hour later they came up for air, and got out of bed and took a shower together. Nicole went out to the kitchen, and prepared them a wonderful Sunday dinner, of roast chicken, potatoes, vegetables, and a homemade apple pie. She set the table with candles and wine, and put on a long flowing dress that fell softly against her skin. It was a pale mint green, and was very sensual with her long blonde hair.

"You look so sweet tonight, and dinner smells wonderful." Samuel was always impressed by his wife's looks, and the fact that she'd become such a good cook over the years.

"I wanted it to be special because I guess this is our pretend Christmas dinner together. You won't be coming back for Christmas will you?"

"No my sweetheart, I won't. I will be starting the new job next week, and there is no way they will let me leave a week later. You understand right?" He looked at her with distance in his eyes.

"I know... but Christmas will just not be the same, without you by my side this year."

"Yeah, I feel the same, some things are just not that simple or easy, and you and I have never had anything given to us easy. We have fought for everything, especially each other, and no matter whatever else happens to us in the future, I want you to remember that I love you, and will always love you. Promise me now you will remember that Lady."

"I promise. But if I do forget, you'll be around to remind me right?" She looked very worried. She was hearing a desperation in his voice, and it scared her.

"I sure hope so, but if anything were to ever happen, then you must remember, that I know how blessed, I have been all these years to have you as my wife." His voice broke into a sob, and he put his head down into his hands.

"Oh baby please don't be so upset. We'll work this out. I'll come there with you whenever you are ready for me. We can still have a life together, just as soon as you're settled there. Just have faith it will all work out."

She bent down on her knees, and put her arms around him. All he could do was cry. He was crying for the woman he was about to hurt, and she didn't even know that the tears he was shedding were for her. He was panicking, and he didn't know what to do anymore. She was becoming more and more afraid now too, because of his reaction and the words he was saying to her. It felt like he was going away and never coming back, but how could that be? Her mind was racing.

"Sam babe please talk to me. What is it really? You're making me feel like you're saying goodbye somehow." She looked frightened.

"I am sorry Lady." He wiped his eyes. "It's just that I miss you so much over there, and I can't be here for Christmas with you. It's all really bothering me tonight." He straightened up, gained his composure, and pulled her into his arms. He hugged her as tightly as he could. Her heart was pounding. She knew something was wrong; there was something he wasn't telling her.

"Lady please just let me hold you tonight. Let's just stop talking; let's go to bed now, and make love and sleep together like we always do. Let just fall asleep in the same bed, just like we always do okay? Please?" He begged. He looked at her like a man who was heartbroken, but she just couldn't put it all together in her head. Maybe he was just tired, and missing her more than she realized. Maybe he was uneasy about his trip back to the US. Or maybe she was just not seeing the truth, which had been staring her in the face for weeks now.

"Sure babe, we can do that. It's all going to be all right. Please don't be so sad. I love you; you're my whole world. I am never leaving you baby. You know that Sam right?"

"Yes, my sweetheart. I know you would never leave me. I love you for that."

She looked at him with a thousand unspoken questions in her eyes, and all he could do was hold her as tight as he could on their very last night together. All he could hope for now, was for her to know and remember, that she was loved by him.

He held Nicole until she fell asleep. He just watched her for a long time as she slept in his arms, tears in his eyes, as he prepared his mind to leave her behind. It was the kindest thing he could do for her. She was still beautiful and young enough that she would find some other man, and move on with her life. He knew a woman like Nicole, would never be alone if she didn't want to be. He also had to make Jane legal in the eyes of the American law, so he needed to divorce Nicole. He hadn't meant to fall so deeply in love with her, but he had, and now he was suffering right along with her. The difference was that he had a life to go to, a woman and a child waiting for him. And the career he loved would be opening up to him. She on the other hand, would have to start over with no one by her side to guide her, only a heart full of sorrow.

The sun came through their window just like it always had, and woke Nicole up just as it always did. She looked over and there was her husband, still sleeping soundly by her side. She quietly got out of bed, and went out to the kitchen, and made them both breakfast. She put everything on the table, and then went back to their bed. Samuel was awake now. He reached out to take her hand, and pulled her back in bed beside him.

"Good morning Lady. Did you sleep well?"

"Okay, I guess. Did you?"

"Not really. I missed you when you were asleep."

"You're so funny. How can you miss me when I'm right beside you silly?"

"I missed your smile and your kiss, I miss those beautiful eyes looking at me." He smiled.

"Really? Well, here's that kiss that you've been missing all night." She leaned over and gave him a kiss. He pulled her on top of him, and they made love. He knew it would be the last time he would ever love her again in his life. She could feel the intensity of his body. It was like he wanted to cover her with all his love, so she would always remember him in her body and in her heart.

"Wow that was the best good morning ever. It's like there's a storm of passions inside of you these days." She looked at him closely, noticing how sad he appeared.

"No storm Lady. Just giving you all of me while I still can."

"I know you're leaving, but we'll be together again very soon, so don't worry so much baby. I'm not going anywhere, and I know you love me. Now how about some breakfast before we go to the airport?"

They ate mostly in silence, and when they looked at the clock on the wall, they knew they had to go get ready for the airport. They stepped into the shower together. Samuel washed Nicole's back, he noticed one last time how lovely and soft her skin was, how soft and wavy her hair fell, and how beautifully curved her body was beneath his hands. He noticed every inch of her; he didn't want to forget a thing about her. As she stood there beside him, she noticed how his strong shoulders were, how his arms felt around her waist. They got out of the shower, and slowly got dressed for the airport.

She looked at him sitting on their bed, she sat down beside him one last time. "What is it Sam? Why are you looking around the room like you're never going to see it again?"

"It's just that I want to remember you here in this room, whenever I think of you. I hate to leave you again so soon. I am going to miss you so much, my heart aches already."

"I know. I feel the same way. But you have to go back, and do what you have to do now. So let's get moving before you miss your flight back to the US." She picked up her car keys, and they slowly walked hand-in-hand to the car. As she drove, he held one of her hands all the way to the airport. They looked at each other from time to time and smiled. She parked the car, and they walked into the airport. He checked in his suitcase and then came back, and sat down beside her. He looked at her and gave her a kiss.

"Lady be careful when you're driving back home. I will call you when I get back, and let you know I arrived there safe?"

"For sure I will, and I'll be waiting for your call. Baby I love you so much – I hope you know that."

"I do Nicole, I have always known that, you can set your mind at ease. I have always felt loved by you. You have been a wonderful wife to me, and I have been so happy to be your husband. I need you to always remember that my sweetheart?"

"I'll remember I promise. That's your flight number they're announcing. You need to go now darling."

They stood up, and he pulled her into his arms one last time. He closed his eyes, and smelled the scent of her hair, he hugged her as tightly as he could.

"Safe journey my love," she whispered into his ear.

He walked slowly away, then he turned for just a moment, and looked back at her. He wanted to take her in one last time. She waved goodbye. Her face was still glowing from their love making. When he turned to walk away again, suddenly strange feeling descended over her. Something in her soul told her he was never coming back. He then turned the corner, and was gone from her sight. Her world went dark as she started to pass out. She quickly sat back down to catch her breath on the bench. What was this feeling? A panic was washing over her. Her gut was screaming out to her now, that he was gone forever.

Suddenly it came into sharp focus in her mind's eye. He was saying goodbye to her. How could she have overlooked it for so long? But maybe she was wrong, she thought. Desperately she tried to make sense of everything. Maybe she was just panicking. She couldn't see anything clearly in her mind now. She got up and ran around the corner to try and find him again, but he was gone. He'd left the gate, and was on the plane. She stood by the window, and watched his plane, taxi out and take off. Within only minutes, it had disappeared into the clouds. She tried to calm herself down. She was being crazy. Of course he was coming back. That wasn't goodbye; how could it have been? She told herself over and over again.

She drove home in a daze. She sat and waited by the phone for his call. She just needed to hear his voice again, and then she would be fine. She needed him to tell her that he'd be back again, that it wasn't goodbye, and that it was just her imagination playing tricks on her. It was nearly six o'clock now; he should have been there hours ago. She picked up the phone, and dialed his cell phone. She let it ring several times, but there was no answer. The panic roared inside her gut again. Why wasn't he answering? She poured herself a cup of tea, and sat by the phone again to wait.

***

Ben picked Samuel up at the airport, and took him back to his little apartment. Samuel opened the door, and there stood his little girl. "Daddy you came back!" She ran to him, and hugged and kissed him.

"Of course Tracie, I came back. I told you I would, didn't I?" He smiled at her.

"Yes you did daddy, I missed you, when you were away."

Jane came into the room and stood in silence, looking at Samuel.

"Jane how was your weekend my dear?" Samuel asked.

"It was a quiet one. Just waiting for my husband to return. But maybe I should ask how your weekend was?" Her suspicions dark eyes held a million questions.

"My weekend was just about wrapping up loose ends back in Canada Jane. Nothing to worry about my dear." He looked away from her, and she could tell that the loose ends, had defiantly been a woman in Canada.

She walked past him, grabbed her purse, and put on her coat. "I will take our daughter, and go out to the market to buy food," she said coldly.

"Okay. I will see you when you get back."

His little girl took her mother's hand, looking back at Samuel as they left, not understanding why they had to leave just when her father had returned. "Mommy, why did we leave daddy behind again so soon?"

"We didn't leave him behind my child. We are just going to the market. He will be there when we return in a few hours. Do not worry so." She smiled down at her child with a warmth and kindness; she knew her little girl was worried about losing her father again. She was never going to let that happen. But she also had to teach him a lesson.

The African way was not to argue, only to ignore until their men came around to the woman's way of thinking. Samuel was actually glad Jane, and his daughter, had left for a few hours. He needed time to call Nicole and let her know he had arrived safely; he had to at least do that much for her. He couldn't leave her to worry, that something bad had happened to him. He took out his cell phone, but the battery had run out, and was now dead. He needed to call Nicole before Jane returned, so he had no choice but to call from his home phone. He would block the number from showing, so Nicole would never find out where he was calling from. He sat there for a minute, thinking of what he could tell her. Maybe it would just be easier to pretend, that everything was still the same between them for the call. He would just tell her that he'd arrived safely, and hang up as quickly as he could. He still had a few days before she would be served the divorce papers. It was the week of Christmas, and he had now wished he'd waited until after the New Year to send the papers, but it was already done. He'd tried to stop them, but his lawyer said he'd already sent them out to Nicole. So he now had to live with what he had done to her. He hoped they reached her after Christmas, but his lawyer had said it would be within a few days. That would make them reaching her, on the day of Christmas Eve. He anxiously checked his calendar again. "Oh God," he groaned. He hoped he was wrong. He looked at the clock and saw it was nearly seven. Jane would be home soon, and Nicole would be waiting for his call. He was feeling so stressed that he picked up the phone, and dialed Nicole's number, forgetting to block his own.

The phone rang out, waking Nicole up. She had fallen asleep waiting for his call. She snapped up the phone, without looking at the number that was calling her.

"Hello?"

"Hi... Lady. You sound like you were sleeping?"

"Yes... I fell asleep. You arrived safely then? I tried to call you on your cell phone, but you didn't answer."

"My phone battery was dead. How are you my sweetheart?"

"Panicking a little. Samuel tell me the truth. Are you coming back home again?"

"Why would you ask me this?"

"I just had a terrible feeling inside my gut that you were never coming back to me."

There was a long silence on the phone, as Samuel wiped the tears from his eyes, and tried to clear his voice to make light of his answer.

"Everything is fine. I love you, and I will always love you, please remember that my sweet wife."

"I will try, but you sound strange Sam, please is everything alright?" She said softly in a voice that tore at his heart. "Sam don't forget about me over there please. I'll be waiting for you to come home to me. I need you to remember that my husband."

"I will remember you always, please forgive me my sweetheart." His voice broke as he tried to conceal his feelings. He had to hang up fast, or she'd hear the truth in his voice. And he just couldn't bear to hear her cry for him.

"I have to go now. Take very good care of yourself my sweet Lady."

"Sam don't hang up, forgive you for what?"

He was silent, and then he just hung up. She was left with silences in her ear. It was a strange way for him to end the call, she thought. The panic was back stronger now than before. She picked up the phone again, and saw that it was a different number that he'd called her from. Not his cell phone. She immediately called it back.

Samuel sat there with his head in his hands. When he heard his home phone ring; he looked at the caller ID and saw that it was Nicole calling from home. Oh dear God, he thought. I forgot to block the number. He didn't know what to do, so he let the call go to voicemail.

Nicole sat on the other end of the phone as the ringing came to an end, and then she was left in utter shock, as she heard a woman's voice say, "You have reached Samuel and Jane's home, but we are unable to answer so please leave us a message."

She hung up, feeling sick. Samuel and Jane's home. Who was Jane, her voice had an African accent. But why was he living with her? What was going on? Her mind was racing. Samuel was visibly upset as he realized that his voicemail would have answered with Jane's voice. He knew that the lie he'd been hiding from Nicole for so many years, was now brought to light. Nicole would now know why he left her. She'd never know he had a child to protect, only that she'd been left behind for another woman of his own kind. He called the phone company, and had the number disconnected immediately. He asked for a new phone number in a different name. He put it under his African middle name, so she would never know enough to find him again.

Jane put her keys in the door of their apartment, and came inside. She saw Samuel sitting on the chair beside the phone with his head in his hands, and when he looked up at her, she saw tears in his eyes. She knew it was not the time to be unkind, or to try to teach him anything. She just put the bags of groceries down on the floor, walked over to him, bent down on her knees, and quietly put her arms around him. She knew that he had left the woman in Canada behind now; it was done as he had said. She was going to love all those tears away in time; he was her husband, he had always been, and always would be. She placed his hands on her stomach and said, "We will soon have another child to love my husband." She smiled up at him, and hugged him tighter than ever. His daughter climbed into his lap, and put her head on his shoulder. Jane and their daughter, had waited a long time for him to come home to them, and now they were about to have another child with God's blessing she hoped.

***

After an hour, Nicole picked up the phone, and called the same number again, but this time she got a recorded message saying "The number you have dialed has been disconnected." She sat there, trying to figure out what in the world had just happened. She picked up the phone again, and called Samuel's cell phone, but got the same message. "The number you have dialed has been disconnected."

She hung up the phone in complete shock, and just sat there in disbelief. How Samuel could actually leave her behind, and worse was living with a woman from his country? She stumbled to her bed, stunned that he had betrayed her this way. How could he do that to her, when she had been nothing but kind and loving to him? She was so confused by everything. That's not how life is she thought. This can't be real. It's all a big mistake her mind told her. She cried and held her pillow, all alone in the darkness of the night. She kept denying the truth in her mind; it was far too much for her heart to bear. Her innocent mind refused to believe the worst. He wouldn't leave her like that, he couldn't. He loved her didn't he? She knew down deep in her soul that he loved her, so why on earth would he have done this? Nothing made any sense to her now, nothing at all. She lay on her bed and cried her heart out, all alone with no one to hear her cries. She had been deceived and deserted, by the man she had loved with all her heart. She was sick in her heart, and now in her soul. She laid there in so much misery that she just wished she would die.

When the morning came, her eyes were still open and red from crying. The morning sun came up as it always did, and was shining brightly through her bedroom window, just like always. But this morning she couldn't move, couldn't get out of bed. She just laid there and cried. She cried for all that she had just lost, she cried for all that would never be, she cried the most because he'd never even said goodbye to her, or allowed her to say goodbye to him. After all those years of struggling, not even a goodbye, she thought. It was like he was a different man, than the one she'd lived with and loved for so many years, because that man could never do this to her. It was totally cold-hearted to have changed the number within a matter of hours, leaving her no way to reach him, or to find out what had just happened. She tried Ben's number several times, but no one answered there either. There was no one to explain, no one to hear her cry, or to hold her as she lay sick and alone in her bed.

Sarah was busy in the kitchen, and she decided to call Nicole to find out what time she'd be home for Christmas. Marilyn had been already back at home, and Nicole was to drive home after work on Christmas Eve. It was only two days away now. She dialed Nicole's number, and the phone rang several times. Nicole just laid in bed, and listened to the phone ring. She couldn't get up to answer it; she was too weak and in shock.

"Good morning Sarah. Who were you calling just now?" Millie asked.

"I was calling Nicole, but there was no answer. Maybe she went shopping early, to get the rest of her Christmas shopping finished. I'll call her again later I guess."

Millie looked at her watch. It was only eight in the morning, and she knew Nicole was not shopping. She had a very bad feeling that her precious child wasn't all right at all. She sat and stared out the window, looking up at the sky, trying to see the child in her mind's eye. But for some reason, she couldn't find her. That's odd, she thought. I can always find her.

What she didn't know was that Nicole's mind, was in such a state of shock, that it wouldn't receive any outside calibration of energy. It was the energy between them, which had always connected them, and brought them together in each other's minds. But today Nicole was all but drained of her natural energy, as she lay there fighting to stay alive. She had not slept or eaten in almost two days, and was in limbo. She knew she needed to get up from bed and eat, and see who had been calling her. Nicole closed her eyes and tried to talk herself into moving. She sat up and put her feet over the side of the bed. The movement exhausted her. But she managed to get herself up and take a shower. She moved out to the kitchen in a fog. She made some toast with an egg, and drank some coffee.

She went over to the phone, and saw that her mother had called several times, and she knew she had to call back. She sat motionless in her rocking chair, thinking of how to handle it. She didn't want to ruin Christmas for her family, so she decided to just pretend that nothing had happened. She couldn't deal with it herself yet, and it would be just too hard to explain it all to her family.

It was Monday morning, and she had to go to work. She walked into the store, and slowly walked around to see what condition it was in.

"Good morning Nicole. Nice to see you back," Richard said as he spotted her walking around.

"Good morning, Richard. How is everything here?"

"Better now that you're back. How was your time with Samuel? Did he get back safely?"

"Yes, he did. Thanks for asking Richard. She walked away as quickly as she could to the back room. She had no desire to even talk to anyone, so restocking the product was better for her today. She had greeted her staff, and told them what had to be done. She spoke politely to them, but she lacked the smile and sparkle she normally had. They all knew something had happened, but not one of them asked her.

That's odd Richard thought, she'd never even smiled. He thought, after a few days with her husband, she would have been happier-looking, but she actually looked worse. He wondered if everything was okay between them. This was the worsted, he had ever seen her look, and she looked like someone had just died.

"Thanks everyone for a great day. I'm off now and I'll see you all tomorrow." Nicole said to them as she left. She slowly walked through the shopping center where she worked. It was all decorated with Christmas lights, and it had a big Christmas tree in the center. The children were all lined up to see Santa Claus. She stood and watched for a moment. Knowing she would never have a child to take to see Santa. At least not Samuel's child. A tear rolled down her cheek, as she walked slowly back to her car. She walked into the little apartment, she had once shared with Samuel, she didn't even bother to turn on the lights.

She made some soup and forced herself to eat it, and then just crawled back into her bed. She had no energy and longed for sleep. At least when she was asleep, she didn't have to remember the terrible thing that had just happened to her. She never wanted to be a victim in anything, and never asked for sympathy from anyone, not even her own mother. The only person she ever really showed her true emotions too, was her Grandmother, but today she couldn't even do that. She wanted answers but there were none. She wanted to scream, and hate him for what he had done, but she couldn't do that either. Yes she hated what he had just did to her, but it was the silence between them, that killed her the most.

She had called and left her family a message late at night when she knew they would be sleeping, saying she would be home on Christmas Eve and not to worry. The message was enough for everyone in her home except her grandmother, who knew that if Nicole was fine, she would have called when she could hear their voices, and they could hear her. But she had not intended for them to speak directly to her. Millie knew it, and she also knew Samuel had left – she could feel it.

She had a cold chill now that went up her spine, every time she thought of Samuel. But she would wait to see her precious child first, before she told her that she knew. She also knew that Nicole needed time alone, to deal with everything in her own way. She wanted to get in her car and run to her child, but she knew she had to wait for her to come to them.

"Damn him," she muttered under her breath so no one would hear. Except Sarah did overhear her.

"What's that, Millie dear? Who did you damn?"

"Oh, nothing Sarah. I was just talking to myself again dear." She knew that half the time Sarah thought she was losing her mind, so she just let her. It amused the old woman to see Sarah look at her like she was crazy.

"Well Grand dear, maybe you should talk to me instead of yourself so much. After all dear, I'm right here in the same room with you. It looks like the weather will be good for Nicole's drive home tomorrow evening. I'm so glad she'll be home with us this year."

"Yes it will be and she needs us more than ever now" Millie just kept on knitting her socks for the boys, but in her heart and mind she was cursing Samuel future.

It was the day of Christmas Eve, and Nicole was working at the store until noon. She wanted to get a head start on her long drive home. She had packed all her gifts in the car, and had put her suitcase in as well; she would leave for home right from the store. She had come into the store only long enough to give her holiday greetings to her staff, and give them their bonuses.

"Merry Christmas everyone. I do hope you all have a very Merry Christmas with your families. And thanks so much for all your hard work over this last year. You've all done a wonderful job, and the store had record sales." She handed each of them a greeting card, and inside each card she had persuaded Richard to give them all a five hundred dollar Christmas bonus. She went into Richards's office. He had his head bent, looking at his bank records. He'd already started sending all his profits from the store to his wife's bank account, leaving only enough money to pay his staff, and store rent, and a few other necessary bills. He paid no suppliers as he didn't need them anymore. He would very soon declare that he had no money in the bank, to continue with his business.

"Wow... Richard, you're still here? I thought you'd be at home today, getting ready for the holidays with Helen."

"Yes, I'm leaving soon my girl. But I have something for you." He handed her a letter.

"What is this?" She opened it, and inside the greeting card was a bonus of twenty thousand dollars.

"Wow Oh Richard! This is an amazing bonus. Thank you so much." She bent over and gave him a hug.

"You deserve it Nicole. You're always here working hard, and as you know we had record sales this season, thanks to you. Just don't mention it to my wife if she asks you." He smiled at her.

"No worries on that one. If it's okay, I'll be off to drive home. My mother is expecting me in a few hours, and I don't want to get stuck in traffic later."

"Sure my girl. I'll see you in a few days then, and Merry Christmas."

He noticed that there was still no joy in her smile, and that her voice was sad. Nicole looked at her bonus. It would be a huge help. She had a long, solitary road ahead of her now, and she'd need the money to figure out her future. She put on her coat and was getting ready to leave the store, when a stranger came toward her.

"Are you Nicole Emeka?"

"Yes I am. Who are you?"

"Mrs. Emeka, I'm sorry to do this today, but you have been served." He handed her a white envelope.

She sat down at her desk, opened the envelope, and read the papers. She couldn't believe her eyes as she read. Samuel had filed for a divorce on grounds of irreconcilable differences, and it said if she wished to counteract she would have 30 days. She sat very still. She couldn't move, she knew many of her staff were watching her. So she stood up, waved to them, and left the store as fast as she could. She walked to her car in a daze.

It was Christmas Eve, and she had just been served divorce papers. She closed her eyes as the tears rolled down her cheeks. He'd just disappeared into thin air. She had no way to reach him, and even Ben's number had been disconnected now too. How could she even counteract? She had no way, and she was too tired to even try. She was so heartbroken, and she just couldn't understand why Samuel has decided to treat her so coldly and cowardly. He never even has the guts to face me, she thought as she put the papers inside her bag. She sat in her car and cried for all she had lost, for all he had promised her, and never lived up to, and for the love she missed so much. She sat and remembered all the things he'd said to her during his last visit. How he knew she loved him, and that she had always been a good wife to him. Yet there it was. She read it again:" "irreconcilable differences."

She couldn't believe her eyes. There had to be something else she was missing here. He couldn't ever be that cruel to her, not her Samuel, not the man she had supported, and stood beside all these years. But how would she ever find out, how would she ever know the real truth? Right then and there she decided to do nothing. She would just let the divorce go through. She would just give him what he was asking for. All the things he said to her came back into her mind. The divorce was something he had to do for some reason. She was sure of that now. She only wished he'd been man enough to talk to her about whatever it was; it would have made things so much easier to understand. The way he'd done it, left her with a sickness in her soul, which she feared would never go away. She would fight for him if she knew how, but she didn't. No the best thing for him, and her family was to let him go quietly away, into the far dark corners of her heart, and pray that one day he would find her, and tell her the truth about why he'd done it. She wanted nothing from him, she knew he had nothing to give her. He had betrayed her, and left her alone with divorce paper on Christmas, and that would take a long time to forgive.

As she drove, she kept hearing the voicemail message play in her head. "Samuel and Jane are unable to answer, so please leave us a message." She knew that wherever he was now, he wasn't alone, and somehow for that she was glad, but at the same time angry. She was happy that he wouldn't be suffering alone the way she was. She'd learn to accept this in time as fate; the hand she had been dealt in life. She had chosen her life, and it was with him for many years, so she had no right to complain to anyone. They would all just say 'I told you so' anyway, because most of her friends and family, never understand the connection she'd had with him. She had to be strong, and yet in the middle of all her misery, she could still hear his voice say, "How is my pretty lady today?" And then he would laugh, and smile at her. Many women in her situation would be angry and want revenge, she knew this. But she was not just any woman, she was a child of God, and she knew he would always guide her. God did not make mistakes. But until then, she would pray for the day, when she would see his face again. To gain some kind of closure, just to somehow know, she had not lived with a heartless man all those years.

It had been a very hard few days for Nicole, and all she really wanted to do was crawl in bed, and hide away from the fact that he was gone. It was all so sudden, and she was so unprepared for what he'd just done to her, and their marriage. It was like he'd died, and she needed time to grieve the loss. But she still had to get through Christmas with her family. It was a hard lesson she was learning. She had been so innocent, and had no experience in dealing with a man like him. She knew he must have loved her somehow; they'd spent too many years together for him not to have had any real feelings for her. There were so many unanswered questions left in her heart and mind.

She was nearly home now, and it would be a relief to get off the road, and see her mother and grandmother again. She pulled into the driveway of her family home, wiped away her tears, put on some makeup so they couldn't see she'd been crying, and got out of the car with her gifts.

The door opened as soon as she got there. "Hello dear welcome home. I've been watching for you," Sarah said. She quickly took the gifts from her arms, set them down, and gave Nicole a warm hug.

"We are so glad your home dear. Come in and sit; I'll get you some food. Your brothers will get your suitcase, and put it in your old room."

"Thank you Mommy. Where is everyone?" She smiled. It was so nice to be home again.

"Grand is waiting for you in the living room, and your sister and brothers are watching a Christmas movie on TV."

Nicole walked into the living room, and there sat her old Grandmother knitting, and beside sat her sister and brothers watched a Christmas movie, eating popcorn and homemade fudge.

"Hi! Merry Christmas everyone." She walked over and bent down to kiss her grandmother's cheek.

"Merry Christmas dear." Grand said.

"Hi sis. I'll get your bags," her brother said.

"Why did it take you so long to come in today?" Marilyn asked.

"Just traffic I guess. What are you all watching?"

"*The Night before Christmas*." She offered her some fudge and popcorn, but Nicole declined.

"Come out to the kitchen Nicole. Your mother will put your dinner on the table for you." Nicole followed her grandmother out to the kitchen. She was dreading having to eat. Sarah had put a big lobster sandwich, and a cold glass of milk on the table for her, and beside it was a large piece of homemade apple pie.

"That really looks good. Thanks so much." She sat down, and in spite of everything, she was able to eat the food her mother had prepared. Just being home made her feel better somehow. She ate it all, and even took several bites of her pie. "Wow... I am so full. That was really good Mom." Nicole got up and made herself some tea. She sat back down at the table, and looked at her Grandmother. Sarah was busy preparing Christmas dinner in the far corner of the kitchen.

"So how are you?" Millie took Nicole's hand and squeezed it.

A tear rolled down Nicole's cheek and she looked away.

"I know child. When you're ready, we'll talk about it. Why not just enjoy Christmas with us for a day or two, and don't think about anything at all."

"Okay Grand, I'll try." Her voice broke and she wiped away her tears. Her grandmother put her arms around her and squeezed her tight.

"Nicole? Are you okay?" Her mother asked as she looked over at her.

"Sure Mom. Just tired. May I please just go up to bed now, and I'll see you all in the morning?"

"Of course dear, see you in the morning." She kissed Nicole on the cheek and watched her walk away.

"Grand something's is terrible wrong with Nicole isn't it? This is the worst I've ever seen her. I'm really worried about her." Sarah sat down at the table beside Millie.

"Sarah... Samuel has left our child, but you must not say a word until she is ready to tell us herself. Now promise you will just love her enough to let her be while she decides what to do next."

"How do you know that if she didn't tell you?"

"I just know. Trust me on this one Sarah. That bastard has abandoned our child to suffer." She looked like a wild woman when she mentioned Samuel name.

"Oh my God! I hope you're wrong. My poor baby."

"I'm not wrong. Can't you just believe me for once? I'm not crazy, or losing my mind, I just know." She left the kitchen, and walked up the stairs to check in on Nicole. She gently knocked on the door and then opened it. She stood at the door and watched her as she slept, she still looked like a small child to Millie. She was curled up into a little ball, holding her pillow. Millie walked over to the bed and covered her up with a blanket, kissed her on the cheek, then closed the door and left. One tear after another rolled down Nicole's cheeks, until she finally fell asleep for real.

Christmas morning came early for Nicole. She was awake by six. She got up and went down to the kitchen, to make coffee for the family. She decided to make a batch of homemade muffins, the kind Samuel loved. She placed them in the oven, sat down at the table, and drank her coffee. A light snow was falling. Soon the whole family would be awake, and wanting to open the Christmas presents under the tree. All she could think of was what Samuel would be doing this Christmas morning, and who he would be spending it with. She closed her eyes, so she could see his face in her mind's eye.

***

Samuel was awake and sitting in his living room. He'd just made some coffee, and had put his daughter's gifts, under the little Christmas tree they had decorated together. He'd even had gotten them a turkey to cook for Christmas dinner. Jane had told him, she didn't know how to cook a whole turkey, as it was not a traditional African meal. But Samuel had told her not to worry; he would cook it. He'd watched Nicole make a special turkey dinner for them for years, so he knew how to do it now for his African family. He just wanted to have a Christmas that reminded him of her.

He thought about her constantly; she was always on his mind. He wondered if she'd received the divorce papers yet. He hoped she didn't, at least not until after Christmas he prayed. Ben was coming over with his sister, to celebrate Christmas with Samuel and Jane. Jane was trying her best to make Samuel love her, and he was starting to, but it was a different kind of love. It had none of the passion, and joy that he'd felt with Nicole. Instead it was a kind and gentle love, which made him feel sometimes comfortable, and other times completely lost.

Jane knew there was some part of her husband, that most days wasn't present with her. But she couldn't think of that now; she was pregnant, and was having their second child. The news had made Samuel feel even more trapped in their life together.

He hadn't thought she'd get pregnant so fast, and he wished he'd used precautions. He wasn't ready for a second child; he still needed to get settled with his career. But he had no choice now. He started working at the same hospital as Ben, doing a year-long internship, and soon he'd be qualified for a medical license in the US. That was what he'd worked so hard for back in Canada, and it had never happened, but here he'd managed to get an internship in less than six months. He was so excited when he got the news, that all he'd wanted to do was pick up the phone and call Nicole. But he couldn't tell her anything, he couldn't hear her soft, velvety voice. He was brought back to reality when his daughter came running out, and jumped up on his lap.

"Daddy! Can we open the gifts now, please?"

"Where is Mommy? Let her come out first; then we can open them okay? Let's have some food, while we wait for Mommy to wake up."

Jane slept later than usual. She was always tired from her pregnancy, and he tried his best to help out as much as possible. He found himself wondering often what his child with Nicole would have looked like; no doubt it would have been a beauty.
 He was becoming a good father to his daughter, and she adored him.
"Soon you will have a little brother, or sister to have fun with at Christmas. How does that make you feel my sweetheart?" He asked her.

"Happy I guess. Mommy says we are a family now, and she is happy to be having another baby. She said she planned it all just right, that her timing was perfect. Whatever that means." She was too young to understand what her mother had done, but Samuel knew now that Jane getting pregnant was no accident. She'd known when she was fertile, and had made sure that she, and Samuel were together then.

He was beginning to see that his new wife was a foxy one, who knew how to get her way without even asking. That was the African way; the women wanted more children and planned the family, and the men just accepted it when told of the impending child. Jane was a doctor, and would work after the birth of their second child. She wanted to do an internship after the baby was born, and get a medical license to practice medicine in the US too. With a growing family, they'd need both incomes. Jane wanted a large house with lots of children, and knew she'd have to help out with the income. She soon joined them in the living room

"Good Morning my husband, and Merry Christmas."

"Merry Christmas my dear, did you sleep well?"

"Yes I did, as long as you are beside me, I sleep well." Samuel smiled and started passing Jane and his daughter a gift.

"I love my new watch, thank you Father." She ran over and kissed his cheek.

"Thank you for my perfume Samuel. White Diamond is that a kind of perfume, you prefer that I wear?"

"Yes I like this sense a lot, and I hope you will wear it for me." She walked over and hugged him like a sister would hug a brother, it was a kind and comfortable love they had between them. Samuel opened his gift from his daughter and Jane.

"Well, now that is a very nice shirt and tie, I must say." He walked over and thanked them both with kisses on the cheeks. The shirt and tie were nice, but really not his style. Nicole had picked out all his clothes for years, and she had impeccable taste when it came to clothing. Although Jane had no idea about this, she did notice the disappointed look on Samuel's face when he opened the box.

"I have just put our turkey dinner in the oven to cook, so today I will be preparing our dinner today. You just relax with our daughter, and leave everything to me." He smiled at them.

"But don't you want our traditional Christmas dinner of goat from back home?"

"No not really, I like turkey better now, and so will you once you taste it." He laughed.

"Living in Canada has changed you a lot my husband. But thank you for preparing our food today. How did you learn how to do all this?"

"I learned from a good Canadian family I spent a lot of time with. This was their traditional meal every Christmas, and I have grown very fond of it." His smile held sorrow, which did not go unnoticed by Jane. She knew it would take time for him to adjust to his new life with them, but she had lots of hope for the two of them, especially with the new baby on the way. She had him for a lifetime, and no matter what, he would be there for his children and her. His whole family was solidly behind their marriage, and loved that they were already expecting a new baby. To them it said that they were happy with each other. But they hadn't seen Samuel's face, or heard his voice since he'd started living with Jane and his daughter. He had refused to call them, he was feeling so unhappy and trapped.

***

Nicole's family all came downstairs at once, and soon the kitchen was full of smiles and laughter. They all had coffee and her muffins, and then went to the living room to open the gifts underneath the tree.

"We've all been very blessed this year with so many beautiful new things," Sarah said. "Let's get ready for church, and then we can come back and enjoy our turkey dinner."

Nicole put on a simple black dress, like she was in mourning. She stood beside her Grandmother at church. As she stood there, her mind once again wandered back to their wedding day. The church was decorated exactly the same way it had been then, with Christmas lights and red flowers. A tear rolled down Nicole's cheek, and Millie knew exactly what she was thinking. She put her arm around Nicole's shoulders as they sang Silent Night.

"Nicole, what's wrong? You look so sad. Has Samuel called yet?" Marilyn asked.

"No, not yet. I'm fine, no need to worry Sis. Let's just go home and have dinner." She smiled at Marilyn, who was smarter than she thought.

"Maybe he'll call later tonight. He may just be very busy." She tried to reassure her sister, unaware of what the real situation was. They sat around the dinner table, and chatted with each other while they ate. Nicole stayed quiet, she felt happy to listen to her family talk, and it took her mind off of her own situation.

The next day was Sarah's birthday, and Nicole's anniversary. They were all sure that Samuel would call her today. Nicole woke up early, and made coffee, and French toast with fruit for everyone. She didn't want her mother to cook on her birthday. She was fighting back the tears again. It was her anniversary, but instead of celebrating with her husband, she was facing the future alone and going through a divorce.

Sarah came downstairs alone, the rest of the family was still sleeping. She found Nicole gazing out the window.

"Oh thank you dear, so much for making us all a special breakfast. That was so thoughtful of you."

"You're welcome Mommy, and happy birthday, she gave her a small gift."

"Oh thank you dear, it's a lovely perfume white diamond, isn't that what you wear dear."

"Yes Mom, I just thought you may enjoy it too, I have worn it for years." Her voice broke and she started to cry. She couldn't hold back the tears any longer. She'd been strong for as long as she could, and she needed her mother.

"Talk to me about it dear. Let me know what the trouble is." She sat down beside her daughter and listened.

"He's gone Mom. He just up and left me, and now I've been served divorce papers. I have no way to contact him, and I don't even know why he did it. I'm so heartbroken I could just die." Tears rolled down her cheeks as she spoke.

"Oh Nicole. I'm so very sorry to hear that. I know it must be a shock to have Samuel treat you this way, and without any good reason. I am so sorry my dear." She put her arms around Nicole, and just let her cry. Sarah got up and made a pot of coffee.

"Here, drink this and we'll plan our way out of this together. Just let me think on it awhile, and in the meantime, you must eat and not let yourself get sick."

"I can hardly swallow food, when I'm alone at home. How could he be so unkind, and such a coward to do this to me this way."

"I wish I knew the answer to that, he's certainly not the man we all thought he was, that for sure."

"At least Marilyn will be coming back with you again dear. You can take care of each other now. And I'll come down next week with Grand, and we'll stay with you for a few days too."

"Thanks Mommy. But he's still gone, and I just can't find a way to accept it."

"Just give it a little time. It's all still new in your head. Do you want to contest the divorce?"

"No. If this is what he wants, I won't stand in his way. Besides... I can't find him." She looked exhausted as she spoke. Sarah was worried for her health, and thought that maybe it was for the best, to just let Samuel go. A long fight with him would surely destroy her daughter. The whole situation made Sarah mad as hell. She'd watched Nicole have no fun for years, she had carried all the worries with her every day, about his damn career. And now he had let her down. He had let all of them down, because they'd always treated him like family. She felt sick that she had let this man into her home and heart too. He had fooled all of them.

"You know that today is my anniversary with Samuel? How could he do this Mommy?" She continued to cry silently.

Sarah just sat beside her. She had no words. Why he'd done this was beyond her understanding, but even worse was how he'd done it. It would have been far better had he been a man, and talked to Nicole about his reasons for leaving her. Why couldn't he explain his reasons to her and her family? What was he hiding that was so bad? They both knew that there was a lot they didn't know, and may never know, but one thing that was certain, was that Samuel had been keeping a cruel secret from them all.

Nicole loaded up the car with her sister's things, and her own the next day. They hugged their mother, and grandmother goodbye, and got in the car. Within minutes they were on their way back to the city. As Nicole drove, she put on music for Marilyn, and they travelled back to her little apartment in silence. Sarah had told Marilyn what Samuel had done, and she was both horrified and furious. It was killing her that he could hurt her sister that way, and she vowed to never let him near her again. Together they would make a new life in the city. Marilyn had a job as a chef in a retirement home, which she loved. It paid the bills and gave her something to do while she went to school part time, studying business management.

They arrived back safe and sound, Nicole went straight to bed as soon as she came through the door. Marilyn called home to tell them they'd arrived.

"How are things there?" Sarah asked her daughter.

"We're here okay, but Nicole just went straight to bed. I'll try and get her to eat later."

"You do that. If she gets too bad, just call me, and we'll come sooner than next week. Love you dear."

"Love you too Mom."

Marilyn went in to check on Nicole, and found her fast asleep on her bed. Marilyn went out to the kitchen, and made them a homemade pot of chicken soup; she knew her sister would eat that at least. She loved soup, and it was the easiest thing for her to swallow right now. She poured her a bowl and carried it in.

"Sis! Time to eat. Sit up now and have some of this." Marilyn's voice was kind.

"Thanks, but I'm not hungry." Nicole rolled over to face the wall.

"No you need to eat. Come on now. Please just take a little," she begged.

"Okay, but just a little." She took a few bites and then set it on the table, rolled over and went back to sleep. Marilyn stood helplessly for a moment, unsure of what to do. She made more food for the next day, hoping that tomorrow Nicole would eat better.

Nicole woke up to the morning sun, looked over at Samuel's pillow and cried. She held his pillow close wishing desperately that it was him. She both loved and hated him now. She managed to drag herself out of bed, it took all her energy to get ready for work. That was the thing about heartache, she thought as she looked out the window. The sun came up as always, the day went on as always, whether he was there or not. So she had too.

She dropped Marilyn off at her job, and then went to the store. It was a big day. Boxing Day sales had begun, and as she arrived at the store, the customers were already lined up to get in before it had even opened. Nicole looked exhausted, when she walked through her little apartment door after work that night.

"How was your day? I made some supper. Come sit down and eat." Marilyn said.

"Thanks Sis, but I'm so tired I just need a shower and my bed," Nicole said.

"Not before you have some food. I just made a simple chicken pot pie. Just have a little piece, then take a shower. If you don't eat, I'm calling Mom."

"Oh fine. Let's eat then." Nicole cut herself a small piece and ate it, drank a full glass of milk, and then went to take a shower.

"Thanks for all the food and stuff," Nicole said as she closed her bedroom door.

Marilyn called her mother that night. "Hi Mom. How are you and Grand doing down there?"

"Just fine dear. How are you doing in the city? Is Nicole doing okay?"

"No Mommy. I can't get her to eat more than two bites at a time, and all she does when she's home is stay in bed and sleep. I think she's getting sick." Marilyn was worried about her, and needed her mother's help.

"I see dear. Grand and I will come in tomorrow then, and stay on for a few days. We'll get her through all this, and take care of you for a few days too. See you tomorrow then. Good night and I love you."

"I love you too Mommy." Marilyn hung the phone up and went off to bed.

Sarah walked out to the kitchen, and sat down beside Millie. "Pack a bag. We're going to the city to see our girls for a few days. Marilyn says Nicole isn't doing so well, and isn't eating. So I think they need us for a few days to get them on the right track."

"We'd better go then. Damn him all to hell for doing this to our Nicole. He's hiding something bad, for him to take off this way. Just like a snake, he's hiding away out of sight. He's not man enough to face all of us. May his soul be haunted by her face of tears forever, and may his future with anyone who stand beside him be cursed," she said cruelly

"You sound like an old witch, for goodness' sake! Stop that dear. We have to learn to forgive others, and Nicole needs to move on, not get hooked up on anger and revenge." Sarah went upstairs to pack a bag. She could swear that the old woman was a little off some days. Grand just smiled to herself. She knew that Samuel would pay dearly, for what he had done to her precious child.

Early the next morning, Sarah and Millie took off for the city. It was about a two hour drive, and they should be there about the same time Nicole and Marilyn, would be getting home from work, if they didn't get lost. Sarah let Millie drive, she always like to be in charge.

"Oh Grand I think you just missed the turnoff dear, we are in a totally different place for heaven's sake, you need to watch the signs."

"Yes, I guess maybe I did, I'll just stop here, and asked this man where we are."

She pulled the car up to what looked like a homeless man. Who was standing by the road, asking for a ride."

"Hello can you tell me how to get back into the city again, I think I miss the turn off."

The dirty looking man who stood there in torn clothing said. "Yes, Mama I can, but I could drive with you there, and then you will not get lost."

"Well... ok then, climb in you can drive there with us I guess." Millie just smiled.

"Millie you cannot let a stranger in this car, have you lost your mind completely, dear God in heaven helps us." Sarah said as she stared at the stranger with her piercing dark eyes. The Stranger guided them into the city, and Millie dropped him off, and thank him for his help, she handed him a twenty dollar bill.

"Grand if you ever do that again, I swear I will walk back home without you. Did you take your meds today?" Millie just smiled and said" We're here now let go in, you worry too much."

They had a key to their apartment, so it didn't matter if the girls were home or not. Sarah had brought groceries, she was going to cook them a good homemade dinner tonight. They were already settled in the kitchen with dinner almost done, by the time Nicole and Marilyn came home.

"Mommy! What a nice surprise!" She walked into her living room, and found her Grandmother knitting in her rocking chair. She went over and kissed her on the cheek. "Hello, Grand! I didn't expect to see you both so soon," Nicole said.

"Well dear we know how hard this time is for you, so we just wanted you to have family support all around you for a while, Sarah said with a warm smile.

"Thanks. That's so very kind of you to come down all this way, just to take care of us. They continued talking as Nicole went off to take a shower. "Just glad it's the weekend, and you're here to cook for a while, because Nicole isn't eating a thing I cook. She's crying all the time too." Marilyn said sadly.

"I know dear. It will take some time for her to feel better. You must remember that she was with Samuel for a long time. She needs to get used to the idea that he's really gone. Sarah went to Nicole's bedroom door, and called her out. Nicole came out and quietly sat down next to her grandmother, and took several spoonful's, of the stew. She drank a glass of milk, and then asked to be excused.

"I am just so tired mom. Thanks for the stew, but I really just want to go to sleep now, okay?"

"Okay dear, we can talk tomorrow. Maybe we can all do something fun like a movie."

"Let's see how I feel tomorrow." Nicole kissed her mother, and grandmother goodnight, and then went off to bed.

"You see what I mean now Mom? That's all she does now – sleep. And she hardly eats anything."

"I can see that dear. Don't worry yourself. She had to think of something to get her out of this, but maybe only time was the answer. The next day was even worse. Nicole didn't get out of bed at all that morning.

"It's nearly noon Grand, and Nicole's not even out of bed. How much sleep does she need? We should just go get her up, shouldn't we?" Marilyn asked.

"Yes, I'll go check on her now. We just thought sleeping in for a while, might help her relax a little more."

She knocked at Nicole's door, and when there was no answer so she opened it. Nicole was awake, just lying in bed staring out the window.

"Good morning child. Time you should be getting up from bed isn't it?"

"Hi Grand. I don't feel so well. I just want to stay here all day."

Millie had never seen Nicole's eyes so depressed. "I know that all this hurts like the devil, but Nicole you need to start to fight back. You need to get up and get yourself going again. You'll get through all this in time, and for now just eat and stay positive, because from every bad thing in life comes something wonderful. You need to have faith. God sends us times in our life when he tests us. It's to give us more courage, and strength to get through whatever is next in life. If you just give up now, you'll never know what wondrous things he has for you next."

"Well, excuse me Grandmother, but I sure hope that it's better than what I just lived through because this sucks, and is just so unfair." She smiled for the first time in days.

"Yes child it sure is. And believe me, God knows that too. So whatever comes next will surely be great for you.

"I think we should get out today, and take your Mom and Marilyn to the movies, or maybe so some shopping. What do you think?"

"Okay I'll try, maybe the movies."

"I think something funny; we could all use a laugh," Millie suggested.

"Yes, let's go see something funny." Nicole was tired of fighting everyone; it was easier to just go along with them. She didn't have the energy to fight them anymore. The shock of it all was starting to wear off now, and she was trying her best not to become too depressed. She still struggled every day just to get out of bed, and not to cry every morning. But with every day she was growing a little stronger, and working hard at the store kept her mind busy.

Chapter Eight

Millie and Sarah finally left after two weeks. They'd made sure that Nicole was eating again, and getting out of bed on a regular basis. They even talked her into joining a gym with Marilyn. It gave them both something to do, and a way to meet new people. Although each day was still a challenge for Nicole, she was slowly beginning to feel better. At least she didn't cry every day; only once in a while now, whenever something reminded her of Samuel, and of the life they had shared.

Nicole walked into the store, two months later.

"Good morning everyone. We need to get ready to do inventory this week, so I know what I need to order for the spring season."

Richard came in the door just in time to overhear her.

"Nicole my girl, I think we need to hold off for a little while on next spring's orders. I think we still have a lot of stuff to sell off first."

"Really, why? Most of the ties and shirts I ordered have already sold out, and we'll be short on those areas within a month."

"Let's just wait for a short while please."

Richard walked into his office and closed the door. He got on the phone to his lawyers, and told them he wanted to declare bankruptcy, and that he would be running a sale to try to clear up old debts with his suppliers. He knew they'd take all the money from the sale to try and pay them off, but at least it made him look like he was on the up and up. He had already put over a million dollars into his wife's account, so they had enough to go and open up a bed and breakfast. They'd found a small place to renovate, in a little place called Chester, a small district just outside of Halifax. It was perfect for them. It was right on the Atlantic Ocean, and got lots of tourists every year. They had put their house up for sale, and it had sold quickly. They'd used the money to buy the small bed and breakfast in Chester.

They'd been living in a hotel for the last month, trying to get through the Christmas sales, and to bank more money before they had to commit to bankruptcy. It was all going according to plan, and they now had enough money to live very comfortably. And if he was lucky, Helen would make money with the bed and breakfast.

Leaving him free to go golfing and boating, whenever he wanted to. The hard part would be when all his loyal longtime staff found out the truth. Some of the men had been with him for over twenty years. They'd raised their families on the income they'd made at the store. And then there was Nicole. He hated letting her down; she had worked so hard to build the business up for him again. He knew declaring bankruptcy would make her look incompetent, because she was the one running his business, and people in the community would think she'd ran it into bankruptcy. He knew it wouldn't be easy for her to get another job in the city after this. The terrible thing was, that it was actually due to her, and the great job she'd done, that he was able to retire. But Nicole would be left with the fallout, as other small business owners, in their small city heard the news. The news would travel fast he knew, and most of them would never trust her to run their businesses. But he also knew she was way too smart, to believe they were actually bankrupt. She was the one person who'd looked at all the sales, and had seen all the money that had come in. He'd have to have a really good explanation for her. He knew she would never be a part of his deception, and yet she was about to take the fall for it all. He had used her, and then when it was convenient for him, he was going to abandon her. His life was now with Helen in Chester. Richard decided he'd better do this now, and give his staff some notice of what was coming up. His lawyers would be in tomorrow. He would call a staff meeting tonight, and tell everyone what was happening. He walked over to Nicole.

"Nicole, can you call a staff meeting for an hour tonight, right before we close? I need to talk with all you regarding the business."

"Yes, I can Richard. Is everything okay?" She was stunned; he never called a meeting without her.

"I will see you all around six." He walked away, leaving Nicole to wonder what was going on now. She was getting a bad feeling in her gut again. Not another upset she thought. She didn't know if she could handle anything else in her life going wrong. But it looked like she had no choice on this one either, so she walked out to the store, and told her staff about the meeting at six. They all looked worried too.

Six o'clock arrived, and they gathered around Richard in the back room. "Thank you all for staying tonight. There's something I need to tell all of you. I have declared bankruptcy in my business. Tomorrow morning, my lawyer and the bank will be coming in to take an inventory, and put everything on a final sale. All the money we raise will go to pay our suppliers, and all of you. I'm sorry. I did try my best, but things just got too backed up in the bills for me to carry on." He held his head down as he spoke; he couldn't look any of them in the eye.

"But I don't understand that Richard. We had record sales this last year. How could we possibly be so behind on the store's bills? What happened to all the money?" Nicole was stunned.

"Yes, we did have wonderful sales – mostly because of you Nicole. But before you came on board, I had a few years of really bad business, and I got very behind in the bills. I couldn't catch up." He didn't look her in the eye as he spoke.

"I had no idea that things were even bad. You never said anything to me about this. How much time do you have? How long will the men have their jobs?"

"I'm not sure. For the next few weeks or so I think. As long as we're still open, you'll all be kept on. The bank will try and sell the store and the name. Who knows maybe someone will buy the place."

He said it without a care in the world, she thought. She was starting to see a whole new side of him now. The men looked devastated by the news. Nicole never even thought of herself; she was more concerned for the men, who had spent so much of their lives working for Richard.

The next morning, the lawyers came in from the bank, and Nicole and her staff assisted them in the last inventory of the store. At noon they reopened the store, with the news of the business going under. The customers lined up in hopes of catching a bargain. Richard was nowhere to be found, of course. He couldn't face them all, especially not Nicole. He never showed his face again, no one, not even Nicole, got a chance to say anything to him again.

"Well folks, we have a bit of good news for everyone. We've struck a deal for the business. It's been sold, and the new owners will be in to speak with you all tomorrow," announced one of the lawyers from the bank.

"That's wonderful! Maybe they will keep all the staff on," Nicole said. Surely they would value the hard work, they'd put into the business for so many years, and the experience they all had. The men were sad for Nicole, because they knew the new owners would probably not keep her on. They'd assume the bankruptcy was due to her management, and wouldn't want her to run their business.

She still didn't believe Richard's story either. She knew they'd made too much money to be in this kind of situation. He had done something with it all. She went into his office and looked over the books. She found that Richard had paid Helen over one million dollars, in wages and consultation fees. She also found a receipt for a boat that cost over fifty thousand dollars, and the sale of his home was there too. She found the address of the bed and breakfast with Helen's name on it. She had found it all in the lock box in his desk, because she knew where he hides the key, so she decided to look and see what he was hiding. Richard came in after midnight, and clear out all his documents, and left for Chester, with Helen.

Though she felt sick with betrayal. That was why he'd given her such a large Christmas bonus this year, it was to ease his guilty mind she thought. She'd banked the money with the rest of her savings, knowing one day she may need it. She guessed today was that day. At least she knew she could draw on her unemployment insurance for the next year, and maybe it would give her time to figure out the rest of her life. She wanted to let Richard know how disappointed she was, but when she called him there was no answer. Just another coward of man, who could no longer face her she thought.

The next morning, the new owners came into the store and introduced themselves to everyone, assuring all the men they still had their much-needed jobs. There was a look of great relief on their faces. The new owners asked to speak privately with Nicole in her office. They walked in and closed the door.

"Nicole… we're sorry to have to tell you this, but your services will no longer be needed by us. We have our own store manager, who will be running the store for us. Someone who we feel will have a better idea of how to manage the store finances, and such. So if you would please, we'd like you to clean out your desk and leave us today."

Nicole was stunned. "Did Richard not give me a good reference?"

"Yes he did, he said that you did a good job for him, but he just couldn't keep ahead of his bills. We think that maybe the men's clothing business isn't your best talent, and maybe you would be happier elsewhere. Someplace where you can be more successful." The man spoke to her in such a condescending tone that it made Nicole's blood boil.

"Really." She stood up and looks him straight in the eye. "Well, maybe I'll be as successful as Richard is now, with his new boat, and his new bed and breakfast down in Chester. I guess bankruptcy really isn't so bad after all for him. You see I seem to have made him over a million dollars in the last year. More than he'd made in the last three years in business here without me. I don't mind taking the blame for the things that I am actually responsible for, like the record-breaking year he just had in sales. But for his bankruptcy, oh no, I refuse. He went under because that was exactly what he had planned to do all along. I am no one's fool. So you want a man to run your business? That's fine with me, and the best of luck with that. But I have been nothing, but successful in this business, and I will continue to be in whatever business I decide to take on in the future. It's really your loss, and one day you will come to find that out, when you're struggling to pay the bills here again, just like Richard was before I came on board to work with him. Because once I am gone, and this place no longer has my magic touch on it, you will be just another menswear store, trying to get customers through that door. Many of these men come in here because of me, because of the kind of clothing I bought, and the way I took care of them. They loved my flare for style and color, and the great customer service I gave them. So you may think whatever you like; it's no longer my concern. I will have my desk cleared out in an hour and be gone. Please have my final paycheck mailed to me. My address will be on my desk when I leave."

"Nicole I'm sorry. I haven't seen all the documents yet. It's nothing personal really. I hope we can call you in the future, if we have any questions regarding the business."

She smiled sweetly at him and said, "You can call as much as you like. But believe me, it will be a very cold day hell, before I pick up the phone to answer." She turned away, and started packing up her things. She packed up the books with all the new business contacts and deals she'd made in the last year, making sure the new owners wouldn't benefit from any of her hard work after she was gone. She was disgusted, and so tired of always getting dumped on. How dare he assume that she had run Richard's business, into bankruptcy just because she was a woman. What a fool, she thought. Richard himself, and no one else had done that deed. She was not about to take the blame, or assume responsibility for what he'd done. What a coward he had turned out to be, to leave her to deal with the fall out. There was a part of her that didn't really blame him either. She knew what a nag Helen could be, and that he was getting old and tired. The one sad thing she had learned over the years, was that it was hard to trust people. Just when you thought that it was safe to let your guard down, they'll turn around, and throw you off the bridge when you're not looking. It had happened to her with Samuel, and now with Richard.

She packed up and went home, and sat rocking in her chair, looking out the window, wondering where to turn next. She hadn't yet told her family, of what had just happened. She needed time to figure out what to do with the rest of her life. She had just lost the man she loved, and now she'd lost her job. She'd be damned if they would get the best of her. Not Samuel, and certainly not Richard. She just needed a little time to settle her mind and her heart down, and when she felt better in a month or two, she would start to plan a whole new future.

There was one thing she knew for sure, as she took out her computer and started to write. There was a story here that needed to be told. When she started writing, the word "Travesty" came to her mind. The word haunted in her heart as she spoke it out loud. Why travesty? She thought. She looked up the meaning in the dictionary. It meant a mockery of justice.

"That pretty much describes my life, and what I've been through, so I guess that is the best title I could give my book." She wrote at the top of the page "Travesty of Justice." And so she began to write night and day. Through tears and laughter, she wrote word after word. There were many times when she questioned herself on what she was doing. She hoped that one day it would be published, and that maybe one day Samuel and countless others would read her words.

She wanted people to see the scars, and hear the heartache of discrimination, and injustice that people like herself, and Samuel had endured. For just as it was done to them, she had no doubt in her mind, that it had been done to countless others in her country, and many others countries like hers.

She enrolled in some evening writing classes at the university in her city, and learned about the business of book publishing. Soon she knew she wanted writing to be a big part of her life. Her family was saddened by the news of her lost job. They supported her in what she was doing; her mother thought it would be good for her to write things down, maybe it would be good therapy, and a way for her to get it all out of her system. Sarah knew that whatever her daughter decided to do, she would somehow come out on top. She was thankful that Nicole had saved enough money so that she could write for a whole year, if she wanted to. Nicole was starting to feel better in many ways. It had been almost six months now, since Samuel had been gone. She hadn't heard a word from him; she'd received the final papers in the mail a month ago. Her mind only focused on him briefly now when she woke up. She had chosen to live with love and forgiveness in her heart. She had decided to let the betrayal and injustice, live in the hearts of those who had betrayed her.

She was reliving her life in many ways, as she wrote her story down on paper. That was enough heartache in itself.

She picked up the newspaper and started reading, she saw an ad for a job working with a jewelry manufacturer in sales and marketing, in the help wanted column.

"Jewelry Hmmm? Maybe she said to herself. Never hurts to call she guessed. Who knows where it could lead. Nicole picked up the paper, and reread the job ad. The more she read it, the more she wanted to call, and see what it was all about. So she picked up the phone, and called for an appointment to meet with the owners, of the jewelry company. They wanted to see her the next morning at nine.

In some ways now, when she looked into the mirror, she never felt good enough anymore. She'd been left behind by the only man she'd ever loved, and that was still taking its toll on her self-esteem. She never noticed all the men that stared at her, or the ones who tried to get her attention, when she was out shopping, or walking in the gardens. Her mind was always so far away, that she never noticed anything except the beauty of Mother Nature around her.

Her grandmother and mother, encouraged her to get out more and meet people, but she still had no desire to do that. She just stayed home, and continued to write. Tomorrow she would go to her first job interview. The next morning she got up, ate

278

breakfast and showered, and dressed in a dark blue business suit, with a pair of high-heeled navy pumps. She wore a pair of teardrop citrine earrings, which had been her Mothers. They were her only accessory. She pulled her hair back from her face, and let the soft curls flow down her back. She looked like a professional business woman. She walked into the office. It was a kind of run down old building, and the office she entered was cluttered. As she entered the office, a small Chinese woman came out to greet her. She wore a white shirt and a pair of black slacks. Right away Nicole knew she was overdressed for this office.

"Hello. I'm Hanna, the owner. Pleased to meet you." Hanna was a soft-spoken, understated woman.

"Hello, my name is Nicole. Thank you for seeing me."

"Please come and sit down, let's talk." Hanna motioned to her desk.

"Thank you." Nicole smiled warmly at her; she liked Hanna right away.

"I'm looking for someone who can be a sales manager here, and take care of all my sales representatives in the US and Canada. It would involve some travelling to trade shows etc. I see you have a lot of sales experience, and I like that. You also look good too – very professional."

"Thank you Hanna. Yes, I have experience in sales, and in managing people. What kind of jewelry do you work with here?"

"We work with natural gemstones. They have lots of energy you know. They're both very beautiful and good for your health. Come into the showroom and I'll show you them."

Nicole followed the small Chinese woman into her tiny little showroom. When she looked at the product carefully, she was a bit disappointed by what she saw, but was immediately drawn to the actual gemstones themselves. She didn't like the designs or the color combinations. But thought that maybe, she just was not aware of what sells well in the jewelry business.

"So what do you think of the jewelry Nicole?" Hanna asked her.

"The gemstones are very beautiful. I love them." She was careful not to criticize the woman's designing abilities. "Where do you sell them? And how many sales representatives do you have now? What kind of sales volume do you have in a year?"

"We sell all over the US and Canada. I have ten sales reps, we do over one million in sales each year. Nicole I like you very much. I want to offer you a job here with me. What do you say? Will you come and work here?"

"Wow Hanna, yes I'd love to come and work with you. When would you want me to start?"

"Tomorrow, if that's okay?"

The truth was that Hanna was beside herself with worry, and needed help in the worst way. None of her sales representatives, had been producing very good sales in the last year, and she just didn't know how to manage people very well to get them to sell her jewelry. Her company's sales had fallen to just under three hundred thousand this year. This was her chance to get the company going again. But of course Nicole didn't know any of that yet. She just liked Hanna and wanted to help her. She instantly loved the natural gemstones, and wanted to work with them. She connected with their energy.

"Okay, I would love to start tomorrow. Would you like a reference to check?" Nicole knew after she checked, she may change her mind about her, depending on what Richard said about her work. Although she suspected he would be kind in that regard, if she could actually get him on the phone.

"Yes, please. You can come back tomorrow at nine. We work Monday to Friday, nine to five. Your desk will be in the showroom, where the customers come in, and I'll fill you in tomorrow on all the sales representatives, and each territory and trade show we do.

"Thank you, Hanna. I'm sure I'm going to love learning new things about the jewelry business, and I believe I'll be able to help out a lot. I'll see you tomorrow."

Hanna smiled. She was relieved that she'd finally found someone to help her with her business.

Nicole drove home smiling. She hoped she was making the right choice with this company, but she really had nothing much to lose by trying. She couldn't wait, to start working with all the beautiful gemstones; she could sense and feel their powerful energy. She was hoping that before long she could learn about designing jewelry. She had a great eye for what would sell and what wouldn't, and she would be absolutely surprised if Hanna, actually did the kind of sales she'd claimed. It didn't really matter though to her. She knew she could make it happen, once she'd learned the business. Nicole picked things up fast, and could hardly wait to go back to work. Tomorrow was the first day of her new career. It was a baby step in making a new life.

The problem was that Samuel still haunted her. She just couldn't get over the fact that someone she had loved so much, and for so long, could treat her the way that he had. She dreamed of the day when she'd be happy again, when she'd no longer remember this strange love she'd had for a man, that turn out to be someone she'd never really known. She wondered if he ever thought of her. So many unanswered questions, still remained in her mind. Most of all she wondered how anyone, ever got over love, especially if it was real. She didn't understand how people moved on so easily. Samuel had, or so it seemed to her. She was trying her best to put all the pieces together as she wrote her story down, but some things were still cloudy and confusing. The fact was that she wasn't getting better. Even after all he'd done, she knew that somehow he loved her still. Sometimes she could even see his face in her mind's eye if she tried hard enough. His face was always sad, and he never looked her in the eye.

Sometimes she'd use all her powerful thoughts, to try to reach him again. She was trying to get him to reach out and contact her. But so far she hadn't been successful. She closed her eyes now, and she could see him standing there again. She held him there in her mind's eye, refusing to let go.

***

Samuel went through all the motions of being a good husband, and father to his child. Jane was now almost nine months along, and soon there would be a new baby in his life. He was working in the hospital alongside Ben, doing what he loved. He had everything he wanted now; and everything he had worked so hard for. He stood looking out the window of his office. He still had such a strong feeling of her. Sometimes it was so strong he'd pick up the phone, and then put it right back down. It was almost like he couldn't help himself. He just wanted to hear her voice again. Impulsively, he picked up the phone, and dialed her number. He let it ring this time.

The phone startled Nicole out of her reverie. She looked at the caller ID, and realized it was a long distance number.

"Hello? Hello? Is anyone there?" And then the line was dead. She quickly dialed the number back, and Samuel answered.

"Samuel it's you. How are you? Do you know who this is?" Nicole asked.

"Yes... I do Lady." He was silent for a moment and then said, "Just a minute please. I need to take this call in my office." He sounded cold. He put her on hold, and went out to whisper something in his nurse's ear.The next voice Nicole heard was a female voice. "Miss, this is Dr. Emeka's nurse. He's asked me to tell you, to please never call this number again. He cannot talk to you now or ever. So please don't call back again." There was a click, and then dead air.

Nicole was stunned. He hadn't even been man enough to talk to her on the phone himself. She knew they were divorced now, but she had spent so many years by this man's side, she had secured his citizenship in Canada, and had helped him achieve his medical degree on the Island. And this was what she got for it. How very cold, he'd been, she thought. He was like a different man altogether. Why had he even dialed her number in the first place, only to hurt her with those words by a complete stranger? Fresh tears rolled down her cheeks. The phone call, had brought back all the headaches again. It was like rubbing salt into an open wound, and it hurt like hell.

Samuel went out to his car, put his head in his hands and cried. He'd hated to do that to her, but he knew they could never talk. She'd find out the truth, and he couldn't bear to hear her voice, and know that she wasn't his anymore. He should have been stronger and not called her; he'd only had made things worse for her. He had everything he'd wanted, and everything his family had wanted for him, but he had no peace in his soul. She haunted him night and day. All he wanted to do was hide somewhere, anywhere, where he couldn't remember her.

Culture is a strange thing, he thought. Stick with your own kind, his family had always told him, and in the end that's what he'd done. But in his heart and own mind, he knew he had never been happier, or more at peace, than when he'd shared his life with this woman, and whose only crime was being from a different culture. He had failed her, and he'd always have to live with what he'd done, to this innocent young woman who'd trusted him with her heart and life. Yes he thought, he should have known better, but then a strange thing happened – you fall hopelessly in love, and it changes everything. All the best intentions in the world, cannot help you make the right decision, when love gets hold of your heart. Sometimes there are things you're not proud of, and sometimes there are things that are so powerful, that they complete your world, and make everything worthwhile and right. He knew he was being a coward; and he was not proud of himself for that. He could tell by how quickly she'd called back that she still loved him, and he felt even guiltier for what he had just done to her again. He knew he didn't deserve to have a happy family by his side like he did. While she was so still so very lost.

***

Nicole sat for a long time, staring out the window. Her mind was trying to figure out the actions of this man, that she had loved so dearly. What in the world had made him turn so cold-hearted towards her? But she knew it was no time to be too shaken by the day's events. Tomorrow she would start a new job. And that phone call only confirmed, to her that it was time to get on with her life.

She never told any of her family of the heartbreaking phone call; they didn't need more suffering. The next morning as the sun came through Nicole's bedroom window, she smiled and thanked God for waking her up, and for the new job she was about to start. She got ready for her first day at work. She had a notebook and pen, in her purse to take notes. She wore a white cotton shirt with a simple pair of black slacks and a red blazer. She put her hair back into a ponytail, grabbed her purse and left for work. She drove to the rundown office building, and parked her car. She was excited to meet with Hanna, and the rest of her staff.

Nicole hung up her blazer, and put her purse inside her desk drawer. She walked around the showroom, opening drawers and looking at different jewelry designs, making notes on them all. Soon, Hanna appeared at the door.

"Welcome Nicole. I hope you're finding your way around okay." She smiled.

"Yes. I've been looking over all the jewelry designs, and making a few notes along the way. Where would you like us to start today, Hanna?"

"I'll tell you what gemstone they are, so you can learn their names. I've also brought you a few books on gemstones and precious metals, so you'll know what each piece is made out of."

"That's great Hanna, thank you." They worked all morning on the product line, and then Hanna took her out to a quiet little place just across the street. They ordered lunch and sat down to talk. "To tell you the truth Nicole, and I hope I can trust you, my company's sales have been going down, for the last six months. I have lost my partner who did most of the designing and sales, and now I'm trying to replace her. I need someone with a good eye, and I can see now that you have that. Maybe you can also help out in the designing department a bit too."

"I'd love that. Of course, there is lots for me learn in order to do that, but I learn quickly when it's something I love. I love all the colorful gemstones. They're so magical"

"That's great. The other side is that we need to get our sales representatives selling more of the product, and maybe hire some new ones. There's a trade show in Chicago in two weeks. I want you to go, meet our sales reps there, and work the show with them. What do you think?"

"Yes of course, I'll do my best to learn what I need to by then.

"Mary is the owner of the sales agency, and she had her sister, and two other representatives working with her. Their sales have gone down a lot in the last few months. Mary is very protective of her business, and can be very stubborn and defensive, when I ask her questions about the lack of sales with my jewelry line. She'll tell you it's our product and not them, so you'll need to decide what the real truth is. It will be your job to get the sales up in that territory again."

"I'll try my best to sell the product at the show. Let's see how I do. Believe me, Hanna– one thing I'm very good at is sales, and building customer relationships"

Hanna took Nicole into another room after lunch, where all the jewelry production took place. Colorful gemstones hung on all the walls. Big tables were laid out with gemstone that were getting ready to be made into pieces of jewelry. There were also several more Chinese girls, who worked in this department. Nicole quickly realized that she was the only white woman, which worked in the entire company. It didn't bother her a bit; she only hoped she would be able to communicate with them all. A few of them didn't speak much English, but they didn't really need to, their jobs were to make the jewelry. They communicated only with each other and Hanna, who spoke both

English and Chinese very well.

"In here is where we design and produce the jewelry. Here's the table of our new spring designs. What do you think of the colors here?"

Nicole looked over the lineup for spring. She made only a few suggestions for now, until she learned more about the company's market and customers.

She worked hard each day, and quickly learned the business. In two weeks, she was packed, and ready to go on her first business trip to the city of Chicago. It would be her first jewelry trade show. She was excited to be doing something so different, and hoped that she'd get along well with their sales team there. She took a cab to the airport, after calling her mother and telling her, she was off and promising to call once she'd arrived. Nicole dressed in a simple, straight dress made of a soft brown jersey fabric. She wore one of the necklaces she'd designed – a lovely citrine pendant and sterling silver combination, with tiny stub citrine earrings that matched. She loved the natural energy of this stone, she could tell they were powerful. When she looked up the meaning of the gemstones she worn, they were said to bring good luck. She liked that meaning, and God only knows she needed it.

It was her first trip to Chicago, and she wondered if Samuel was still living there, with this woman Jane. She wouldn't have known how to find him, even if she'd wanted to. She had already called the phone directory, and there was no phone number listed in his name. But she still looked at every black man that passed her, searching for his eyes or his smile.

She checked into her hotel, and then took a cab to the trade show. She registered, and found the booth where her sales team was set up. "Hello I'm Nicole from Canada. I work with Hanna's company, I'm her new sales manager."

"Hello Nicole. I'm Mary. This is my company, and this is the spot where your line is set up, so you can try and sell it for a few days here with us if you like." Mary was somewhat condescending, and Nicole had a feeling right away that this woman would not be easy to work with. But she was going to do her best to sell the jewelry in the next few days, and just keep an open mind and see what happened.

Nicole walked around, and looked at all the other jewelry lines that Mary carried. She could see that the others lines were much better priced, and better designed, than her company's. If she was a buyer for a retail store, she knew she would have not have bought their line of jewelry, but would have bought others in Mary's showroom. That bothered Nicole a lot, because if the competition was so stiff, then they'd have to make a lot of changes to their own line, in order to gain more customers.

The day flew by, and soon Nicole left them, and went back to her hotel. She took a shower and put on a pair of jeans, a white shirt, and a black leather jacket. She decided to go walking, and look for a place to eat dinner.

As she was coming out of the hotel, she noticed a hospital just a block down the street. She unconsciously walked in that direction. It was just getting slightly dark, and she didn't want to go far from the hotel, so she decided to eat at a little burger place just across from the hospital. She took a chair next to the open window, and ordered a hamburger. Suddenly she felt very alone, and just wanted to go to her hotel and sleep. She paid the bill and walked back to the hotel.

Samuel was working late tonight and he was tired. Jane had just given birth to a little baby boy, and he wasn't getting much sleep. He was on the evening shift tonight at the hospital, and as he looked out his window with his tired eyes, he noticed a beautiful white woman walking slowly along the street. Her walk reminded him of Nicole's walk. He also noticed the woman's golden hair. For just a moment, he thought his mind was playing tricks on him. He could have sworn it was her. He ran down the stairs to the street, but she had disappeared. He looked up and down the boulevard, but couldn't see her. He noticed the hotel, and thought maybe she was here in his city, but then quickly decided that he was being crazy. Why on earth would she be here, so far away from home?

Nicole had a strange feeling come over her as she entered the hotel lobby, briefly she stopped, and looked back over her shoulder. She wasn't sure what she was looking for, she just felt something say stop. She could feel him here in Chicago, and she knew he was close, but she had no idea where to look for him. She fell asleep dreaming about him. Several times that night she woke up, and looked out the window, and across the street at the hospital.

Samuel's night was slow, and he found himself looking out the same window most of the night, hoping to catch another glimpse of the woman. But he never did, and soon his shift was over. He left and drove home to his family. As he entered the apartment, he could hear his little baby boy crying for dear life. Jane was beside herself, because this baby hardly slept at all at night, and she was growing exhausted hearing him cry.

"Jane my dear, just give him to me. You go get some sleep. I will settle him down, and then sleep too."

She handed him over, and very soon his little boy was fast asleep in his arms. He gazed at his child, grateful for them all. He loved them, and owned them as his family. It was rare that he thought of Nicole now; it was too hard to let her in his thoughts anymore. But sometimes no matter what he did, she would slip out of the corners of his mind, and come back to haunt him when he least expect it. That was what had happened to Samuel tonight. She stayed in his thoughts, and visited him in his dream as he slept. He woke up from time to time with a heavy feeling, which made him just wanted to go back to the same street corner, and wait until he saw the woman again.

Nicole got up the next morning, and put on a lovely blue dress with a matching scarf swirled around her neck and flowing down her back. She put on a pair dark sunglasses. She walked back to the same little coffee shop, she'd had dinner at last night. She wanted a coffee and maybe a muffin to start her day. She ordered and sat by the window, and look out into the busy street as she ate. For some strange reason, she felt comfortable in the little place. She wondered if Samuel had ever eaten there, and if that was his hospital across the street. For just a brief minute, she thought of going into the hospital, and asking human resources if they had anyone working there with his name. But she knew he had disappeared from her life for a reason, and if he wanted to be found, he wouldn't have done things the way he had.

So she just went on to the trade show, and worked all day trying to sell her new company's jewelry line. It was a difficult sell. There were a lot of competitive jewelry lines on the US market. She was beginning to see that perhaps, it was the product that needed to be changed, and not the sales representatives. She would have to have a serious talk with Hanna when she returned. She left the building later that evening, and walked slowly back to her hotel, but instead of going to her room, she went back to the same little café for dinner. She took the same seat by the window, and looked out at the hospital. She ordered a chicken sandwich with a glass of milk, and slowly ate her meal.

Samuel was running late for his shift. He'd wanted to run into his favorite little café for a quick bite, but his little boy had been up crying again, and now he was late. Maybe later, he thought on his break. They made a muffin he had grown to like a lot. They were a lot like the ones Nicole used to make for him. So he got one almost every day with a coffee on his break.

"Will that be all miss? Any dessert for you?" The waiter asked.

"Yes, I'd like one of your blueberry muffins with a coffee. I make ones like these myself."

He came back a few minutes later with her order.

She sat eating it slowly. She kept her eyes on the hospital entrance across the street. She saw a tall black man go in, but she didn't see his face. He was moving too fast, and he could have been anyone.

She constantly thought about Samuel. This was the city she'd last heard from him in. And the fact that she was staying beside a hospital, made her think of him even more. She knew there were so many different hospitals in the city, that the chances of him working at this one were a long shot. She still felt the need to go inside the hospital for some reason. It was only seven o'clock, and she didn't want to go back to her hotel room just yet.

She crossed the street and went inside. She stood in the lobby and looked around, then sat down and watched everyone moving in different directions, going about their work and business. She stayed there for a few more minutes, and then decided to go back to her hotel room, and take a long hot bath, and go to bed. She stood up, and turned around to leave.

Samuel stepped out of the elevator. He was taking a break, and was on his way to get his regular muffin and coffee. As he walked out, he noticed the same woman, just as she was going out the main entrance of the hospital. He jogged down the long hallway, and went through the same door, but he could no longer see her.

Where did she go so fast? He wondered. It was as if she disappeared off the street in a matter of minutes. He stood on the sidewalk and looked all around him; there was only the hotel across the street, and the little café next to it. There were a few shops up the street, and then it turned into a busy shopping area. Maybe she goes shopping he thought, or maybe she is staying in the hotel. He crossed the street and went inside the hotel, but he couldn't see her. He went to the café, and got his muffin and coffee. He took the same seat he always did, beside the window, and looked out. The vision of the woman played in his mind. She'd been wearing a scarf up around her neck, the same way he'd seen Nicole wear those millions of times.

Nicole took a hot bath and climbed into bed. But she couldn't sleep, so she got back up and took a seat by the big window. She noticed what looked like the same black man going back into the hospital. She wondered if it could have been him, but she hadn't seen his face, and she knew the chances were slim. Yet she could feel him somewhere close. She knew this man, and she knew that he was still thinking of her, at least today he was she could feel it in her gut. The next morning, she checked out, and got in a taxi to go back to the airport to fly home. It was still very early in the morning, and the sun was just coming up.

Samuel had just finished his shift. He was coming out of the hospital entrance, when he noticed the same woman getting into a taxi cab. She had her head bent down as she was getting into the car, so he couldn't see her face. But as the taxi drove by him, he saw her. Her beautiful face was looking out the window, and up at the sky. He could see her lovely hair, flowing down her back. It was Nicole. She had been staying only minutes away from him all this time. He couldn't help but notice how very sad her eyes had been. In only moments, the taxi turned the corner, and went out onto the busy highway. And then she was gone again.

He hated himself all over again for what he had left behind. He sadly got into his own car, and for just a brief moment he thought of driving to the airport in hopes of catching another glimpse of her. But he didn't, he knew Jane would be waiting at home for him with their son. He drove home to the place where he laid his head, where his children called him Father, and where a woman of his own kind, called him her husband. That was his world now. He knew there was no way to reach out now to Nicole, there was no way to hold on her anymore. Nicole boarded the plane, and took her seat. Her life was so different now without Samuel. She lived each day without any thought of the future. She took each day as it came, just hoping to get through the day.

The plane landed, and she took a taxi home. Her sister was waiting for her with dinner on the table.

"Hi Sis I'm home," she yelled as she put her suitcase in her bedroom. She was so glad to be back, and sleeping in her own bed tonight.

"Hi, Nick. How was your trip? I have dinner ready, and a special surprise."

"Really? What?" She walked into the dining room, and there sat her mother and grandmother smiling happily at her.

"Oh! What a lovely surprise! I'm so happy to see you both."

"So what brings you guys here so soon again?" Nicole asked

"It was your grandmother. She insisted that we come in. So here we are dear," Sarah said with a smile.

"Is everything okay Grand?' Nicole eyed her, wondering what it was really all about.

"Yes child. I just missed you, and kind of had a feeling you were missing us." She didn't smile. She just sat and ate her food. The truth was, Millie had seen Samuel in her mind's eye, and knew how very close they had come to connecting with one another again. She knew any contact with Samuel would have taken Nicole back into a deep depression, and she was so glad they hadn't. Or at least Nicole hadn't. She didn't care if Samuel had; he deserved to be haunted by her memory.

Nicole just smiled at her old Grandmother. Her mother recognized the sleepless look in Nicole's eyes again. She had only had a few bites of dinner, and then kissed her mother and grandmother Goodnight and went to bed.

"Now you see why I insisted we come here Sarah? She's run down and upset again. I see it in her; can't you?"

"Yes, I can see it too. Maybe after a good night's sleep, she'll feel better. She could tell that Nicole was still not back to her old self yet. No matter what anyone else did for her, or around her, she had to want to heal herself, and be willing to let Samuel's memory go. She knew that writing their story was helping Nicole in some ways, yet in others ways it was holding her back. She hoped she soon finished the book, so she would no longer visit the past. Nicole's confidence had been shaken, and she now felt like she wasn't good enough in so many ways.

The weekend passed quickly, and they had helped Nicole focus on happier things. They shopped together, and watched movies that made them all laugh. By Monday she felt rested again, and ready to go back to work. Her mother and grandmother returned back home, and her sister went back to her job at the retirement home.

"Good morning, Hanna. How are you this morning?"

"I'm okay. A little tired; I haven't been sleeping well." Hanna was looking very stressed.

"I'm sorry to hear that. Is there anything I can do to help you more?"

"We really need to get our sales up. We can't survive long if they keep declining like this."

"I know Hanna that concerns me as well. We do need to talk about this. I'm sorry to tell you, but our product line isn't strong enough. There are so many jewelry lines that are more attractive, and better priced. If we don't make serious changes in the product line, I don't think I can do much with the sales. I am willing to do my best, and help redesign the line with you, if you give me a chance. And when it's great, I'll go back, and sell it to the best of my ability, everywhere and anywhere I can. What are your thoughts on that?"

"What kind of redesign do you have in mind?" She asked, feeling even more downhearted.

"Let's make everything in real precious metals, and real gemstones. Most of the customers I spoke with, wanted real sterling silver and gold. So let's start by changing all that over. Let's also start making it, mostly here in Canada, not back in China. I know you have over half of the line made there now, but our customers are complaining about the poor quality, and too much of it breaking on them. An unhappy customer doesn't repeat business with you. I can sell them once and well, but if they don't come back then we're dead. We can't grow this business, and I can tell you love this little company so much. So that's where I think we can start." Hanna could tell that Nicole was a woman who didn't like to lose, especially in business, so she was inclined to trust her opinions on this.

"Let me think about this for a little while, and see what I can come up with. In the meantime, why don't you see what you can come up with in the design room, and I'll have a look at it tomorrow." Hanna left the room feeling discouraged. Nicole's suggestions had made a lot of sense; now all she needed to do was to figure out a way to make it happen without spending lots of money. Nicole went into the design room, picked several gemstones, and started creating different designs. She learned quickly from the production manager, on how to physically make them. It made the job of designing samples easier.

Now that she was working full time with Hanna, she could only work on her book early in the morning, or at night before she slept. She wanted to complete her novel as soon as she could. She believed, that one day she would get published. She engraved that though in her mind. Her only hope was that it would allow other people, to open their hearts and minds to injustice, and to see it for what it was, and how devastating it could be. She was living proof of that, and it was by the sheer grace of God that she had survived, and was now growing stronger.

She was almost at the end of the story. She wanted people to read her book, and see how discrimination, and the lack of equal opportunity had affected two people's lives. How it had left them broken, beyond any words she could ever write on paper.

But she was determined to put the pieces of her life back together. She was so excited to be learning all about the different natural energies that each gemstone held, the different kinds of powers they stood for, and the different effects that they had on people. She felt the gemstones energy, and used the different powers they held to heal, and to command success in her new business life. Hanna loved her new designs.

"Nicole I think you have a good eye for design, and I think we should put a few of them into production, and see how they sell at our next trade show."

"Oh really, that would be wonderful! I'm looking forward to meeting the rest of our client base and seeing if my designs sell. I promise I will do my best to sell them."

Hanna liked Nicole a lot, and was pleased that she was so passionate about her business. She could see that Nicole was working hard, and had learned a great deal in a short amount of time. Nicole had a way of making other people feel important, and was always happy to listen to their problems, and offer any solution if she could. When Nicole wrote now the last end of her book, it was almost like in her mind that she was writing about characters, and not herself or Samuel. She had to do it that way, or she would never have been able to function in her day-to-day life.

She was researching how to successfully market a bestseller. She knew she had lots to do if she wanted as many people as possible to read her book. She was busy with her new job, designing, and finding different ways that she could get the sales up in her new company. She buried herself with work, and filled her mind with new dreams, of one day becoming a published author. She visualized this on a daily basis, until she knew it would one day become reality. She believed that love, and gratitude were the way to achieve all her dreams. She was a woman who had been through hell and back, and was still standing. She had loved and lost much in her life, but had been given many gifts in return, and soon she would take the biggest step yet – she would send her book out to a few publishers. She had a book that listed agents and publishers, and the kind of work they were interested in. She just had to decide where to send her story first. She prayed constantly for a divine connection with the right agent and publishers. And she knew that very soon, they would appear in her life. She knew God was never late, but instead was always right on time, with his flood of blessings. She worked even harder with Hanna, and finally they had come up with a winning collection of jewelry, or at least Nicole hoped so. Soon it would be time to send them out on the US market again, and see how well they did there. The Tradeshow was in Chicago again, and was in less than a week. She was hoping to go and sell the line herself, to see how it would do. She asked Hanna to book her back in the same hotel.

Around the same time, she finished her book. One night as she sat down in her big rocking chair, and scanned the pages of the big book of publishers and agents. She closed her eyes and prayed again for a divine connection, to the right agent and publisher, and then lets the pages of the big book drop open. She looked down, and there was a publisher, and agent listed in Chicago.

She thought to herself, I'm going to be in that city at the end of this week, so maybe I should send out my query letter to these people first. She'd prepared a query letter with a brief synopsis, and a chapter outline for Travesty of Justice. She wrote down the email of both the agent, and publisher in Chicago, who just happened to publish her type of work. She addressed the email to the people's names that were written down in the big book, and attached her letter and chapter outline. She hesitated for a few minutes before she sent it out. Maybe she wasn't a good enough writer to be doing this. She didn't know if she could handle more rejection in her life right now, and all the negative thoughts, she could possibly have were coming to her mind, yelling out to her to retreat back to safety and out of harm's way. She prayed for guidance as she always did, in her mind's eye, this is what she heard. A little voice inside her gut yelled out "just push the SEND button!"

She pushed the send button on her email, and never looked back. She wanted to show others, that there was a light at the end of the tunnel, and that no matter how long the journey was, or how bad the situation is, there was one thing that could save you, that could pull you out of the darkness, and back into the light. That thing was love, and gratitude for the gift of life, and the talent that God gives you.

She went on about her day, busy designing new designs that they would try out on the US market in Chicago. Before she knew it, it was already six in the evening and time to go home. She packed up her laptop, and off she drove. Nicole washed up the dishes and crawled into bed. She opened her laptop and went to her email, and she couldn't believe her eyes. She had an email from the agent, she had emailed early that day, and he was asking to see her whole manuscript. She smiled for the first time that day from ear to ear. Maybe her dreams of becoming a published writer would come true after all. She quickly emailed him back the manuscript in an attachment, and said a prayer as she pushed the send button. She knew it was rare to hear back so soon.

She was so excited that she found it hard to fall asleep; all her hard work was at least getting read by a real agent. For the first time in a long time she felt like she was right where she was supposed to be. She went back into work and prepared for her trip to Chicago. She kept checking her email, but she hadn't heard back from the agent yet.

The night before her trip, she opened her email and there was a message from the agent. He was interested in representing her, and asked her to please call him. She couldn't believe her eyes. She quickly called the number.

"Hello, Goodman and Goodman agency."

"Hello, this is Nicole Butler. I just received an email from you asking me to give you a call; that you're interested in representing me with my book, Travesty of Justice."

"Oh, yes. Hello, Nicole. My name is Ryan Thomas. We like your novel and would be interested in setting up a meeting with you."

"That's great, it just so happens that I'm in your city in the next two days. I arrive on Friday morning, and I am there until Monday night. Can we meet then?"

"Yes we can arrange a meeting for around four on Monday afternoon, if that's works for you. We're located in the city, right next to Northwestern Hospital. We're just across the street beside the Fairfield Hotel."

"Oh wow, that works out just great. I'm staying at the Fairfield. I can meet with you on Monday. My flight doesn't leave until later that evening. And Mr. Thomas, I just want to thank you so much. I am so grateful to be meeting with you, and I'm so glad you like my manuscript."

"We like it very much, and we're looking forward in meeting with you too Nicole."

She didn't want to say anything to her family yet, until she was sure they would represent her, and they'd gotten her a publisher. She only told them that she was going away on another business trip for Hanna. But she could barely contain her excitement.

She felt almost sad that her writing had ended; she would miss writing every day. So she opened her laptop, and starting writing the next chapter in her life. It would become the sequel to Travesty of Justice .What could I possibly call this one? She thought. Then out of the blue, the words came to her. "The Magic in the Little Gemstones Kiosk." I work with all these lovely gemstones now, and I can feel all the power and positive energy all around me every day, so this is a great title I think", she said to herself out loud. And so she began writing again. Her next book would be written as it unfolded in her life. She was sure it was going to be a very exciting one.

She zipped up her suitcase, and called a taxi to take her to the airport. Before she knew it, she had landed back in the city of Chicago again. She could hardly wait to get to the trade show, to see how well their new designs were selling. She checked into the hotel, dropped her suitcase off in the room, and took another taxi to the tradeshow. By the time she got there it was already noon, and the booth where her sales representatives were set up was very busy.

"Welcome back Nicole. Your line is selling way better this season. We're much happier with the jewelry sales so far," Mary said with a smile. She was starting to actually like Nicole now. She could see that she had made a difference already, with the quality of the jewelry that she was sending them to sell.

"Thanks so much Mary. I'm so glad to see that it's selling better. I'll sell our line now for the next few hours for you," Nicole sat down at the table with a heart filled with gratitude. She took a cab back to her hotel after work, changed into a pair of jean and cotton blue t- shirt; she decided to walk back to the same little café to grab a bite of dinner. She liked the place and for some reason it felt comfortable to her. She ordered a bowl of chicken soup, and one of her favorite muffins. As she ate, she looked out the same window. But for some reason, she couldn't feel Samuel there with her anymore. She looked over at the hospital, and it didn't feel the same as when she was there the last time. The last time she had visited the little café, it was almost like she could feel him there, and this time she couldn't feel his presence at all. In some ways, it was a relief, and in other ways it made her feel sad. Maybe she was just no longer in tune with his energy.

***

Samuel was busy at his desk early this morning. He'd just taken a new job as the director of a substance addiction center, counseling and working with people who needed help with drugs and other substances. It was across town, but closer to where he lived. He wanted to give Jane a chance to go back to do an internship, and get her medical license too. With this job he'd be doing nine to five hours, enabling him to get the children after work when Jane was busy doing shift work at the hospital. She was now doing her internship at the same hospital, which Samuel had done his last year. Samuel would drop her off and pick her up when her shift was done, with the children in the car. They had somehow managed to have a routine family life, mostly with Samuel picking up most of the parenting duties. He knew just how hard the one-year internship could be, and he wanted to do all he could to make life easier for his wife. In many ways now, being a good husband to Jane, and a good father to his children, helped to ease his conscience. Samuel was more in touch with his own culture now. He knew what a terrible husband he had been to Nicole. He'd always been captivated by her sensuous allure; and the strong sexual pull between them. Whenever he'd seen her, he wanted to pull her close to him, to touch her in any way he could. He hated himself some days for that, and others days he just carried on with his daily life. He was growing to love Jane more now, and he was beginning to realize the benefits of being with someone of his own kind. There were fewer judgmental eyes that stared his ways; he was just a normal couple of the same race, with children and a busy career. Samuel was living the life he'd always envisioned, but the thing he'd never counted on, were the visions of the beautiful white woman, which still haunted him from his past. The one he had only planned to use for a time, but instead had fallen in love with. The one he had wished he could forget, but in other ways was afraid to lose even a single detail of her face. His memories were all he had left of this woman, and to lose even a single detail of their life together, was like losing a dream, which he was still trying to keep alive in his heart.

***

It was Monday morning, and Nicole was done with the Tradeshow. She was busy in her hotel room, trying to prepare herself for her meeting with the agency Goodman and Goodman. She was going to meet with Ryan Thomas, the man she'd spoken to on the phone. He worked with the agency, and had been chosen to work with Nicole. She was so excited that her business trip for Hanna had been successful, and she was now praying that her meeting with the agency would be just as good.

She prayed "Dear Father in heaven, I am asking for your favor for my meeting today. Father only you know my story just now, and only you know the need to tell it everywhere. So please grant me this favor. Make a way for countless others, who have suffered a great loss at the hands of those who are blinded by race and color. Be my bright guiding light today. Be so bright that I cannot miss you, and let me shout from the rooftops, look what my God can do! May your will be done, Amen." Little did Nicole know, that her prayers had already been answered, and she would receive more than she'd asked for.

She dressed in a light gray tailored suit. She wore only a small pair of pearl earrings that her grandmother had given her for good luck. She walked out into the hallway of her hotel. Her long golden hair fell softly in curls down her back, she was now a mature woman with elegant style.

Ryan Thomas was ready to give Nicole great news. They had already provisionally sold her book to a publisher, and the movie rights to a movie production company. Which was a very rare opportunity for her. Movie production companies rarely did that, until the books hit the bestseller lists. Ryan was just hoping she would agree to the terms, and sign off on the deals they were about to make for her today. He knew he had to get her signed with his agency as soon as possible. He also knew there was a lot of money at stake for his company. He was under pressure to get her on board with their plan. He had read her story, and he was full of curiosity to know, what kind of woman she was. He was wondering how much of her story was fiction, and just how much was fact. He also knew, that may well be the question that would be on many people's minds, after they read her story. It also may be, that she would never answer those questions for anyone. He wasn't sure about anything regarding this woman. He was prepared for a woman who had been through a lot, and he wasn't sure what kind of frame of mind, she would be in, but he was happy to be the one chosen to work with her. He was wondering what she would look like in person, what kind of personality she would have, and whether or not she would be strong or fragile from all that she had been through.

Nicole walked into the building, and went up to the tenth floor where the agency was. "Hello. My name is Nicole Butler. I'm here to meet with Ryan Thomas."

"Oh yes Mrs. Butler. Right this way please."

Nicole was shown to a large meeting room, with a round table and chairs. The room had large windows with the most beautiful view of the city down below. She stood in the far corner of the room looking out the window, admiring the view her back turned toward the door. She was lost in her own thoughts.

Ryan came into the room and stood for a brief moment, observing the woman he was about to speak with. He stood completely quiet, looking at her. He cleared his throat and walked towards Nicole.

"Hello Nicole. I'm Ryan Thomas."

She quickly turned around and stood looking at him, and then suddenly, just as if someone had just turned the lights back on, she begins to walk toward him with a warm smile. "Mr. Thomas, I'm so very glad to meet with you. Thank you so much for reading my book, and seeing the value in my story." She spoke with such passion, that he instantly liked her. She drew him in, with her voice as she spoke.

"Not only did I like it Nicole; my agency has sold it to a publisher, and we are also about to sell the movie rights as well. I just need to get you on board with us, and sign some of the paper work. If you would like a lawyer to go through the details with you before you sign, I understand that as well." He looked at her and beamed.

"What did you just say? You've sold my book and the movie rights as well?" She looked stunned.

"Yes that's right. You are going to be a very successful woman, and one that everyone will remember, if this book and movie are as lucrative as we all think."

"Oh dear God, thank you." She just sat quiet for a moment, and gave thanks to her God for making it all possible. He had given her just what she'd prayed for: a divine connection with the right agency and publisher. He had given her what she was meant to have. A writing career, and a story that would in the future help and inspire others, to find their way out of the midst of a storm.

"Where do I sign Ryan? I can't wait to work with you on this, and thank you so much for making all this possible." She sat down and read over the agreement of the legal papers, and then signed them all. Nicole and Ryan made plans to begin working together on the movie script; they would work back and forth over email until it was finished. She couldn't believe her good fortune, and that something was finally going terribly right for her after all. She had been through so much in the last few years, with so many doors that had never opened, when she had knocked in the past. And now finally, this door was wide open and full of bright lights. It was maybe the only door that was ever meant to be opened, she thought as she walked out of the building. The agency had provided a car for her to go back to the airport, it was waiting in front of the building. As she was slowly walking down the steps, she looked out into the parking lot, and saw a familiar-looking person standing in the lot beside a car. He was standing with a small child in his arms, and there was an older child, who looked just like him standing by his side. She was about to run to him, when a black woman came walking toward him, looking happily up at him, as he handed off the child in his arms to her. She got in the car with the children. And as he was closing the door, he looked up and saw her standing there in the parking lot, a short distance from him.

Samuel's eyes locked into Nicole's on the steps of the building. She walked down the stairs, and out into the parking lot, their eyes still locked. Hundreds of unspoken disappointments and words, that had gone unsaid between them, were all there in her eyes as she stared at him. They stood facing each other with only a small distance of parking lot between them. They communicated with just one look, that only they could understand, for only they had shared the same loss, and the same destruction at the hands of others. And in a single moment with just one glance, a thousand words were spoken, and a thousand unanswered questions were answered, that only they could hear. A love that had faced all odds, with a bond that one experiences only once in a lifetime. As they stood there, they both knew it was all lost forever, buried now in their hearts and minds. The life they had lived, and shared was only theirs to remember, for now it was nothing more than a distant memory, a bad dream of a true life travesty of justice.

Nicole was still in shock, as she walked slowly over to the car. Her eyes held his, and then she softly smiled, and got in the car. She put her hand on the glass of the car window and then to her heart, as she drove slowly past him and then off into the distance. He now knew, that he had been forgiven, by the woman whose heart he had broken, whose trust he had betrayed, and whose soul he had wounded. Samuel stood there with his eyes wide open, staring at the woman he had once loved as she drove away. Remembering all the times they had laughed and cried together. But most of all what he remembered was her amazing ability to forgive, and her kind spirit that had held so much love for him.

The mystery was now resolved for Nicole, who'd had so many unanswered questions. She now looked at the world through different eyes. The kind of eyes that knew what it was like to suffer, yet still lived to face another day, with strength and courage to carry on with a life that had been all but been destroyed. Her hope and faith were renewed, that one day she would find happiness too. In her heart all she really ever wanted was for him to be happy, to be free to pursue his medical career, and to have the family he'd always dreamed of.

Samuel now looked at the world with more compassionate eyes, and grew more hopeful with each passing day that his future was bright. His heart was relieved that in the eyes of the woman he had once loved and lost, he could see her forgiveness as she drove away. He wasn't sure how on earth she could have forgiven him, but he'd always known down deep in his heart, that Nicole was no ordinary woman; she was an extraordinary woman that had many gifts.

Nicole knew that there are many people in life, that will try to break you down along the way, but she also knew that fortunately in life, there are more who will help you to succeed. They live all around you, and are often complete strangers. They will open their eyes, and be blinded by the bright light that you carry inside. They will be inspired and touched by a special kind of love, which only lives in a heart that is purely good and kind.

She closed her eyes as the plane took off for Nova Scotia. She held a peace in her heart, as she travelled home, back to the loving arms and care of the ones she called her family. As Samuel looks up into the sky, as he stood at the door of his home, and watched a plane until it disappears off into the clouds, wondering if it could be hers. He knew it was not over, that it would never be over for him. He would always hold onto the memory in his heart, of a woman who he knew was truly one of a kind.

Author Heather Butler   Photographer Arnold Caylakyan

Twitter- HeatherButler@thebutlercollection
Instagram- thebutlercollection
Facebook- Heather Butler
Heather's Website- www.authorheatherbutler.com

Heather's depute novel Travesty of Justice was inspired by a true story. Still today less than 15% percent of International Graduates gain access to their chosen professions in North America. Travesty of Justice's Sequel is called "*The Magic In The Little Gemstone Kiosk*". This book will be released in the near future. Heather has also written an inspiring book of poetry, called Thoughtful Moments, which is also available on Amazon.

Heather now lives in Toronto Ontario Canada, but travels back frequently to her home in Nova Scotia. She own and runs her company The Butler Collection, and she continues to write every day. She is presently finishing "*The Magic in the little Gemstone Kiosk.*"

For more information about Heather Butler please visit her blog, and website at

www.authorheatherbutler.com

www.thebutlercollection.com for Heather's Jewelry designs and jewelry blog.

86285022R00183

Made in the USA
Columbia, SC
12 January 2018